Llyfrgelloedd Caerdydd

www.caerdydd.gov.uk/llyfrgelloedd

Cardiff Libraries

www.cardiff.gov.uk/libraries

Bethany Bettany

FRED D'AGUIAR

Bethany Bettany

Chatto & Windus
LONDON

Published by Chatto & Windus 2003

2 4 6 8 10 9 7 5 3 1

First published in Great Britain in 2003 by
Chatto & Windus
Random House, 20 Vauxhall Bridge Road,
London SW1V 2SA

Random House Australia (Pty) Limited
20 Alfred Street, Milsons Point, Sydney,
New South Wales 2061, Australia

Random House New Zealand Limited
18 Poland Road, Glenfield,
Auckland 10, New Zealand

Random House South Africa (Pty) Limited
Endulini, 5A Jubilee Road, Parktown 2193, South Africa

Random House UK Limited Reg. No. 954009

A CIP catalogue record for this book is available from the British Library

ISBN 0 7011 7382 3

Papers used by Random House UK Limited are natural,
recyclable products made from wood grown in sustainable forests.
The manufacturing processes conform to the environmental
regulations of the country of origin.

Typeset in Bembo by SX Composing DTP, Rayleigh, Essex
Printed and bound in Great Britain by Mackays of Chatham PLC

For Lillian Dalton

I can flatten myself and slide under doors. It is the only sweet thing about being sixteen in a body that attracts spit, slaps, jabs, curses and sneers from adults and their offspring. Do not call me the girl with the same two first names. Two names, yes, the same, no. I bypass locks of every kind. I see what girls my age dream about in their wildest sleep but dare not remember when they awake. But I remember. Adults parade before me in the fleshy poses of love and its loss and every action in between. A flat version of me roots around in their private lives. I do all this with my five feet three inches and ninety-nine pound body because a grown woman, my mother, light years away from me and destined to return for me, lives through me, inhabits my body with her spirit, my head with her worldly-wise thinking. She must come back for me if only to comb my hair twice daily with a brush picked by me from her huge collection. But not my father. There are photographs of him, his concrete grave nearby, and somewhere, a letter he left for me that I must see one day, a letter that will tell me everything I need to know about my early life with him and about his death and whom to blame for taking him from me. This is what I have been told countless times by the grown-ups around me and by their children. They do not say, 'Bethany looks like her mother's child' or, 'Bethany takes after her mother.' They say, 'Bettany is her mother.' And never Bethany, the way my mother would say it, the way I write it at school.

I

BETTANY

I live in my grandparents' house surrounded by my father's two brothers and four sisters, their wives and husbands and some two dozen children between them. Everyone around me knows my mother had a hand in the death of my father and she abandoned me here when I was five so that I might live as a daily reminder of her among the people closest to my father. Not one of them is willing to brush my hair. No adult can bear to touch me in a kind way: to touch me would show consideration to the woman who drove my father to an early grave.

I refuse to name these people. Not people but rock, stick, glass and bone. No names, only words for the things they have done to me. Here comes The Sneer, I tell myself, and I avoid that body's stone-rendering look. Beware of The Jab, from another body in a narrow corridor, those two fists are known by various parts of my body for planting roses in them. Be wary of The Slap, her hands, their ambidexterity stamped and re-stamped on my face, left a ringing in my ears. There are no corridors wide enough to dodge a leg, no yard, no field with sufficient acres to contain a curse. And The Spit, with a wide gap between her two front teeth that she fired spittle through farther than a child could throw a stone.

These people are blood. Aunts and uncles. They have names for me. Wretched child. Possessed child. Abandoned child. I am all of these things. Each insult adds itself to me one piece at a time to complete the puzzle of my body. Body of black and blue flowers. Red roses planted on me. Bad looks burned on my retina. Pieces of me broken and scattered about the house, in the yard, across the surrounding fields. Each piece so far from the rest of me that I can never assemble myself again into the mother creature parading as a child.

Tucked away in the middle of their scorn is their belief that I am a miniature of my mother. I compare the description the grown-ups give of her with how I looked the few times I bothered to check in a mirror. Her brown eyes, her straight, thin nose and her pouted mouth adorn my skull. I even carry her shoulder-length hair, with the natural reddish tint, not too thick not too thin and so suited to brushes as my mother would say. Her bone structure underscores my face and the same number of dark freckles decorates my brown skin. My bony body is just like hers. I harbour no memory of my life with her except the bits and pieces that I pick up from others.

Seeing photographs of my father dotted about my grandparents' eight-bedroom house, I understand their loss. When the priest visits my grandmother – out of eternal gratitude for the church my grandfather's money built and one of only two things my grandfather could not gamble away because he did not possess the deeds, the second being the house – the priest blesses the photos by carving a cross in the air. In all of them my father wears bright colours, shirts unbuttoned down to his level stomach and felt hats angled to the left or right of his scalp and drawn forward a little over one eye. His chest sticks out as if he held his breath and a pose. All his two hundred pounds are balanced on one leg and the other leg is slightly forward of his body. His right arm rests on a mahogany cane while the left is held akimbo. In pictures taken without his cane both hands are on his hips, and his feet, planted more than a shoulder length apart, share the glory of his six-foot height. Or else his right hand strokes his chin with rings on four fingers and a watch and bracelet, all made from Guyana's bright, world-renowned gold. In one photo he wears the skimpy animal skin and feathered regalia of a Macusi or Wapishana warrior from a part of the continent's Amazonian interior explored by his father for diamonds. My father actually spent time there charting rivers for their hydroelectric potential in his travels as a river surveyor, trained in Cuba. How can a woman even dent, never mind destroy, such a man? What possesses my mother to leave him? Where on

3

earth does a woman find an improvement on him in the males of the species?

On their rum and ice Friday night gatherings on the balcony I hear my aunts and uncles.

She drag him and the miserable child to England say she making a life for them.

We all know she really out for sheself.

What so wrong with making a life here in Boundary?

London welcome to her.

The miserable child should have swiped at her with the razor, not at him.

And the fire set by that damn child.

On purpose no less.

You can't plant cassava and expect to reap plantain.

I am that child armed with a razor. And after I brandish the razor, within a year, I strike that match. And all this before I face five candles on a cake. They cannot bear to say my father's name or my mother's, just as I refuse, in turn, to utter my aunts' and uncles' names. At this point when they reach the part about the fire set deliberately by the no-good child, I cork my ears. Let me sleep in my father's closet in peace. I listen to the same curses against my mother again, and against that child that I used to be but who assaults my ears every time I hear about her.

My mother drops me off here like a parcel and continues on her journey. She leaves me with her eucalyptus smell. No one wants me. I keep asking them but they all refuse to brush and plait my hair. Then my brushes disappear one by one. I hide the last one. I see a brush in an aunt's hand pulled through another child's hair and I recognise that brush as mine but never for my hair. But if my mother says, Keep her for a while, it has to be so or else an orphanage in the country's capital for me where the children reputedly fight with broken bottles and die from their injuries. Better a blow under a roof and in a yard whose kindness my father knew, than the mercy of a stranger's roof and yard. Better the back-hander from the odd neighbour familiar with my lot than a life dependent on the whim of

4

strangers. Here at least I have flatness. And locked doors, many, many locked doors – since doors never open for me – to slip under as a flattened child and the right of a body punished at random and relentlessly to change from a target to the viewpoint of a firearm.

I learn how to make my body flat when I find that in my everyday shape no one wants anything to do with me, except in one way. Otherwise I am universally ignored. In the village school for children age five to eighteen I cannot be distinguished from any of the other voices repeating a golden rule of grammar, mathematics or government. Whenever the teacher tells me to hold out my hands for his cane or he will double the number of lashes I obey, knowing that my body earns no praise or comfort from adults. Women look at me and fail to see a child with needs, like all the children they bear. They hardly notice the girl who desires all the usual things a budding adult seeks out in older people. Other children, even those in their late teens, earn the praise and affection of these same adults who treat them so differently to the way they behave towards me. I try hard to act just like those children and not to be the tongue-tied one who takes too long to spit out her words for anyone to catch them. I copy all the endearments of the other children that I see gain the good girl or clever girl compliment, or an approving smile (teeth shown or lips kept together does not matter) or quick shoulder press and on rare occasions a bear hug of a cuddle from an adult. I scrape my knee soon after I arrive at the house (quite badly I think going by the drops of blood that flower and run down my shin). I cry and hobble to the nearest adult. I hold up the afflicted area for that adult to see the legitimate cause of my distress. But when I reach to within arm's length of that grown person instead of a hug or a look of concern, that aunt pushes me away. She complains that if she finds one speck of my nasty blood, meaning my mother's blood, on her good dress, I will answer to her right then and there.

The sign I carry by virtue of the arrangement of my skin, flesh and bones, all replicas of my mother's, says REPRISALS

HERE. And the adults in the house oblige. Kick That Woman's little wretch. Slap her hard across the face. Make her fetch water from the standpipe that serves the village until she fills an entire rain barrel, before she eats any breakfast, before she picks up her slate, her exercise book, and her mother's self and shuffles off to a school wasted on her. Send her with fatigue and hunger to church, to school, to bed. Tie her up into a reef knot of rules. Her in her mother's face and body. She must pay. Straighten her out. Even the unsmiling boy my age, who lives in the next field but loves the big house more than his own home, joins in with my blood relatives in my correction. Flattening me out cannot be further from their minds.

This Friday night I awake to the more raucous than usual talk of my aunts and uncles. 'That blasted child not ready to see,' – so my uncles and aunts keep shouting at the solitary dissenting voice of an aunt – 'that damn letter', from my father to me. They will know when the time is right then they will let me know it too. The day will declare itself to all of them and then they will declare it to me and that will be that. Then and only then, they will hand me the letter. I can inspect it for all the things I want to know about my father's life surveying rivers and everything about his London life with my mother and I will be answered once and for all. They speak as if the letter is theirs to give away. In fact, Grandfather took it with him when he left. They embrace a facet of one person in the family as if it belongs to all of them, including the letter from my father.

Their argument widens to other matters. Apparently, when asked by my mother if he can love one woman at a time, my father answered No, instead of Yes. My uncles and aunts debate the rightness or otherwise of this honest answer. Most think that my mother was not enough of a woman for my father, that he was bound to stray but his straying, even if it had consequences, did not mean he loved her any less; that something evil in her refused to see that. And why after leaving him did she insist on using the family name and spreading it all over the country with her warped politics?

6

They find this last fact the most noxious of the many terrible things about her.

And she end up back here with her tail between her legs, calling herself politician.

When monkey catch trouble, baboon trousers soon fit.

She make a name for herself all right.

He should never have left this place with her.

I wish she never set foot in Boundary.

London should-a keep she ass.

I miss him all the time.

Me too.

Me as well.

They toast to three things – my father's continued peace in the grave, my mother's rapid demise, and the aversion of a border war. I cover my ears but I still hear them. I blink the salt from my eyes, pretend the spread fingers of my right hand is a brush and run them repeatedly through my hair for the noise of a downpour that fills my ears and the scrape of bony fingertips on my skull. I hum a calypso in which the only words I know are *Ring, ting, ting*. I conjure eucalyptus.

MOTHER

When I delivered you to your father's house – you will hear many versions of why he wanted you there and why I had to comply with this last wish of his — I remained by the roadside. It was not safe for me to set foot on property owned by the parents of the man whose death they blamed me for. The car pulled up to the front of the house in a U-turn that spanned the entire two-lane road and ended with the car facing the capital it came from, its engine idling, its wheels half-on, half-off the grass verge. You tried to stand on the back seat and look through the back windscreen at the children sprinting towards us from the two-storey whitewashed house. I climbed out the car and hauled you after me. I literally slipped my hands under your armpits and scooped you up. You bent your legs thinking that I intended to carry you just as I lowered you to the ground and I frowned at you because I had to bend my bad back to accommodate your weight. You soon caught on and you straightened your legs and took the strain off my poor back. I swiped at the hem of your pleated dress knocking away the untidy folds of the road trip. Then you smiled at me with your upturned face and I inhaled deeply to give myself back-bone to go through with giving you away as I was obliged to do. All your lovely teeth and bright brown eyes trusted me so completely that I found it hard to breathe knowing what I was about to do with you. My eyes narrowed. You must have recognised this look of mine. I put it on or it took over me when I worried or took on resolve. You clung to my leg.

Your uncles wore various items from your father's wardrobe, even his muddy boots. And since they resembled him your father appeared split into two, his features distributed between them. Everyone looked up and down at us. Aunt

Ethel, the eldest (since you always like to know precise ages, she is much older than I) approached us and signalled the children and everyone else to stay back in the yard. All obeyed. They perched on one leg or leaned on the fence and the gate or on each other and they stared without smiling or any expression other than complete curiosity. The children ranged in size from so small they had to be carried to so big they appeared to be the parents of the children wedged to their hips. From your lip movements I could tell you counted them with all your fingers and toes and still failed to account for all the adults and children. You braced against me and kept your arm around my leg during the minutes of negotiations between your father's eldest sister and me. She repeated clause by clause the dictation of your grandmother locked away in an upstairs bedroom, running things as ever from a distance as if by remote control.

My narrowed eyes must have made crow's feet splay towards my temples, crow's feet that I try hard to hide by keeping my face as still as a mask in this glaring light. I miss you rubbing my temples with your bony little fingers after I come home from work, as you must surely miss me combing your hair. I grimaced against the glare of the midday sun and must have looked bad-tempered. I hoped you knew I guarded against the people here and not the sun. I could not take my eyes off your Aunt Ethel as I talked to her, not once, not even to glance at the sun or at you. I could feel you hugging my leg and feel too the lean of your body on me that I had to brace against a little to stop us both toppling into the trench at the side of the road.

Then I unclasped you from my leg, kissed you on the lips, cheeks and forehead, and would have consumed you then and there if I could, but your Aunt Ethel unhooked you from me to help me separate from you it seemed. Or she did it to put a stop to our long goodbye. I handed Aunt Ethel a suitcase packed with your clothes, and, knowing how much you share my love of brushes, I secreted some of our old favourites in various parts of the suitcase, in your shoes, or wrapped with your clothes. As I packed for you I itched to be a fly on the wall when you unpacked and came across our brushes one by one. Last thing, I pressed a valuable bundle of British pounds and American dollars into your aunt's hand. I stipulated that the money was for you and not for any other child. You might have overheard this. I said, 'Write to me. I will write to you.' And I added quite loudly for those nearby to hear just what they could do for you: Ask someone nicely to brush your hair in the morning and at night. You nodded and then you screamed at the top of your five-year-old lungs at the sight of me climbing into my chauffeur-driven car without you. I cried to have to leave you in a strange place with strangers. You know how much I love you. I write this to fill in for you things you cannot possibly retain in your young, impressionable head. But you should know from me that you are a part of me and I feel your absence every day. I will explain everything a little later when you are old enough to judge for yourself. Enjoy as much as you can the house where your father was born and where he grew into a man. Pay your respects at his grave on his birthday and the day of his death and on your birthday and on mine too if you think of it. You can pay your respects on my behalf any time.

If you see a bird, especially a flock, think of him. He loved them as much as the rivers he surveyed and believed he was a kingfisher in a previous life. I teased him by saying he struck me more as a pigeon in a flock at Trafalgar Square than a regal kingfisher. He never failed to retort that whatever species of bird I cared to make him I would still be the desirable worm he pulled from a lawn.

BETTANY

Eleven years of hearing from my aunts, uncles and cousins about my arrival and not a word from my mother, not a single reply to my almost weekly letters to her, makes me believe that I recollect my arrival and her departure without me the way I hear it. How my mother turns from me and climbs into the back seat of that government car and does not even bother to look out the back windscreen at me, her child, in the arms of an aunt holding on to me to keep me from chasing the official car taking my mother from me. How the driver toots the car horn as he accelerates away. And I scream and wriggle to free myself from that aunt's grip but she holds on to me tighter as if my struggle tightens the knot of her arms around me. My aunt orders me to stop my foolish behaviour. I keep up my elbowing and kicking of my legs. When I find I can hardly breathe, I stop fighting. Sure enough her arms slacken around my chest. But she looks down at me to check that it is not a trick that I play on her and to let me know in that raised eyebrow stare of hers that she knows what I am up to so I should think twice before trying anything. Her look seems a little surprised too as if my little body displays too much strength for its size. Can a five-year-old body fight so hard? Answer: Yes, if the mother shelters in there. The mother is the one who fights and not the child.

A part of me says to the rest of me that I am wrong to put on such a show for these strange relatives. All I have to do is watch and wait and in a little time the peaked-capped chauffeur and the special government number plates will reappear because my mother cannot bear to leave me anywhere she is not. That part of me wants to walk away from the side of the road the second my mother hugs me and turns her back on me and climbs into the back seat of the black Mercedes. This part of me assures the rest of me, she'll be back, mark my words, so in the little time it takes for her to make up her mind to return for you why not see what you can of this quaint place. Be quick before she bundles you in the back seat with her, and the chauffeur toots twice as he zooms from the village towards the capital. That's the part of me that looks on and sneers as I writhe in my aunt's bear hug, the portion of me that believes I am showing the worst side of myself and all for nothing. Because I should know that my mother could not live without me, just as I cannot live without her, two portions of a lung, two halves of a heart, two aspects of one mind.

I try to make a sudden break from those slack arms and run after the Mercedes as it approaches the bend that would take it out of the village and out of sight. But as I tense and dash forward the arms around my chest simply spring their trap and pin me to my aunt's body. I thrash my arms and legs and my aunt clasps them with her limbs. She wraps her legs around my legs and her arms around my body. The government car's brake lights flash as it hugs the corner that leads out of the village. The part of me that most resembles my mother, my grown-up side, disapproves of my actions by shaking her head in dismay and almost walks off and leaves me but thinks twice about it, knowing she will not last long without the rest of me to feed her. I fight with my aunt at the sight of my mother's disappearance and almost faint from my aunt's powerful grip. The two parts of me reunite as a reminder that no one can help me now but myself.

I believe right then that my mother in me, the part of me that behaves like her, will surely perish away from the real figure of my mother to model herself on. I struggle even harder in my aunt's arms wishing for more of my mother to involve herself in my fight, lend me her strength, that of a woman who buried a strapping man and who lives her life without relying on anyone. All this done with a little dependent body. Another mouth to take the food out of her mouth, another back to clothe and deplete the layers on her back, another body to keep safe from traffic, from ponds, open windows, yellow fever, and scorpions. But the gleaming black car that brought me here disappears with my mother. I stand among strangers in my aunt's knotted arms. Again my aunt tells me in a rapid, loud voice to stop my foolishness. I gather myself for nights and days away from my mother in my father's house, the house where he sprouted from my pint size into an adult and in whose grounds he lies in peace. The road wavers emptily in the heat, empty as far as the corner that leads back to the capital, except for me and my parts in that road, my mother in me and the sneering portion of myself, crying to be back in the car beside my mother.

My aunt scoops me up and carries me into the yard and to the house. A bunch of children follows us. I scream into my aunt's face, *I want my mother!* She shakes her head and turns her face away. I shout at her, I hate you! Then she puts me down and just as I wish I had employed the slur earlier, before I can dart from her, she grips my right arm and pulls me back to her and slaps me hard on the right side of my face. I fall silent. But she is not content with this immediate result. I tricked her before and I might trick her again. She aims at me, this time with her right hand, as if she expects me to dodge her and she slaps my stock-still face a second time, the fresh left side of my face. Then she talks into my stinging features but I cannot hear a word. Her lips are white and her eyes narrow as my mother's eyes often narrow in concentration. My aunt ignores the urine that trickles down my legs. Her two slaps, one from each hand, both delivered with equal force, knock all the words I know up to that moment out of my head. She pulls me by my left arm and I trip along after her. We walk past the house to the back of it, past a few tall coconut, mango, tamarind and guava trees until we reach a well-tended spot shaded by a huge jacaranda tree and there in front of me is a neat rectangle of concrete, newly laid and spanking white. My aunt says my father lies under the ground right there and that is why I am here. That he wanted the best for his daughter and only Boundary could offer it to me just as the house offered it to him. Were it not for his dying wish to have me live in his childhood house and gain all the same goodness from it, I too would be underground. I have the bad manners and devilish looks of my mother and none of my father's good ways and decent blood. Then she flicks a tear from her cheekbone and spins me around and to my surprise all the children and adults looking on at the spectacle of my aunt disciplining me, they too flick tears away. The sight of them all upset on my account renews my bawling. I look at my surroundings through this eye water and stop seeing one thing as distinct from another. My aunt keeps her firm grip on my left arm and marches me into the cool shadows of the house.

The sneering part of me looks on resigned. I switch to its frequency. I wipe my face dry on my right forearm and drop that wincing look for a mask of impassivity. My sneering self nods at the rest of me as if my newfound quiet and calm is a place it has been waiting in all along for me to arrive and join it. This is my mother's body, not mine, I tell myself, not in words but pictures. I have no words for what is happening to me, just pictures. Of a VIP's car driving away with my mother snug in its plush leather interior. Of my aunt's arms wrapped around my body. And of a steel cable snapping when my aunt's left hand, then her right, connected to my face. And my father, dead at twenty-nine, buried in the soil under my feet, deep below ground, hearing nothing of all this, his ears sealed with wax, his eyelids clamped shut.

My mother swears to return for me at some distant point in the future. And she promises to write. But I do not receive a single letter from her despite my weekly letters to her which I dutifully hand to my uncle, Boundary's one and only postman. Less letters, more notes at first and drawings scratched on any piece of paper I lay hands on and put into an envelope. He promises to take care of everything. Notes and drawings become detailed recapitulations of my punishments at the house and of my dreams to be back in my mother's arms. I sign, fold, seal and hand over these letters to my uncle and always without any prompting from me exact from him his promise to personally place them in the hands of the right people who will in turn deliver them into her hands and only for her eyes. My aunts and uncles say she does not write to me because she does not care one iota about me. I would be lucky if she knows who I am. That she dropped me into the world and walked away from my mewling. And who can blame her shunning a wicked and unbearable miniature of herself. My aunts, uncles and their children ask me about my likes and dislikes. From my frank answers (for instance, I like green and hate red, prefer furry things to smooth, love savoury things, not sweet, and loathe all things bitter or good for me), they decide to take up my instruction in country life by means of a series of reprimands. They see how a couple of slaps works miracles on me. My aunt strips me of my good clothes, as she calls everything I own, and she gives me faded and patched replacements since she knows 'as sure as day follows night that you will soon be scratching in the dirt like a chicken'. She passes a hand over my hair to ascertain its texture, its coarseness. From the look that plays for an instant around her mouth, as if she tastes tamarind, I must fail some complex indices of hers defined by the mix of our South Asian, African and European antecedents.

After a few days of leaving me to wander behind the other children, another aunt looks at me and decides it is time I learn a skill around the house. My instruction does not involve any explanation or demonstration of a task. I am simply handed a tool or pushed in a particular direction and expected to founder or prosper. This method of instruction by trial and error costs me dearly. If I get a particular thing wrong I earn a blow and a reproach, like the day I spill too much water from the buckets I fetch from the village standpipe and pour into a water barrel. The electricity, water supply and sanitation systems to houses break, and with no foreign currency for the government to fix it the countryside reverts to oil and gas lamps and to fetching water from standpipes and using outhouses. I return from the standpipe with the buckets less than three-quarters full and gain a blow. I reach up and tilt the bucket into the water barrel and a little water spills and I earn another blow and my aunt tells me I must repeat the trip. When I plead with her she slaps me on the mouth and slaps me again in her two-handed delivery of blows when most people would use one hand or the other for the enterprise. I have no idea where the next slap will come from. So I keep my mouth shut and dart from her clutches with the clanging aluminium buckets.

My father's oldest sister, The Slap, who is said to be closest to him, decides from day one of my arrival and after she hears me describe my likes and dislikes that I am a five-year-old blabbermouth. She slaps me every time she catches me talking in her presence, no matter what I say. In a few weeks after my arrival at the house when I try to speak in her absence I find myself stuttering.

I watch adults and other children as closely as I can in order not to fail. But everyone I look at feels uncomfortable under my scrutiny, since it is too much like my mother's, and they tell me so, chase me away or hit me. I practise seeing without looking. My peripheral vision becomes better than a direct stare if only because it involves my total concentration. As I pretend to unravel a bundle of twine I actually study how an aunt with a thimble on her index finger sews a button on to a shirt.

I do this seeing-without-looking thing again as I sit in the shade of the house picking spoiled rice grains and gritty bits from a bowl of rice everyone in the house is destined to eat that night. I use the occasion of my closeness to my oldest uncle, The Lash, sharing the same patch of shade, to observe how he shortens a slack bicycle chain. He services his collection of bicycles from around the world, the aluminium Keppler from Germany with its noisy sprocket slightly faster than the second hand of a clock creates the impression of accelerated time so that a sensitive rider may feel himself ageing as he rides it. The cast iron Raleigh from Birmingham, England, with its fixed wheel that the rider must keep pedalling to stay upright weighs a ton. The Gazelle from Holland with its quaint bell, narrow saddle and dropped handlebars seems built expressly for sprinting off the saddle. You can pull the body weight up using the leverage of the ram's horns for handlebars. No one but my uncle can ride these bicycles unless given special dispensation from him.

My aunt feeds the needle through each of the four holes of the button in turn and finds her way with the needle back through shirt material and through the buttonholes using touch alone. She concludes by wrapping thread around the base of the button and makes a simple knot and bites through the thread with her front teeth, biting so close to the button that I think she might accidentally swallow it. I find out later when I watch her teach another child how to sew buttons on to garments that this technique of biting close to the button is to make sure the bitten-off end of the thread does not show.

First, my oldest uncle slips the chain off the big sprocket connected to the pedals of the Gazelle, whose 23-inch frame mounted on 27-inch wheels stands as high as my head. Then he hammers with a chisel using precise taps very like tuning a piano, until the main link that joins the chain into a closed circle pops and releases a very small clasp with one open end and one closed end. Until this moment I have never seen a broken bicycle chain. Laid out on a cloth in a rough straight line it looks like the bare bones of a poisonous snake and though just a skeleton somehow still capable of destruction. I fight an impulse to move farther away by sticking both hands into the bowl of rice and squeezing handfuls. The uncle removes two links and replaces the clasp with the same delicate taps. When he puts the chain back on the big sprocket and turns the pedal with his hand the chain is tight. It hardly shows any slack as he presses the chain midway between the pedals and back wheel with his middle finger.

Older clothes patch newer ones. No one except me ever seems to throw anything away. Everything applies in some fashion to some function other than the one designed for it. A massive jar full of buttons contains one button someone will need sometime. An old shirt or pair of trousers provides just the right patch for a newer shirt worn at the elbow or collar or trousers worn at the knee or in need of a zip. The entire house relates in this way, one part to another, item by item, person to person. And I extrapolate from there that it must apply from house to house until it engulfs the entire country. Except for me. I stand alone, ungarlanded. In that jar with a thousand buttons none suits me. In all the cupboards, drawers and boxes of old clothing and bits and pieces, not one patch suits what I wear. Or so it is presented to me over the years. The bolt of cloth I am cut from has to be stored in some other far-away place. In some distant place a jar full of buttons has my name written on it and every button in it is for me. But not here in my grandparents' house or any other house in this country.

My uncle glances at me with a look of satisfaction after his successful repair of the bicycle chain, but I am obviously engrossed in cleaning rice for the evening meal.

Come ride this thing for me, make sure it work all right.

Me?

Yes, you.

I move extra fast for this uncle, The Lash. His lashes sting the most because he delivers them at twice the speed of everyone else. His hands make reluctant contact with my flesh, they hardly touch down and they are off again only to descend on me with the same rapidity, as if beating eggs for an omelette. His technique of rapid descent and ascent rather than creating the impression of a light touch really stings. I jump on the Gazelle, from Holland, painted a beautiful red with white tape around the dropped handlebar and he says not to ride anywhere, just balance on the spot with my weight on the pedals while he inspects his new link on the bicycle chain. The children call this 'stickling' after the habit of the hummingbird, its sudden stop in mid flight to tread air. The bicycle wheels are kept on the spot and the rider balances on the pedals. Only the handlebar swivels to keep the bike upright and the body tilts left and right, forwards and backwards in small fractions and rapid adjustments. With all the weight on the pedals the chain must be sturdy. I stickle. I know this has to be my best effort to avoid a beating from him. I pretend the bicycle has three wheels and I have merely to stay poised over it. I distribute my weight between my feet and my hands and draw an imaginary straight line from my navel to a point halfway between the arc of the two wheels. I shut everything else out of my head, the birds, the traffic, far-off cackles from children playing, an enamel pan dropped on the kitchen floor, a donkey braying, cows calling and answering each other. My uncle stops examining his handiwork on the chain and shifts his gaze to me instead. I drop my left foot off the pedal not sure what else to do and he nods and almost smiles.

The chain good, Uncle.

You think so.

Yes, you fix it good.

He seems about to say something kind, even to surrender to that smile, but a cloud of recognition passes over his face that I am the girl child of that woman, the one who killed his brother. He tugs the Gazelle from my grip and wheels it away. I watch him less overcome with sourness at his dismissal of me than with his adult trick of pushing a bicycle by the saddle and somehow managing to guide the steering wheel with little jolts of the hand gripping that saddle. He toggles life into the frame or the frame serves as an extension of him.

The belief prevails throughout the region that one cannot reason with Guyanese people. They believe in God and in an array of spirits with equal alacrity. They speak the Queen's English on a sliding scale of imperfection that ranges from passable to incomprehensible. But I grant their accent a certain sonority making the most banal report sound like the Cambridge church choir. The temptation to a leader who thinks Guyana's plural use of English puts the people at an intellectual disadvantage must be simply to pass legislation against certain types of primitive behaviour. Our leader legislates on the basis that the habit of reason will supplant blind faith, even as she relies on the latter for political survival.

My school – I should say the school I preside over – brought the idea of reason into the countryside in an attempt to replace an ingrained superstition that governed all practices and impeded progress. More to the point, my school bought Bethany a few hours of relief from the big house but thrust her into another crowded building. She seemed the only child every other child in the building refused to acknowledge. Her cousins passed her in doorways and in the playground. They showed a stranger more consideration. They failed to register her existence even when her name came up. A new teacher always expressed surprise to hear that this child bore the Abrahams name and lived in the biggest house in Boundary and was a blood relative of the twelve children of school age who attended my school. The surprise soon turned to concern that the girl did not appear to exist around her cousins.

When I started this school I held ideals that governed the thinking of certain sections of the educated elite in the region's newest republic. We had the highest literacy rate in the region but we were dirt poor. The rich would climb higher as riches do but governance of the soul also in pursuit of ethical wealth meant giving a helping hand to those less fortunate as we progressed. In this way everyone would improve. We would not rely on legislation to do all the work of building a nation. To this end I became a government schoolteacher. I put aside my private pupils and the glut of their privilege that seemed unmindful of the importance of my Cambridge classical education brought back to this country, less a country and more a shared jungle. I embraced the humble and less fortunate, though equally able, children secreted in the countryside. I did this for my new country. A new start for it and for me. A clean slate. When it all turned sour and the big split occurred in the party, driving a wedge between family and friends, had I stayed in the capital I would have killed a man or he murdered me.

Bethany started at my school already well versed in her alphabet and most of her multiplication tables. I asked her about it since illiteracy and innumeracy were more common in a pre-school child. She informed me in her English accent that diminished with every day she breathed republic air and was replaced by the telltale singsong-like intonation of pot-pourri English, that she learned her tables and alphabet from the years she listened to her father and mother. Apparently, while they resided in England her mother sang everything into her ear. Her mother could sing. I'll testify to that. Many years ago I heard her sing the new national anthem at a government rally in the capital. She sounded much like Lady Day with her interpretive cocktail of tonal clarity and emotional venom. And her father, brandishing a theodolite (he taught her how to say the word) looked at the sweet Thames and made her repeat everything he read there in his job as a river surveyor.

She relayed to me in a public-speaking class the story of her first day home from school. According to her testimony Bethany showed her slate to two of her aunts. To Ethel, going by the child's description, the second oldest woman in the house, if I omit the child's grandmother, and to Vera who is younger than Ethel though not the youngest of the four daughters. Bethany wrote her name on the slate. She pointed to the words and said aloud, 'My name is Bethany. I was born in England.' Something startled her aunts both of whom recoiled from her. Ethel blurted out, 'You can't spell.' Before Bethany could ask her aunt where the mistake was located her aunt daubed her finger with spit and swiped it through the letter h and with the same spittle added a second t next to the first one. Bethany said she began to protest that the head-teacher – meaning me, I supervised her penmanship – thought the spelling was fine. But Ethel chased Bethany away by raising her hand as if to unleash a slap across the poor child's face. Bethany said she kept running long after she was out of Ethel's reach because the younger aunt, Vera, could project her spittle the length of Wimbledon's centre court. When she reached a safe distance she examined the slate. Bethany reported that her aunt's wet finger marks dried and left an empty gap: Bet any. Bethany rubbed her index finger lightly over each letter for a little chalk and made that missing t that her aunt said should be there. She took from one to add to the other and made her name almost illegible. She ran to find her aunt spelling her name over and over: B-e-t-t-a-n-y; B-e-t-t-a-n-y; B-e-t-t-a-n-y.

She told this story about her name before what was a mild speech impediment worsened to unintelligibility and she ceased saying anything to anyone unless forced. I made her tell me what happened and only got it out of her one syllable at a time when I threatened her with a taste of my cane. She said an aunt hit her in the face every time she spoke. It puzzled me that the child's face was clean and unblemished. She described the blows as fists and kicks. I volunteered to her that if these repeated beatings were true then she ought to have scars to show for it. Other children turned up with black eyes, black and blue marks on their bodies, even broken limbs. She took a long time to reply between her stuttering and sobbing but all she said was that she would not be here, meaning alive, were it not for one thing that saved her life every time she was subjected to a beating. What, I asked her, what? Her shoulders and chest heaved in the full throttle of distress. I may or may not have heard her say 'flatness'. I should have asked her to write it for me because it made no sense as explained by her, and by pressing her I drew an inordinate amount of attention to her speech defect. At this point and in light of the lack of visual evidence on her of a beating, I put her story down to three things – first, a child's fertile imagination, second, her need for her absent mother, and, third, the absence in her life of a male substitute for her dead father.

I never encourage the children to think that I have a favourite among them but that tale of hers about the spelling of her name told me that she loved to obey authority and for her own good that authority needed to be benevolent otherwise she would suffer. We preached this in the capital in those heady days of nation building when the newly independent country was the child and those of us in charge of governance its parents. I found myself showing her special attention. She is very like her mother, able to draw you in and before you know it there is nothing you can do but be drawn in.

This report on my newest and most promising pupil would be incomplete if I did not declare my partiality in this case. For political reasons I am unable to set foot in the Abrahams' compound. For the same reasons I cannot send this report to the house but must keep it in confidence until the child's mother returns to claim her. But I will have another teacher make discreet inquiries about Bethany's situation at the house. I may be banished from the capital for my views but I can still exercise benevolent authority when I see the need for it.

The first time I become flat I think I am drowning in my own blood. I feel some evil force walking me very slowly through the various stages of asphyxiation. The incident involves the uncle I call The Jab, who everyone says cannot exert himself any more since his accident.

The Jab calls me over to him. He shows me a glass marble with a swirl of blue trapped inside. I want that marble. He sees it in my face. He smiles and holds his hands behind his back and fidgets for a while. Then he presents both hands to me, closed into fists, palms facing downwards. I realise I should choose one of his two hands. I stare at them. I know them as fists, their deep bruise, yet now they hold in the same shape the very thing that I most want at that moment, the promise of the blue sea trapped in clear glass in what air would be if air were solid. Choose one. I want the treasure that one of those fists contains, some good thing offered to me for the first time in my dealings with them. The risk of picking one, the wrong one, and losing the gift wrapped inside it seems worse than anything those fists have done to me up to this point. I use both of my hands to slap the backs of both of his hands. This astonishes him. His jaws drop wide open. He looks at me quizzically as if to say, What have you done? He has the choice right then to become deadly serious with me or to shrug off my action as that of a child who cannot bear to lose a marble. He decides on the former.

As he carries out the action of his decision I hear a lot about my father from this uncle. He talks as though he read the letter my father left for me to learn all about our life together when I was too young to recall it. That's how this uncle sounds from all the pieces of his chatter as he tries to breathe with faulty lungs and deal with me at the same time. He talks about my life in London with my father and mother. *Before his body was flown home in a box.* My father posts the letter to the big house with my name on it (care of my grandfather) and it is delivered after his body arrives at a house of disbelieving screams, shouts, howls and moans, followed closely by my mother's delivery of me. *He shaved every morning for work and at night too before he went out. He had to. The hair grew so fast on him you could practically see it sprouting on his face.* If he shaves so often I must have seen him. But I only summon up what this uncle says about him. Then I pretend that I do not hear it from my uncle and it becomes a part of my recall about my father. In our past life together my father often shaves twice a day and I like to watch him and he takes his time liking me there by his side. My earliest memory from age two is of my father standing in front of a mirror and sink shaving. I consume everything this uncle says about my mother and father, no matter how terrible, and write myself into the middle of it in this way. I become convinced that I remember it the way it really must have happened rather than hearing my uncle say it to me. I decide I am the one who knows and not this uncle. *He took more care over his appearance than most women.* I think of my father and mother quarrelling over which one should have first use of the bathroom. He complains that she steams up the entire bathroom and it is impossible for him to see his face in the mirror in order to shave properly. She says he takes so long he makes her late for her nurse's shift at the hospital. He maintains that a man must be clean before he faces the outside world. She replies his account of clean is more like a pre-operative sterility since no woman she knows takes so long to get ready to face the world. They both laugh during these exchanges and I join in their laughter. Bethany-Bettany laughing on behalf of her absent mother and dead father.

A normal child would have played by the rules of the game and chosen one of my two hands, not both. I shouted at her that her action mimicked what her mother would do, that she deceived just like her mother, that my dead brother would still be here if it was not for her murdering mother. What she thought of as clever, I reminded her, was simply force-ripe, way ahead of her years through some deal on her part and the part of the spirit world, some contract between her and it.

I would teach her to be smart with me. The same hand that displayed the marble to her, before I placed both hands behind my back and pretended to shuffle the marble from one to the other, now opened with the marble in it. I plunged my hand into my right trouser pocket and pulled it out empty. Let the spirits and her mother protect her from what I had to do. Let them strike me dead. Nothing can hold my hand.

I said a lot more to her as I dragged her towards the bushes at the back of the house. I chased the other children away, including my own son, Rick. The children still followed at a safe distance. But Rick walked away from me hanging his head as limp as the day I pulled him half-drowned from the pond. I dragged her past the few trees that dotted the yard at the back of the house. Bushes began a little further down the yard and shouldered up to the fence bordering the right side of the property. The trees cast broad shadows. The children sometimes played a game of seeing who could get from the back of the house to the bottom of the yard by jumping from one shadow to the other without their feet touching the ground baked by the sun. The backyard became a narrow path as the bush encroached into it and took over. Most of the chopping with cutlasses that we did around the property was a losing battle against this proliferation of weeds, bushes and vines. I did not have to drag her too hard. She ran to keep up with me as best as she could. I suppose she knew that any resistance on her part would simply add to her punishment. I walked at top speed now and I looked down at her and continued our little talk. I made a note to myself to find Rick and explain why I did not want him to witness this side of me. His temperament changed since his near drowning, from warm and outgoing to the reticence of someone wound up like a coiled spring. I hardly recognise him. I need to try harder with him.

But right then I had to contend with her. I reminded her that she was her mother, that she had killed my older brother and that whereas the law had failed to do a thing about it, since her mother paraded scot-free, I would knock some sense into her. How long had I waited for this moment? How long bided my time and watched her parade as her mother? I cringed as the woman in her skulked about the house and hopped on the concrete grave of my brother. And early one morning I found her asleep on my brother's grave, its sunned concrete from the day before cooling all night with her on it.

But as I dragged her she screamed like a child. The time that it took me to transport her to the bushes allowed more time than usual for her to think about the beating. Usually when threatened with a beating it happened right away, even as the threat was uttered. Or else the threat remained like a remote and fading possibility that allowed her to carry on with her chores with it at the back of her mind. This time the person who made the threat conveyed her to the place where the punishment would be carried out. She had no means of escape and the time that it took to reach the bush, which could not have been more that a minute, was enough time I suppose for her to conjure up the worst kind of beating in her mind. I think I convinced her somehow that she would be killed this time, that there would be no nursing of her wounds, that one badly aimed blow from me would send her into the hereafter to join her father and she would never see her devil mother again. I broke a long stem from a branch with the hand that had started all this when I held out the marble to her. I did not bother to clear the stem of leaves and small twigs. My marble hand lashed at her. She wet herself. She stood as still as possible, offering her back, shoulders, legs and arms to me and shielding her face by turning it away from me. She screamed. I struggled to breathe. The whip broke. I picked another and lashed at her again. I promised to beat her mother out of her. The normal child must be buried in her somewhere. I would find that child today or kill that murdering woman in her. I punctuated each of my words with a swing of my whip. This second whip broke too. I hit her on her arms and back and about her head with my open marble hand and steadied her folding body with my other hand. I reminded her that her body was a temple of evil and the devil was in her and the priest would have to exorcise the devil from her. That my brother would be alive today if only he had stayed away from her mother and gone to the other woman and stayed. I no longer aimed at her back or arms or legs. I jabbed her in her face and chest and stomach. She fell to the ground. I kicked the woman. She yelped like a dog. But she dared not bite back or snarl or bark. She curled her body and absorbed all the swings from my arm and leg, two arms, two legs. What chance did she give my brother? I ignored her howls and then her whimper. She turned her back and shielded her head, crotch and ribs. But she needed the arms and legs of a spider to shield herself from my blows. And more than a government to protect her. Her hands were too late and too few. They served merely to map the places where my fist or foot landed, mapping my blows with her lighter touch that hardly touched down before it raced after another blow from me. Where was her government now?

She glanced at me through the crook of her arms, her spread fingers, through the curl of her body she peeped out to see where the next blow from my arms and legs would land. This was for my brother, in honour of his memory. And no army, no law, no government or headmaster behind her this time to stop me.

KIND AUNT

Bettany always in the middle of something. Even when she nowhere in sight she enters the conversation of my sisters and brothers. I think we talk about her more than anyone else in this house, even my absent father and lock-away mother, more even than my dead brother and the woman who put him in the ground. I have my own children to worry about without taking on Bettany, yet I look to be the only one willing to defend her.

I hear the commotion from the kitchen window above the noise of cooking a meal for a small army of mouths. I hear my brother shouting at the top of his bad lungs between his exertions. If he chopping wood, something he has not done since his accident, then his voice calls out just before the axe falls on the wood. His voice strains. He growls and shrieks, fights for each breath and fights someone all at the same time. Whatever he swings comes down on its target at twice the speed of an axe. I lean from the window as far as I can without tumbling out of it but the angle is wrong. I cannot see that deep into the back yard. I see the children. All of them it seems, except for my brother's son, Rick, who wanders to the front of the house with his head hanging, all of them crane their necks and hold on to each other and wince as they watch. Their faces tie and untie and their bodies flinch as if their flesh counted something or had something counted out on it.

Right away I think of Bettany. My brother's voice, his laboured breaths, his exertions as if he swings an axe all have to be with Bettany as the hard wood, greenheart wood, Bettany or the stubborn donkey. I want it to be the donkey because the donkey often stops in the middle of carting a load and no amount of beating can induce him to move off the spot. Cajoling him becomes as much of a spectacle as the sight of him nailed to the spot and oblivious to the bribing and bullying. The usual comic laughter from watching someone try every trick to win the donkey's favour is absent among the children. It must be Bettany, she always in the middle of everything bad.

I run from the kitchen and manage to dry my hands on my apron and remove it as I run. I hope to bump into one of my two children coming to fetch me instead of forming a part of the crowd of children who simply stand by and watch the girl's punishment. I fling my apron on the banister of the back steps as I bound down them three at a time. The habit of never being seen outside the house in an apron stays with me even in an emergency. I sprint and shout at the children as I approach them and they part obligingly for me. I order my two into the house. I see Bettany on the ground, curled up with her head tucked in her arms and her hands stretched over her groin, her knees drawn up too. She lies quite still. Except when my brother's fists and feet connect with her and then she jolts.

I throw myself between my brother and her. I collect a few of his blows. I fought him all the time when we were younger and sometimes I won but he is a man now and far more muscular. His bad lungs help to even things between us. He tries to push past me and get to the child again but his need for air weakens his resolve. I hold on to him and brace my body against his so that he cannot move without dragging my entire body with his. He cries and keeps fighting to get around me and hit the child. He pants for air and begs me between panting in a broken string of words, each word separated with a breath, to release him. I say I am older and therefore he should listen to me. I beg him to forget the scrawny child and think about the people who will grieve for him if she died by his hands. The idea of her death and our grief for him puzzles him. I cannot think of anyone around here apart from me who might grieve for the child. Through my tears triggered by his, I shout at him that a child should not have to pay for the sins of the parent. I repeat that the child is not the only one to think about.

Rick needs his father. But he pushes at my arms clinging to his body and says he sure Bettany not an ordinary child but the very woman who killed our dear brother. I tell him I do not want to lose another brother over the same woman and spread more grief among us all. I think the idea that he might become the second victim of the child's mother quiets him a little. He no longer thrusts me away from him. That is good because my arms slide down his midriff and I am on the ground holding on to both of his legs and on the verge of releasing my grip for lack of any strength left in my arms. He presses his fingers to his forehead and shakes his head to clear it. His chest heaves as he gasps for air. He turns his neck alone since he cannot move with my arms around his legs and he looks across the field at Mavis's house and then at her son in the crowd of other children. Whatever he thinks about the fact that Mavis's son is watching him as he beats Bettany, that and his difficulty breathing more than my grip on him and my reasoning with him, stops him. He takes a marble from his pocket and drops it on the child. One of the other children detaches from the crowd of onlookers. It is my second sister's child, a spiteful little brute of a girl if ever there was such a creature. She runs up to us and grabs the marble. I am too out of breath to talk to her about it and she ignores my wave of my arm. Bettany remains in her crouched position except for her head, which she raises and stares at me. Her mouth and nose are bloody and her eyes swollen. Even with her face smeared red she bears a striking resemblance to her mother. The way she stares at me I have to remind myself that this is a child facing me and not a woman. She soiled her dress. I scramble to my feet and turn my brother towards the house and guide him back to its shade before he changes his mind and returns his attention to the child. I have no strength left to hold him off her. When I look at Bettany again her head is turned towards the house. I follow her gaze to my three sisters and two sisters-in-law all of whom move away from the upstairs windows and back into the shadows. I want just one of them to help me, but even his wife fails to lift a finger to stop my brother.

I pull the apron off the banister. I shout at them asking if our brother's death is not enough, if our father gone from the house is not enough and our mother locked up in her room unable to face the light of day because she thinks she caused both disappearances. I say all this near our mother's bedroom window, almost below it, as I guide my brother into the house. My brother despite his breathing problems has the wherewithal to put his hand over my mouth to silence me. I do not have the strength to push his arm away and I have nothing more to say anyway. My brother moves his hand off my mouth to allow me to pull the apron over my head. I take a small step away from him and tie the apron string around my waist. I lift a clean corner of the country's map faded on it and wipe my face and we walk into the house. He holds on to me to keep me by his side and prevent me from returning to help the child. I stay with him unsure what new calamity my going to the child might bring down on her head. I promise myself to go to her later or send one of my children to make sure she is on her feet and ask her to come to see me.

A girl says to me, Look what you do, you make uncle cry. I ignore her and try to stand and find it easier just to sit for a while. I lift my left arm, not my right. I use the good arm to brush the front of my dress. The rest of me feels numb. A group of six children or so, including the gangly boy from across the field who seems to spend more time here than at his home, looks, not at me, but all around me. There are tears in his eyes and his eyes dart about him. I think he is about to take up beating me where my uncle left off. Then I realise he may be searching for Mad Rick, the only son of the beating, crying uncle. Mad Rick is nowhere in sight to see his father cry over beating me. The children look for him knowing he will fly into one of his famous rages when he hears about it. They cannot be sure what he will do to me. Perhaps some of them are glad he is not around or else sorry not to see his reaction to his father crying because of me.

The numb parts of me begin to ache and it supersedes any thought of Mad Rick's absence, until the children say his name. I think of him just to take my mind off my condition, him at the bottom of the pond with his head stuck in the mud. Mad Rick because of his terrible temper. A docile boy until he dived into the shallow end of the pond and hit his head so hard on the mud floor that he stayed under and his father had to drag him out and resuscitate him. And when he came around he flew into a temper because he thought that his father bent over him had something to do with his giddy condition. Left alone from that day, the mad epithet stuck to his name. I conjure the alligator none of us ever laid eyes on but all of us are certain lives in that pond. I have it amble over to Mad Rick and nibble at him. First his flailing arms then his kicking legs, before devouring the rest of his body. The alligator misses the final morsel of Mad Rick's head because it is hidden in mud. Mad Rick who never bullies me. Mad Rick who looks on with the boy from across the field while others jeer me. Or else he joins in with the others and then only for a short time before he leaves off jeering or talks the others out of it, Rick who never isolates me for special punishment as is often the case with the older children. So I like him a little and must be the only one who does not laugh when he flies into one of his rages at the slightest provocation. The child responsible for the outburst has to run behind an adult or risk being killed by Mad Rick. He always grabs the nearest weapon and gives chase with no regard for what might happen if he catches the child he chases with a blow from the stick, hoe, shovel or cutlass he carries raised above his head as he charges after his fleeing target. But not me, never me.

If I can make a grown-up cry what evil might I do to a child? In the children's eyes I must seem capable of the most unimaginable things. They are sure I cannot be like them, a child, but that I harbour the very woman everyone complains about. She who took from them the person few of them met but all of them hear about all the time from everyone. The man whose photographs are the most numerous about the house and whose grave is the first in the family plot designated by his parents initially for themselves but now housing the most promising of their children.

I crawl in the direction of the boy who likes this place more than his own home and he takes several steps away from me. I ask the little girl who is the first to grab my marble to show me what she hides in her clasped hand. Her black eyes widen and her jaws hang apart at my injuries or my soiled dress or both. She uncurls her fingers to reveal the coveted marble my uncle threw at me, not a chip on it and luminously blue with the promise of the horizon where the blue sea meets the sky.

Give me it.

She obeys then runs off crying. I look at the others. They obviously interrupted a game of marbles to witness the

34

spectacle of another beating for little Pissy-Missy. All of them
carry marbles in their hands or bulging in pockets. Give them
to me, I say spitting blood and with a sweep of my swollen
eyes over their faces. They empty their hands and pockets.
Now, go away. I manage to blurt out through split and fat-
tened lips. They back off and turn and walk away briskly, a few
of the small ones crying for the loss. I pick up the marbles from
the dust, wipe them off on my dress and look at each for the
blue swirl that is the blue sea my mother flew across in her
search for a place for the two of us. The blue sea that will yield
her up one day to me.

Before the thought forms that I must follow that uncle, I
find myself following him. Flatness takes over my body. I
think I am dying. My chest tightens and my mind forgets
about the marbles and the sea and turns wholly towards the
goal of catching up with him. I stand but without the help of
my legs. I remain upright though not an ounce of me rests on
my feet. I weigh as much as air. The house draws nearer
matching the thought that I must enter it. I glance back and
see the children scrambling in the dust to retrieve their
marbles. I climb – more float – up the back steps, and wonder
what became of the usual breeze that sweeps around it. Inside
the house looks cool because of its shade, but there is no body,
or obvious me to register this coolness. Only a mist of me
exists, smoke of my flesh, blood and bones, wisp of my body.
I look down the long part of the L-shaped corridor and hope
that my uncle's bedroom is before my grandmother's. The
biggest of the eight bedrooms, on the corner of the L, where
the long part of the corridor meets the shorter part, houses
Granny. Children never enter that room under any circumstances, I hear repeatedly, not even if the house is burning
down and the only way out is through that room. Granny
retired into the master bedroom and closed its two wood-
slatted windows and took to her four-poster bed and vowed
to remain in it until her husband returned from the jungle of
the country's interior. Grandfather, missing among vines, trees
high as hills, waterfalls that descend like smoke from the

35

heavens, volcanic rapids, and Arawak, Carib, Macusi and Wapashani tribes, departed on a diamond-prospecting mission to recover the fortune found on an earlier diamond-prospecting mission and lost at gambling. For all my childhood years at the house she hides in that room. She blames herself for my father's death because she blessed the union of my mother and her son when no one else in the house wanted it. My father's death nailed the darkness to the door and window frames. My grandmother, sealed inside her room, only unseals its tomb to admit her eldest daughter who cares for her daily needs and for the weekly visits of the priest who gives her the sacrament and absolves her of her sins. Whenever I sneak upstairs I run past her door. I have no idea what she looks like. Her seven living children and two dozen grandchildren all refer to her as the princess. An early photo of her shows that she stands tall and thin and indeed regal in her bearing if her straight back and slightly raised chin are to be believed. And because her skin resembles onyx and shines in the photo, I conclude she definitely must be an African princess.

The first door I approach makes my already tight chest even tighter. I guess or recognise from the worsened tightness that I do not need to look further. I knock and wait. Then I turn the handle – locked. Do I really knock or imagine knocking? A picture of the door handle enters my mind but without really turning it I see the lock. A picture springs to mind of me turning the handle, but only a picture. My body fails to follow through with the action of opening a door. I crouch down level with the floor and listen in the space left by the door for a thick rug ripped up long ago in preference of polished wood floors. My nose edges towards the gap, the polish makes me think of old shoes, and just then, to my astonishment, my face floats to the other side of the door and pulls the rest of my body under with it.

I squeeze my eyes and hold my breath. I expect an adult to shout my name. I hear the muffled tones of speech right there in the room and only a few feet away. I try to breathe without a sound. Air rushes amplified up my nostrils. I fancy I hear my ribs crackle as they separate for my lungs, which fill with a sound of feet over dry autumn leaves. My eyelids relax – I wonder if my face can be heard as it softens – then lift. I expect to be reprimanded or something, anything but the blind oblivion from the adult seated on the bed muttering to himself. The disappointment of being ignored clouds my head, and, equally, I quake over the prospect of having just transported myself from one room to another through a locked door. I float before the full-length rectangular mirror the uncle stares into as he sits on the end of the bed. I block his view but he looks right through me. He begs God to forgive him for beating a child as if he were fighting a man. He wants God to take care of his dead brother in heaven. Tears scramble down his face. His nose drips and he ignores it. I walk back and forth in front of him, between him and the mirror he stares into without blinking. How much can he see with his eyes full of water and how does he think straight with his nose running? I fight an impulse to lift the hem of my faded green cotton dress and wipe his nose for him, but not his eyes. The thought leaps into my head that if I dry his eyes he will see me.

What he does next I do not expect of him in his state of grief and penitence, though I will witness this thing in my changed state again and again. In adults when they choose to be alone or in couples, no matter what their state of mind, which can be anything from despair to panic to glee, with adults it always comes back to their bodies. He loosens one button, raises his arms and pulls his shirt over his head. He wipes his nose and face with the shirt bundled in his marble hand then throws the dirty bundle into a corner with such purpose I think that precise spot designated from this moment and for eternity for laundry. I glance at the shirt and back at him as he runs his hands over his nipples which are almost black on his dark brown skin and wrinkled somewhat more than his shirt but not as bad as a raisin or prune. He stands and slips loose the waist of his trousers, and pulls the waistband wide so that the zip works itself open with the sound of tearing and he steps out of his trousers and is completely naked. I marvel at the fact that he does not wear underpants. He kicks the trousers into the same corner as the shirt. The hair on his crotch, shades lighter than the black hair on his head, arms, eyebrows and around his nipples, forms an upside down funnel. Nor is it as curly as the hair on the rest of his body. He is not circumcised. I take a step or two away from him and almost spread myself smooth on the mirror against the wall. I order air into my lungs. I want to look at a part of the room where he is not but wherever my eyes swivel he looms centrally in its sight. He fills the entire room with his naked body. The bed loses its usual dimensions, miniaturised and slotted into a corner next to the shirt and the trousers he kicked towards it. He cries again but this time to himself, that is, soundlessly, or so it seems drowned by the wheeze of his injured lungs. I turn my back on him and see in the mirror and through my flat body just as much as if I still faced him. He falls back on the bed and digs his heels into the mattress and groans. Then his limbs freeze and only his chest heaves. The room reeks of something sulphurous. He rolls off the bed on to his feet and retrieves his shirt and wipes himself clean. Next he drops the shirt, picks up his trousers and steps into them. As he zips himself up in the corner the bed resumes its dimensions as the major piece of furniture in the room. My body, cured of its numbness and bruises, now tingles all over. I think *door*, not the word but a picture of it, and find myself back in the corridor with the speed of that thought. I walk as quickly as possible into the yard. In one corner children play marbles and fail to notice my appearance a few feet away. I trot to my father's grave at the back of the house where my uncle dragged me. I feel drained. I sit in the shade of the jacaranda tree and look at the bushes peeled for switches by my uncle. *Mummy, Mummy*. This said to myself seeing her airborne over a blue sea and I fall asleep right there on the warm concrete, almost immediately and think it makes a pleasant change from the closet crammed with my father's things and me.

Days fly by, not singly, but in flocks too high up and remote to distinguish one from another. I attend school and church. I like the headmaster about as much as I hate the preacher probably because the desire of the headmaster to see me reunited with my mother matches the preacher's indifference to my wellbeing. I walk the L-shaped corridor of the house just for its coolness and isolation. Except for the door to my grandmother's room, which I always rush past. If the upstairs corridor is blocked by an adult's presence in it, then the route to the front porch, the second source of coolness, becomes round about. I have to go out a door on to a landing surrounded by three doors. One door leads from the L-shaped corridor, a second opens into the combined dining room and kitchen and a third door leads down the busy back stairs, my last-resort cool source, where my dress always fills with a constant draught. At ground level I have two choices. Either I turn left into a door with a top and bottom half and walk along the ground floor of the house through the large living room. Or I turn right and continue from the back steps and walk in the yard along the side of the house until I reach the front of it. A second set of stairs leads directly up to the large front porch. Wide double doors open into the shortest section of the L-shaped corridor with nine doors dotted along it to eight bedrooms and a bathroom.

One day that lulls and lingers rather than sails past, I stroll the L-shape corridor thinking nothing of the delightful cool and shadows when something, call it a sixth sense or my mother in me, my guardian angel, tells me to look back along the longer part of the L. What I see makes me freeze on the spot and in a flash of emergency thinking I visualise the route around the house. For there is Mad Rick standing at the far end of the corridor with a cutlass raised over his head looking like another government statue commemorating slavery. No doubt he heard that I made his father cry and after days of thinking about it and listening to countless retellings of it arrived at the belated conclusion that I must die. Everyone says he is simple-minded but such a prolonged deliberation qualifies more as studied revenge. Otherwise why wait until the incident leaves my mind before he decides to strike at me? He should know it was not me, but my mother who made his father cry. I imagine the tale relayed to him by a few of the children who shared out the phrases of the story between them. They probably volunteered it to him every minute of every day. Mad Rick grabbed the cutlass on the hundredth re-telling of the tale when the order of events broke down as children interrupted each other to get in the most shocking part of the story about his father's tears. I take one look at him and know this is not an occasion for reasoning or capitulation.

Mad Rick

I see she but she not seeing me. I stand and watch she. I looking for a sign of she mother on she body. All I seeing is a little girl. How come such a slight thing make my big father cry. I watching she skinny self running she hand along the corridor wall and daydreaming even though we always get tell by the grown-ups, do not run your hands along the wall, and I considering whether I should just use my bare hands on she. I thinking maybe my cutlass too much for this bony, little girl. She look so slight yet everybody talk about she and treat she like a big woman. I don't see she mother nowhere on she skin and bones. Just a small girl. But she make my father break down and cry.

I wait till she see me and panic then I charge at she. She run towards the kitchen. I give chase. I not thinking straight. I just want to chop she until all the talk about my father crying because of she come to a stop. I expect to bump into a grown-up wrap up in the usual chores. But not one. Not one of them kneading bread, or standing over a steaming pan of stew or a pot of soup. Not a soul setting fruit in jars or picking rice clean for the giant rice canister, or churning butter, or scraping the long wooden table clean with a metal scraper, or mopping the floor, or cutting up vegetables. Where they all gone? I fling myself down the stairs after she, I taking two and three at a stride. I like to linger for the cool breeze that always blow there. But not today. The girl faster than I realise. She run like she getting help from jumby and buckoo. I start to wonder whether she might have a bit of she mother in she after all. They say she mother got wings on she foot them. She mother big with child and still she outrun the iguana that chase she. And not a scratch on she body after she dash through a fence, break through it, only a little bad back.

I tear after she through the living room. It empty as well. I climb the front steps two at a time and jump over two aunts spread out on the balcony. I glance behind me to see if they intend to give chase and stop me doing what I intend doing but they just duck they heads and crouch down like they expect a convoy, in case somebody chasing me while I chasing she. I carry on past the bedrooms. I see she a short way up front banging on the doors as she pass them and screaming *Murder, murder*, but she smart enough to know not to stop or even look back for me since I sure she hear me curse she mother as I chase she.

I dash pass the kitchen door and I start to run down the back steps a second time when I stop halfway and realise she not in front of me. She must still be in the blasted house. I scramble back up the steps just in time to see she open the kitchen door and run back along the bedroom corridor. And so the chase start all over again but in the reverse direction. I chase she back along the corridor past the bedrooms. I push open the double doors to the front porch and again jump over the two aunts horizontal on the floor surrounded by bundles of baby clothes with thimbles on their fingers and pins in the corners of their mouths. Then down the front stairs two or three steps at a time with one hand on the railings and the other swinging that cutlass in the air for balance. And around the corner and into another set of double doors. Then through a living room now full of men, women and children standing around as if planning a rice harvest or the movement of cows to the slaughterhouse, some fanning themselves or nursing bottles of cold beer or glasses of lemonade. I point my cutlass ahead of me at she and none of them move quick enough to grab me and disarm me. So I find myself on the steps up to the kitchen a second time and along the entire L-shaped corridor as far as the front porch thinking, Chop she! Chop she! To she screams of *Murder! Murder!*

She slowing down for me now. She mother draining out she legs. She wings them clip. The gap between my cutlass and she back getting less and less. If I chop she hard enough she going die on the spot. Should I chop she in the back of she head or on she shoulder? What if she stop and turn and look me in me eye? Should I chop she between she eye? She shouting she mother's name. Three uncles grab she and then throw themselves in front of me when I fly through the double doors and over my two aunts with that cutlass raise over me head. They drop me to the floor and hold me down. I fight them as hard as I can then I switch from fighting to crying. My father push away his brother and two brothers-in-law and he take me in he arms. He rock me all the time talking with he lips almost press up to my left ear and I can breathe again.

BETTANY

Mad Rick collects himself and his father who whipped me and cried promises me in his aspirated voice that I have nothing to fear from his son. They remark how fast I am for such a skinny girl. Then they change their minds and find it not so remarkable after all since my mother was a sprinter when she was young, and she and I are one and the same. Didn't she outrun a rabid iguana and her belly seven months big with the good-for-nothing child leaving her with a bad back? Meaning me. I walk backwards away from them and their words until someone shouts at me to stop walking like a mad person before I bump into something and break it. I turn and run out of earshot just as they reach the part of the story where my mother scoots from the iguana through a hedge so cleanly she leaves the exact gap of her body in that hedge. My stomach feels empty and my mouth dry. I pick a water barrel at random and drink to my fill. In the kitchen I find a plate covered with a dishcloth and I assume the setting is meant for me. I uncover the plate and eat the rice with peas and shredded beef mixed into it as fast as I can and run to my cupboard and snuggle among my father's things for the rest of the night. I dodge people for days. Nights I listen to them always a little distance from them. They seem happy with this arrangement. They bother me less when I am out of sight and correspondingly out of their minds.

They look at me and see a child of no common sense, no ability to demonstrate that I follow the reasoning of a teacher when asked a question because of my severe stammer. A child of no promise, of a mother's broken promise. 'Not much topside', as the adults like to put it, about my gross stammer or what they see as my demonstrable lack of intelligence and with a bladder always emptying itself, unable to hold anything for any length of time. Pissy-Missy, the children jibe. Here come Pissy-Missy. And they pinch their noses and scrunch up their faces. Head with the same propensity to empty. A body only good for blows, that catches the hands of passing strangers; people strange to me but who knew my father when he lived. My body invites mockery and strokes for wrongs strangers with their punishing hands know I am destined to commit.

I keep the print of a hand, a scent, an address, and I find the owner usually in a locked bedroom. Hands punish me on behalf of my mother who reduced a man in his prime to rubble. She dropped me, eucalyptus from her perfume on my skin, her child, dropped me from her body, bit through the cord and walked away from her baby without any outward show of concern. That's what everyone says to me about the woman who is my only road out of here. Mother road; father bird.

To clear my head I conjure a picture of my mother and send it across the ocean to her in the hope that I would succeed in making her think about nothing else but wanting to be with me, her daughter, her mirror image if a mirror can be found that reflects for the adult the child she used to be.

Flatness has its limits, just as the country comes to an abrupt end at the coast. Flatness only permits me to raid the private lives of those who beat me, just as the country should only have dominion over its willing subjects. Not only a beating, the blow must leave evidence of a bruise. Once hit by a cousin, uncle or aunt, teacher, stranger or friend of the family the combination to the safety deposit boxes of their secrets is mine. It is as if I were the keeper of their conscience. I follow them home. I avoid detection by walking sideways in my flattened condition so that the whole of me is no thicker than a long strand of hair. If I feel bold and I walk in full frontal fashion as it were, all they detect is a mist the size of a pillow case, a mist equidistant from them in the open where mist should not logically be present. What can they say or do? Comment on the fact of a mist under the hot sun and then run

45

after it? They force it to the backs of their minds. They literally deny the evidence of their eyes, shrug and walk off in their perambulation towards privacy, towards another body as a finger-explored map, lip-surveyed map, places sought and found for burying and unearthing protuberances, breathing places, saliva-slicked places. And me in the middle of it all barely able to contain myself, my thin self seemingly too slight to witness so much and maintain flatness, my body becoming like a coastline eaten away by the encroaching sea.

I watch and my bruises heal. If I fail to go and see for myself I keep a rosy bruise for several days and my attention relocates to that painful spot on my body at the expense of my ability to perform the simplest tasks. The bruise lingers, the rose of it plunges into the vase of my body where it feeds happily on my body's nutrients unable to distinguish between me and a stem and therefore flourishing for days. I might as well stay rooted to the spot and allow insects and birds to travel about on my behalf. To clear up my body of this patchwork of kicks, punches and slaps, scratches, pinches, ear-twisting, finger-bending and even hair grabbed and pulled from my skull, I follow the planters of these roses on my body and witness them asleep or at play in bed, or both. Only then I am able to heal fast and become a child who walks without a limp and who can stretch and not wince or be accidentally touched and not cry.

HEADMASTER

I remember the feeling that she was actually there in the school as the only student one morning during my school assembly. Everyone else fidgeted on the wood benches. She sat stock-still. While their eyes roamed out the windows, she locked eyes with me. And for one morning only in all my years as a teacher up to that moment I felt wanted for what I had to impart. Up to that moment all my work with students gravitated towards their duty to me, their desire to pass such and such a certificate or entrance examination necessitated their attendance to what I had to say on the subject. Everything changed for me that morning. I decided to break from the traditional assembly for prayers and a lesson from the Bible on one of the Commandments or seven cardinal sins to tell them, actually her, about an alternative creation myth. An alternative, I suppose, to the usual fare dished out to promulgate national pride.

This creation myth varied between the Carib, Macusi, Wapashani and Arawak tribes. It originated in the country's famous jungle interior, brought out of the bush by an anthropologist distant relative of mine from England at the start of the twentieth century. The tribes this great uncle twice removed had lived among were numerous and they shared creation stories that involved trees. Before I began to tell it I cleared my throat then picked her face to latch on to. Her eyes became pinpoints. I say her eyes because I decided then and there that the republic needed a youth with questioning eyes, eyes thirsty for knowledge, not cowed and compliant eyes. I suspected there was some truth to her plight at the Abrahams household, even without a shred of physical evidence, from the behaviour of her cousins towards her. I decided to help her the best way I could. With a story. I banked everything on her ability to understand the deepest, most profound things while her peers foundered in the shallows. That morning for the duration of my talk hers was the only other face in the large hall with my face.

Two sticks, no more than twigs, fell from a tree in the rainy season after a particularly heavy shower had softened the earth from stone to sponge. Both sticks landed upright and one foot apart. A third twig worked loose by the pounding rain and the twisting of a constant breeze dropped directly on to the two upright twigs. A long time passed, rain, sun, and another rainy and sunny season at whose end two more twigs fell and landed on top of the table of the third twig and they too stuck vertically. And yes, a sixth twig worked free by the wind came to rest on top of them. And the tree, which bore nothing, suddenly sprouted round fruit. One fruit fell on to the platform of the sixth twig and balanced there. With the passing of seasons the fruit did not decay. And with the next strong breeze and heavy rain the body of the sticks thrown together uprooted and walked away from their moorings in the earth. The collection of sticks with a fruit stuck on top called itself a collection of limbs and because it had no leaves and bore only one fruit, and, therefore, strictly speaking, did not qualify as a tree at all, it called itself human. This myth applies today. Our leader's status as human, as distinct from a collection of sticks with a fruit on top, may become doubtful if a border war begins. But I digress.

BETTANY

I abandon the idea of a world where one leader determines the fate of a people and where my father dies and my mother lives elsewhere and everyone around me beats me and shouts at me every day. I become a stick, a twig, and an accidental collection of these. I do not recall ever being embraced. I see people do this squeezing thing to each other, this locking of arms around each other's torsos in a careful making of a knot of flesh and then the way the knot falls apart just as easy and quick as it is made. How they know where to lay their heads without their heads clashing and how to interlace the feet without stepping on toes, or plant those feet just at the right point in front of another pair of feet. All this tells me that the embrace, for all its lovely benefits, the way it brings on a deep smile and the soft closing of eyes in the two people, takes too much studying to master. I am better off without it. If I get one part of it wrong and step on toes or butt heads, I earn a beating for my error. Even with flatness on my side I cannot bear the thought of another opportunity to court another beating. So I decide to let them keep their secret society of hugs to themselves. I place my arms around a young tree or a post or a pillowcase stuffed with my father's clothes without thinking about the position of my feet and head. I hold on for as long as I like. I squeeze with all my strength or as light as a feather without drawing a complaint. There always comes a point when I forget the nature of the thing I hug or forget myself in the act and I thoroughly enjoy myself.

The best wood for hugging is greenheart, no splinters and no little pieces of bark that fall away and stick to clothes like the splinters and bark of oak, ash, birch and cedar. But any greenheart not put to good use is hard to find around the big house. There are few single posts without nails jutting out or red ants marching up and down them. Greenheart wood is so durable that long after a shed or house collapses the greenheart posts in its foundation or corners remain standing. If my mother is anything, I want her to be greenheart wood and not the oak, ash, birch or cedar of my father. I want the sticks that fell off the tree and made her to have originated from an old greenheart tree and if I can remake my father I will have him stand under a greenheart tree and collect its twigs for a more durable body.

My uncles and aunts hear about the headmaster's twig, stick and fruit lecture and they promise to teach the headmaster a lesson for bringing what they call 'family politics' into the classroom. They swear they will burn down the school they built because he insulted the Abrahams family name. I have little idea what all the fuss is about but it seems important to the headmaster and vital to the house. From what I overhear the headmaster played an important role in the previous government in the capital before the party split into two and one half assumed power while the other half fell into permanent and powerless opposition at which point he became head of the school. The priest mediates between the headmaster and the Abrahams family. In exchange for the headmaster's word that he will never refer to politics in the classroom at the expense of the Abrahams name, the priest extracts a promise from the uncles and aunts to leave the headmaster in one piece and the school untouched.

Around the time of this lecture from the headmaster and my search for alternatives to hugging people, I win my first fight. A cousin, head and shoulders above me, squares up to me with his fists raised in a boxer's stance. When I first arrived he was one of the children who learned to hit by watching grown-ups beat me. He practised his strokes on my body. Like most of the adults around him he saw how he did not require me to do a wrong before he struck. Like many of the children he used me to perfect his aim. My body was apprenticed to his body. I existed to improve his ability to inflict pain. He flung his darts and some hit bull's-eyes. I tried to be a moving target. A few missed me altogether if I dodged. But he pursued me so I practised how to stand quite still for him and the others knowing it would be over sooner than if I dodged or tried to run away. He is another of the people to whom I owe something of a debt. Without the attention of his punches I could not have become numb and then angry and developed the ability to see without being seen. I would still be trying to duck and dodge rather than standing still and crying as loud as I could when I come across the many varied offerings of arms, legs, mouth and eyes.

I stand sideways in front of him and I throw one kick. It surprises him that a girl kicks so straight and hard at such a little concealed target between his legs. He hobbles away howling. I make myself scarce. He does not swing at me again when I walk past him. I no longer grant him the privilege of watching him from a long way off out of the corners of my eyes. I walk up to him and look into his face as if examining a cockroach for signs of life and he scuttles away perhaps thinking that I might squash him.

Sometimes an aunt or uncle tells me a particular beating is for my own good, and more than all the previous ones it will definitely knock some sense into my wood head. One aunt (I refuse to name her) even makes me look up the word *punishment* in the dictionary before she dishes out her dose of it. The dictionary, next to the Bible on the mantle in the living room, explains everything. But first she makes me wash my hands. Better a blood relative doing this beating thing than an uncaring stranger, I am told. Strangers beat without an agenda, without any long-term strategy since the chances are slim of their ever seeing me again to continue their variety of physical education. Therefore they perform their one-off instructions more energetically. Blood relations beat but their hearts are rarely in it; otherwise I would be dead by now, their minds absent themselves from the present purpose of my immediate punishment. Their hands still land heavy on me but they take a long-term view of my prospects, the fact that I am available for future beatings reduces the urgency of the present one, though not always. Their thoughts become so intent on the next chore of the day that I feel the definition of that chore in the shape of their hands. Their palms and fingers tense not for me but the bread they must knead in a short while. Or the cutlass they must swing to clear a path. Or the exact angle of the crowbar they sink into coconuts and rip the husks off. Or the precise grip on reins they are destined to slap on the hindquarters of a donkey. All this just as soon as they step over the hurdle of my body.

I stare at my aunt directly during my beating because I am rarely granted the grace of eye contact. My aunt, The Slap, selects a portion of me to punish and off she gallops raising and lowering her arm that is already clearing weeds from a path or throwing up unclean rice in a pan for the lighter husks and other minuscule debris to blow away. Her leg kicks at me when I pull just out of her reach and her eyes dart around in search of someone's approval as if to say, Look at me taking precious time out of my busy schedule to straighten out That Woman's child. Every time I dodge and dance I end up worse off. A kick or punch aimed at my leg or upper arm in an absent minded fashion lands in a more delicate area such as my stomach or face because as I move evasively the aunt or uncle tries to catch up with my body with a late adjustment. Moving robs them of the softer target they chose, the backside, legs, arms and back of the head, places that would bruise but not easily break or bleed, moving presents them with the delicate ribs, the soft nose-bridge, the readily blackened eyes or bruised crotch.

Since this beating is inevitable I offer my back for her famous slap, my arms for a pinch and another slap, my shoulders for a karate chop, even an ear for twisting. I follow her and I feel better because I witness her exertions over her husband's body and his departure from the room and then her alone in the room without clothes crying herself to sleep, and I heal. Alone in the room with only grief for company makes me feel sorry for those hands that swung at me earlier. Take a

52

grown woman curled up in bed and rocking like a child, her stinging hands filled with the bedding or her hands full of her hair, those hands pull and pull and the sheet tears or hair comes away in tufts from the skull, and eyebrows. I cannot look any more, but I stay to heal from the beating those very hands administered. God, or whomever, let those hands become leaden and drop to her side. Not her but her hands are to blame for my bruises. Wring the hands until they drop off, the grief rests in them, not in the head and heart. Those hands lash and tear and pull the rest of her to pieces just as they swing and beat me.

I absorb her punishment, all the time wishing my bones were longer, harder, older. Then there would not be a need to convert my body from something into nothing for anyone. But I am new in my skin, a child's easy-to-tear skin and short, brittle bones. But the child is merely a shell housing an evil woman's spirit. I hear my aunts and uncles after dark, mix me into their talk about troops gathering at the border and the threat of an invading army. The voices of my aunts and uncles burrow into me. They say carrion crows circled the house without moving their wings the afternoon my mother dropped me off and forks fell from the hands of adults, static crows overhead and flying forks announcing the arrival of misfortune. The uncles all swear they will join the army and help the coalition government repel the threat of invasion and would have done so long ago were it not for the fact that Granny would not countenance it. (Their word, countenance.) Their tones are sad but when they switch to talk about my mother they become angry.

Open windows invite their voices into the house and my open ears grab the relay baton of those sounds and bury them in my skull and down my neck and my spine. I tremble with the idea of my mother using me for shelter. My fear that I am nobody away from her worsens. I want to abandon my body and leave it to my mother to do with it what she pleases, anything but this dual residency of her and me in the same body and her always with the upper hand over me.

My relatives believe that I am dough they have to knead and shape and finally bake to perfection. And then maybe I will be as sweet as a product of the famous village bakery. Others think they can beat the devil out of me. Others still convince themselves that I am among them to work around the house as compensation for the crimes of my mother. Only one aunt, the youngest of the four, ever mentions the fact that my father is not entirely without blame in the affair since he committed a wrongful act, what she calls an indiscretion, with consequences no one can afford to ignore. Her single hope for me is that something of him lies buried somewhere in me, instead of me being my mother inside and out. And with a little kindness and time that small thing might grow and surface one day, if I am not driven to my death by all the cruelty shown to me, and everyone will see him in my smile.

The others shout her down, those big bodies in small causes, or small causes in big bodies. They hold sway over me by virtue of those big bones that bruise me, cause me to disappear and follow them in order to heal. I tell myself as the years accrue that my mother must return for her own flesh and blood, that I am far from forgotten, that no one in their right mind would forget their own offspring. I repeat this in my head during a beating and last thing at night before I curl up in my father's closet, my sleeping place, then again first thing in the morning, when I emerge from it aching to straighten from my all-night folded sleep.

Dream One

I smell eucalyptus in this dream. I roam the capital fragrant with it, a city where I have never set foot and in a government building never visited by me. Corridors without end where I dodge my uncle and his jab and run from my cousin brandishing a cutlass and when he grows tired of chasing me an aunt takes his place except that she stands on the spot and she fires her spit after me. Narrow corridors without end. I throw out my hands to the walls on two sides. The ceiling stretches to the sky. Strip lights built into the ceiling and equally spaced some three feet apart, flicker like aircraft stacked above an airport. When I reach a corner, always a right-angled turn, I think someone, perhaps my uncle, waits there for me, someone who wants me dead, someone waving a fist or aiming a mouthful of spit. I approach each bend on tiptoe, unable to turn back because behind me a wall replaces the corridor, rounding each bend with the finality that it is the last thing I will see. And always not a soul greets me there, only the feeling that next time it will not be so, the next right angle is destined to produce someone. So I edge to the wall opposite the right-angled turn and jut my head forwards, ready to spring back. And the nothing that greets me helps me to breathe again, and the something or someone that did not meet me makes me tense for the next twist in the corridor.

Did I say I try the handles of doors in the walls as I pass them in this recurring dream? I pass doors in the walls. I turn each door handle as a way of getting past them. All are locked. And no name plates outside them. No keyhole to peer through, nor a gap under the door. Not the government building in the capital but the house in Boundary. I glance back just in case a door opens after I pass and my grandmother's head peers out to check my progress towards my mother.

55

Pieces of a wheel, a rotten broken wheel from a donkey cart, are strewn along the corridor and the parts of that wheel reconstitute from old to new and reassemble into a perfect whole which blocks my path. I walk into it and it falls apart and scatters in my path as before and again it repeats its remaking of itself, the barrier of it that I must walk into and through as long as I dream.

BETTANY

My eyes open with the promise of more corridors ahead in a capital I must visit and behind me only countryside. I wake hungry. I unfurl my bones folded all night in the closet. Rather than face my relatives in the kitchen I decide to try my luck at the bakery. The children speak often of the free samples they collect from the bakery just by identifying themselves as my grandfather's grandchildren. Perhaps the new owner feels sorry for the way he acquired the bakery, not sorry for my grandfather, a merciless gambler who never took pity on the men whose property he won, but sympathy for the children whose grandfather's recklessness cost them their daily bread.

I walk from the back yard and hopscotch on my father's grave as I pass it, duck through a gap in the paling fence and pick my way across a field of razor grass until I reach the main road. I picture the bread, cakes, buns and biscuits cooling in infinite rows and my pace quickens. One second the bakery is conjecture, the next I hit the perimeter of an aromatic fence made up principally of cinnamon, yeast, sugar, flour, almond, vanilla and coconut and thrown up hundreds of yards away from the door of the bakery. My mouth waters. I almost break from my fast walk pace into a sprint towards it.

Approaching the bakery is like wading into the slice-space of a giant crusty loaf not long out of the oven. I breathe in slow and long and hurry the air out of me just so I can drag on it again. My mouth pools with saliva that renews moments after I swallow. My stomach squirms and complains for a morsel and I chew on the air in the hope that air might magically coagulate into a small loaf, or a little slice or a cornstick or sticky bun. My hands and feet operate independently of my

57

will: feet turn off the road; hands unhook the wire that fastens the gate to the fence post. I trot up the path to the bakery front door. My mind does not dwell on the fact that I should have nothing to do with the bakery. I am too hungry to be reasonable. Instead my mind becomes preoccupied with my grandfather. What kind of a grandfather gambles away the paradise of a bakery? I speculate as I wade deeper into the perfume of flour and sugar, cinnamon, spice and yeast. And the imagined smell of salt when it is not sweat but the industry of rising dough, baking bread. Perhaps he lost his ability to smell. Maybe his stomach was surgically removed and his tongue scraped clean of taste buds or ulcerated beyond belief, beyond recognition of the heaven it was made to detect by taste alone. In which case he was dead on his feet and would have sold my grandmother if he could to procure a little more credit for another round of gambling. No wonder he left for the wild. When he came around from his stupor and saw that he lost the bakery he must have felt like swallowing his tongue and ending it there and then. Losing the barbershop is one thing but to lose the bakery seems sacrilege beyond recompense.

The path runs out. My hand raps on the door unilaterally of me thinking I should knock. My knuckles compress against the weathered wood door. They throb from the three raps that sound urgent and too loud. I hear a couple of dogs barking. I consider spinning on my heels and darting out of there. I decide not to knock again and begin my count to three. At three I will leave. One, I drag it out and pause before I mouth two. I almost spell three the length of time it takes me to say it. Now turn away, I order my feet. Just then the door swings open a fraction and a head – white as if dipped in flour – juts out. He wears a thick moustache dipped in flour and so long it covers his top lip and fences off his bottom lip and chin from the rest of his face.

What you want, child? The bottom lip separates from the moustache with four small puffs of flour. *I name Bethany. I mean Bettany. From the big house.* He recognises me all right.

His eyebrows jump and his forehead wrinkles and unwrinkles. The merest hint of a smile peeps over the fence of his moustache. His head pulls back inside the door but he leaves it ajar. I feel certain he is on his way to fetch me a treat. With years behind me of being told I do not belong to the household I stand on the threshold of gaining an independent witness who will by his recognition of me and my name corroborate my birthright. Rather than eat that cake or cornstick or both that is about to be mine, it crosses my mind that I should save whatever I gain as evidence to show the other children at the house what my name earned me. I visualise a group of them begging me for a share of my treat and me squeezing an admission out of each of them that I am indeed their cousin before I dole out pieces of my bounty won from the bakery by the mere utterance of my double-barrel name.

I hear growls and barking. I count two dogs. Two heads shoot out the door and it flings wide to accommodate two dog bodies barrelling through it. I turn and sprint for the gate. A man's maniacal laughter fills the air. I feel two big tugs on my dress and underwear and chunks of both rip from my body. I scream so loud the dogs halt and let me run out the open gate. I keep running. I glance back and watch the man covered in flour as he secures the gate. The dogs bark and jump against it. Out of breath I slow to a trot. I brush my hands around my back and realise my bottom and thighs are exposed. I stop and peer around and twist my dress forward. A large portion of it is torn away. But the dogs' teeth missed my skin. I look about and see no one, but rather than risk bumping into someone on the road I decide to make the rest of the journey to the house across the fields. I use the front of my dress to dry my eyes. My legs feel twice as heavy and each step demands much effort.

My name makes me my mother's child. Hearing me say it causes a man I never saw before to set two Dobermanns on me. My name pollutes his bakery so he drives me off his property. First the house shuns me, now the bakery. No hiding place, no refuge, exists for me. I duck sideways through a loose paling in the fence into the back yard resigned to my fate as the replica in miniature of the woman who killed the most loved man in the house besides my grandfather. I wonder how she managed it, if she employed her teeth and claws to bring the wild beast of him down and then tear him to pieces as he fought to escape certain death.

My mother must return for me or I will be killed here. I know no one can save me besides her. I realise I must serve the sentence of my name right here in the house and by extension the village. Serve it and earn my name. Day by day. One hour for the cloud, my mother, to cross the horizon. One minute for the bird, my father, to fly from one end of the sky to the other. One second for the light to ratchet up its brightness as a glare in a field, a wall of light I see through before I see the plane of razor grass swept in waves. A blink of an eye for a beating to break my skin. Dogs bark my name. A ghost plastered in flour laughs at me. I should say my name more often. See if I can raise bats from the rafters. Send mice squeezing through the floorboards into the surrounding fields. Empty the house of all those who cannot bear to hear my name. Reverse nails in walls with the hook side of my tongue and my name in its sling, depopulate the country of quarrelling people and start again to build harmony from scratch, one agreeable soul after another.

Aunt The Spit

First I call the godforsaken child. Then she call me. She talk over me. She call me to come and see what happen to she at the bakery. She talk when I talk as if she use of me name should take pride of place over me need to talk to she. How long the kiss-me-ass child need to learn respect for big people? She turn she back to me and show me she bare backside and thigh. She say big man who should know better set dog on she and she only a child and what make big people bad-minded so. I repeat she name even as I hear she shout me own louder than before. I call her one more time to make sure she hear me. And she answer loud and brazen 'Yes!' I swear I never in my life hear any single word in the dictionary sound so insolent and impatient to my Christian ears as when that devil child sheself answer me. 'Yes!' I had to tell she right then that it embarrass me to hear a child reply to me in that manner. I wanted to know from she ripe mouth if she thought she was a big woman. Did she sweat smell any other way but sour? Did she grow hairs on she crotch overnight? Had she even bleed one time yet? No, no, no, no, she shout with alarm sensing that I just want to start beating she ass and me questions them only serve to work up me appetite for the task.

I know right away she want to run from me and keep running. But the road that I see she running on, run out fast, and only swamp there for she, only jungle, forest, savannah and a river, wide as the sea. She out of arm's reach but I talking to she and edging up to she and she backing away. But she not looking to avoid what damage me arms and legs might do to she. She plant she eyes them on me mouth. I tell she, attend to me child. Clear you head and listen good because as God is my witness you got a beating coming to you for sure. There is no

61

escape. But first I list she wrongs. I list she bad names. I tell she how she take after she mother, that evil woman. I warn she if she run I multiplying she punishment ten times. But she keep edging back, back, as I edge forward, forward. She keep staring at my mouth. I tell she how she head like a open book to me. And I see she mother inside, taking up all the room in there.

She cringe and cower like a dog accustomed to the stick when I walk up to she. But she more devious than a dog could ever be because she keep edging back, keeping me at arms length and keeping she eyes them lock on my mouth. I make she know I don't have energy to waste chasing she around so she better stand still for me. I list some of the things wrong with she. She force-ripe. She stammers but she behave just like she politician mother. She got no right to cut eyes with big people. Is for me to wipe the smirk off she face. She nose turn up against everyone around she. She always poke she pug nose into everybody business. She ears too quick to attach to other people talk. She walk like she own the place. She can't even learn how to make sheself scarce like other children. She chin jut too high in the air for a child. She condemn to repeat the ways of she mother. I intend to beat she mother from she or kill she trying. I tell she I don't want to hear a word from she about she dress since it was just another thing wrong with she, failing to care for sheself. She back away from me and I decide not to take another step towards she. I stand with my hands on my hips and dare she to run from me. And the girl defy me. She turn and she run.

All this happen outside the house in the front yard below the window of the master bedroom. So I keep my voice low, low. The last thing I want do is wake the old girl. She heart break and everybody know to tiptoe near she room and whisper. And here this child stand under the window in front of me say she talking back to me at the top of she voice. The child close enough to me for me to whisper but she just out of reach even if I throw me body and leap at she. She take off for the side of the house. She dash for the corner to escape me and not just me. She eyes on me mouth for good reason.

The little wretch sprint from me. She high-tail it thinking she reach too far for me to catch she. She bony legs fast like she mother. But I keep she in me sights and I roll up one of me specials with she mother name on it. Just as she turn the corner and ease up to make the turn and ease up too because she thought she safe from me and she look back at me over she left shoulder to flick that look of she mother at me, I strike. A look like that could never come from a child. Baleful and with malice in it. And with raised eyebrows, arched above that look in a gesture of eyebrows almost, if eyebrows could form fingers and flick the rudest sign at you. Right then, in me move to blot out that look and gesture I let fly a perfect, sticky ball that I roll on my tongue as I watch she fly from me. I curl me tongue round it as she dash round the corner of the house. Her mother speed make she nearly overshoot the corner. I make me move just when she think I miss she and she gone and she good and safe and she dash that look of she mother over she shoulder and it splash over me, like a bucket of cold water dump on me in me sleep. Just then me spit. I let that thing fly through the gap between me front teeth. I send me thing at top speed with a curl on the end so that it travel in a slight curve. It turn that corner with she and hit she flush in she face. I mean square on, in she mother face, splat-tat! A sound I hear above everything going on round the house. And she fall on she backside as though when she turn that corner she run bah-dam! into a brick wall.

It sweet to me ears every time I tell it, sweet like it just happen for the first time. I get she mother good, good. Me brother on the other side looking at all this. Laughing, he laugh.

BETTANY

I resist the temptation to claw at the mask on my face. Use my torn dress to wipe my eyes. Open the clothes cupboard stuffed with children's clothes, next to the cupboard I sleep in, and select the most faded dress, the one with the most repairs, the dress least likely to be contested by another child. The same rules govern my choice of underwear. I slam the torn clothes into the basket for storing old clothes used as patches for salvageable garments. Except for the torn underwear. I sink those in my pocket with the express intention of disposing of them where they can never be found.

I leave the house and shut the back door almost soundlessly. Four children skip rope in one corner of the yard, another two children play hopscotch and three more roll marbles at a line of holes dug equidistant apart. My usual way of moving among them without drawing their attention proves unsuccessful. One of them looks at me, the boy from across the field who practically lives here, and he remarks at the fact that I dare to linger in their presence. Do I want some cake? He has some. He will show me if I follow him to the path behind the house. I shake my head and prepare to sprint in case they all chase me. But he seems keen for me to accept his offer of cakes. He becomes so persistent I wonder if he knows about my recent trip to the bakery. Why the path at the back of the house? I do not care to find out. I refuse his offer and hurry away from them thinking they might change their minds. They sometimes abandon their games when they spot me and turn instead to chasing me. If they catch me before I dive into the house they usually push me and call me names or else hit me until I admit verbatim some crime of mine to do with my mother or some name my mother deserves. Then they release me and return to their games laughing about my reaction. *Bettany she mother self.*

This time I just walk away from them and they stand around looking indecisive about whether to resume their games or pursue me. I disappear into the outhouse and sling the torn underwear into the pit and sit there wondering what I should do next. I hear the children laugh. The song of them skipping breaks off if someone's leg catches the rope and resumes when the rope turning resumes.

> Bring me, fetch me, make me come.
> Run come bring me, fetch me, come.
> Make you bring me, run come fetch me,
> Don't you drop me, throw me down.

Who would miss me if I jump into the latrine pit and sink into oblivion? The aunt who always needs me to fetch a bucket of water or the uncle who hopes to hit me and shake off his sad feeling of always missing his brother, my father. A cousin mired in boredom and in desperate need of some entertainment at my expense. And maybe just as I sink out of sight some small thing about me might cross my mother's mind or an involuntary shudder run through her body wherever she may be and in the middle of whatever preoccupies her so much she cannot spare a thought for me. I listen for the children and hear the odd twitter of a wren and whistles from a canary, robin and sparrow and the clank of adult industry but not a sound from the children. I almost hold my breath and my eyes fall on one crease in the door pierced by a sliver of sunlight as I listen harder. Nothing. Have all of them wandered out of the yard at the same time? Something might have happened in the road to interrupt their play. Things often happen with traffic speeding through the village. Occasionally livestock wanders unsupervised across the road and a car or truck collides with it. Two cars passing each other too closely often smash their driver's side wing mirrors making the sound of gunfire, and if they bother to stop the *kapow* is followed right away by the screech of car tyres on tarmac. Or a laden-down tractor trundles by at a speed too tempting for the children not to chase it and clamber on the back of it. They enjoy a free ride to the bend of the road at the edge of the village where they all jump off and wander back to the house laughing and discussing the various aspects of the ride. How they jumped up. How they jumped down. How sweet to watch the road as it unfolded under them. How they nearly missed the trailer altogether on the leap up. How they almost took a tumble on their leap off the trailer. And all along the driver knows nothing because he failed to notice them hiding in the trench waiting for his tractor to approach before they sprint after it. And those drivers rarely look back anyway. They must calculate that if a child is foolish enough to jump on to a moving trailer loaded with sugarcane or coconuts at the risk of life and limb that is the stupid child's affair.

I hear my name whispered. Then one of the older children shouts, *Bettany come out of there.* I keep still. *You have up to three, Bettany.* I maintain my silence. *Oonnee, twoooo, threeee!* I open the door a fraction and the first stone hits the zinc close to my head so I close the door again. The stones rain down on the zinc outhouse like grenades and I crouch on the floor and hold my palms over my ears and squeeze my lids. I hear someone try to lift the door handle and I turn to jump into the pit. I close my eyes but I cannot move. The door handle jiggles a couple more times and I guess they must be restocking on stones. With at least one of them near me I calculate that this is the best time to make a break for it. I open the door and grab the nearest child who happens to be my size and who is so surprised by my move that he tries to run away. But I keep hold of him and we run together wildly. None of my cousins dares throw a stone and risk hitting him. I steer him towards the house and they give chase. When we reach a few yards from the back steps I push him away and dart up the steps. A wild breeze flings my dress up and my hand wanders to the back of my dress and flicks it up some more at my pursuers. Not one stone is hurled at me since no one wants to risk hitting the house. They halt at the bottom of the stairs as if my climb of them represents a kind of sanctuary for me, and the children threaten me with all manner of punishments next time. I lean out of the kitchen window and poke my tongue out at them. I cross my eyes and twist my tongue out of my mouth. I stick my thumbs to my temples and flutter my fingers at them. I pull up a chair and I am about to stand on it and turn my back to them and flick up my dress but the aunt who spits at me comes into the kitchen and I back away from the window. She looks out and orders the children to disperse and even allocates chores to four of the older ones as she complains that they have too much time on their hands. I smile. She tells me to wipe the smile off my face or she will do it for me. I ask her quickly in a move to curtail her anger if there is some job I can do to help her around the kitchen. She looks at me sharply and says, *Disappear.*

My tongue flaps independently of my mind. I retort, *How? Like Granddad.* And run for the kitchen door. A plate or saucer shatters against the door as I slam it behind me. I bolt the door leading to the upstairs corridor and dash into my kind aunt's bedroom and crawl under the bed. I hear my aunt on the landing banging on the bolted door and an aunt from an adjoining bedroom unbolts the door for her and asks her what the commotion is all about. And what is she doing with a kitchen knife. She swears she will cut that wretched child's tongue out of her mouth. I squeeze myself further under the bed. Another aunt joins them and they persuade her to relinquish the knife and they lead her into a room with soothing talk about my worthlessness. I am worth less than the bother of knifing me. Expending anger on me is anger misspent. My unworthiness extends to the fact that my own mother wants nothing to do with me. I cannot listen to any more. I cork my ears and hum my calypso reserved for these moments of total immersion in myself at the exclusion of further damaging sensory input. *Ring, ting, ting.*

MOTHER

My darling Bethany, you will hear things about me that you must measure against our time together. When you pick up scraps of bad talk about your mother ask yourself: Is this the woman who raised me for five whole years in London? If you are told something that makes you feel bad, square it against some good thing that you remember. Bring to mind London town. Imagine your poor mother sick with you growing in me and your father arriving there in bleak midwinter and seeing the sooty brick houses huddled together for warmth and not a leaf on the trees, both of us thinking some huge fire had scorched the land. And then imagine yourself between us two going to every corner of the city in our free time to see if we could find where the city ran out and when the countryside began and finding nothing but street after street after street of brick and concrete and no decent hairbrushes in any of the shops, and not enough birds, nor water either, according to your father. Water that would claim him; bird he would become.

BETTANY

When the corridor clears and the voices die down I run from the house to my father's grave under the flowering jacaranda tree, not far from the bush where that uncle beat me, and where I turned into air for the first time. A place I later christened *the beating bush*, based on a sermon I would hear the preacher give in his church one Sunday.

I lie on concrete showered in blue and white petals, inhale the honeyed air, stare at the clouds and drift off with them into a light sleep. A dreamless sleep. A sleep with my mouth open like a salamander. A wind-pick-me-up-and-set-me-down-in-some-other-place sleep. A drooling kind of sleep with my thumb half-in, half-out of my mouth and poised on my bottom lip. A black-eyed-bean-shape looking sleep in the sense that I turn on to my side curl up and become as compact as a bean.

Bones a pack of cards, flesh folded like laundry, fingers lax and slightly curled, eyes soft, head emptying, always emptying in a bid for peace, heart slow and in my neck a butterfly for pulse and at my wrists the merest flutter of powdery wings. Tongue without speech, lolls. Strings in my neck slack. Just like my father under packed earth, under cooling petal-strewn cement, under me.

MOTHER

I wait for my turn to bathe, wishing we had a second bathroom.
I lean on the doorframe and make idle talk with your father in
sentences we hardly attend to and sometimes do not even finish.

You pick up the thing for me?

Yes, I put it on the dresser.

You expect me to find it in the middle of all your brushes.

Well last time I checked aftershave was hard to confuse with
brushes.

You know what I mean. It could be buried under a pile of
brushes.

We are talking about the surface of the dresser and a couple
of baskets of brushes, right?

Yes. And?

And I did go out of my way to pick up your aftershave.

And?

Well, thank you would be nice.

Thank you.

With feeling.

Thank you!

With a little love thrown in.

T-H-A-N-K Y-O-U.

Maybe a cuddle and a kiss.

I must shave and shower and so do you.

I do not have to shave, darling, unless you are trying to tell
me something.

I meant shower, after me.

Bethany, if you have been reading my letters over the years
then you are ready for what I have to tell you. You are old
enough now, only a few years younger than I when I gave
birth to you.

Your father stands shirtless before a mirror mounted over a white porcelain sink in our narrow bathroom. The top of your head reaches his belly button. His body is hairless exactly to the point where his white Y-fronts begin. There, thick curly black hair peeps out of his brief's broad elastic waistband and along the double-threaded corners over his thighs. His crotch draws your gaze only slightly less than the neat curlicues of each hair strand lying independently of each other on their little beds of flesh, up and down his leg.

He shaves with brisk strokes first on the left side of his face by leaning as close to the mirror as his upper body allows with his thighs braced against the sink. He holds his breath when he leans forward because his breath steams the mirror. When he rights himself it is to immerse the razor in the sink of warm water and jiggle it a few times as if baiting some form of life in the sink's shallows. And he breathes. Two deep breaths quickly become easy and soundless and hardly visible as anything more than a rumple of movement around the smooth area of his ribs. Once or twice he glances at you and then at me without taking his eyes off the mirror. He simply lowers his eyes fifteen degrees or so to take in the reflected portion of your head nestled somewhere in the bottom left hand corner of the mirror's cracked, oak frame or else looks to his left or right to take in me leaning on the door frame. His wink snaps at both of us in what must be a camera shutter's speed assessment. And because his eyes dart away before either you or I fire off a smile of our own, I can only assume that his instant conclusion is that we are a picture of contentment. I try to catch his eyes before he glances down and catches you staring at his crotch, hairy legs and smooth, clear torso.

The left side of his face shines like a newly minted coin. He chews on his cud, not in anger this time, but in concentration, as he twists his face and leans into his reflection. His thighs press against the sink and whiten with the pressure of his weight. They look huge and muscular, like a professional cyclist's, with the muscles and flesh splayed like this. He twists his mouth to the left and stretches his right cheek in readiness for the razor that you are never allowed to touch. He raises the steel blade to his sideburns and pauses to twist it at the angle his sideburns are trimmed at, which is about as steep as a children's slide. His right elbow is cocked in the air in an awkward manner. His bushy armpit is the only visible place where hair appears to sprout in a wild fashion as if on the neat garden of his body he has cultivated twin beds where all hell is allowed to break loose. The same is true of that other bed, his crotch.

Right now, it occurs to me that he has two faces and were he to abandon the process of preening himself to a spanking newness, and remarkable youthfulness according to the repeated testimony of my friends, then I would have two husbands, and you, two fathers, immersed in one body. The first is the shining youth who passes for my younger brother when we go out, and the second is the man with the five-o-clock shadow.

I will the razor to scrape off the face with the shadows and feed it with little jiggles of the wrist to the creature nestled in the shallow sink water. And as sure as thought his arm comes up to his face and drags off the man who shouts as he flings his fists, with one, two, three deft strokes and plunges him into the sink. I breathe for my husband, your father, restored to me and to you. He is singly, truly youthful. He looks down and winks at you and you wink back and he laughs and says, Girl, where you learn to give sweet eye like that! He pauses with the razor in the air beside his cheek and shakes his head in mock despondence. He is swift now to bring the job to a close. His hands work independently of each other. The left pulls the plug while the right turns on the hot and cold taps in turn. The left splashes his razor under the running water while his right cups and sprinkles around the sides of the sink to clear away the hairs peppered there. Left opens drug cabinet and puts away razor as the right increases the flow of water and proportionately a waterfall noise adds to its decibels. Left and right unite behind a towel and dry his face in unison. Right steadies the aftershave bottle while the left uncorks it and puts down the cork, relieves the right of the bottle and pours a little in the curved upturned palm of the right. Left discards bottle and shares the perfume with the right in a quick rubbing together. Now both slap the cheek on their side rapidly as your father sucks in air. And if there could be a noise made by perfume filling a room then it is his lips pursed and split a fraction to allow sucked air to rinse his front teeth with a swishing noise. I breathe deeply and from your flared nostrils I see you take the same deep breath. This is the sweetened oxygen made by my husband, your youthful father.

Dream Two

Not for long do I sleep without dreaming. They come unwarranted. They recur. I never laugh in them. And once more I find myself in a government building in the capital and since I have not visited either of them in my waking life I surmise that I must have picked up pieces of both in textbooks at school.

In this dream I move in all directions in a corridor and whether I travel up or down or sideways to the left or to the right I remain in the corridor and progress without climbing or descending any stairs or obvious slope.

Aunt The Spit appears, the whole of her just a massive head. Her tongue flicks between that gap in her two front teeth, lassoes my waist and pulls me into her mouth. Her teeth are pillars in this dream, her tongue as huge as a sail.

Next I chase a shadow, nothing more definite, or follow a shadowy figure that convinces me by its indefinite shape that I must follow it or give chase because it is my mother or some agent of hers and it will lead me to her hiding place.

The green walls of my aunt's giant mouth shine. I assume moss grows in her mouth. But my reflection warps and wavers as I move. A dark roof by contrast reflects nothing of me. The earth-coloured floor suggests carpet but I know it is really my aunt's rough tongue underfoot.

Her tongue revolves like a globe with me balanced on it or a conveyor belt that propels me forward. The shadow remains just ahead of me no matter how fast I run.

MOTHER

Where is the cannon hidden in which he loads his voice and fires volley after volley of insults at me? Where is the man on that clean-shaven face who knocked over a lamp, two chairs, a coffee table and broke as many of my precious cut-crystal glasses and bone china cups as he could lay his hands on? Who hit me, a grown woman, with his fists and the back of his hands before he slumped down on the sofa and stared at the opposite wall? Bethany, believe me when I say he is under the skin of your youthful father. Biding his time. Making preparations for a spectacular comeback. Planning to emerge as stubble on your father's face and then forming a fist and forked tongue, red-eyed rage and a bull's body for stampeding through our house.

The night in question when you became involved he came in late as usual after struggling to thread the key into the lock as quietly as possible. I met him the only way I knew how when my husband was several hours late for the fourth night in a row without a proper alibi. When he hit the light switch I was there with my arms folded over my breast, there with all the furniture in the room which moments earlier was one dark mass of peace. There and ready for the fight he was happy to oblige me with as a merciful deviation from the offering of false explanation after false explanation disproved by me faster than he could offer them.

Woman, get out of my face.

You take me for a fool. I don't intend to put up with you even if she does.

What you going on about? You crazy or something.

I realise now, Bethany, that you must have caught snatches of your father and me rowing. I thought you were asleep but you may have been listening as hard as you could in the dark of your bedroom. Words soak through walls. Even if they reached you in fragments you could piece them together. I know your father and me fighting frightened you. The words you could not quite make out must have sounded worse than the ones that you clearly heard.

If you want to leave then just leave, but don't play me for a fool.

You throwing me out of my house for coming in late.

Be a man and admit you just come from her bed. Be a man.

Shut your mouth. You hear me. Shut up.

And here my memory fails me. I forget what he says next. I cannot recollect my replies. I shriek when he breaks something precious of mine. He grunts with his exertion. My ears fill with blood. My chest threatens to burst open. I want to grab you from your bed and rush out of the house but my body weighs as much as all the furniture in the room. To move I would have to pick up my cabinet with its crystal and china, the bed with you in it, my baskets of brushes and pull up the floorboards from its bed of nails. I tell myself my daughter needs me. I order my legs and arms to sweep away the threat of your father and cross the room to the front door and fling it open and bring an end to your father and me warring. I want to take off my clothes and run and stand in the middle of the street. My naked body in the middle of the street would silence him. The broken things in the living room would mend with me standing naked in the middle of the street. Throughout the house the silence of sleeping things would reign once again, reign in peace as it did before your father's late appearance which produced with the flick of the light, me, standing, arms folded in the middle of the furnished room.

Don't come back here after you climb out of her bed.

Stop trying to provoke me tonight.

Get out of here. Go back to her. If you want her that much stay with her. I don't want you around me.

Shut up, woman.

You make me sick with your sneaky behaviour and your lies.

I said, shut up with your insults. Get out of my way.

Bethany, the walls of your bedroom retain pieces of these words, an imperfect shield, held up around you against the possibility of this kind of onslaught. But wood and plaster are too weak. They underestimate your father and me, the lash of our tongues, the slap of his fists against my flesh penetrating wood and plaster as if the two were conductors of his moves against me. I cry when I think about our words filling your head and heart and driving you to do what no child should be impelled into doing to bring an end to her parents fighting. I love you more than words can say. Forgive your dead father even if you cannot bring yourself to forgive me. I love you more than I love anything else in my life. Do not blame yourself for what happened. Your father and me drove you to do what you did.

Bettany

I wake breathing hard with rain and petals falling through the jacaranda tree and stencilling on to me. I sit up to see the children dashing in every direction chased by four uncles swinging belts at them. The children scream and scatter. Aunts try to stop the uncles. A couple of children dodge behind me and the uncle chasing them lashes at them without hitting me until they scoot towards the house with him close behind them and swinging his belt. Even the boy from the field next to the big house earns some lashes. It seems appropriate somehow. He spends so much time here he resembles the other children. The uncles probably mistake him for one of their children and beat him with the rest of them. But for doing what wrong? Rain pounds the dust, which flies up and sinks back to the ground as more rain rattles down. The sheds on the far side of the yard with their corrugated tin roofs sound as if all the marbles in the world landed on them. Pigs in the sheds squeal. Then I see the source of my uncles' anger. They drag the donkey from the narrow path at the back of the house. Its braying sounds more like a squeal. They support its twisted front legs, carrying it for a change instead of it always carrying them and their things. The rain pounds them and the donkey. They and the donkey disappear behind some bushes. They chase a couple of the children who are curious despite their recent beating. A long bray issues from the donkey and it suddenly ends in mid-flow. Sunned clay and grass perfume the rain. The four uncles reappear, one carries a hammer, while another brandishes a foot-long iron spike used for slaughtering animals whose throats are not easily cut. They sprint across the yard through a gauze of a downpour to the house. They huddle with their wives and the whimpering children and watch the rain and comment on it and the donkey. This is the first rain for two months. Everything craves its appearance: the rice fields, vegetable farms, mango and guava trees, and the empty rain barrels dotted around the big house and every house.

Rain slides petals off my father's grave, and with a slight breeze, I grow uncomfortably cold on it. I walk to the house slowly. The rain massages my head, neck and shoulders. I feel my dress cling to my flesh. The children point at me and exclaim to each other, their misery driven from their minds by my appearance. My aunts and uncles laugh. As I draw near the children order me to find some other part of the house to shelter under. I look at the boy who does not even belong to the house and he pitches in a few insults of his own. He suggests I crawl under the house. Another child says I belong there with the frogs, spiders, leaf-cutting ants and worms. They sing *Bettany! Bettany! Better you than me!* My aunts and uncle applaud. *Bettany! Bettany! Better you than me!* I skirt around them and find a dry spot beside a rain barrel fed by a gutter from the roof of the house. *Bettany! Bettany! Better you than me!* The rain chokes the gutters and tramples into the water barrels louder than all the voices joined together in song. Sun begins to shine even as the rain falls. Slanted rain seems to shape the light so that sunlight falls at the same slant. I start to sing to myself, *Rain in the sky, sun open he eye. Dust lie down low, time for seed to grow!* Do the others hear me? The children change their song from the one about me to the one I sing. The adults join in. The kind aunt who stopped that uncle beating my mother in me steps out of the house and the moment she spots me standing alone she beckons me over to join her. I edge along the house to avoid the rain draped over the sides of the house. I lean as close to her as I can without touching her so that her warmth grazes me down my entire side nearest to her.

The rain's volume increases from a quarrel into a brawl, and its mass, from a thin see-through drape to a thick screen. Clouds pack the sun away in their crate and ship it elsewhere.

The sky turns from late afternoon into moonless, starless midnight. An uncle orders all the children into the house. The Kind Aunt and Aunt The Spit stand by the door and hand towels and dry clothes to every child as each files into the kitchen. I make my body small and inconsequential so that I too earn a towel and flimsy dress just like the other girls among the children. We towel ourselves and change into our dry clothes right there in front of each other, the girls struggle to keep the towels round their bodies and wriggle into panties, dresses and skirts, the boys with towels around their waists step into underwear and trousers. Laughter and shouting break my concentration to stay covered while I dry myself and dress when someone temporarily loses their grip on a towel and unwittingly reveals too much. Our discarded wet things make a huge steaming pile. We sit on benches at the long table in the kitchen and the others bump and push me off the end of the bench until my kind aunt intervenes on my behalf. I notice my cousins allow the boy from the small house across the field to sit with them but not me. Each of us receives a cup of tea already sugared and whitened with fresh cow's milk, and a fat slice of brown bread already buttered. The first couple of bites take place in near silence as we all relish the lovely homemade bread and butter, trying to sip the very top of the tea and avoid the hot enamel of the rim of our cups. A series of slurps arise. On a different day an adult would order us all at this point to stop eating like hogs, but today with these first rains and this early tea, none of them seems to care about our table manners. An aunt actually smiles as she says we are noisier than a gaggle of geese. Something about the picture of us all in feathers and with beaks, or the onomatopoeia of the phrase, or the fact that we are hungry and it is raining hard and the food and the rain combined cannot be timed better, or all of the above, tickles us. Suggestions fly around the table of other creatures our collective slurping might resemble. We purse our lips and suck tea and air off the rims of our enamel cups and chew buttered bread with our mouths open as if the very air we breathe is a condiment. Someone volunteers that we make more noise than ten pens of hens. Someone else adds that we are noisier than frogs on logs. Another child quickly says noisier than rigs of pigs. Yet another chips in with than a blimp of chimps. And so it circles the table – than thickets of crickets, than boats of goats, than streets of sheep (my rows of cows is rejected), than flaming flamingos, than flocks of peacocks, than a city zoo of cockatoos. An aunt begs us to pipe down and we fall quiet. Now we all listen to the rain. We drink without slurping and chew with our mouths closed. We maintain a quiet each of us appears wedded to, as though all we want is just to sit speechless around a meal and hear the outside world being replenished.

Two new conversations start at the table. The children discuss a previous beating of mine (a favourite subject among them) and marvel at my capture and abandonment of their marbles. Both conversations conclude that my behaviour is evidence, if more evidence is needed, of my stupidity, my oddity. I try to look pleasant, not smiling but with an expression farther away from a frown than from a smile. I want to communicate something akin to obliviousness but avoid seeming nonchalant since that will draw their hostility. I appear too stupid to care that I am the topic of their talk as I sit right there at the same table. Somehow my thick skin makes me immune – that is the gift of my mother – to the content of their talk. I am not the child I seem to be outwardly. I harbour a woman who deserves all the scorn poured on my head so much so that even the boy from another house joins in.

My kind aunt asks me to collect all the cups from the table and put them in the plastic basin in the sink. The children drain their cups and bang them on the table in a hurry to leave the crowded room in case more chores are handed out or before they can be roped into washing up with me. Or they rush off to join the other children in a window or on the balcony. From there they watch the rain and talk about water gathering outside. How it changes things, turning the grass green and throwing up weeds and flowers where dust ruled and filling the pond for swimming in with tadpoles, sprats and minnows, so many we scoop them up with our bare hands. How rain helps everyone to sleep deeper to its sweet drone.

I soap and rinse the cups in a basin of clean, cool rain. The white enamel cups and plates, badly chipped, show the years of their tumble against each other in wash basins and repeated falls to the wood floor. The blots of chipped white paint feel rough like a scab healed over a wound. I have the sensation touching them that if I rub hard enough they will come off and the bruised enamel will bleed, so I imagine the utensils as very young birds and I give them a bird bath by wiping the wash cloth gently over feathers. The Kind Aunt calls me and says I should not take all day to do such a simple task. She adds that I might miss all the fun and games unless I hurry. She walks about the kitchen fetching things and putting them away in cupboards, jars and pots and pans, as she chews bread with some delicious spread on it. When she passes me she says open up, and sinks a large chunk of her bread into my mouth. I relish the sweet and seeded guava jelly, and guavas are not even in season. The jelly comes from a jar reserved for adults alone and visitors such as the priest. I know better than to make a fuss and try to thank my aunt. I chew slowly. I put her kindness towards me of all people down to the fact that she is pregnant. She has no choice. Her swollen body gives itself over to sacrifice and with it an offshoot of sacrifice – kindness towards young birds tumbled from nests. I move my hands very fast over the bodies of what I decide are now fully grown birds, tough and worldly wise. I raise the noise level of enamel cups and plates banging into each other to heighten the sense of industry around me. I churn the bread with my tongue from a ball to mush then to watery bits and unable to hold it in my mouth a moment longer I swallow and chuckle involuntarily, a spasm of happiness washing over me. My aunt passes close to me a second time and deposits on to the draining board a cup of ashes she must have scooped from the wood-burning oven. She says I should use the ashes to scrub the two aluminium pots covered in soot on the outside, and rice and other bits glued to the bottom of the inside. The ashes blacken the basin of water but restore the pots to shining originality.

I empty the basin and turn it upside down in the sink. I squeeze the washcloth with both hands, wringing it with all my strength, and spread it out on the draining board beside the cups and plates. Then I lower the slatted window, glancing out one last time at the early darkness, and rest the wood used for keeping the wood slat ajar on the floor by the draining board. I hear her say that the bread thing must remain between us. When I turn from the sink I am alone in the dark kitchen. My aunt who expects me to be right behind her takes the lamp with her and slips out the door and on to the landing then through another door that leads to the L-shaped passageway of bedrooms. I want to run and catch up with her and join the others but in a larger crowd she becomes distant and I will be at the mercy of everyone else. Instead I drag my feet on the wooden floor and allow the glow from her lamp to retreat from me. She calls my name. I dearly want to run and stop beside her and take her hand but I know the most I can do is catch up to the glow of her lamp.

She disappears around the corner of the L-shaped corridor and leaves me in complete darkness. Days, weeks, months, pass with me feeling trapped in this dark. My body seems outfitted with this darkness. I exhale it even in broad daylight. Months accumulate into years: years of me dodging my shadow; years with me careful not to allow my shadow to cross an adult's path.

Kind Aunt

I hear from her mother how she think Bettany might have reached the bathroom by sliding around them, by sticking close to the walls of the room the two of them turning upside down.

Uncle The Jab

How come a little thing like Bettany manage to reach the drug cabinet? Must be she climb up on to the sink and balance on it, crouched or something, and she manage to steady with one hand and grab the razor from the cabinet with the other.

Aunt The Spit

With all the screaming she mother doing no wonder the poor man never hear she when she jump off the sink, how? – in a backwards jump, and land on the floor.

Aunt The Slap

She runs, she jumps. What else she good at?

Kind Aunt

Her mother was sitting on the floor right where our brother pushed her while he was standing next to the cabinet in the living room reaching in and smashing crystal and china on to the wood floor.

Aunt The Sneer

I don't see how she can cross the room without cutting her foot.

Aunt The Slap

And you can't tell me the woman fail to notice she daughter crossing the living room from the bathroom brandishing a razor.

AUNT THE SNEER

She turn a blind eye.

KIND AUNT

Imagine what going through the child mind. What will her father do next when the china and crystal in the cabinet runs out?

UNCLE THE JAB

None of what you say on her behalf excuses a child taking a razor to her father.

AUNT THE SPIT

The miserable child wanted a taste of her father's blood.

AUNT THE SLAP

And that woman calling herself a mother looking on. Not lifting a finger to stop the child.

AUNT THE SNEER

Willing she on, more like.

BETHANY

I walk into the light of the living room. There is the small table and lamp lying on the floor. I read beside them sitting in my mother's lap. The lampshade is broken in two and the bulb into smithereens and the table overturned. She sits on a dining room chair with her face in her arms and sobs. He stands next to the cabinet in which she keeps her china and with precision timing he reaches into it and brings one piece at a time and smashes it on the wood floor and curses. I walk over to him. He fails to notice me. He is rapt in counting out the precious china and crystal that measure his swearing. I hurry to him before the china and crystal run out. I reach up with the razor. It is like pelting a stone with a wide overarm swing. I swing again at my father, quickly. I shout or I think I shout, *Do not hit my mother. Do not break another piece of her china.* He knows and I know that she dusts her china piece by piece every Sunday morning, depending on her nursing work rotation. She sings or hums a tune as she dusts and holds the polished pieces up to the light. And if there is a stubborn spot she exhales on it and rubs her breath away vigorously and holds the china a foot from her face as before. We know not to disturb her. We edge around her if we have to cross the living room to get to the kitchen or bathroom. I shout or think, *Do not make her cry. Do not. Do not.*

He lifts me, my father, with one hand full of my nightdress, and throws me. The razor flies from my grasp and I feel it graze my forehead and burn. I land against the sofa and slump to the floor. My hands cannot decide which part of my body to hold. My mother screams. I cannot look. I feel her sweep me up and lay me on the sofa and then she is gone from beside me. She picks up the razor and runs at my father who turns on

86

his heels and darts out of the front door. She bolts the door and comes to me and looks into my face. I see her with my left eye. The right eye is blocked by the trickle from my forehead. She takes the hem of her green cotton nightdress, smelling of Johnson's Baby Powder and wipes my forehead. She actually tears a portion of the hem of her nightdress off with two wide sweeps of her arms and ties it around my forehead so tightly I feel a clasp of arms there in some unshakable headlock. She gathers me up and kisses me and cries. I do not cry. I want to say something that will soothe her. But my head spins and I think my father will raise one of his muscular legs and kick the door off its hinges.

Bethany, he will never touch you again. He will never see you again.

But I cannot move from my bed. I convince myself I am pinned to it. The sheets are made of lead. They press my body to the mattress. I can hardly breathe. The silence in the house is mine with my ears blocked by my noisy blood and heart. My flesh becomes lead. I am impervious to outside noises; immobile too; too heavy in my protective gear to lift a muscle. The silence is thick as if silence were a material, a heavy, purple velvet curtain, metres and metres of it draped from ceiling to floor and gathered in thick folds. In this condition I levitate from myself and imagine that I put my body between my parents armed with my father's razor. I picture myself leaving my bedroom and interceding on my mother's behalf. When I cut at my father's crotch I rid him of the shadowed half of himself that surfaces again and eclipses his youthful self. I am my father's apprentice barber. In the bathroom he wants me to watch him shave and learn his trade.

Save me from myself, my daughter.

Yes, father. This is my best aim. This razor is a stone.

MOTHER

I tie your favourite green cotton scarf around your head and pack a few things in two suitcases with samples of my remaining china and crystal wrapped in clothes. I make two quick phone calls. You obey my instruction to run to your room and put on your best, pleated white skirt and lime-green blouse. You walk a little unsteady on your feet. I run to you and offer to dress you but you tell me you are fine and you can dress yourself. My independent little missy. I discard my torn nightdress and step into a tight pair of beige slacks and a loose-fitting, pleated blouse, without bothering with a brassiere, not exactly early autumn gear but who cares at this hour. We leave the house, the overhead light still burning in the living room. Just as I start to think I called the wrong cab company the headlights swing into our street. I tell the address to the taxi driver. I see the back of his head and a cloth cap.

You all right, missis?

Yes, thank you.

Is there . . .

. . . Please, I don't want to talk.

OK.

He pulls on the steering wheel to get more comfortable and that's the last his head and body moves. I dab the inside corners of my eyes with a section of handkerchief wrapped around my right index finger. You fall asleep in my lap and embrace to the drone of the car.

We come to a stop and you sit up. The black taxi is bathed in red. My arm around you is suffused in red. We stand at the lights with the engine idling and the road ahead dark and clear. The driver steers us out of the green haze that succeeds the red. He pulls up to the emergency entrance of the Greenwich

88

hospital surrounded by parked ambulances and I assure you that all I want to do is get someone to look at your forehead just to be sure the cut is not deep. I carry both suitcases and you drag a smaller black bag with straps that are too short to lace over your shoulders. We enter fluorescent lighting and squint after the wide-eyed dark of the taxi interior. I tell the male nurse that you were playing with your dad's razor and you cut yourself. The nurse peers into your face and winks. *What's your name then?* You look down at your sandals. *You're a shy one, eh?* His fingers flick one of your plaits. You step back out of his reach. I fill in the liability form. You look at the nurse and he winks again. *Go on*, he says, *wink for me with those sweet eyes of yours.* I glance at you and wish I could write faster. I hand the form back to the nurse who then leads us into an examination cubicle. He tells me that things have been slow tonight. I do not know him or anyone in Emergency. I tell him I work on the Oncology ward. We exchange small talk, people we might know, doctors we hate to work for, as he unwinds your bandage and says to me, *Oh yes, she needs a few stitches to close that up.* Then to you, *You won't be playing with your dad's razor again, will you princess?* You nod when you mean to shake your head. I hug you. The nurse brings in a kidney-dish with iodine, cotton swabs, needle and suture thread on it and he asks you to look up as he dabs at your cut. The ointment makes you wince as it burns for an instant. *Not to worry, love, you won't feel anything now.* I catch your eye and wink at you and smile and mouth *Love you.* You close your eyes and try to ignore the little tugs of the nurse's stitching action. His hand has tufts of fair hair on the back of it of roughly the same thickness as the black thread that closes your cut. What makes me think right then and there of my body as a container and of you as my precious cargo? I see my body with you in it on the end of a crane at a seaport being hoisted high into the air and swung over the empty hold of a cargo ship and let down gently. The repair is good. In the momentum of the lift and setting down none of the stitches break. I wanted you right then back in my belly as the safest place that I can offer you. *There, good as new,* the nurse says. He winks at you and you try on a half-smile for him. He puts a pink plaster at a thirty-degree angle to your eyebrows over the three stitches.

We board another taxi. In the engine-noise dark I look down at your face and catch you winking a few times before you lapse into sleep. We stop at the low terraced houses shouldering each other for more elbowroom. I carry you to my friend Evangeline's front door. She flings open the door and thanks God that we are safe and says she was worried sick from the moment I phoned her. Our bags wait on the pavement to be collected. Just then your father pulls up in his Bentley and immediately I set you down and stand in front of you and before Evangeline or I can think what to do next your father is on his knees crying and begging me to forgive him and come back home. He calls you and says he is sorry he hurt his precious little daughter. He promises you this will never happen again; and me that he will do whatever I say to make things better if only we would come home with him right away. My back starts to play up and I see the traffic lights changing from green to red with each throb, green, red, green, red. Malfunctioning lights that I am stuck in. Evangeline, still in her nurse's uniform, pulls you to her and asks me to come in off the street at once. Your father begs us to give him just one minute. He says, if a man deserves one chance in life the woman he loves should give him that chance. *I am a fool. The most precious thing under my nose I didn't see, you, my darling and our beautiful daughter, I am sorry, I made a mistake. You have my word it will never happen again. I love you. I've never loved anyone else.* He is shaking and crying and still on his knees. I giggle. My friend too. Your father pauses. I must say, you look totally puzzled. I take two steps towards him and punch him on the chest. I tell him he is a very foolish man.

Lucky for you your daughter missed your goods.

Yes, he says emphatically. Yes.

He stands up, tugs at his crotch then hugs me and kisses me all over my face and neck. Then he steps around me and bends on to his left knee in front of you and inclines his head to the right, *Your daddy is very sorry he hit you. Your daddy loves you. You are more precious to me than my own life. I promise, cross my heart, never to lay a finger on you and your mum or I will cut off my hand. Forgive your daddy.* He holds out his arms to you and you look at me and I nod my encouragement and you fall into his arms. I feel as if the chains on that crane are still attached to me and before I can settle in the hold of the ship that crane, your father, hoists me out and back on land. If I can kick him I will. If I can break those chains even in mid-air I will break them and crash to the ground rather than be set back on land. Evangeline pushes me in the back, gently, towards your father and I fall into his embrace. The alternating lights stick on green and red so that the dark behind my eyelids is a prism of this mixture of the two.

The sky is the darkest blue imaginable as the first signs of morning emerge. I cannot be bothered to listen for birds. They begin singly at first then others join in and soon it becomes a joyous chorus. They literally sing the day into being along with your father whistling a chorus from a calypso. I help you with your seat belt as you lie on the back seat. Your father holds the door open for me and I climb into the front passenger seat. He pushes the door shut with a flourish of raised hands as if the metal were on a hot stove, then he half-shuffles, half-skips around the front of the car to the driver's side. I love the sound of a car door when it is closed with just the right amount of force so that it does not slam but clanks shut. Your father manages to repeat this exactly beautiful thump with the door on my side and his. And it's the two of us, my darling Bethany, who are precious cargo in your father's container.

BETHANY

I listen for the engine and when it starts, panicky at first before settling into its telltale rhythmical hum, I stop listening. The leather interior of the car fills with warm air and their voices. I lie on my side with my back nestled into the back of the seat and my hands over my ears and my eyes tightly shut. This is the smoothest, most cautious drive ever made by my father. I hardly budge lying on that back seat with a seatbelt around me. It is something I am never allowed to do. But usually at this time I am in my bed and on my tenth dream.

I refuse to open my eyes when he scoops me up. My mother leads the way, obligingly holding the gate and then scooting ahead to open and hold the front door. He swings me through the garden gate then the front door by turning his body so that he walks sideways through both since both are too narrow for his shoulders to pass through square-on. I flinch in the brightness of the living room. I fight to keep my face relaxed since my natural inclination is to squint. He lowers me on my bed and pulls a sheet then a blanket up to my chin. He does not tuck them in like my mother. His lips and the tip of his long, thin nose, brush my cheek. He smells of his beer-coloured aftershave until he talks. The 'h' dropped from my name, his four words said as if they were six syllables in one musical chord.

IloveyouBettany.

Then I smell tobacco. I peep as he backs out of my bedroom and pulls the bedroom door reducing a flood of light from the living room to a wide band then a strip then a sliver then nothing but a glow at the bottom of the door.

Who will be there in the late morning to greet me? A dead mother on the living room floor and a father standing over my bed with his open razor? A dead father slumped by the cabinet with china in it and my mother covered in blood and asleep on the floor beside my bed? I stare at the door until it bulges like an eyeball. The oak wood softens to a sponge while it retains the look of a door but one seen in a distorting mirror. I blink to restore the door. I don't feel my eyelids blink. Instead the sensation is of my eyes rolling upwards in their sockets and then my body in a slow somersault, rising or falling, I can't tell. Rising and falling. What is up, what down, eludes me. The walls mimic the bedroom door, they soften and become convex. Soon my body takes up the entire room. I am not suffocated at all. It is the most comfortable place I have ever been in. A room built just for me. No sharp edges to the walls. No need on my part to push against them. The entire surroundings seemed imbued with an eyeball's delicate nature. This is me in my mother's belly, without a mother and father to lay claim to, having not yet staked my claim in the world. Keep it like this, dear Lord. Let me sleep so long and so deep that I don't wake in the morning.

But I do wake. To the smell of toast. Burnt. The sweetest smell in the world. My mouth waters even as I surface from sleep and it elicits a grin from me – I never rise with a smile on my face. I raise my hand to my forehead and the feel of a plaster brings back last night. I trace the contours of the plaster and the ridged stitches underneath with my fingertips. Do I smell toast or burning flesh? One of my parents could be burning the other. I dash the bed sheet to one side, jump out of bed and lunge at the bedroom door. Just then it opens and I charge into the legs and waist of my mother. She reaches down and hugs me and laughs.

Whoa! Where's the fire?

Where's Dad?

Preparing breakfast. Let's go eat.

He burnt the toast.

Yes, I think he was trying to send you a message in your sleep.

It worked.

93

How's your cut?

Doing fine, thanks.

Let me have a look.

She steadies my chin with her left hand and uses her right index finger to lift a corner of the plaster and peer underneath. Just as I think she is about to replace the lifted corner of the plaster she swipes the whole thing off in a quick retraction of her hand from my face. I don't feel a thing but I say *Ouch*, and I crinkle my eyes and grimace. She hugs me and apologises and says there is no other way to remove a plaster.

What neat stitches!

Can I see?

Sure.

She points my body to the mirror on the living room wall and lifts me up to it and I look at my three little stitches in a row like miniature furrows and I feel ashamed that I made such a fuss when she removed the plaster. It looks like an insect, perhaps a centipede, fossilised on my forehead. Something as worrisome as a mosquito that I reached up and swatted and did not bother to wipe away so that a part of it dried and stuck right there above my left eyebrow. I quite like it. It could pass for a botched tattoo. A part of me feels proud to be cut by my father, for visiting the emergency wing of Greenwich hospital and receiving stitches, to have a battle-scar, something to show for my bad dreams and interrupted sleep.

Dad walks in wearing Mum's pinafore and holding two plates loaded with eggs, beans, fried tomatoes and buttered toast. The smell of toast is superseded by that of thyme, Dad always puts thyme on baked beans.

Come and get it!

I sit in my usual place opposite my mum and he comes around to my side of the table just to kiss me on the top of my head and when I glance up at him I see both of his eyes are focused on my ornamental tattoo.

I don't even know it's there, Dad.

Good. I am sorry.

No, you're not, I think. Then I'm not sure he isn't really full of remorse. I mean look at these two eggs done the way I like them, turned, but still soft inside and the triangular toast and the hill of beans. And a tomato cut in half and softened on the stove in butter. I am even allowed a cup of tea instead of the usual medicinal glass of milk. He sits down and Mum tells him she can't eat without laughing unless he takes off her pinny. He obliges and stations himself at the head of the table and we launch into our late-morning feast and everything really seems idyllic. I pop a section of the slippery albumen to the back of my throat, and, without chewing it, I gulp and feel it slide down my neck. This is the bit when I get told to chew my food and not wolf it down. I wait for it. Nothing. I repeat the swallowing trick with more albumen. Again nothing. Instead, they ask me what I'd like to do with my day. They make suggestions. They list all the wonderful places I might want to see in a year but plan to fit them all into one afternoon. Part of me thinks, Yippee! I have them where I want them. Another part of me wants to run and hide from them.

Can we go shopping and buy back the things that were broken last night?

That's not me talking. That's not even me thinking. That's the reply I never give, because it is beyond me to give it. It's what I say now, looking back at then. It's what I say on the confused girl's behalf, the version of myself struggling to find something on the list that pleases them both.

One of you pick, I can't. It all sounds good.

I look around and realise that the house is shipshape. Apart from the odd gap where a lamp or side table once stood there is nothing to suggest last night's tempest. I look in the direction of the cabinet with Mum's china and know what I want to do with my day. Mum reads my mind. Why don't we go shopping and buy a few things for everyone? I nod, along with my father. There are smiles all round. Egg and toast between our teeth sort of smiles. Things we say with our mouths half-full, dispensing with the usual decorum because what we have to say seems so much more important than how it is said.

I fried everything in butter. I was so busy trying not to overheat the frying pan that I forgot about the toast and it burnt. I hope I scraped off all the burnt bits. Is it all right?

It's the best, Dad.

My mum agrees. Dad drops egg off his fork just as he is about to put the fork in his mouth and in his usual quick fashion his nimble fingers dart and catch the falling egg before it lands on his shirt.

Mum, do I have to shower before we go out?

Not if you don't want to.

Great, I think. Get as many concessions as you can while you can. I feel bad immediately for thinking this.

I didn't want to wet my stitches.

Don't worry, darling, you can take a bath later and keep the water off your cut.

Dad says he has to shave before he shows his face in public. I hadn't noticed with all his smiling but his face is overcast with black bristles. Mum declares that she is glad to hear he will get rid of all those prickly, scratchy hairs. I see she has a red mark on her neck. A love bite, no less. After all the warring last night to have produced a love bite in the same span of time defies comprehension. I wonder when he found the time to switch from abuse to charm and how she managed to turn off her defensive invective to become a receptacle for his lovely attentions. With the furniture scattered about and overturned – is the sole reply I offer to myself.

In an instant the baked beans switch from a sugary taste to dry and pebbly the next. I detect acid in the fried tomato, cardboard in the charcoal toast. I gulp the rest of my tea to clear my mouth and excuse myself from the table. This is where I am scripted to tell Dad the breakfast is wonderful and thank him, I know by the way my mother pauses to look at me with that narrow-eyed stare of hers, her chin slightly lowered as if studying me through her long eyelashes, but I don't. Dad seems to be operating on the plate so locked is his attention on the orchestrations of his knife and fork. I hope he feels rotten. No, I don't. Yes, I do. Both. I try to take my plate to the kitchen sink as usual but he tells me to leave it and get dressed. I scoot to my room, happy about the prospect of a day of shopping in their company and the chance of procuring a few goodies in this general atmosphere of guilty recompense.

From my room I listen as I dress to the two of them clearing the table: plates clink, knives and forks chime, cups and saucers plunk as they are piled up, the scuttle of chair legs on the tiled floor, her voice and his in a ping-pong repartee. And hot and cold balanced water running into the kitchen sink. One washes while the other dries. This is the music of domestic bliss. The small movements of two people harmonising in closeted space. I pull a T-shirt over my head and without feeding my arms through the sleeves, slump to the floor. I can do nothing but listen to the two of them in the dining room and adjoining kitchen. Their sounds are the equivalent of a noisy hunt, beating the undergrowth to drive out the prey, in this instance chasing last night's bad behaviour from the walls of the house where it skulks, banishing it from the still corners of their heads.

I freeze in this crouched position on the floor. I hide in bushes this way. In games of hide-and-seek, I make myself small and wait patiently to be discovered, unable to see anything but what is immediately under my nose. I find myself listening so hard for someone's approach that I begin to hear my breath rustling along my nostrils. And soon, as I concentrate on my breathing, I come to believe that each exhalation adds little by little to the inflation of a big balloon in which I play, a balloon whose walls cannot be seen, one so big it accommodates buildings, trees, animals and children. Then my parents quieten and I think they stop to listen for me. I wait for another second. Hearing nothing, fearing that one of them is heading to my room to check on my progress, I spring to my feet and punch my arms into the sleeves of my T-shirt. I head for my bedroom door while I step into my skirt with interchangeable hops and half steps. I pull open the door and meet my mother standing there.

Hey, you're dressed. Well done. Stand still for a moment.

She straightens my skirt and pulls a little of my tucked-in shirt over the waistband.

Don't want you to look like you've just come off the toilet, now, do we?

This is our private joke. I cannot remember if it is my mother or father that first points out the fact. The idea is that clothes on the body must look natural, hang in a relaxed and roomy way, rather than seeming to be just the right size as if the cloth for making the particular item has run out. Whenever we see someone with a shirt or blouse tightly tucked into trousers or skirt we cast each other knowing looks. He or she has just come off the toilet, dressed hurriedly with no attention to his or her appearance in the eyes of others. What a shame.

Where's Dad?

He's about to shave.

I want to watch him.

The door is open as usual when Dad shaves. I see him long before I reach the bathroom, in my mind's eye, stripped down to his underwear for the shower he always takes after his shave. Why wash all that aftershave off right away? It smells too strong, attracts wasps, and funny comments from his colleagues, and, anyway, its job of closing the pores along with any nicks from the razor happens the moment he slaps it on. He likes me to watch him shave but then he ushers me out of the oblong room and shuts the door for his shower.

Six months after this big fight and reconciliation my father is dead. Another six months later my mother delivers me to the big house where I spend the best part of twelve years expecting her minute by minute to come back and claim me. Flesh of her flesh. Her mirror image if a mirror existed that showed a younger side of an older person staring into it. Her penitence all these years through me at the house her husband grew up in and lies buried beside. And my father's people there to watch me grow and pay for my mother's sins. For the death of my father take me his daughter and mirror of her mother, his killer.

HEADMASTER

Maps, timetables, modes of transportation, points of embarkation, ports, docks, airports, jetties, ferries, bridges, railroads, roads, canals, rivers, schedules, fares, methods of payment, minimum age of passengers, whether unaccompanied minors are allowed, safety records, insurance liability, anonymity of travellers, documents required, provision of bathroom facilities for the opposite and fairer sex, size of compartments for sleeping, luggage, storage, inspection policies, immunity to highway robbery, criminality, transport police, fuel consumption, fuel capacity, availability of fuel, import and export differentials, trade fairs, International Monetary Fund and World Bank meetings in the capital, deaths of women under age forty, missing teenagers records, post office deliveries, cost of a standard letter, international letter, small package, disposal of garbage on various modes of transport, provision of drinking water and meals on trains, airplanes, buses, hitchhiking practices, police attitudes to minors away from home, brushes and combs, clean fingernails, posture, bank accounts, and money laundering are some of the things that interest her.

She is an omnivore, her mind roving while her tongue sticks in one place. Perhaps she researches every possible angle of her escape from that house. I do not blame her but her interests are too diverse to make the appropriate impact on the examinations that can open doors for her. I suppose she relies on the master key of her name. In that respect she is an Abrahams through and through.

For years I wish to have her tongue but not her stammer. Her mother's tongue I should say. One I can call my own. Mine missing long ago. Already cut out. When I married my husband he told me I used mine too much. I blurted out all the things that formed on my tongue about the kind of wife and mother that I wanted to be and the sort of husband and father I expected of him and he said, *It no go so*. And he hit me. My sisters make it plain to me, You the woman, he the man. You can't wear the trousers and he the skirt. He wears the trousers and the marriage works. Then this child comes along and she saying things that a grown woman, like me, cannot get away with saying.

My children envy her because of her sharp tongue, a quick and wicked tongue; a tongue that forever causes her grief. I curb it for her, still it for her, as mine was stilled. She ignores my warnings. She sings calypso as I talk so that she does not have to listen to the sirens of everyone around her, including me. I cast her one of my stone-cold-dead looks because whatever jumps off her tongue and out of her mouth always causes offence. She seems to find it hard to think before she talks, as I learned how to do. Like me she has no idea what she thinks until she hears herself say it. Her tongue thinks for her and she plays catch-up with it just the way I behaved a long time ago. Her tongue provokes me. I do not wait for her speech to be unleashed on my body. My hands wash her mouth in soap and water. My fingers twist her lips. My look seals her mouth.

I wear the same seal. Except when my husband comes to my bed in one of his moods and wants me, but from behind. I scream into my pillow when he drives into my rear. He puts his spit there with his tongue sometimes or his fingers. He bites the nape of my neck and says I am sweetness incarnate. Sweetness, he says, between bites and thrusts, biting the back of my neck as if to tattoo the word there with his teeth and pinning me to the bed with his arms, legs and body. Only then the moment I must concentrate to bring about happens. He forces his way into me. Then I feel only the jolts of his waist. Not long after I open like this for him he grunts and groans and floods into me. And he flops down on my back and kisses my neck and tells me he loves his sweetness. For an instant with his seed running out of me, and with no sense of soreness, maybe I love him too, maybe it is not much to ask of me. I stop screaming into my pillow. Words fail me.

Bettany walking into the same kind of trouble. A man will fight her and win before she loves him. His love for her will hurt her more than it will comfort her. Either that or she will be alone with only her tongue for company. Talking to herself. Alone or dead.

GRANDMOTHER

Lord, forgive me for thinking this but I am disappointed in my children, dismayed by their choices of husbands and wives and dejected by what they do to their children in the name of love and blood. They fill my house with their progeny and deceit and lust. The one room I eat, wash, read, sleep in and never leave is the only place in this house that they have not defiled with their ways governed by the flesh. They pay lip service to the Good Book and Father Nichols because they are more afraid of me than of anything in that book or what the priest might tell them. But they are grieving, Lord, over the loss of their brother and so they are not themselves. And they have to live with the child as a daily reminder of their loss and of the woman responsible for it. The child is a cross we must bear, a test by God of our faith and charity. I miss my husband and I miss my son and I am ashamed to say not one of my six children and their husbands, wives and two dozen children or all of them combined can replace those two. God, forgive me. I am old. When I cross the room I hear the creaks and cracks of my brittle bones. My brush chokes with grey hair. My skin peels off like clothing. God, save what remains of my soul. I believe my son's dying wish to have his child reared here was meant to console us all for the loss of him in our lives. When we demanded the child we wanted to punish the mother. We did not expect the child to look so much like the mother. It was like we had invited her here as a daily reminder of what she had cost us, our beloved son. Now she wants her child. She insults us by offering us money for the child. Her price is really what she thinks my dead son is worth to us all. I should pray for her soul.

BETTANY

Most Sundays I hide until everyone, except my grandmother, leaves for the morning church service on bicycles and in the donkey-drawn cart. But this particular Sunday I stay under my kind aunt's bed where I watch her dress her big round belly with the skin stretched over it and her navel poking out. When I think she's gone I emerge from under the bed and she hops off the bed as if her belly is full of air and she grabs my arm and drags me out of the house. She settles herself on the crossbar of a bicycle and orders me to pedal a pregnant woman to church! We catch up with the replacement donkey and cart. An uncle slaps the reins on the flanks of the unco-operative donkey until it gallops. The children loaded on the cart beg him not to allow the bicycle with a pregnant woman and Pissy-Missy, killer mother girl, on it to beat them to the church.

My aunt declares that she understands my intention to avoid sweating on the ride to church because she does not relish the prospect of arriving hot and flustered. Nevertheless, she maintains, there is a race to win while I pedal as if I have prosthetic devices for legs and smokers' lungs and would I start working my legs this instant or leave us both mired in shame. I pedal as hard as I can with my aunt lying low on the crossbar of the bicycle to mimimise air resistance. I feel certain that the donkey and cart loaded with jeering children will surely pull away and leave me in its shadow. But my aunt says that she knows a challenge when she hears one and she is not a woman to turn her back on a challenge. She orders me to stop and she takes over the pedalling and I sit on the crossbar. I lower my body on to the crossbar to avoid her belly pressing down on me. I worry that I might damage her baby. But she leans forward and practically drapes her big belly over me – to lower the air resistance you understand – and she yelps like a cowboy taming a horse. I have never in all my years at the house been this close physically to someone else, never mind two people, except in a fight or at the receiving end of a beating from them. She pedals so hard the bicycle rocks from side to side. We draw alongside the galloping donkey with its payload of bouncing children and they urge my uncle to beat the new donkey some more and not allow a pregnant woman to beat them but he refuses. The bicycle pulls ahead of the cartload of children and we leave them behind. I peer back and delight in their long faces. My uncle shouts at my aunt to stop behaving irresponsibly with her big belly. My aunt ignores him and begins to tell me that I made her do the one thing she did not wish to do this morning of all mornings, that is, arrive at church sweating like a donkey. Both of us are drenched. Just as I search for something to say as an offer of my exculpation she adds, But how sweet the victory.

The whitewashed steeple of the wood church points one clean wooden finger into the face of heaven. Benches in neat rows mimic the idea of an orderly and purposeful universe or a field of corn and each of us seated on them an ear of corn. The benches dig into the pelvic bone. The adults sit on their hymn books between songs. The children perch on their hands. Every few minutes I shift my weight from my left to my right side to ease the pain and pins and needles. All the children squirm in this way throughout the service and sometimes an adult taps the child to still the fidgeting. The priest towers on a platform at the front of the congregation drawn from all quarters of the village and outlying houses. He launches into his readings and lesson. As usual he seems to be addressing me when he sermonises about the devil's ways, if only because his words match those launched against me at the house by the adults and children. The hem of his frock at the front ends a few inches higher from his ankle than at the back due to his protruding stomach. I am surprised one of my aunts all of whom are so deft with a needle and thread has not corrected that gown. His habit of resting the Bible on the top of his paunch as if on a tabletop annoys the hell out of me because I cannot help looking at the Bible, which shakes as he speaks. I wonder if the leftover sacrament ends up in his belly. Like everyone else around me he looks at me and never smiles. And along with everyone at the house (except my kind aunt) I find it hard to attach a kind word to his body. The way his eyes pass over me makes me look at him with the same neglect of the usual social graces, the demure glance and soft smile to acknowledge another's eyes, perhaps even a nod of recognition. I stare at him and try not to blink or only blink when I am sure his eyes are on someone else so that the trick becomes to avoid blinking while his eyes are on me and to fit in as many blinks as possible while he scrutinises someone else. His entire sermon about the burning bush and our need to keep the faith and resist the temptation of doubt can be plotted as a series of quick-fire winks and long swathes of eye-watering, dry-eyeballed and therefore eye-stinging stares.

I was beaten beside a bush whose whips never ran out. The bush supplied fire to my uncle who applied its burn to my body. It was a burning bush. It burned for me. The fire that does not burn, that leaves the bush in the Bible intact, as if fire dances around the thing it engulfs rather than consumes it, sounds nothing like the fire on the stove my aunt held my fingers over. My fingers reddened and blistered and the blisters burst and scabs formed. The fire ate my skin as fast as if it were a wafer. This fire with my hands in it like that bush, would preserve me. I could pass my eyes through it and the moisture would remain untarnished. My mother in me is like this fire. She blazes but she does not burn.

After the collection plate passes up and down each of the twenty aisles, he makes us all stand and repeat the Lord's prayer and then we file to the altar for the sacrament. My stomach growls. I hate it that I actually want the wafer and wine to assuage my hunger. In fact one tastes like paper while the other recalls vinegar. I try not to look at the baptismal font. I washed my face in it once to cool down and freshen up after a race to the church by the children ended with all of us arriving there hot and sweaty. All the children were so amazed they said nothing to me or to anyone. They may have secretly admired me for it. At the end of the proceedings the children speed from the wood building and make their own way home on foot which sometimes includes a detour to the bakery for what they call variously, freebies, girts, manna, baps. I forget about pedalling my aunt back to the house. I run especially fast taking the short cut across the field just to get home before everyone and find some real food, something that lingers in my mouth a little longer than a wafer, something I can consume without it burning me.

PRIEST

I look for the child on Sundays during my service and when I visit her grandmother. Her grandmother and I grew up together until I got my calling and turned my back on the world of flesh for all things Godly. The child looks wiser than her years but she remains a child. She may or may not have her mother's ways as everyone at the house maintains. The simple fact that she is blood cannot be altered. I see her father in her, fleetingly. She looks at me for answers. I speak to her as I must speak to everyone in my congregation. Her grandmother should not have married an inveterate gambler and heavy drinker. His good head for business remains his only saving grace. He gave the woman grey hairs and lines on her face. She never had those downturned lines around her mouth. She was a sweet young woman. He turned her sour. I know he put the roof over my head and God provides in mysterious ways but I wish he would stay lost in the jungle. I do not wish him dead. That would kill the poor woman. Just lost. She buried her eldest son. One funeral is enough. The child must live as much as he must live. Just do not come back.

Her mother promised to return and then got caught up in affairs bigger than her responsibility to the child. Someone needs to sit that child down and tell her the truth about her mother. They need to stop taking it out on the child and put their name to better use. But who am I to ruminate on matters I have no influence over. I cannot even talk a lifelong friend out of confining herself in her bedroom over a worthless husband. With all my religion I cannot bring her around from her grief over her son to the greater love of God. I love her all the same. We were childhood sweethearts.

Bettany

Flatness saves my life the time my aunt beats me and draws blood from my left ear, even before I open my mouth for some offence caused to her by some unwitting action of mine. Bleeding from my left ear, and walking in a daze along the same L-shaped corridor, its dark thick and cloying, I wade against a knee-deep current or weeds tangled against my legs. I want to turn back, afraid to pass my grandmother's room but I succumb to an even greater impulse to free myself of the drag of that current and the pull of those weeds. I throw out my right hand against the wall, deliberately place one foot directly in front of the other so that the heel of the forward leg always makes contact with the toes of the other foot. I follow the smooth wooden wall with its little knots and dents and creases under my fingers until I arrive at the bedroom that belongs to the aunt who made my left ear bleed. I stop and listen. My chest tightens. But I hear nothing except rain and a ringing in my ears like the muffled laughter of children. The usual lamplight does not leak from the gap under the door. I press my good right ear to the wood and touch it with all my fingers lightly so that the whole of me is no more than an ear and ten fingertips.

What if the door opens now? How do I explain my presence? My breath skims the surface of my chest and my heart sprints away from me. The part of me that always looks on from the sidelines at everything that happens to me calms the rest of me by brushing the questions aside. That part knows that these transitional questions or questions asked by one side of me as I cross over to the other side, become irrelevant the moment I abandon my earthly form for air, a heavenly body. Before the next thought occurs I find myself transferred to the darkness of the bedroom, filtered from my body, become ethereal. I melt and slide under the door in a state of disembodiment, a feather's weight, the expanse of one exhaled breath on a wintry morning, the thickness of a playing card, and resume my listening pose in a flattened state. The switch from one state to the other is as fast as one thought succeeding another. I break into an immediate cold sweat at the notion that I might be in the wrong room, my grandmother's room. If she lays eyes on me and I am within her reach I convince myself that she will grab my neck and strangle me for the loss of her son. I may be a child but I am still the eyes and ears and looks of the woman who took her son from her and put him in the plot of land reserved for her and her husband first before any of her children. She will tear me limb from limb, sink her teeth into me and eat me.

My grandmother fills my head to such capacity that I take a few seconds to register the presence of my aunt in her bedroom. She curses the day I was born as she massages her hands bent out of shape by my body. Then she begins to smile. She unhooks the eyelet of her dress by reaching behind her neck. She unzips the dress down to the small of her back and steps out of it completely naked. She places the dress on a wood hanger and hooks the curved end of it on the top of the doorframe by stretching up on to her toes. Her long tubular breasts look much fairer than the rest of her except for two dark circles around her prominent nipples. Flesh around her hips and buttocks shake with the effort of that stretch and only settle when she lies back on the bed.

The outline of my aunt's naked body and her movements are clear because she left the window open and the little light that lingers outside pours in with vapour from the rain. She glistens with moisture. Her skin is pale except for black patches of hair under her arms and her crotch. Her thick long black hair fans open on the bed. I want to brush it. I wonder why she does not take the time to get under the sheets. She made the bed so well the corners of the sheets form neat angles of sixty degrees to the bed frame. There are no blankets. I learned from the carefree talk of my aunts that only my grand-mother's bed has blankets on it, everyone else makes do with sheets. The bed must be very old. It creaks above the noise of the rain every time she moves. She reclines on it but her legs from the knees down dangle over the end. Her feet do not touch the floor. She runs her hands over her breasts and around her nipples where her fingers pause and pinch before continuing down to her belly and up to her breasts and neck and face and hair, which she spreads with her splayed fingers that act like a long-toothed comb through her hair. I think I hear her hum a tune, a recent chart-topping calypso, but only the chorus of it over and over again, a couple of lines about a couple taking turns to be on top and in the confusion, somehow both of them ending up on the top. The children sing it a lot too, but uncomprehendingly or just for the tune, or so I believe from the tone of their singing.

A door I fail to notice before, in the wall that the bed braces against, opens. A man enters from an adjoining room. The woman hardly turns her head in his direction. *He* startles me, rather than the presence of another person. All my fears of adults leave me the moment flatness takes over my body. But I jump surprised less by the sudden intrusion and more by the fact that the man is not her husband. He waltzes straight for the bed with a smile. I put my body between him and the woman to stop him. He steps right through me bringing his hand up and across his face to clear the flimsy web of me. In my changed state I resemble a few strands of web, or the slightest mist. He pulls his shirt out of his trousers, changes his mind about undressing licks his lips and simply kneels at the foot of the bed and buries his face between the woman's thighs. My aunt grabs his head and widens her legs. I move around the bed to the end where the man kneels. I look up and see he did not shut the door properly but merely pushed it until the door came to rest against the doorframe.

The room he entered from is equally without lamplight. My mind spins on the fact of my presence in this room in my flattened state. I wonder how long it will take for me to heal before I am allowed to leave the room. The woman claws at the man's shirt buttons. He looks up at her face and raises his torso over her and pushes his hand between her legs. She rushes to unbuckle his trousers. She takes his head into her hands and licks his face. Then he lowers his torso on to hers. I want to get away from them before another second passes or another person comes along, but I cannot form the command in my head that operates my body. I hear a noise above the rain and the creaking bed that is not the breathing of these two people. Something akin to the click of a lock sounds from the other room. Again I order my body to retreat and this time it obeys me. I conclude that my left ear has healed from my beating by my aunt. I walk backwards and keep an eye on the couple on the bed and I stumble into the door. But because I am less than smoke I find myself on the other side of the door and in the glow of a lamp. Before I can speak or turn around a hand slaps me gently on the back of the head and a soft voice orders me to stop playing the fool by walking backwards. It is my kind aunt in the corridor with her hand on the door handle about to enter the room the man she is married to left to join her older sister in bed. My aunt carries folded clothes. What am I up to? She inquires. I tell her to come with me this instant to the place where I just saw a scorpion. She brings the lamp closer to my face, sees the shock on it and asks me to lead the way. I scrape my foot on the wood floor and clear my throat as I pass the bedroom and all I hear from inside it is the loud rain. At the L where the corridor shortens and ends on the verandah I point at the ceiling. Her lamp picks up a large scorpion at the top of the wall. She raises the lamp and pulls me behind her. She grips the folded clothes in her hand. As the lamp rises above her head and its rays define the scorpion more sharply with its arched back and poisoned tail hovering inches above its back, the scorpion dives at her face. She shrieks. I crouch behind her. She dashes the clean clothes to the floor and stamps on them with both feet. I leap from behind her and on to the laundry and stamp. She pulls me off gently by my ear and complains that she does not want me to stamp on her clean clothes with my unhelpful dirty feet. She peers under the clothes one corner first then the other. She lifts up one item at a time and shakes it at arm's length. Then she tells me to go and fetch her husband from the bedroom. I run and pound on the door and he emerges neatly dressed and with an angry expression for me but when he turns his head and sees his wife at the end of the corridor his face softens and he walks briskly towards her. I follow him and glance back in time to see a woman step from the bedroom next to the one he just left. She trots away from us on tiptoe, towards the kitchen, clutching her dress to her body.

My aunt tells her husband a scorpion hides here somewhere and the child should keep her distance. He turns and shoots me a look that stops me in my tracks. Then he advances more cautiously looking all around him. I wonder how I made her see that scorpion. This must be some charm left over from my condition of flatness, some ability that is mine to use for the benefit of my smooth return to a child's body. Her husband asks if she saw the wretched thing with her own eyes or whether she heard about a scorpion from the wretched child. I visualise a scale of wretchedness and see the scorpion and me on it but I cannot decide which of the two of us is the heavier wretch. My aunt says she saw the scorpion herself and now she cannot find it in the very clothes that saved her from it. Has he known a scorpion to dive-bomb someone? And has he seen her older sister? No, no he has not. When was the last time they found a scorpion in the house? He could not remember, but he thinks its appearance may have something to do with the long wet season disorienting insects after the prolonged drought. Where has he been all this time? Doing things. What is it to her? And he has not seen her sister? No, he is not her sister's keeper and is it wise for her to become so riled in her pregnant condition? They fall into a silence just short of exploding at each other. He helps her to shake out the clothes one piece at a time. She says she hopes his hands are cleaner than that child's feet. He tries to touch her big belly but she slaps his hands away.

Georgetown Calling

I convince myself if I get away from the house then the jumbled pieces of my mother and father associated with it will sort themselves into two neat compartments, one for each of them, and I can approach each and take from it what I will as I do my father's sarcophagus. I dart from the side of the house, duck through a gap in the fence and sprint along the main road until I reach the rum shop. Two trucks, parked facing the direction of the capital, lean on the grass verge, half-on, half-off the road, their drivers in the rum shop enjoy a beer and catch up with each other's news. I look around and see no one in the immediate vicinity of the trucks. I climb up the back of the open trailer and crouch in a corner of it. It feels huge to me despite the bundles of rope and a few bags of mangoes and cassava and some loose coconuts all collected by the driver on his return from the interior to the capital.

The driver's door slams and the truck shudders and splutters to life. I almost bolt from my hiding place but by the time I picture how to jump to the ground from my high perch in the trailer the truck works through its low gears and begins building speed. I stand with difficulty and hold on to the side of the truck. The wind whips water from my eyes. I trap my flying hair with one hand to keep it out of my eyes. The road below blurs. The grass verge blends into one mass of green and brown. I look into the trees and fields far away to stop my head spinning. When I see a town coming up ahead I crouch down again and hear people hail the driver and some of them slap the side of the truck and the driver beeps back or sounds his horn in reply to a beep from another truck passing inches away. The second the driver passes a town's main road he climbs up through the gears and settles at a breakneck speed I guess to be about sixty without really knowing how sixty actually feels.

The distance closes between towns and then little or no gap of countryside opens up between one group of houses and another and I guess that this must be the outskirts of the city so I do not bother to hide from people. The driver stops sounding his horn for people he knows and starts to use it to warn other traffic or object to another driver's manoeuvre. Streets run into other streets. Traffic lights hold back cars, bicycles, motorbikes and horse-drawn carts for us to pass. The air thickens with exhaust fumes and engines. My eyes dart everywhere. As soon as I settle on a group of people or a tall wooden building I dart to something else equally riveting. The driver pulls into a market square and jumps out of his truck. I take this as my cue to bail out. I lower myself down on the opposite side to his and people immediately begin bumping into me but not one of them remarks on the fact that a girl of twelve just jumped off the truck. I need to ask someone where I might find the central post office. I want to know why I have not received a single letter from my mother in reply to my countless letters. My uncle took an honesty and loyalty oath when he became Boundary's sole postman but I suspect that he destroys my letters to my mother and intercepts her letters to me. Surely I can find out something from the main post office of the land.

I face people and speak to them but they ignore me and bump into me, as if my only function in that public square is to be propelled by them from one spot to another. Not one person in the crowd sees me. I feel flat again, incognito, but with the exception that my body lacks all the benefits. Perhaps we are all blind to one another's presence for some reason to do with our enforced proximity. What would I do if someone decides to beat me in this city? Perish in the invisibility that I hold in common with theirs. I convince myself that I cannot be seen and therefore I am free to do as I please and I meander among the crowd looking into people's faces and standing beside them as they bargain at a market stall. Then a boy my age asks me to help him collect some bags of produce, that's the word he uses, produce, from a stall for his house. I shrug off my surprise that someone notices me after all. I follow him from stall to stall. He has a way of walking sideways on in the crowd like a prow cutting upstream that makes it hard to follow him since the stream closes immediately in his wake. I ask him if he can direct me to the main post office, the central one for all the country. He shoots me a quizzical look and says matter of factly that he knows of two post offices and both seem equally important. I think about this for a moment. Perhaps I should start with the nearest one and work my way to the farthest.

The vendors wave their arms full of fruit and vegetables and call on women and men to stop and buy the sweetest and the freshest produce in the city. The shoppers browse and sneer at what they see. But the same vendors usher the boy away the moment they set eyes on him, until we come to a fruit and vegetable stall run by an old woman with an unlit pipe in her mouth and hit on some luck. He hands her a piece of paper with a few notes and coins wrapped in it. She barely glances at the money before she buries it in her apron and fills two sacks with the worst looking fruits and vegetables she can find. I wait for the boy to react but he just concentrates on keeping his sack open for the vendor. The boy pushes one of the sacks at me and I swing it over my shoulder and follow him, since no one seems to bump into him, away from the market square and down a narrow street with tall three-storey buildings on both sides. He says his name is Fly, and when I tell him mine and he repeats it, the first time doubtfully, and the second time as if announcing fresh fruit to a buyer who needs coaxing to part with his money. I say right away that I have no mother or father. He replies that he does not know of another child who has parents. Ha, I continue, but my mother left me to go and better herself in another country. The plan includes me eventually. At some point in the not too distant future she will send for me and we will be together once more, surrounded by the prosperity of her labours in my absence. He interrupts me by pointing out that all the children he knows expect to be rescued at some stage of their abandonment. They all spin tall tales like mine. I cut him off with a fact. Whereas these children lack parents and dream of being saved, I have a mother who knows where to find me and who promised me she would return for me. I continue irritated by the way I feel goaded by him into launching my defence, somehow this reward – too much for me to experience in one lifetime – will justify my nights and days stuck among my relatives who want nothing to do with me. And me with nowhere to run and hide that does not involve an embarrassing return for food and water, and that beating that I try to evade still there waiting for me. I am the child who will one day be going overseas. A blue sea trapped in a glass marble reminds me of it.

He listens and adds that he dreams about the same things but all the children he knows who also nurse these dreams never go anywhere. There is nowhere to go but another part of the city and if a child leaves the shelter then only the open air remains for that child. And children do not last very long in the open unless they stay with other children. I listen with half an eye on the endless stream of windows with washing hanging from them and the other half on the bicycles and cars that brush my side. The stink from the narrow roadside trench makes me sneeze. Bless you, he shouts every time I sneeze, which forces me to suppress the next sneeze since no one ever blessed me when I sneezed and I want to bank the few from him for good luck. At last we stop in front of a large four-storey building full of children and he inclines his head towards it for me to follow him into the yard. I tell him my journey with him ends right on this spot and can he give me those directions to the nearest of the two post offices he knows. He points out that the post offices are closed for the day and with nightfall almost upon us it is obvious that I have nowhere to sleep. What makes him rush to such a conclusion? I interject. He rolls his eyes and reminds me that he was not born big so. Since I seem to be hardworking he will put in a good word for me with his Super, but if I walk off now there is no telling what might become of me. There are things a country girl needs to learn about a city sooner rather than later. There are places he could show me that would make my hayseed stomach turn but right now I should follow him inside and meet the Super. I should secure a bed for the night before all the beds are allocated to the many children who will soon turn up looking for shelter that night. Enough of the country girl, hayseed stuff, I tell him, I lived in the most exciting city in the world before I ended up in this . . . before I got dumped in this country. I change my mind about saying dump instead of country since it could never be true of this land trailing off into the sea or else into dense jungle and sectioned by many rivers some wide as the sea, this land could never be anything but beautiful.

In the crowded yard a game of marbles erupts into an argument between two boys who stand close to each other and shout insults and move around without opening any space between them. Fly drops his bag, tugs mine out of my hand and flings it on top of his, grabs my arm and pulls me deeper into the yard to join the group of onlookers. The two boys circle each other like cocks about to pounce. The taller of the two jerks his head forward and butts the nose of his shorter but much stockier opponent and blood spurts from it. They punch and kick each other, grapple and tumble to the ground and roll around less like cocks in a cockfight now and more like two coral snakes in courtship, with the rest of the children stepping out of their way. The boy with the bloody nose pulls a flick knife from his trouser pocket and the taller boy springs away from him.

Fly says now things will get interesting. I think the boy a cheat for introducing a knife into an otherwise fair fight. Fly reminds me that this is the city and people fight any way they can. A shrill whistle rips through the commotion and the boy closes the knife quickly and hands it to another boy who sticks it inside his shirt. Everyone turns towards the house. A tall man with broad shoulders seems lodged in the front door whose dimensions could barely contain him. He lunges into the yard and I am afraid his leaving the building may have robbed it of its main support and it will collapse. His handlebar moustache bobs about as he walks with a stick and a whistle in his mouth. He pushes the children from his path or they scatter from him and he points his stick at the two boys. When he raises his stick at the other children, they run to the side of the house or out of the yard altogether. Except for Fly, who grips my hand, and the two boys in the fight, the yard, crowded a moment ago, instantly and completely clears of children. The man turns and the two boys follow him into the building. Fly pulls me out of the way and back to the corner of the yard where we retrieve the two bags with provisions then march back to the front door. I try to hide my upset about the fight. Fly peers into my face. He says I should know that if those two boys meet outside the yard to fight no one would stop them. They fight to the end. One of them walks away and leaves the other one on the ground or both boys finish unable to stand after it. The whole non-refereed arrangement means it is all right to use whatever comes to hand to defend yourself because it is live any way you can or die like a dog.

We step inside the house. Disinfectant stings my nose. The worn and clean wood floor creaks under me. I follow Fly into an office to the left of the front door. The man with the stick (the two boys are nowhere to be seen) raises his eyebrows quizzically and his fashionable moustache follows suit. Fly explains about the produce he procured from the market and the supervisor nods his moustache and Fly turns to me and says I played a pivotal role in the successful transaction, and as it happens, I need a bed for the night.

Where you from, girl?

B–B–B–Boundary, mister.

Boundary. Nice little place. Who your family?

I say I have none. He lifts his stick in my direction and asks me again and adds that I slept somewhere before I turned up here so name the house. I tell him and he sits upright, looks at his watch and writes a quick note on a piece of paper and orders Fly to walk me to the bus station right away so that I can catch the last bus home. I say, on no account do I intend to return to that place. He ignores me and asks Fly if he needs help to get me to the bus station and Fly declares he can handle a girl. The Super looks at me sternly and I swear the hairs on his moustache stand on end. He says I should open my eyes and look around me and see how lucky I am to belong to a family with a famous name in the capital and a quiet place in the countryside. Then he orders me to get on that last bus because if he learns that I am still in his city after sundown he will personally see to my punishment.

'Government money come to me to run this place because the minister with your name pull strings and make it so. If you turn up here and we don't send you back what happen to us?' Before I can react he answers himself: 'We finish.'

He stands and his chair falls to the floor. The way he leans over me I feel he is about to sweep me out of his office with his moustache. Fly grips my arm and pulls me outside.

I-I-I-I ca-ca-ca-can't go back there.

You must, Bettany, or all of we finish, you hear, all of we done for unless you go back.

I-I-I-I d-d-d-don't un-un-underst-st-st-stand.

If I know your last name back at the market I tell you for free that your people open this orphanage.

I want to ask, What minister? I feel stupid not knowing that a relation holds high office in the government. The rest of the walk I cry and Fly just shakes his head at the fact that I am the luckiest child he knows but I do not know my luck and he wishes we can swap places.

At the bustling bus station everyone carries a bag in each hand, something on their backs and a bundle balanced on their heads. Fly asks me to help him look for Mable on the front of the buses. We pass row after row of blue and white buses, imported from Cuba and walk up and down long lines of people jostling to board buses. Fly grips my arm and asks me several times, if I see Mable yet. I see the word but I do not tell him as he keeps checking my face to see if I see it. We almost walk past the bus when I realise something must be wrong with his eyes since the letters are big and bold on the bus. Do you need glasses? No, why? Does he watch television a lot as all city children are known to do with all their spare time? No, but he sits through as many matinees at the local cinema as he can slip into undetected and the screens are so big he could see the action from a street away rather than ten feet away as is often the case. He wants to know how much television I watch? I tell him I do not have television where I live but that films come to our village once every week. If he is not blind why couldn't he see the word bold as brass before us? He confesses he cannot read and write, but he intends to remedy that soon. As we wait for the driver to open the doors I write his name in the dirt plastered on the side of the bus. That my name? I nod and get him to copy the word. He writes his name not once but all over the side of that bus. The driver opens the doors and people climb aboard. I wish Fly well and thank him for taking care of me from the moment I landed in his city. He waves me away. If I come back to town I know where to find him. He might even look me up one day in the country.

I show the mustachioed driver my note and he shakes his head in despair and puts me in the seat just inside the door and adjacent to the driver's seat so that all he has to do is glance across at me. He wets his bottom lip and feeds it over his moustache every few seconds so that the hairs are moist and lie over his hidden top lip. He resembles a younger type of the supervisor. He tells me I am not very smart to leave a house with everything, for a city with nothing but misery to offer a child on her own. Do I know that people kill to belong to my family? I am glad when the bus fills up and it is time to leave simply because he stops telling me how lucky I am to have my last name and what it means for my life, a charmed life, if I take proper advantage of my name instead of running away from it. And do I not realise I can never escape my name.

As we slip from the capital orange streetlights glide over the wide windscreen and houses hold their furnaces close to the passenger windows. Gradually, dark spaces open between hamlets and it takes longer for the generator-powered bulbs leaking from rich houses to interrupt the ubiquitous dark. All I see is the defined sweep of the headlights as it swallows the dark and finds only more of it ahead. And then a sweep or curve that seems to obliterate not just any dark but one I know, a familiar dark, a way known to me because I see it with my eyes closed, no matter how much dark or how thick the dark spread over the objects. This is the dark of Boundary; its kerosene-lit and gas-lit houses; shapes I associate with it in daylight. Except at the abnormally bright rum shop that swarms with people the way insects gravitate towards a lamp. The church steeple resembles one of those satellite rockets on a launch pad in neighbouring Suriname, waiting for weather other than the common fare of the rainforests of the Amazon to permit it to launch into space. The bakery ovens fill the night air and people on the bus steer their conversation towards the far-flung reputation of Boundary's bread. The driver slows before I tell him anything. Everyone knows this house, he laughs, then he switches back to his stern disposition and remarks loudly for everyone left on the bus to hear that I am lucky to leave his bus without a stinging lash as a reminder of my stupidity and he winks at me. He pushes his bottom lip very quickly several times over his moustache and turns his body from the steering wheel to watch me disembark. I pray that everyone in the house is anywhere in it but on the balcony overlooking the front yard. I thank the driver and run into the yard, and knowing every inch of the way, I close my eyes and picture my feet as two headlights feeling out the dark.

I grab a ladle tied to a rain barrel and scoop out a drink. It is as if I placed the tip of my tongue on the end of a battery for I feel a charge emitted by cold water that hurts my teeth and tastes mildly of rust. How odd that not a single child or adult bothers me. Thank you, Mother. The back stairs up to the kitchen still damp from a recent scrub-down cools the breeze so much it is uncomfortable on my thighs. But the door to the kitchen is locked. I stand there in the dark and wonder what to do about the growl in my stomach. The bag of bruised fruit and vegetables from the market that I carried earlier suddenly seems dear to my empty belly. Fly must enjoy his food knowing exactly how it comes to be on his plate. For my part I see the rice fields, the coconut and plantain groves, the sugarcane fields, the orchards of mangoes, sapodillas, breadfruit and guavas and yet there is no guarantee that any of it will be earmarked for me. My plate remains empty from day to day. I find it or I do not. If I am lucky it is there for me because I attach myself to a bundle of children, otherwise I go hungry. I should have struck a bargain with Fly and found a way to stay in the city. But I must return and investigate the post office. I pace the landing outside the locked kitchen door wondering what I should do next. I must eat or I will not catch a wink of sleep. Maybe there is something lying around somewhere that someone forgot to finish. My belly growls at the vague prospect and grumbles loud and long as if to let me know it must have something to settle it and soon, and not just a drink of rusty water, however numbingly cold. I look out the window at the dark pond below, not quite below actually, and at the fence along one side of the pond that separates the pond from the house. I stare further out into the dark field whose only crop right now appears to be the insect-riddled night. There might be a corridor into this dark, a way through its thickness with no possibility of return to daylight and the house. Perhaps I can search for the corridor, just walk into the dark and not stop until I lose my way and lose all thought about turning back. My mother might be out there waiting for me to arrive at this conclusion and act on it. And maybe my father can act as my guide. Oh, emperor of darkness ensconced in your airtight, light-tight coffin for years now. I belong to my mother but the second I die I will be yours. I turn to go back downstairs and bump into the swollen breasts and tremendous belly of my kind aunt. She says she does not want to know what I was doing on a bus. She slaps a chunk of bread and a fat slice of cheese into my hands and tells me to make myself scarce before everyone returns from the film show at the school. I run downstairs and count the steps and think the breeze warmer perhaps because the steps are dry. I lie on my back in my allotted cupboard and nibble the bread believing that the longer it lasts the more full my belly becomes.

Mad Rick

The girl hide when Aunty call she name. I hunt for she with the others. I find she in the barn. She crouch behind a broken wheel from the donkey cart. I want to shout for the others to come and see who find she first but my head full of that day when the wheel break. The cart hit a rock and overturn and crush my father, vomit in his mouth and the old donkey still running, harness dragging on the ground. The cart roll on top of my father in the trench. The mute plantain man lift the cart off my father. Nobody know where he find the strength to lift that cart and save my father, I don't think even he know, but from that day the plantain man the strongest man around. They keep the wheel in case they need a part from it to repair another wheel. My crushed father breathing hard from the least exercise from that day. He must look at that wheel every time he go in the barn. When I see she behind the wheel I see my father under the cart and I feel sorry for she. I just stand there and look at she and I say nothing until other children come up and drag she from behind the wheel. Another aunt decide to beat she for not answering her sister's call. Aunty swing the belt and she dance to avoid the swings. She skip-skipping over some kind of rope, she hop-hopping in a game of hopscotch. She jigs on hot coals under she two-foot them or to someone taking pot shots at she legs. All that left for she to do is click she heels in the air to crown the dance. She gyrations make Aunty double the beating. I want to tell the girl to keep still and the beating soon done. But she will not or cannot be still. Aunty aims even more and puts more effort into each lash. The girl twist and turn and she dodge one or two blows but catch plenty more all over she body. She end up worse off like she pin under a wheel and no strong body around to free she, not her poor dead father, not even she good-for-nothing mother.

BETTANY

I follow her, not wanting to particularly. I cannot help myself. The impulse to stick close to the body responsible for my latest aches overpowers me. She turns around and chases me away. At first I think she cannot mean to chase me since I expect her not to be able to see me. But she heads straight for me and I just evade her grasp and dash along the side of the house with the fence so close to it only a child can fit in the gap between the house and the fence. Then I crouch behind a rain barrel taller than me and peep at her as she saunters to the back of the house and deep into the yard and into the latrine.

She looks around before she ducks into the small zinc shed and closes the door behind her. I comb the ground and pick the biggest stone I can grip. I tiptoe to the corrugated zinc latrine thinking about what I intend to do and what it might bring down on my head. But I do not care. I pelt that large stone with all my might at the galvanized zinc. The noise of a large stone dashed against zinc sheeting is nothing like thunder but more like an amplifier in an empty stadium turned up full for a sound test where all six strings of an electric guitar are struck at the same time. A shriek bursts from the shed and my aunt erupts from it tripping over her skirt and panties around her ankles. Standing only a few feet away from the shed and in the open and obviously the guilty culprit, I will surely be the victim of a murder that afternoon. But she rushes past me as she pulls up her clothes and grabs at the children who gather to see what the commotion is all about. She chases and beats as many of them as she lays hands on until out of breath. The laughter subsides succeeded by crying children. I stand in the middle of it all and no one registers my presence. I cannot be seen. Invisibility is not instantaneous this time but gradual.

KIND AUNT

I shout in the middle of the night and wake the house. I hear people say to each other again and again, *Her time come!* As though I missed the fact. I scream every couple of minutes. During the quiet between my cries, so much quiet at 2 a.m. my lone voice in the big house belongs to the house itself, I make myself comfortable, sip on crushed ice and cast my husband baleful looks. The house in birth pangs. The house, burgeoning another room under its roof. And then the small cries of a room with so small a voice that it is not much bigger than the cupboard full of her father's things that Bettany elects to sleep in.

My other two children find another bedroom to sleep in during the long night. By morning all I want to do is sleep but everyone files in to see the baby, all except Bettany. She knows her place. At last they leave the baby and me and take their broad grins with them and their palms held out a few inches apart to denote the small parcel size of my darling. When they are all gone I call for Bettany. My husband asks me if I am mad. I ask him if he has something, anything better to do and he sucks his teeth and walks out of the room and scowls at what I take to be the doorframe. I call again and right away Bettany runs into the room and almost falls on to the bed. I look at her to see if she is hurt but her face retains its usual softness. I hold my child up for Bettany to see and she peers at the wrapped bundle and seems surprised by my baby's pink, scrunched face and swollen eyes and look of utter contentment. Bettany appears more upset than pleased. Say hello to Augustine, I urge her. Hello, Augustine, she says, Welcome to the world. She scoots out when my sister – who nearly always spits in Bettany's presence – steps into the room.

GRANDMOTHER

Mother tastes afterbirth then offers the father some. He eats it off her fingers with a look on his face as if tasting frogspawn. My eldest daughter brings me the screaming child right away. Nothing wrong with his lungs. I hardly glance at him before I order her to take him back to his mother and make sure he latches on to the right breast because she is right-handed. The father buries the placenta under the back steps then the navel string when it drops off a few weeks later also under the crowded back steps; everything done according to my instructions conveyed through my eldest daughter.

Father Nichols to bless child on next visit, then the baptismal font for the official ceremony at the church. I will not be there. By the time that man returns to me his house will be full of grandchildren all strange to him. Serves him right for taking off at his age. God bring him back to me safe and sound just let me set eyes on him and if I get close enough to him land one slap on his face for leaving me alone in this godforsaken place.

Bettany

The baby's cries measure my nights and days, a sound that begins as small and choppy then grows loud and clear. Between the breast milk, boiled water, gripe water and more breast milk, Augustine expresses an endless discontent. His knotted face makes a noise for each knot in his face. I will him to be quiet. In my direct telepathy to him I point out that he should be happy with two parents to look after his needs, in particular, a mother with kindness for a name.

The other children return from one of their hunts for empty tin cans (I heard about it, I tried to follow them but they chased me away), all rattles, clanks, chinks, and full of big talk. I loom into sight again. They boast among themselves that their cars qualify for the Brazilian Grand Prix. The unopened end of each tin can contributes to one half of a wheel. Hacksaws cut away the intact bottom quarter of a can and two of these ends fit together with little taps from a hammer into a tin wheel. A child runs the risk of a dreaded tetanus injection if cut by the jagged end of a rusted can. This makes the children work like diamond cutters, brain surgeons and chemists handling explosives or poisons. They cock their little fingers and peer closely at the tins and younger children entrust their cans to older children to mould into wheels.

I watch them and as they play I make my own car. I beg my milky and slow-moving kind aunt for a few tins. She says only this one time and she hands me Augustine to hold while she empties tomato purée, condensed milk and California prunes into plastic containers. Augustine sits in the crook of my arms. He stares up into my face with his big dark eyes. I stare down into his with my mother's brown eyes. He smells milky and his bare arms and legs, butter-soft, exude a fresh-bread warmth. My kind aunt tries to take Augustine from me but my arms refuse to open and surrender the baby. *Please, Bettany!* My aunt's appeal loosens my hold on Augustine. I grab the tins and run from the kitchen. I work at the back of the house knowing if I cut myself on the tin no one will care enough to make me have a tetanus injection. I will contract lockjaw, fever and paralysis from my poisoned flesh and blood and save them all a lot of grief. Then I can join my father and that will bring my mother home to me.

I drive my car in a race of one. I imagine myself in a time trial for pole position in the Brazilian Grand Prix. The other children watch me and return to races among themselves. I try to look engrossed in my driving around the yard away from them. I wait for the invitation to join them in vain. When they grow tired of me playing near them they chase me away. And when the strings break on their cars or the wheels come apart or the axles separate from the steering columns they find me and take away my car and as I plead with them they pull my car apart for spare parts for their own cars.

I run to my aunt but she feeds her baby and her husband chases me from the room. He says I should not say one word to him, just get out of his sight.

I descend the stairs from the kitchen so quickly I leave layers of my body behind me. I close my eyes because when I look down at my body I see all the layers of it segmented into the various angles of a body descending stairs. I try to ignore the cold breeze crawling up my legs. I linger in the living room to allow the stripped parts of me to catch up and rejoin my body. As I wait for my body to become whole again I open a dictionary and read its pages at random:

syncretism\'sin-kre-,ti-zem, 'sin-*n* [NL *syncretismus*, fr. Gk *synkrētismos* federation of Cretan cities, fr. *syn-* + *Krēt-*, *Krēs* Cretan] (1618) 1: combines different forms of belief or practice; 2: fuses two or more orig. different inflectional forms − **syncretist**\−tist*n* or *adj* − **syncretistic**\,sin-kre-'tis-tik, ,sin-\\ *adj*

abiogenesis\,a-,bi-o-'je-ne-ses\ *n* [NL, fr. 2 a- + bio- + L *genesis*] (1870): the spontaneous creation of living organisms from lifeless matter — **abiogenist**\,ā-(,)bi-'ä-je-nist*n*.

GEORGETOWN CALLING

I exit Boundary across fields, walking away from the house and its knotted mass of things about my mother and father towards the simplicity of two people each storing facts about themselves and each other for me to find out about. I duck under barbed-wire fences or climb over paling ones, the two varieties of territory markers my grandfather cooked up to demarcate land for grazing, crops or human habitation. The trails are hoof-trodden, tractor-driven and always meandering. I wait out of sight of the road but with a clear view of traffic leaving Boundary for the capital. That is how I see the bus from Mable with its Georgetown banner at the top and in smaller letters the towns it plans to stop at along the way.

Imagine my surprise when I board the bus and there is the same mustachioed driver who dropped me off on my first foray to the capital. I immediately show him my legal tender procured from an uncle's pocket I emptied before a wash and inform him that I intend to return home that very evening. He says he will never take money from an Abrahams. I insist but he ignores me and we spend a few moments throwing my money back and forth between us until eventually I give up and thank him. I even ask him if he will be driving the last bus to Mable as before and he says yes. I tell a small lie when I quickly add that I like the way he drives. He invites me to sit near him in his seat reserved for family and friends but I excuse myself by saying that I need to catch a little sleep before we pull into Georgetown. Really I hope to be out of his sight fast to avoid his questions. I head to the seat at the back of the bus and slip in beside a woman already resting her head against the window.

I find the orphanage like a second home. I ask the first boy

132

whose eyes make four with mine if he knows where I can find Fly. The boy tells me that whatever Fly is doing for me he can do bigger and better. I tell him if his big mouth is anything to go by that may well be true but that Fly gives me everything a girl could ask for. He tries to add another rejoinder and I interrupt him by saying he should tell Fly it is the Abrahams girl. Saying my name plunges the little burning coal of his prowess into deep water for he immediately shuts up, apologises for his freshness, begs me not to mention it to anyone, apologises once more, genuflects and may be about to get to his knees and beg my forgiveness when I tell him to forget it but do get Fly for me right away.

He returns with an open-mouthed Fly who runs up to me and hugs me then thinks better of his enthusiasm and steps back. I wave the other boy away and he trots off. Before Fly can fire his questions at me I tell him if he has not been to market for the day then I would be honoured to accompany him and in exchange would he mind showing me the nearest of the two post offices he mentioned to me on my first visit to his fascinating city. Fly bows. I ask him to keep my presence confidential, by which I mean he should not broadcast it to his Super. Again he bows and dashes off to pick up two sacks and an envelope of cash from the front office and we depart.

The usual wing mirrors of cars and trucks almost knock off my arm or head. I smell traffic and sewer in equal measure and occasionally the aftershave of a sweet boy on the prowl for a woman to chat up, or the perfume of a dolled-up couple of women who attract whistles every few steps they take. No one whistles at me because I am chaperoned by Fly. Not that I would welcome such a thing. I am no one's puppy.

We both try to secure better-looking provisions from the stall holders but mostly get told to move ourselves and what do we think this is, charity or something, so settle for what we get, the usual spread of bruised fruit and vegetables. Fly takes me down a main street pass the United States embassy where all the palm trees are painted white to a height of about three feet up their trunks and not a single piece of litter blows in the street. He informs me that the Americans think the street is US property along with the embassy. Fly adds, *They think the whole country American property.* We laugh but we like what we see of the neat and clean surroundings and the heavily armed and clean-uniformed soldiers at the gate.

The post office is not as well kept. It is a large wood building in need of a lick of American decorum. I ask about overseas mail destined for East Coast Demerara. The clerk informs me that mail for that region is sorted at another office. I want to know if it is possible to have one's mail held in the capital if it is destined for an address in that region. He is not sure but he can find out for us if we wait a moment. I nod after a quick glance at Fly who shrugs his shoulders.

As we wait we share an overripe banana and I ask him what he has been up to in the interim. He says meeting me made him set certain goals, which he cannot discuss with me until he fulfils his plans since to talk about them before they are realised would jinx them. I understand. I tell him I too have a scheme up my sleeve but to tell him about it now would surely jeopardise its chances of success. He understands.

The clerk returns and informs me that companies pay for this service but it is not available to the general public, the latter must go to their district sub-post office for the same service at a small cost. This is not what I want to hear from the clerk. I thank him and ask him if there are any exceptions to this rule. He looks at me and looks over his shoulder and says I cannot quote him but certain ministers and top-notch civil servants use the mail-holding service for their own private purposes. Again I thank him and we depart.

I buy a crushed ice and syrup cone for Fly and myself but not before I almost have to twist his arm to get him to accept my offer. What is the big deal, Fly? I don't want one, I'm not thirsty, I'm fine, thanks, everything but sure, that's nice of you. Is it because I am a girl and you cannot accept a treat from a girl? Maybe, could be, perhaps, well, yes, you are a girl and I should be treating you but I cannot. Fly you are my friend. Can I not buy my friend a cone? Well, yes.

We drop off the provisions at the orphanage and he walks me to the bus station. I find the Mable bus and my driver with the walrus look and I hug Fly and tell him I hope to see him before too long. I promise to write to him and want to kick myself for saying it when I remember almost as I say it that Fly cannot read and write. But he says he would love to get a letter from me if it is short and I do not use any big words. He might even reply to my letter but he cannot talk about that right now.

He waits for the bus to pull out of the station and we wave to each other until we lose sight of one another.

BETTANY

The priest arrives for his weekly visit. He asks after my grandmother with a glance up at her window. My eldest aunt shows him to the master bedroom. From my aunt's reports to her sisters I know that the priest prays for my grandmother's speedy recovery and attendance at church soon, that he chants a canticle with her for the return of my grandfather, and blesses the spirit of my dead father. My grandmother always howls. My eldest aunt whimpers outside the bedroom.

She takes a break to slap me several times for slamming a door and disturbing my grandmother and the priest, then she resumes her station in front of the master bedroom. The beating from her makes me stick to her.

When the priest emerges from the master bedroom, almost an hour later, my grandmother is quiet and probably asleep with exhaustion. My aunt pounces on him as he sidles out of the shuttered room and tucks the door soundlessly into its jamb. She tells him she wants to discuss a matter of life and death. She dives into the next bedroom, her own, and he follows her into it and she steps around him and closes the door.

I am there beside her invisible as a message written in lemon juice that only shows when passed over a flame, a flame that does not burn.

AUNT THE SLAP

Father, the child wicked. I saw her with a mirror looking at herself. The girl wicked. Her body in the hands of the devil. Her body his instrument. His fingers pluck her nerve-strings. She his child. She dance for him. Not him, her. The devil her mother. The child speak with her mother fiery tongue. She open she mouth and scorpions jump out. Father, she stares into you. She sees right through you. She look like she ready to turn us all into stone with one blast from her red eyes.

No child behaves that way. Walks with her head in the air. Swings her arms like a soldier. Takes too long to answer to her name. Like she don't know is she we calling. When she hear she name she must think something but she say nothing. If she decide to answer her tone questions the adults for daring to shout her name.

That's the child we contend with, Father. What should we do? Will you look at her for us? Tell me what we should do about her. We beat her to rid her of the devil. We beat her to distraction but she continues to look straight through us. My arms tired of beating the devil out of that child. One of us might kill her while trying to kill it. I don't want to end up trying to kill the devil with the child in the way. She knows what she is, Father. She want to be that way. She enjoy acting on the devil's behalf. Father, I know the church. I know your power can drive the devil from this child. Tell me what to do Father. We want the child back. Tell me what to do.

We must drive the devil from her and convince her it is for her own good. To restore the child and rid her young body of the wicked she-devil riding her flesh and bones. I see the child sometimes. Asleep with her child's face. And I wanted to cut out her tongue. Father, do something to help us restore her to herself. Help us to drive the devil from her body. Father, she bound to die from one of these beatings unless you help us. The devil cannot win in this house again. She take our brother from us. She drive our father into the bush and our mother to her bed. Now she here in this brazen way, in the body of that child. None of us wants the blood of a child on our hands but we all agree that the devil cannot win this time. Not again, not in this house.

Knock the little devil off her cloven feet. Put out the fire in those wicked eyes. Lash her, slap her, not her, but her mother in her. Beat the devil in her. For our dead brother. And our father lost in the interior. For our mother locked in her bedroom and our house sour with grief.

It won't be a single blow from one of our hands that kills her. Each of us will hit her until the devil flees her lifeless body. And when we surrender to the authorities we will say, yes, we killed the child, but not before we turned to the Church for help and the Church turned us away.

PRIEST

Ethel holds on to me and I do all I can to stop myself from tipping forward. I keep my left arm by my side. My right hand clutches the Bible to my chest. The book sits between her and me. I expect her to take a step back from me at any moment and apologise for clutching on to me but she stands her ground and talks about the child. *Push her away*, I order my body, begging the Lord for strength in my dealings with this woman. She steps closer and my left arm grabs her to keep me from toppling backwards with her tipping forwards into me. But my left arm is not enough. The right that clasps the Bible frees itself from between the crush of our bodies and hooks around her shoulders. I would have rocked back and fallen over otherwise. I steady her and myself with both of my arms around her and the Bible still gripped by me. It works. We stay upright and she calms down.

If my neck were a microphone Ethel's lips reported right on to it. My white collar moistens with her spittle. She looks up into my face, her eyes wide and full of water, her face soaked. I keep my face averted from hers. She speaks even quieter than before, her upturned face still searching mine. I keep my face averted from hers then she looks away. I think she grows too tired of searching for an approving look from me. But she glances down to my waist and she holds me tighter.

I struggle with her for a moment and push her from me. She slumps to the ground and looks up at me, her voice louder than before. She looks up and grabs me around my legs. I stoop a little and pull her to her knees. Then I straighten to my full height and clutch my Bible in both hands and pray for both of us.

I pray for flesh too weak for words, for blood brought so

easily to the boil, for bones no sooner bent that break. I thank God for the inviolable spirit and lament that it shelters in a house of sand for bones, this wavering flesh and blood for temptation.

BETTANY

I feel someone behind me on the landing but before I turn my head a hand grabs my shoulder and when I look around at the source both the priest and my aunt appear to share the one grip with me in it. The priest speaks from one of two mouths linked to the arm. 'Don't be afraid, child. You have nothing to fear. Only the devil is afraid of God's messenger.' I try to run and his arm pins my shoulder. My aunt grabs me around the waist. The priest opens the door to the kitchen and they drag me into it and slam the door. My aunt tightens her grip around my waist and the priest bolts the kitchen door. I scream. Another aunt in the kitchen, The Spit, dries her hand on her apron and bounds over to me and holds my arms. The priest directs them to put me on the table. I scream louder and kick. My aunt moves her arms down my waist and pins my legs. The priest thrusts his face into mine. 'Listen, child. I need to check your body for a sign. Answer me. Do you touch yourself down below?' He signals towards my crotch with a swing of his head. 'No,' I shout. 'No, Father.' My eldest aunt shouts at me. 'No, Father,' I repeat. 'Has anyone, child or adult, touched you there.' 'No, Father.' He looks at my aunts and asks them if they believe me. Both shake their heads negatively. The priest moves towards my legs and asks my aunt in the apron to pull up my dress. I scream again and kick and elbow them. They pin my arms and legs more tightly. My aunt flicks up my dress and pulls down my panty to my ankles.

Look what being my mother brings down on my head, one part of me says to the rest of me. Damnation at the hands of the priest. No part of you for you to call your own. All of you public property now. Next he will look into your heart, my argumentative self informs my compliant and shocked other half, and for that they will cut you open. The priest will dip his hands inside you and pluck out your mother's devil heart.

The priest asks my eldest aunt who holds my legs to pull my feet apart. To do this she eases the panty off my left foot and then she spreads my legs apart. The priest peers at my crotch and they look too to see what he stares at. The three faces of concentration calm my struggle a little. I wonder what they see on my body. He touches my right ankle, the one with my underwear around it and my aunt nods and pulls my legs as wide as she can without losing her grip on them. They continue to stare at my crotch. My aunts glance at the priest almost as if they hope to read his face for some clue of what he seeks on my body and to be ready for his next command. I stop screaming and sob now and beg them to stop. I am afraid that I am damaged in some mysterious way. I picture washing myself earlier that day and how I fail to feel anything on my body out of the ordinary. But because I do not think I am looking for anything unusual I cannot recall the specific moment of washing and how my crotch felt at the time. I only know that had my left hand come across something unusual I would have registered it. This lack of specific recall on my part leaves me feeling that I must have missed some crucial over-night change in my body. The priest keeps his eyes pinned on my crotch and begins to pray for my soul to be rescued from the devil. He makes the sign of the cross as if hanging a notice over a condemned part of me. I panic. Whatever mark he sees on me causes him to pray for my salvation. I stooped over a mirror once to see myself up close and I parted the skin of my vagina as I crouched over that mirror to see what I looked like inside. This picture replaces the one of me washing from a bucket with a cake of soap and a small calabash bowl to dip the water and my hands lathering all my body before pouring and scrubbing away the soap suds. How I always finish by gripping the bucket with both hands and lifting it over my head then pouring the last of the water over me. The priest stares. Does he see the brown skin, slightly darker around the lips and the pink inside peeping out because of my parted legs? He raises his voice in his prayer. What does he see? Something must have happened to my body. Is a prayer sufficient to cure me? When will I start to hurt, first in my crotch and then all over? There is no perpetrator to pin this damage on to. I cannot cure by attaching myself to someone? I am doomed. My bladder opens. Both aunts shriek and lash me but the priest stops them by holding up his arms and praying more loudly. My aunts ease their grip on me and I sit up and pull on my panty and smooth down my dress. But I remain sitting in my urine since they still hold me. We all wait for the priest to finish his prayer. He says, 'Amen', makes the sign of the cross and nods and they release me.

I jump off the table and bolt out the door only to bump into a crowd of children on the landing. I push through them out the door to the stairs and skip them two at a time with one hand on the railing and the other wiping my eyes and smoothing my dress. The breeze coming up under the stairs feels cold on my wet dress. I run blindly into the arms of my kind aunt. She grips me and I fight her grip but she hugs me tightly and I stop fighting her and fall to the ground and howl. I struggle for each breath. She keeps asking me what happened. I cannot speak. My chest tightens, my throat dries completely, I cannot swallow.

She grips my head and tips a glass towards my face. I hold the glass with two hands to steady it and drink the cool cultivated in barrels stored beside the house from whose roof rain funnels down into them. The cool begins on my palate, spreads to my throat, spirals down my neck and radiates outward in my stomach, back up to my chest and down into my pelvis and last of all walking on tiptoe and fingertips along the little bones of hands and feet. My aunt spots my wet dress and still she lifts me and carries me into the ground floor of the house. Her lift of me, the way she bears me, the heat of her body pressed to my cold body, amounts to an embrace. She peels off my clothes and I hide my body from her. She hands me a clean dress and panty. I hurry into them. She glares at the children who creep near to look and listen and they retreat out of sight. She touches my arm and I shrink from her touch. She hugs me and I push her away with all my strength. I lean against the wall and cover my face and turn away from her.

She walks to the door and shouts at the children to stay away from me or face a beating from her. I hear her shouting at her sisters asking them if they want to drive me mad. She trails off in the middle of her talk when she sees the priest who emerges from the kitchen. From her deference to him it is clear she realises that he must be behind whatever it is that upsets me. He announces to everyone present. 'There is nothing on the child's body to show any allegiance with the devil. By all accounts her ways are uncommon for a child but she is not especially evil. I prayed over her young body to keep her from the clutch of the devil. Discipline her as you would any child. Treat her like one of the children. She may simply be missing her mother and grieving for her father.'

BETTANY

The midday sun, obliterated by patched cloud, throws my day into night. I slip out of the house and walk in the westerly direction of the sea. I know my east from my west. I know that the sea is straight across the road from the house because that is where the best breeze is said to originate by the adults when they sit on the veranda at night. And since the sun sinks into the horizon over that road I put the fact picked up at school that the sun always sets in the west with the other fact that the sea is over that road, and I come up with a westerly direction.

I say this because I know that I live in a country that revolves, shuffles its poles and shifts shapes. Night is one aspect of this shuffling process. Day another. When rain loosens its cloud-grip on the sky, sunlight appears to climb wavering chains of water hanging from sky to earth so that sun and rain weave into a glittering fabric strung between earth and sky. I stare hard and soon enough the rain starts to climb back up the rays of sun, using sunlight like a rope ladder. Staring hard makes the whole downward swoop of water switch from a conventional downpour to reveal its opposite and secret upward climb on ropes put down by the sun.

I walk out the front gate, cross the bridge over the trench without looking down at the planks of wood that shuffle underfoot and through the gaps in them into the gully choked with weeds, ignoring my need to count how many logs laid side by side complete the bridge. I should pause at the roadside and look left and right. But I want to get to the sea and as far from the house as my legs will take me. I walk into the road, just step into it. I hear the long blare of a car horn. A man leans out of his car, gestures wildly and shouts an incomprehensible warning or curse at me. The breeze that speeding cars drag behind them like a parachute, rushes by me as if to include me in its forward propulsion. Another horn blares and brakes lock tyres, which screech on bitumen. I stump my big toe on a stone and hear the bone crack as I fall. The chassis of a truck passes over me. Tyres smoke on the road. More men's voices shout. A woman screams. I stand and walk quickly on the hot tarmac and only look over my shoulder when I feel the grass verge on my bare soles. I run down the bank and balance along a fallen tree trunk over the gully that ends in a field. I trot through the tall razor grass following a narrow winding path cut by cattle.

My big toe throbs. The nail hangs off it. I stop, stoop, grip the nail between my thumb and index finger of my right hand and tear it off. I learned this technique from my mother who, I know (or think I know because I heard someone report it) ripped a plaster from my skin with a similar flick of the wrist. Or I imagine my mother removed a plaster from me with a similar flourish. I feel nothing. That big toe too belongs to my mother's foot, not mine.

I jog with that left big toe raised above the other toes. I lose my footing on the mud path studded with hoof prints and twist my left ankle. I switch from running to limping as fast as I can. When I look back a green sea of tall, wind-swept razor grass greets me. I smile thinking it will not be long before I see blue water meeting a blue sky, one shifting, the other still, the two stitched together by the thread of the horizon.

I pass houses on stilts two storeys high. Women and children bend ankle-deep in flooded rice fields and straighten from planting rice shoots to massage the small of their backs and nod and wave at me. Men at the edge of a river pull ropes from the water, gather nets and shake fish that spring and glitter around the fishermen's feet. They arrange the nets neatly before they fling them out again and the nets form perfect circles in the air and plop into the water.

A man flashes a smile at me brought on by the glittering array at his feet. Another dashes off a quick salute from his left temple as he hauls on a cigarette. I ignore the ones who merely stare in my direction. I duck through a series of rusty barbed wire strung between rotting posts and my dress snags and tears. My mud-stockinged feet disguise my bloody big toe and create the impression of boots on my feet.

I pause to watch an iguana try several times to crawl into a hollow log but the entrance is too narrow. I say out loud, Someone changed the locks, buddy, or you have the wrong house. I look closer and see the problem, poor iguana. I shoo the iguana to the other end of the log where the opening is bigger and it scampers into the log. I wander on, glancing back at the log house with the iguana in it and almost step on a frog in my path. I pick it up and place it in the grass away from other feet liable to be as careless as my own. I put the notion out of my head that the frog might be poisonous.

Then I happen upon something I have never seen before, but there it is, a dead starling hanging by one wing in a tree and looking like the last fruit of its kind rather than a creature gifted with flight. I grab a long stick and jiggle the branch to free that fruit, or try to. Instead of falling at my feet, the second the tip of its wing is free from the limb that hooks it, the bird falls and rises in an arc, an upward curve and it starts twittering, circles once overhead and darts across the field. I follow it with my fingers interlaced over my eyes until the starling is a speck, then less than a speck.

I hear bees, their engine revs, before I see the tree alight with them and the crown of their nest where the flame of them seems hottest because most of them concentrate there. I tiptoe around that tree. Razor grass with one cricket clings at my ankles. That cricket jumps ahead of me and keeps exactly three feet from me by hopping away from me as I step towards it. I get accustomed to that cricket keeping me company when it veers off the path in a way that expects me to follow or dares me to try. Two courting butterflies shadow me in that zigzag dance of flight where the wings almost collide or tie themselves up but never do. I wonder how the powder stays on their wings with all that bustling movement. Both are yellow with black stripes (or black with yellow blots) and their bodies appear no bigger than ripe rice grains but with the largest coins for wings. They leave me at a turn in the path as they gyrate over the sugarcane. I want to follow them. I wish for a pair of wings, with or without powder. And someone to fly with me, preferably my mother or father, ideally both. But not this neither of them near me, this solo way of being me, this always wishing for what I cannot have, and the best thing for me, the best I can do is wish, watch and wait.

Walking like this, moving instead of standing still in one place, makes the wait a little easier. If only I could keep moving until one or other of my parents – the dead one and the living one that may as well be dead – catches up with me. If I can be sure that one day I will turn a corner and see one or both of them standing there waiting for me rather than me waiting for one or both of them, my wish and watch and wait would be more bearable.

I approach the next turn in the path with only my thoughts to keep me company, all the wildlife suddenly absent from my immediate surroundings, and I wish that when I turn the bend I will see one or both my parents. I clear my head of the iguana, the frog, the cone of bees, the bird-fruit, plaiting and un-plaiting butterflies, everything except the path curving out of sight in a sharp left turn and the prospect of those two waiting for me around the bend of sugarcane.

I almost stop in my tracks at the sight of a man in muddy, ragged three-quarter trousers walking towards me. He carries a tree limb laden with green plantains over one shoulder and a broad cutlass swings in his other hand. He appears to sweat oil, his forehead, bare arms, bare chest and bare stomach shine. His features are plain except for a massive head of dreadlocks, which appear to be alive as he walks and the knots and plaits and twisted ropes undulate. His nude upper body flexes its latticework of muscles. There is no room in the path to pass him. If he touches me and I bruise I will never reach the sea, I will be compelled to follow him. I dive into the tall sugarcane, duck and run around the cane stalks. I misstep and press on my big toe and it throbs. I stop and see the cane rustling behind me and run again. Wind sweeps the tall canes in patterns that resemble a current, tides, and the green acres turn into a kind of sea. I fight my way through it. The cane leaves act like seaweed and claw at my body. I look back and the whole crop behind me sways. I slow and limp. A raw smell of blood fills my lungs. I look at my toe covered in mud. The sky and sea of cane glosses my skin green. I lunge forward and break into a clearing of sunlight and a sea sound. A long jagged waterline bars my way. Brown waves crumble in soft mud and foam with the effort of climbing the beach. And the sea, soup-thick, mud-stew, sprawls out into a brown plain and stretches upwards, rises until it joins the sky.

Though brown the sea reminds me of blood, perhaps because both smell raw. The horizon presents itself to my sixteen-year-old eyes as one long timeless line in the distance. I expect the sky to bow down to the horizon, a blue sky mottled with cloud-clumps, rather than the brown sea to curve up to the sky. The sea's giant basin of water, muddy from a particularly dirty load of laundry, appears tilted to rid it of its contents, except the dirty water miraculously refuses to spill and drown the land.

This is not the sea my mother crossed to make a name for herself. I pass crab holes in the mud and crabs poised by the holes. The crabs reverse into their holes when I approach. Waves claw at my ankles. I hold up my torn dress and wash my legs, arms, face and neck. I wet my dry lips loving the salt. Another sea lies somewhere beyond this sea. My mother finds it and crosses it. She must find her way back to me over the blue sea miniaturised for me in a marble and then across this big brown world of a sea.

I turn my back to the sea and walk away from its noise, towards the edge of the cane fields then along them until I reach a path skirting the cane fields with coconut groves along one side. I head up it slowly, limping more and suddenly desperately thirsty. The sea dries on me. Sea-mud cakes my skin. Mud head. I laugh knowing there is nothing to do until I find fresh water. The dry mud on my face stiffens my skin and encourages a clownish grin just to feel the slight pull of my face muscles against the dry mud mask. The coconut trees, taller than the church steeple, sway ever so slightly. The coconuts stored in the heavens seem intended for the gods rather than ordinary earthbound mortals. The sky's orange from the late afternoon sun burnishes the fruit orange-ripe.

I look ahead of me and there is the man again marching towards me with his bouncing dreads, his cutlass that picks up the light and the biggest bunch of plantains ever carried by a man.

I think I should bolt from him but I decide to stand my ground. I will test flatness tonight or die. Since none of my relatives who have tried have been able to kill me up to now, why should that change with this stranger?

I decide to challenge him. I do not even wait for him to walk to me I pick up my pace and close the yards between us. I narrow my eyes and soften my lips in case they tremble or part and say something stupid. When beaten by my relations I dodge and end up bruised far worse than they intend to inflict on me until I learn to stand still for their blows. I survive fists and feet. My arms carry two buckets of water a quarter of a mile from the standpipe to the house. My feet kick a boy bigger than me between the legs and immobilise him. These eyes pick up what no sixteen-year-old head should carry around. This body belongs to a grown woman who killed a powerful man and sent her young self into the viper's nest to live among his blood relatives. Six feet from me the man locks eyes with mine. I match his glare and I do not blink or look away. He points to his plantains and hits his chest. I do not want your plantains. They are as green as I am young. I can almost smell the starch in them. I have nothing to offer you. There is nothing you can take from me. Let me pass.

Plantain Man

I never lost my tongue. I born tongue-tied, a cleft palate. I sign to get something across otherwise I let my actions speak for me. I farm. I know nothing else. If you drop a stick on this land the stick put down roots right away and sprout something. If you watch close enough the rice and cane fields you can see them growing. That's how green this country is, green and ripe.

I grow on the land and cannot live anywhere but on a farm. I cultivate a little plot of my own but mostly I work the fields for the Abrahams. Today I cut select hands of plantains and now at day's end I carry a hand of my own back to my family for a meal of boiled plantains, yams, cassavas in an onion and pepper purée when I see the famous girl-child. She run from me and I forget her, even laugh at her fright. Then she appear in front of me for a second time. I slow my urgent pace home that aims to beat the rapid fall of the dark just to show her I am not a threat. This time she does not run from me. We face each other on the grass path with a trench on both sides. I guess she walks to my left so I move over to the right to show her I mean to pass her on my way home, not block her path.

I make out her face in the failing light, girl-soft I think and not the shock of a mud-mask, woman-child, hard-faced like her mother. To my surprise she veers to her left and back into my path. I move to the left to avoid her but walk at the same eased pace. Again she crosses into my path. I stop and stare at her unsure what to do next. She draw closer and spreads her arms showing me her empty palms. Does she mean to tell me she is unarmed? I drop my cutlass but keep a firm grip on my plaintains. I tell myself not to worry I wrestled alligators before now. But I do worry that she takes after her mother though she remains a slight-looking child. I worry too about what she plans to do and what she might say to people at the house who I depend on for my livelihood. Six feet from me I see she limps and she is covered in mud. I look at her and what I mean to say comes out of my mouth sounding like a coyote baying at the moon. I point to the plantains and then touch my chest. I repeat the gesture. Surely she must have heard of my single claim to fame in the region? My picture made the paper the next day under the headline: local Samson. I almost cut off my dreads after that story to stop people talking to me about it and then joking about some demolition job they have for me at a good rate. Her uncle was lucky I came along when I did, another few seconds and he would have been crushed to death by that loaded cart settling on his chest in the ditch. I think the soft mud he fell into delayed what would have been inevitable if I had been a few seconds late.

I jump out of her way to the right side of me and run from her. Who want trouble from the Abrahams family? She say nothing to me. She must live in Venezuela not to recognise me. Everyone knows the plantain man. I turn and watch her as I hurry from her. Then I miss my cutlass and promise to return for it the next day. If it is not where I left it I will go to the house and ask the child for my cutlass and maybe even lodge a complaint with the uncle who owes me one of his nine lives.

BETTANY

The horizon ingests the sun slice by slice. An orange flame paints the sky, the fields, the trees, the plantain-carrying man, his cutlass and me. We are all inside the fire of this giant orange tent. It does not burn. The orange gives the fire a solid look, a ladder I fancy climbing to the roof of the sky. I hold my hand in front of my face and the fire fills the spaces between my spread fingers and webs my hand. I guess I need to make a right turn soon to reach the main road then turn left and follow it to the house. The dark sprouts in the cane fields and among the coconut groves. A coconut falls like a star and splashes into the mud. I rush to it and chop it open with the cutlass dropped by the plantain man. The water tastes warm and sweet and insufficient. I shake the coconut in disbelief when it runs out. I chop the shell into two pieces, cut a spoon from the hard outer husk and scrape out hardened jelly that coats the inside of the shell. I look up into a dark blue sky and a horizon that has eaten its fill of the sun. I hear frogs and cicadas and the first of two bats fly near me in ziggurats. Facing a man with a cutlass in daylight is one thing, but in the dark it is quite another to face jumbies, buckoos and Old Higues. I recall the stories of children whose spirits are sucked out of their bodies by these night creatures. They lead children to ponds on full-mooned nights and the children drown in them even though the same children swim lithe as minnows in those very ponds during the day. These ancient evil spirits cherish the blood of the young who stray too far from home and get caught in the open in the dark. They might take control of my mind and make me turn the cutlass against myself. I sink it into the ground and leave it there for its owner.

The path narrows and the fields close in on both sides. This is just the dark, I tell myself. I try to breathe deep but my chest tightens and each breath is shallow. I wipe away the tears that come of their own volition. I remind myself of the kind of child people tell me I am from the very day I appear at the big house. Not a child at all, merely the body of a child with the mind of my mother stuffed inside. Who should such a child and woman fear? *No one and nothing.* No one and nothing. I repeat aloud. And an engine grows in the dark. I jump off the path and crouch with the toads in the roadside gully. I peer through the tall grass verge and recognise the headlights and engine of a tractor pulling a trailer loaded with something. The moment it draws alongside I sprint from my hiding place and race behind it and grip the trailer and jump on to it. But I slip and fall and a sharp sting rips along my forearm. I recover my footing and ignore the sting and leap again and land in the trailer full of coconuts already stripped of their husks. The tractor turns right and I lie back. Headlights of traffic on the main road brush the countryside with their momentary brightness. I cross my fingers and hope the tractor will turn left at the main road. The driver slows to a crawl and heads right but just as I am about to jump off he makes a wide turn to the left. I almost cheer. My arm aches. It is wet. I wipe my entire forearm on my dress and it stings even more and becomes wet again. I taste a little of it on the tip of my tongue and realise my slip while climbing into the trailer cost me dearly. The injury takes my mind off my throbbing big toe.

I look for the house on the right side of the road, its two storeys easy to spot in an area where houses are small and low to the ground or else high up on stilts if nearer to the sea. And while most people paint their houses in bright primary colours my grandparents stick white paint all over theirs. In the dark the brightest spot is the rum shop owned by my absent grandfather and managed by an uncle. It boasts the only generator in the village. When the engine breaks down, about once a fortnight, the patrons strike matches and light oil lamps on every table. Houses are wired for electricity (I hear the headmaster's fond reminder in his lessons on macroeconomics) but the minority ruling party, made into a majority by its coalition with two smaller parties against the larger opposition, cannot afford the foreign exchange necessary to maintain a national grid. So the wires and bulbs in most homes are entirely decorative. The same pertains to the dry plumbing in every house. After the rum shop I pass the barbershop owned by another uncle. Its red-and-white striped sign spun in the past when there was electricity. Now it is streaked with rust. In the next plot of land I smell but do not see the bakery set back from the road behind rows of tamarind and sapodilla trees, yet the easiest of places to find because of the strong smell of its ovens. When I see the field that adjoins the whitewashed house, a large pond where sheep, goats, cows and the donkey graze, I tense for the jump off the trailer. By now everyone will be on the balcony listening to an aunt or uncle relay some odd event from the day. I doubt if anyone notices my absence.

I grab a couple of coconuts just in case the kitchen is out of bounds to children as happens frequently at night after an adult finishes tidying and putting things away. I curse the fact that I left the cutlass stuck in the ground where I feasted on the coconut. As I hop off the tractor the driver sounds his horn, slows to a crawl and waves at the people on the upstairs balcony. I stand by the roadside not knowing where to put myself. Everyone rushes to open the two halves of the gate and the driver steers the tractor and trailer into the yard. When questioned about me the driver takes off his wide-brimmed hat and I see it is the oldest of my uncles. I nearly faint. He says the plantain man warned him about my presence alone in the fields and he kept an eye out for me and he saw me jump on to the back of the trailer at the coconut groves. There is loud laughter when someone says that the stammer met the mute and what a conversation that must have been, and I recall hearing about the strongest man on the east coast of the Demerara river who was reputedly born without a tongue but I failed to associate him with the plantain man. Someone says I look like a ghost, another that I smell like a crab. I want to dash under the house but they surround me. A child pulls the tear on my dress and takes half the cloth off my body. I run into a wall of flesh and bounce back and drop both coconuts. A chorus begins.

Bettany! Bettany! Better you than me.

Bettany! Bettany! Better you than me.

A foot steps on my toe. I hop and howl. A hand pushes me in my back and I stumble forward. More hands push me in my chest and I fall back again. I throw out my arms for balance and others' arms knock mine away. I fall to the ground and land on my cut right arm and scream at the top of my voice. They chant louder.

Bettany! Bettany! Better you than me.

Bettany! Bettany! Better you than me.

I scream at the top of my lungs. I call my mother to help me and cover my head and pull my knees up to my chest. Someone dashes a bucket of water over me. The sudden cold combined with stings all over my body from scratches I surmise happened in my run through the cane field jolts me to my feet. I feel brittle and about to shatter. I renew my screaming. Hands and feet push me every time I stumble forwards or backwards or sideways. *Help me, Mother!* To save myself I decide I should run at the nearest body and sink my nails and teeth into it and never release my grip and bite. Just as I lunge forward a voice bellows from above our heads, *Leave the child alone.* The voice, deep and gravelly, loud but a little shaky, belongs to a woman. Everyone freezes. I never heard the voice before. It comes from a room whose locked door all the children fear. We all look up at the source of that voice. My grandmother's bedroom window is open and her tall dark shape fills the dark window frame. Her white hair shines in the dark but her features are obscure. Granny repeats, *Leave the child alone.* She sounds quieter than the first time but with the same command in her tone. The upstairs window closes. Seconds elapse with everyone standing and staring up at the window. I shout, *Leave me alone!* And they all jump out of their skins. The ring around me breaks into several pieces and they disperse in whispers. I stand there and look up at the window and gradually become aware of my cold, stinging, wet body and my aching big toe and right forearm.

Bettany! I recognise my kind aunt's voice from the upstairs balcony. I limp across the front yard and up the stairs to meet her. She holds a lamp close to me with her mouth open and eyes wide. She leads me past my grandmother's room where I speed up and overtake my aunt, and into the adults' bathroom. There is no running water, just two full enamel buckets and a calabash bowl to dip into them. I wash and cry at the touch of water on my skin. I struggle not to wet my right forearm and left big toe. My aunt waits at the bathroom door with a lamp and leans into the room to pour the last of the water in the buckets over my head. I thank her as the water falls over my head and face and into my open mouth. Then she leads me into her bedroom. She whispers so that she does not disturb her youngest, Augustine, now four and still a small bundle of a child asleep on the double bed. She needs to wash my toe and arm properly before she bandages them otherwise they will not heal. I know there is no one to follow to accelerate the healing process since both injuries are my own doing. I bite the fingers of my left hand not to make a sound as she daubs at my big toe and forearm with iodine and then bandages them.

You brave like your father.

How-how-how you-you mean?

He never show it when him hurt.

He-he got-got-got hurt?

No. He never show it.

Then-then how you-you know he-he hide-hide his hurt?

Everybody must get hurt sometime but only a few people can hide it. You that way too, just like your father.

Me-me-me?

Yes, you.

He-he per-perfect like-like everyone say-say-says?

Yes! He loved everybody and everybody loved him.

What-what else a-a-a-about me remind-mind-mind you of-of-of he?

The way you stand when you angry with one foot forward and your chest puffed out.

He–he stand like–like that?

Yes. He was a very proud man.

M–m–my mother really ki–ki–kill him?

Yes, and no. Is a scorpion you say there in front your eyes any less real because I can't see it? Let me get you some bread and a drink from the kitchen and then you can catch a little sleep.

I consume the sliced bread using a couple of fingers to pin the thin slice of cheese on top. My smallest finger and the one next to it that are not needed for the job of keeping the cheese in place hover above the bread and resemble a scorpion's tail. The bread is the scorpion's head and body. I gulp the lukewarm tea, thank her with a half-smile and leave the house by the back stairs where a cold breeze runs up my legs like ants and makes my skin goose up. I wonder if my aunt really did see the scorpion? If not, why did she pretend to kill it and make me fetch her husband to help her?

I enter the ground floor and pass through the living room with the photographs of my father in his wide-rimmed felt hats and in some of them holding a polished cane. His forward foot and puffed chest belong to both of us. I stand there and hold that pose for a moment pushing my bad big toe forward and raising my bandaged arm for an important catch. I am more than just a replica of my mother. A man who strikes a few brilliant poses takes up residence in me. And like his father who left town to find diamonds in the bush and redeem his name and so far failed to return to his other debts inherited by his children, my father abdicated from his kingdom of my mother and me. I abandon my father's pose. Was he just like Granddad? Yes, he gambled with my mother's love and lost. No, he paid the ultimate price for his debt. I fasten the cupboard door wide open by sticking a piece of folded cardboard under it and curl up inside. I hate sleeping on my back. I find it difficult to get comfortable on either my left or right side, so I keep turning every few minutes, but with extreme care to avoid bumping my bandaged right arm and bandaged left big toe against my father's knick-knacks.

DREAM THREE

I am my father in my mother's eucalyptus-anointed body. Every time I move it hurts so I strike a pose and hold it and it is like holding my breath. I puff out my chest, put my best foot forward and I fly without wings or an engine and keep my position before the camera of my dreaming eye. As my father in my mother's body. I bump into aluminium clouds. I bounce off the curved and elastic blue wall of the sky. The limbs of trees, fingers that project from the body of the earth, grab at me. A mountain range nudges me and I know it is my mother's shoulders. I comb the landscape of my mother with my father's eyes for their only child but see nothing that looks even remotely like me. Herds of cattle, goats, horses, donkeys and mules, a capital's streets of jammed traffic, a stadium of spectators, a military parade, all scatter as I swoop low but nothing suggests my shape or size or look. I land on my mother's ground with my father's feet in the middle of a procession and the earth does not open and swallow me. The people who dance and parade along the street pour buckets of water dyed red and blue and yellow on my head. Flour and talcum powder flies from bags into my face and sticks to my body. Hand drums and flutes, whistles and clapping bounce me along with the crowd, which chants in Hindi and English. *Abka nam kyaa hai?* And I reply in a language I hear from one of my uncles' wives and in corners of the playground at school and from films. *Meera nam Bethany-Bettany hai.* Parts of the crowd break away from the main street and run into yards to soak onlookers with coloured water and flour and powder. Speakers mounted in boxes big as chests of drawers blare out tunes from Hindi films shown on Friday nights to the village in the one-room school that during the day after the morning school assembly, doubles as multiple classrooms separated by fold-away screens. Calypsos mix with the film music. I hear both, one in each ear. People float in dances to both sounds. Children fill cups with this dyed water, grab handfuls of flour and powder and chase each other. Not a soul remains untarnished. It stuns me that strangers take as much liberty with one another as they take with me. I pick out a faceless old couple standing on a balcony and know right away that they are my grandparents, reunited and doused in flour and dyed water and smelling sweet caked in talcum powder. I smell in a dream for the first time. I search in my disguise as my father trapped inside my mother for me, for their child, but no child, no me appears. I thrash my arms and legs to free myself of the web of my father trapped inside my mother and no me to be seen anywhere in their world.

This is the city where my parents are two names and two people rather than their conjoined lives at the house in Boundary. I wait for Fly to return to the orphanage. He bounds up to me and I step back from him and he knows not to touch me. He looks at my bandaged arm and toe. Don't ask, I say as I shake my head. He nods and presses his lips together. I ask him why he did not answer my letter.

What letter?

The one I wrote to you months ago.

He swears he did not receive a letter from anyone or from me. In fact he has never received a piece of mail in his life. I check the orphanage's address with him and it is exactly as I put it on the envelope.

We skip the market and head straight for the second post office. I ask to speak with the district manager and after a long wait I am greeted by a man with a half-moon hair loss and matching spectacles, which he peers over. My question causes him to take a couple of steps back and to push his spectacles up the bridge of his nose in order to look through them. What recourse would be available to me, a member of the Abrahams household, if my mail was being pilfered by the postman and by pilfered I mean both letters intended for me and letters written by me and faithfully deposited in said postman's hand?

You have proof of your name?

I am living proof of my name.

I continue my bus trips to investigate the fate of my letters to my mother and her letters to me. The district manager helps me because of my name. All he needed to hear was my name.

I catch my usual bus, meet Fly as usual, and the district manager opens a ledger for me to examine the arrivals and departures of government-sealed documents and letters through the postal system. When we cannot bear to look at another name and date and signature we head to a café for a dhal-pouree washed down with mauby. But lunch lasts so long it runs into late afternoon laced with mugs of bush tea and drops (as the pieces are called) of coconut cake.

We swap more news and views. Fly thinks something must be cooking in the government, some war brewing, because more soldiers appear daily on the streets and many of his older friends have been conscripted into the army. Do I know anything about it? Of course I do not. He says he might volunteer.

I want to be with my friends.

You might die if a war breaks out.

War with whom? The border dispute with Venezuela is a national fixture, nothing new. I do not know. This surprises him. He thinks my name determines the course of the country. I tell him I come from a house in the countryside and that I know nothing about the running of the nation. He tells me I need to look into the true meaning of my name.

We reach the bus station before I can question him further. *My bus*, as I like to call the last bus to Mable with the driver-friend of mine, awaits me.

My mustachioed friend knows to leave me alone. Drive the thing, man, I tell him once and once only after a quizzical look from him. I wave back to Fly until he doubles as a speck of dust on the window. I sit at the very back of the bus and cry my no-sound cry, water streaming from the outer corners of my eyes, all the way to Boundary. When I reach the house my eyes dry up and all the things that happen there fail to raise another drop from me.

BETTANY

I hop up breezeless back steps. In the kitchen I find room on the end of a bench and the teenager next to me does not push me off it. An aunt, The Spit, places a steaming cup before me and an even steamier plate of porridge. She blows on the spoon and polishes it on her dress before handing it to me. I thank her with a stunned nod and a questioning smile. Her face twitches but she fails to muster a reaction that qualifies as a smile. Hers seem more of a scramble together of muscles around the mouth just short of the seventeen needed to qualify for the noun. The children finish before me and wait by the door for me to empty my plate, I help clear the table and they pitch in with me so that the task takes no time at all. They rush out of the kitchen and down the steps and glance back to make certain I am there and I look behind me to see who this person could be that they are looking out for. The boy from the small house in the nearby field joins us and he is greeted warmly by a couple of cousins who explain to him the new orders to leave me alone issued by Granny's mouth. He looks me up and down as if he might detect some outward change on my body in keeping with my new status. I poke out my tongue at him.

We meet another group of children also on their way to school and fall into a name-calling match based on the most pronounced features of each child exaggerated into a curse. A long neck makes one child a stork, a giraffe, a stick insect, nothing but neck and a stump for a body, more long bones in that neck than in the legs, arms and back of that child. Another child's protruding front teeth turns him into a blind mole whose sole facial feature are those two big teeth put to good use by its tunnelling everywhere. And maybe that child should consider hiring himself out as an earth-digger clearing more jungle, uprooting whole trees and boulders big as sheds to make way for more pot-holed government roads. And perhaps more ivory skulks in those two teeth than two giant male elephant tusks. And it will help that child if he brushes those two lethal weapons once in a while, but then he faces the added problem of finding a brush suited to the task, one big enough and with bristles tough enough.

My bandaged arm and toe mean I am a mummy someone forgot to unwrap fully. I smell like I am two thousand years old. Except that I have nothing to show for it, no riches, no name to speak of, and no parents.

My cousins look at me and I try to hide the wince that claws at my face. Mad Rick announces that the last comment went beyond a joke and amounts to a declaration of war. My cousins and I back away from the other children who also group together and step back widening the gap between us. Mad Rick, not content with speaking up on my behalf reaches for a stone and everyone scatters and picks up stones and the pelting between the two sides begin with volleys crisscrossing the gap. We duck, jump and skip and even catch stones and send them back with a swing of the arm that lifts us off the ground. I hear a rumble and feel it too, rising from the road up through my feet. Everyone else hears and feels it. We stop in the middle of our stone fight. We look down the road towards the capital. The noise grows louder and the slight tremor in the ground worsens. Then the source of the distur-bance rears its enormous head around the corner and enters Boundary. We scatter from the roadside into the trenches and across the dry trenches into adjoining fields. The trucks group together into an unending body. Each truck is a segment of the giant body, with wheels for legs and rifles for limbs. Soldiers wave with their rifles and I wave back with the others afraid that the trucks might stop or the soldiers open fire. I count twenty-three trucks full of soldiers. The last truck disappears from view dragging the noise away with it.

We run back to the road and glance in the direction of the

interior where the convoy disappeared. We wonder why so many soldiers head there. Then we resume our pelting of each other. Though right-handed I throw with my left arm and my left leg lightly touching the ground. This requires a degree of effort and concentration to stop me from toppling over. Instead of trying to take aim I simply throw my stone high into the air and practise different angles from the overarm bowling of a cricket ball, to a sideways baseball throw, to an underarm swing reserved for rolling marbles into a hole twenty feet away. I do not watch for stones coming at me. I do not even follow the trajectory of the ones I launch. I puzzle over the sight of the army and feel overjoyed to find myself included in the middle of things. I look up and a stone from the other side or even one of my stones that I send straight up claps me between the eyes. I fall to a sitting position and the throwing stops and the other children discard their stones and run to join my cousins gathered around me.

Mad Rick, who leads us in the battle, gently but firmly lifts my hand off my face to inspect my war wound. I grimace and look up at him through the white morning sun.

I-I-I-I-it ba-ba-ba-ba-ba-bad?

No. Just a bump.

Someone's shout of, 'Three eyes!' falls on deaf ears.

Mad Rick wipes my face with his shirt and places his arms under my armpits and lifts me to my feet. Did I see who threw the stone? No I did not. I should add that I believe I am the casualty of a stone thrown by me since I do not feel my usual immediate compulsion to follow someone who inflicts a wound on me. I brush the front of my dress and tense as other hands brush my back. I expect them to change from open hands brushing me to fists pounding on my back bringing to an end their kindness and consideration of me, but the brushing continues. I nod and raise my arms for them to stop and they peer into my face. I smile and we walk on to school, the two groups now one group, with me applying pressure to the bruise on my forehead, my third eye, with the back of my hand to limit the swelling.

HEADMASTER

I call out names and line the two groups of stone throwers in front of the rest of the school assembled for morning prayers. What a pity to find Bethany among them. Never mind. I arrange them in a straight line beginning with the oldest to the right and progressing by junior years to the left. My attempt at order and symmetry is spoiled by the fact that some children who are younger are taller than a few of the older children. She places third from the right end of the line and about seventeenth from the left junior corner.

I talk about the shameful conduct in public of so many of the children from the Abrahams household who behave as if they own the entire world. Such reprehensible behaviour gives the school and everyone associated with it a bad name.

I ignore Bethany as she crosses her eyes. She has never shown such disregard for my authority. I can only conclude that her many years under the roof of that house have brought her completely under the sway of its skewed moral compass. I tell them all they defy categorisation, in my rage I call them, variously – pelters, barbarians, cave dwellers, tree-swinging primates, heapers of shame on the school and bringers of disrepute to the school's uniform. For homework I order them to make up a list of important things all under one heading. A list poem. They must learn to handle words not stones. They should think of the sounds words make and how the words relate to each other in sound and in looks. There should be two sides to the list. The second part should be the mirror opposite of the first in that everything in it must show something quite different about the first list, something none of the words in the first list could have predicted. This homework would teach them to love their enemies, their opposites, that thing furthest from them, which they rather stone than try and name, pelt at rather than try to acquaint themselves with it. Everything on the two-sided list must be drawn from experience. I add that the list, both parts of it, could be anything so long as it maintains decorum. I tell them my idea of what keeps on the right side of decorum does not include anything that would contravene the strictures of the Church and State. I order one boy to look up 'contravene' and 'strictures' and read out the definitions, and I ask another boy to put what he just heard into his own words as he understands it for all the school to hear him. I ask Bethany to agree with the formulation of the second boy but in her own words. She stutters and takes a long time to spit out the truth but the accuracy of her recapitulation is second to none. She says she understands decorum to mean no swear words, no rude body parts, no lewd acts and neither religion nor politics should feature in the list of important things. They must keep the homework personal and avoid crude and bad language.

I nod approvingly, then I proceed to cane them.

He instructs us to hold out our hands. He walks down the line and delivers six lashes, three to each hand of the first two older boys. Mad Rick and the boy from across the field who may as well be one of us, both hop and skip and suck on the air and pin their palms under their armpits, a dance of hot coals under their feet, a look of ice caught between their teeth. Sixteen younger boys and girls who wait in line screech and cry at the prospect that it will soon be their turn.

He draws level with me, stoops a little so that his face juts into mine and he says how disappointed he is to see me in the middle of the fracas. He tells me to lower my bandaged right arm and keep my left hand still for all six lashes. I cannot help focusing on the protuberance on my forehead. I name it, 'Fracas'. His cane, he points out, will surely cure my crossed eyes. 'After this you will think twice about misbehaving in public.'

I obey hesitantly by keeping my elbow slightly bent and my fingers half-curled. *Tongue of my mother, uncurl and help me.* He reaches out and jerks my arm straight and opens my hand, palm facing up. As he flexes his cane a thought flicks across my mind and before I can stop it from reaching my tongue I hear the thought launched into the open. I ask the headmaster if a child is always beaten with the nearest thing an adult can lay his hands on. I surprise myself by speaking without a stutter. From his reaction he seems surprised too. He jerks back his head and forgets about straightening his cane. Instead, he fits and unfits his pointed chin in the V between his right hand's thumb and index finger. His black eyes roam in their sockets. He takes so long to speak I begin to worry that he might punish me for some wrong committed in the manner of my asking the question or in the question itself.

HEADMASTER

Is a child always beaten with the nearest thing an adult can lay hands on? As far as I know, no. For example, the habit of asking a child to pick the switch he or she will be punished with is unique to our region. But it makes so much sense I cannot imagine other people in other cultures at times earlier than ours or simultaneous with our own time, not coming up with the same idea. In Mable where I live it is widespread and in the capital too. It teaches a child responsibility for his or her actions and discipline and proportion.

BETTANY

I want him to stop right here but he carries on. My arm aches so I let it drop a little and bend the elbows. He does not seem to notice and continues talking.

HEADMASTER

Discipline is about conduct, control, cultivation, development, restraint, self-mastery, and order. The word's Latin roots, *disciplina*, means learning, not punishment as it is taken these days, from *discipulus*, which means pupil. So you see discipline of the pupil is instruction of the pupil. Its military use, invented around the fourteenth century, trained soldiers by a system of punishments as inducements into the art of warfare. Children need to learn order through discipline. Without it there would be chaos. Children would grow up without direction.

BETTANY

He releases his grip on his chin but his hand keeps the shape of a fork. He points at me and with his thumb cocked and index finger spread away from his thumb he appears to aim a handgun at me. I keep my attention on his other hand with the cane resting along the side of his leg as if embroidered into his trousers.

HEADMASTER

A lash instils obedience. A severe correction of a child saves
the adult in that child from certain disaster later in life. If
authority is absent in that child's life the adult who emerges
from it is doomed. Corporal punishment applied to the child
literally saves the embryonic adult from capital punishment. A
beating is medicine for an illness that must be cured otherwise
it becomes epidemic and consumes a child, sends that child
into an adult life of criminality and despair. The way the state
handles a bad adult damages that adult far more than any
beating a child receives. A beating prescribes while the state's
punitive action serves merely as a corrective. Beating a child
intervenes in a child's life and changes the course of events in
that life. Not so the actions of the state. It corrects one wrong
action with a similar wrong-doing. And what is the reason for
your enquiry, Bethany? Do you require an additional beating
other than the one you have coming to you to save you from
some later misdemeanour?

BETTANY

I straighten my arm and lift it level with my shoulders. *No, sir,
I just wondered if children were always beaten the way I am beaten at
my house, that's all.* (Again no stutter.)

HEADMASTER

That's all, child! That's everything. The Bible says, spare not
the rod and spoil the child.

BETTANY

Where in the Bible, sir? (I only think this. I bite my tongue.)

HEADMASTER

The ancient Romans who knew a thing or two about combat
and adversity believed a regular beating formed the soldier in

the child. The Greeks showed less enthusiasm for it but the subjection of the wild spirit through the systematic beating of the body that housed it did not escape the pen of Homer.

BETTANY

I think, test this speech impediment to see if it really is gone for good. I ask him about the use of leather and wood and various parts of the body by adults against children.

HEADMASTER

What about it, child?

BETTANY

Is it all right to discipline a child with wood and buckles and fists?

HEADMASTER

Leather is just a convenience that has become a rule. A belt around the waist is near at hand. Ropes bear the same relationship to lynching in America before World War Two: it is more a question of proximity than any scientific efficiency. It goes back to the tradition of hanging in the Wild West of displaying the wrongdoer high in the air for all to see. The wrongdoer's feet are off the ground, he hangs there out of touch with the ground, lifted away from the right to walk the earth, he is held up for all to take note of the course of justice.

But I digress. By wood, I take it you mean the cane and switch cut from a branch.

BETTANY

I nod because I feel ashamed to admit that a piece of wood can be anything from the wooden spoon used to stir a pot to the broom handle to a broken paling lying on the ground. Once it was almost a bicycle chain. But that is not wood. And once, the contents of a chamber pot, most of it missed me, thankfully. Not leather. For years I thought it might be the sharpened blade rather than the side of a cutlass because the uncle who swings it at me might forget or not bother to twist the blade from its cutting edge to its side. But I digress.

I drop my aching arm to my side and wait for him to say something about it but he ignores my arm and continues his talk.

HEADMASTER

Each time the switch or belt connects with skin there is a transfer of knowledge. The swung belt or switch connects the adult to the child. It shows care by other means. You have to realise that the adult must steady the child and beat at the same time and even as the lashes sting the child and the arms of the adult tire there is this passing of knowledge between the two souls involved. This lightning and thunder exchange, between enlightened and knowing adult and unenlightened and unknowing child, saves the child from adult doom and despair. The only drawback may be that the child cannot see the exchange happens for his own good. But is this not a symptom of ignorance and blindness? The blindness of being uninitiated, the kind of blindness where the scales over the eyes need to be removed to result in true sight. The child needs repeated beatings if he is to become fully cognisant of what the swinging arm clutching that switch, cane or belt is trying to convey to that child. A regular beating to avert some future greater disaster demonstrates love. If the adult gives up on the child and stops trying to straighten him out you can be sure the adult does not care one iota about the future of that child.

Evil preys on young bodies. Wickedness controls the child unless a parent or guardian beats it out of the host body. Evil and wickedness would love to set up house there. A lash shocks the system and sends the two packing off to some other shelter. For the adult to abandon beating the child would be to surrender the innocent to certain doom in the tentacles of evil and wickedness. Am I lying to you? The responsibility of adulthood cannot be pleasant under these circumstances: drivers of evil from children's bodies by administering countless beatings; haranguers of children about the dos and don'ts of this world. It is a wonder that adults do not die sooner of kidney stones and liver cancer and brain tumours with all the worry we grown-ups have to carry day and night. It may well be the responsibility of species: some ancient impulse that demands the obedience of adults, their servitude to its strictures or else the extinction of species by the indulgence of children.

BETTANY

Please let the cane stay by his side, I nod as he speaks. And please stay off politics or it will bring calamity on his head.

HEADMASTER

Souls are at stake. Beatings save souls. The responsibility runs for a lifetime. The soul hides and stays hidden in a child's body and may be extinguished by evil unless the adult coaxes that soul to the surface by driving evil from stifling the soul in that little space for flesh and soul to cohabit. The soul may never show its face in a child unless the child is prepared bodily for such an excursion of spirit. I see a school full of children every day and I rarely see a single soul. I trust that the soul lives there, in hiding, but I can only be sure of this by the accompaniment of that body with a set timetable of beatings. If I know those children are subjected to corporal punishment I know that evil and wrongdoing will not triumph over that body. The soul may remain hidden or show itself fleetingly in a smile or little childhood gesture such as ducking the chin and covering the mouth when smiling up at me but I know it is blossoming right there because the sweetest child needs a beating every now and again.

When an adult beats such a sweet child, as I am about to

punish you, he must wonder about the squirming, screeching child in his grip and doubt the efficacy of what he is doing. Of this you can be sure. There is doubt. But luckily for the species their conviction outshines their doubt. What is the alternative? Abandon the child to the devil or the more destructive authority of the state? Those two routes signal the end of hope for the child. A child should thank the grown-up who bothers to beat him. That child is blessed. He is in the process of being rescued from adult despair, saved from the clutches of the devil or the correction system of the state. Try saying thank you the next time you are whipped and see how much better you will feel knowing what has just transpired is good for your soul.

BETTANY

Sir, at what point does the beating itself become an act of evil?

HEADMASTER

Child, when the devil himself wields the rod. When the devil sees God's children as temples to be vandalised, altars to be desecrated. That's not a beating, but an act of evil. Had such a thing happened to you, my dear girl let me assure you, you would not be here to talk about it. You would be in heaven. A child cannot survive a beating from an adult when the devil himself swings that adult's arm. You are maimed by it, child, maimed then killed. From the sight of you, healthy skin, bones, shining brow, hair, white teeth and clean fingernails – I trust your bandaged arm and toe were accidents from your childhood fun and games – there is no way on God's earth your experience can be anything other than a good beating.

Consider yourself lucky. You live with a family, not in an orphanage. You could easily be among strangers who think you owe them something and who extract that debt from your body in a string of punishments unleashed on you. In the primitive societies if you committed a crime you were handed over to the people affected by your crime. They mutilated you as a matter of course. Whatever happened to you at the house does not approach the scale of any of this. Were this the case, were you the recipient of undue punishment, physical or psychological, I could take one look at you and see it that instant. And even if it was well hidden, like a soul buried in flesh and bones, I would smell it on you and even if there were no smell or sign on your body, your eyes would betray it. Your eyes would tell your story. Just as I sometimes see your soul flash from your eyes, Bethany. Or do you prefer Bettany in your present display of family unity? A country cannot run by favours linked to a name. A government works by merit not privilege linked to said name. Your name will be your ruin, young lady, and it will poison the land.

Bettany

Before I can say anything in reply he orders me to hold my arm straight out. He says he wants my fingers to be so straight and my palm so even that the joints show through and whiten my hand. The cane whistles and burns my hand. I hop and squeeze it under my right armpit. I offer my hand tentatively and he reaches out and straightens my fingers and raises my hand higher. Again the cane whistles and the smack of it against my palm and the deep burn convinces me my hand has split open. I yelp and run from him. He orders me back into line. I shake my head and beg him to spare me. I promise never to do another wrong thing for the rest of my life. He shouts above my pleas that unless I rejoin the line immediately he will double the number of lashes and start my punishment from scratch. I look up without crossing my eyes and see from the shadow on my forehead that the swelling has definitely worsened. The bump earns a second name. *Fracas Augmentus.* I shuffle into the gap in the line and offer my hand but when he raises the cane and twitches in his preparation to bring it crashing down I pull my hand away. He tells me, Young lady you just earned yourself another twelve lashes.

A little girl at the end of the line urinates and a teacher drags her out of the hall through a side door. A second teacher sends a boy to fetch a mop. Murmurs ripple up and down the hall. The headteacher turns and glares at the assembly. That look of his – his small head holds two big black eyes with an inordinate amount of white around them – seals all lips in the assembly. When he stares the exposed whites increase and his eyeballs protrude a little. He trains his eyes on me creating the impression of a jumby or buckoo or Old Higue that is about to ensnare me with its hypnotic stare and pounce on me. I feel faint. I offer a limp right hand. I no longer need to look up. I stare straight in front of me and see the shadow adding to itself on my forehead. The headteacher straightens my fingers, raises my palm a little, and brings the cane down with a whistle and a small explosion that rings in the bones of my hand and ripples up my arm. My head spins and the room darkens as though the swelling on my forehead has grown so big no matter where I look I see its shadow. A new last name suggests itself, *Fracas Augmentus Olympus.*

MAD RICK

We all walk out when she faint. I fetch she in me arms. When she come round she look frighten. I promise she we going make the headmaster pay for the things he say about the Abrahams. She don't like what I say or she don't like me holding she because she struggle in my hands and I stop and release she on she wobbly legs. Everybody group round she and me by the roadside. I almost ask she what we should do next. She say like she reading my mind that she heading for home and we all cheer. She add that she feel a little like vomiting. I offer she a piggyback. She turn me down but ask us all to run ahead and explain to we parents and every other grown-up present that the walk out of school not she idea. I smile and run ahead chased by the other children. Our bare feet in the roadside dirt raise red dust. The headmaster has not heard the last of this.

BETTANY

By mid-morning the tarmac on the main road becomes unbearable to bare feet. Cars and trucks move so fast and unpredictably along the two-lane road that children know better than to try and walk along the edge of its tarmac. One time a car's wing mirror clips a neighbour's child on the arm and shatters the rotator cuff of the elbow and leaves the child with a permanent crooked elbow and an arm that cannot straighten and only looks natural when the child places it on his hips. A convoy of trucks ferrying road-building materials and imported food supplies from the capital to the country's jungle interior runs over a child and leaves nothing of the child for the open casket of a funeral. If two trucks passing each other collide, as they sometimes do because one or other of the drivers hogs too much of the road, the crash is heard throughout the village and metal and glass scatters from one end of the main street to the next. Groups of men sometimes fail to move the buckled vehicles, supposing they turn over in the road and no tractors are readily available, then donkeys and oxen roped to the wreckage drag it to the roadside. Passengers riding on top of the open truck fly into front yards and surrounding fields and ponds and surface days later when children playing hide and seek or some other chasing game stumble upon them.

The cream bandage on my arm is only cream in my memory. Every part of it is covered with dirt. My big toe is similarly plastered with dust. But the rest of me I cannot explain: a bump on my forehead so prominent it acts in effect like a visor against the sun. I veer off the roadside down the gully and into a field in pursuit of the boy who lives in the small house in the field. I look at my reddened palm, clearly it is not in urgent need of my attention. The headteacher must wait.

What has the boy done to me to merit my spying on him? Maybe he threw that stone at me after all. Why else should I follow him? He is nothing to me. His age and build approximate to mine, and his hair, long, wavy, brownish and thick, looks like mine might look if my head were fussed over by a parent as his must surely be. I wonder if I am losing my ability to flatten and cure my hurt. It never occurs to me that my ability to transform might be a temporary condition. Perhaps it relates to my mother's imminent return for me. I picture myself how I think my cousins see me when they look at me now, if not in the likeness of my mother and father. The girl who looms into my head remains the one who looks like her mother and on the odd occasion poses like her father. Her bony and sinewy body moves with the caution of a bird. Her chiselled features, though plain, hold the promise of beauty. If stubbornness is a virtue then she carries an abundance of it. I cancel all that and decide my injury from the stone takes precedence over the cane and the boy must have pelted me with a stone otherwise I would not be compelled to see him.

The boy crosses a field whose perennial grass lies in various directions as if the wind practises its cardinal points there. He never looks back. Why should he? He is on his way home and the last thing he expects is someone following him, least of all me. He reaches a one-roomed hut, on a small plot carved out of my grandfather's land as so many small dwellings are allowed to exist for an agreed payment in labour at harvest time or some other form of barter. The boy stands on tiptoe and unhooks a piece of wire fixed into the door and threaded into an eyelet embedded in the doorframe. He steps over a door mound and disappears behind it. I stoop as I approach the single wooden window to the left of the front door. I tiptoe and peep into the hut and the moment I begin to distinguish objects in the room I find myself on the other side of the window frame. The people in me, my mother mostly and a sliver of my father, fall away from me leaving me weightless and transparent, my whole body refines to a thought.

The boy – I cannot bring myself to name him though I know I must sooner or later make this small concession to him – walks over to his mother and hugs her and cries. She appears shocked both by his appearance in the middle of the morning and by his tears. She eases his body away from hers just so she can look into his face, places an arm on his shoulder, pins her thin black hair with her other arm and asks him what brings him home like this. When he says my name she lets her hair fall and reaches for a chair and lowers herself heavily on to it. He relays the events of the school morning. She wants to know every last detail of what transpired. Did the children say anything to him about his past? He shakes his head.

She complains partly to him and in part just thinking aloud, how, of late, everything has to do with me. Bettany this! Bettany that! Bettany the lot! She sighs. She looks at the roof of the one-roomed shack and summons the help of the Almighty for what she must say next, takes a deep breath then she pins her attention to her son's face. She tells him there is something he needs to know about me before he hears it from someone else since it concerns him too. She glances around the cabin at a slight loss it seems for words or if not words *per se* then the right words.

I feel naked under the sweep of her eyes. I move out of her field of sight by the window and position myself behind her, beside the table where she sits. She warns him that what she is about to reveal is not bad so he should not feel bad, it is good, no matter how he feels about it after he hears it. She loves him more than anyone, more than she loves herself. Does he know that? Yes, he nods. His wellbeing over the years has always been uppermost in her mind. Does he know that? Again he nods. If he has the slightest doubt about her love and dedi-cation he should speak up. *No, Mummy*, he cries, more out of alarm than anything, and not loudly, but to himself. He says he pelted a stone at me because I poked my tongue at him, but that I do not know that the stone that hit me came from his hand. Water springs out of my eyes. She wipes his for him. She kisses his face repeatedly using her lips to stem the flow. After this preamble she breathes deep and launches into her explanation. She says his father, though unknown to him, was a great man. Had his father lived instead of dying young in a strange country far away who knows what the result of that greatness would have been. But the man failed to listen to what she had to say, for men rarely listened to women. The man who everyone at the big house talked about in the most respectful of ways because all the wonderful things everyone says about the man is absolutely the case, this man loved her once, really loved her. And he, Brian their love-child, resulted from that union. But the man was trapped in a loveless marriage and the girl, me, came out of the lust of it, out of that loveless union of the flesh. If he takes one thing from this talk it should be that he is the product of passion born of love. The same cannot be said about me. Then she hugs him and he rests his head on her shoulders but keeps his bony arms by his side.

My eyes fill with more water and the room blurs. The back of my hand and the hem of my dress mop my face. I back out of the hut, fall through the walls, turn into my usual self and run into the field. My bandaged big toe hits a clump of grass. I stumble and sprawl on to the grass and vomit. This is Bethany Bettany being sick. My father knew. My mother knows. They would not be sick. None of this would be new to their ears. But Bethany Bettany only just now knows. I lie there on the swirl of grass, on my back and look up at the sky with a few clouds in a sea of blue and sunshine. My mother and father drift away from me with the clouds and I cannot join them. My back is sewn into the ground. All I can do is watch their departure on separate clouds, one for the dead and another for the living but both heading in the same direction. I break the spell when I turn my gaze to my arm and my toe. His mother licks his face clean. Where is mine? Riding on a cloud and moving even farther from me, far away as my dead father.

I tear myself off my back and limp away from the hut towards the end of the field, away from the big house and the main road and deeper into the bushes that begin to hug the path kept open by cows, sheep, goats, tractors, and donkeys and carts. I pretend I have hoofs and so the ruts in the mud path are not strange to my heel. I even attempt to walk on my heels. When I step on to the lip of a hoof print it crumbles and my feet sink into the impression left by that hoof. The feeling of hitting one level of ground and sinking to another pleases me.

The boy, Brian, lucky to have both parents equal in his body. Me, I am a woman, said to be my mother, then a girl named Bethany Bettany, and last of all, my father's daughter. Not much of him can be found in me because the woman, my mother, present in me does not allow any space of hers to be inhabited by the man who strayed from her. Palls of black smoke much lower than cloud drift in the distance. More of the smoke rises above the trees. It seems like a fire, more smoke than a fire, advances along a narrow path and heads right for me. I run to meet it forgetting about my aches until I reach the railway line. I look and the smoke above the trees grows darker and closer but I hear nothing above the wind in the trees and the occasional parakeet. I kneel and place a part of my skirt on the hot metal rail then my ear and sure enough a very quiet hum occupies that line. A nail placed on this track flattens into a knife when the wheels of the train run over it. The rails themselves are spring-loaded and bolted on to sleepers which allows them to lower a little under the weight of the train. I see myself squashed by the train not like a nail into a knife but into my special way of being flat. The noise of the wheels rolling over points where two rails almost join is of stampeding cattle on slate. I close my eyes and the approaching wheels grow in volume as if the rails swelled with them. A whistle sounds far away, but closer than my mother and my father ever were to me in all my days. The sound bursts from the track and fills the air around me. I want to look and see the front of the train for myself, the metal grille on the front that bats cattle and cars out of its path, the plume of black smoke rising above the trees then thinning out as cloud. The singing in the track runs up and down my spine, a sensation that makes me grit my teeth. I share my father with a boy and now the boy can keep him. My mother is overseas and lost and my wait for her return can end without further disappointment. The singing in the rail welds my ear to the line. There is nothing I can do now about the train. My body collects in my ear, in that singing sound and joins me to the rail making the whole of me just the one ear pressed to the line. The singing is the only sound in the world, deafening now with a thin and persistent whistle leaking out of it all. I see my transformed body doing what I have always done, walking everywhere, hitching rides, looking into everything, but unseen by people. It will be me unhampered by my body, an edition of me without my mother and not a trace of my father.

I open my eyes hoping to see for the last time as my mother; she who looks through me at the world. I expect the train to be the last thing in my sight, the train and a shrinking length of track with no difference between us. I mean the short space left between us made insignificant. The time allotted for that space measures so little, there would be many zeros after the decimal point. All that remains is for the train to be seen by my mother's eyes looking out of me and then for it to enter my head through their portals and fill my body. Then the real train will meet the flesh and blood of me. And between the two, between my seeing the train and it reaching me, there is this minuscule passing of time, as my mother would phrase it. Time for a particularly sensitive instrument to measure, and for a brilliant mathematical mind to write up as a series of zeros and decimal points before a number. A mere theoretical possibility (so my mother would surmise) that is impossible to prove in an experiment using matter. And then no more me. No more Bettany for my father, no more Bethany for my mother and no more Bethany Bettany this and Bethany Bettany that. Bring an end to the residency in me of my mother alongside the sliver of my father. Only flatness, the purity of it and its undetectable nature, its floating past all instruments of human measurement of things in the world (this said the way she would say it), its defying of all theory of probability. Bethany Bettany, less than mist, less than a strand of hair, less than a shudder induced in the backbone by someone wishing that body into a grave. Bethany Bettany less than a crow's porous feathers and bones resting on a roof before a life under that roof disappears, less even than what rises from the body as the soul when the body shuts down its machinery (my mother's phrasing). My heavenly body thriving next to my earthly flesh-and-blood self and no one the wiser.

My eyes meet the serious gaze of the uncle who collects foreign bicycles, The Lash, standing on the tracks in front of me with his arms on his hips and his head leaning to one side. He blocks my view of the train but I keep my ear pinned to the line. He looks small compared to the sound of the train. I close my eyes and hope that when I open them again he will not be standing there. But he scoops me up and jumps off the track. The engine rumbles past. He stands with me in his arms and we breathe smoke and watch the long line of carriages rattle past full of soldiers whose helmeted heads and rifles jut out of windows.

My uncle looks sharply at the sky in the direction of the school building. He says nothing and I withhold my explanation about the collective walk out of school. Instead I hold up my hand still red from the cane and touch my forehead forgetting the fact that my visit to the stone-throwing culprit Brian cured it and I point at the faraway hut and then I say how I just learned about my half-brother. My uncle's face relaxes and in the middle of my talk he props me on top of the cart-load of bundles of sorrel and sticks of sugarcane, pulled by the donkey he walks beside and guides along the rutted path. The back of the train disappears towards the interior and its trail of black smoke dissipates over the trees. My uncle interrupts me to say I am not to worry about a thing and he ruffles my hair and my tongue wraps itself up completely in my

mouth, just like the plantain man's tongue. A sob I cannot
control shakes my body and he stops and cuts a piece of cane
as long as the bandaged part of my arm and he peels the hard
outer rind with his teeth and hands me the soft, syrupy centre.
I stare at the piece of cane for a long time and sniffle. He urges
me to bite into it and he demonstrates with a piece by baring
his teeth and biting off a huge chunk with a loud crackle. I
copy him but with less relish. When cane juice runs down my
chin and arms I perk up a little and chase the drops with my
tongue and bite and chew some more. My stomach grumbles
for all that cane. I examine the piece of cane closely, surprised
by its sweetness and how much juice is locked inside it.

My uncle removes his sweaty wide-brimmed hat and drops
it on my head. He squints in his search for the damage to my
forehead. I shoot him a look that says, do not ask. He returns
his attention to guiding the donkey along the path, careful to
keep the cow track between the wheels of the cart, and when
it cannot be avoided, slowing the cart down to a crawl until
the wheels are safely through them. He spits each mouthful of
chewed cane into the bushes and I copy him, craning my neck
and throwing my body behind the effort. When he switches
his delivery of chewed cane husk to the other side of the path
I switch too. I think of his name for the first time in years and
think of his brothers' names too just to be certain I have the
right one, Uncle Joe, the oldest of the uncles, Bicycle Uncle
from now on with his special shed of bicycles under lock and
key. The sugarcane runs out and he asks if I want more and I
shake my head and lie back on the sorrel bushes and pull the
hat over my juice-stained face and breathe the sweat and oils
off my uncle's head. So this is the smell of a living man's scalp,
old and new rolled into one, a dark, portable place surrounded
by plenty of sunlight. This is how my father would smell. I
breathe deep. The cart rocks and sways with the occasional jolt
from pothole to pothole. My face heats up under the hat, even
though the swelling from my half-brother's stone is gone. I
begin to sweat and a faint sweeps over me. I surrender to it and
sink into a sleep.

Not a sleep in the ordinary sense of the term but more an enforced rest since no sleep ever finds me in a bed. I wake in my uncle's bed. My left foot hangs in a sling and my right arm dangles over my head in a pulley. I know immediatcly that I am naked under the white sheet. So much sweat pours off me the sheet clings to me yet I feel cold and I shiver and my teeth clatter. The dressing on my toe and arm are clean, the heat of my body radiates from those two places throughout the rest of me that feels cold. My kind aunt sits beside my bed licking the lead of a pencil and solving a long sum on a brown piece of paper with a large figure at the top of the page divided by seven. She adds numbers from seven columns and the total of that number is taken away from the large figure at the top of the page. She checks and double-checks her answer, erases and corrects individual numbers. The figures blur and my lids close and every effort put by me into raising those lids fail so I give up.

A cold breeze levers my eyelids open. The sheet no longer covers my naked body. Now my kind aunt squeezes a cloth and rubs my chest and then she rinses the cloth in a basin and strokes under my arms. Again she rinses the cloth and the water trickles into the basin and rings a little against the basin's enamel and she wipes my crotch. Wherever she touches with the cloth, a marvellous coolness blossoms on that place. She sponges me from head to foot. She soaks a clean cloth in Limocol and rests it on my forehead, covers me with a clean sheet and leaves the room with the basin of water. I turn my head to the shut window and the sun slices through the slatted wood and falls on the floor in neat strips no bigger than the window. The sun fades and another aunt, The Slap, leans over me, cradles my head and spoons a bitter liquid into my mouth by pushing the spoon so far to the back of my tongue that I must swallow or choke. I try to turn my head away but she holds it still. Then she makes me sip water from an enamel cup and she spoons soup into me. I say water and soup not because of the taste but because of differences in their consistency and temperature. I cannot taste anything but the strongest bitter of that medicine. I listen for the spoon against the enamel bowl but The Slap dips it with such care there is no contact between the spoon and the bowl. I look at the floor and the sun is not there, only the dark spread evenly. When she drops my head gently on to the pillow I close my eyes and forget my promise not to shut them since I find it too hard to open them again, and I sleep.

A bugle and a marching drum wake me. *Left! Right! Left! Right!* A rasping voice commands. An army of boots thunder past the window as if marching past just below the window and all I need to do is make my way to it from the bed to see the parade of soldiers. Sunlight pools in the room and warms me but hurts my eyes. I raise my head off the pillow and a boulder on my forehead forces me to lower it again. The marching drums fire rapid volleys and the feet, keeping time, cannonade. I open my mouth and call, *Aunt*, but my dry throat issues nothing. The parade moves away from the house. Marching feet and drums diminish, along with the voice controlling them. I listen to the house for the usual peregrinations of aunts and uncles, and only hear my laboured breathing. I know that if the house is empty, if everyone has abandoned it to watch the parade and follow the spectacle for a part of the way out of the village, there will still be one other person in the house locked in her room. I call or imagine I call, *Granny*, several times. The effort makes me pant. My eyes roll back in my heavy head. I order my arms to throw off the sheet and push me off the bed and my legs to swivel to the side and stand. But the unchanged pressure on my back tells me I am still lying in the bed. Suddenly I feel a presence next to my bed standing beside me and blocking the sunlight. This blocking of the sun leaves me feeling cooler. I try to open my eyes and convince myself that I manage to prise them open, but my eyes roll back in my head and they look inward into darkness. My jaw drops open, unfortunately the words stay trapped below my tongue. A cool, dry, soft hand rests on my brow. I give up trying to see, speak and breathe. I wait for what the hand does next. It moves from my forehead to the side of my face, this time touching me not with the palm as before but with the back of that hand, with knuckles and veins and a hard spiky ring brushing my face. I incline my head towards that hand and listen for other signs of her presence, perhaps her breathing, but only hear my breath, which is the house breathing.

Houses do not breathe. They lack what I can only call the necessary apparatus, although breathing happens in them because of the presence of people, mostly. Houses could be bustling with life but they can never *be* life.

Life or an organism's ability to reproduce itself, the life cycle, reproduction, if you will, deserves our special attention. Homo Sapiens produce live young. Only one textbook with pictures exists so you must all benefit from my artwork. The red arrows belong to the male the white circles to the female. These squiggles represent the key body-parts of the parties involved: arrow for male, aperture for female genitalia.

My chalk diagrams on the board resemble a battle plan for two opposing armies with arrows pointing along corridors and through doors to the target, the kill, but rest assured it is the life cycle, the perpetuation of the species.

For a house to breathe the perception of the person making the claim would have to be altered. Mind-altering substances are illegal and here are the reasons for their illegality. The individual loses his grip on things, where his body ends and the world around him begins becomes blurred.

The house, as a result of his drug-induced altered view of things, transforms into an extension of his body. When he breathes the house breathes too, or so he thinks because of his subjective mental state. The only natural occurrence of this condition is during a bout of yellow fever.

I experience for a while an eight-bedroom house breathing in unison with me. I dearly want to see the face of my grandmother. I blink for the darkness to clarify with her face but the same featureless dark remains. The hand retreats and the presence moves away from me. To my mind I shout, *No. Don't go!* Without any hint of a stutter, although I do not hear myself. Sunlight stripes my bed and warms me again. My eyes swivel in the dark as I listen for footsteps or loose floorboards or a door opening and closing and hear faint drums and the house breathing.

The sun slips behind clouds.

Is thinking the same as dreaming? If yes, why is it so? And if no, why is it not so?

Let me venture the following, consciousness is an act of will. Every other mental activity is subconscious. Therefore it follows that when I am thinking I am not dreaming and when I am dreaming, although it is a form of brain activity it is not thinking, just as I can daydream while awake, and in the middle of thinking, without confusing it with dreaming itself. Understand? From the youngest, aged five, to the eldest child, aged eighteen, all carry a dream life alongside your waking lives. The same rule applies to the country. There is the country we see all around us and then there is the country that we dream about and wish to make into a reality. Our country remains undreamt. We live the practical side of it, the side we find ourselves in and tolerate because we lack the dream, the dreamed alternative. The youth, all of you, must dream this country into being.

BETTANY

The house stirs from its night slumber: doors creak open and clack shut, floorboards croak as feet strike them, a voice calls a name in one key and the name answers in another. I stretch and feel my fingers and toes. I kick off the sheet and push myself upright on the bed. My head swirls and clears. I swing my legs off the bed and stand and wait for my head to stop swimming. My left foot is swollen and stiff but the right leg compensates for my weight without complaint. I spot a lime-green cotton dress draped over a chair next to the bed and I hold the shoulder straps and steady myself on my strong right leg and climb into it and reach behind me to feed the large cream buttons halfway down the back into their eyelets. My kind aunt puts her head round the door, exclaims happily when she sees me on my feet and dressed and bounds into the room and hugs me and welcomes me back to the land of the living, as she puts it. Then she becomes morose and informs me that all the men of the house were summoned into the army to join the border defence effort against the foreign military invasion.

All of them.

Yes, every last man. They gone, Bettany, gone. If one don't return, Mummy never coming out her room, never.

They must come back, Aunty, they must. Just like my mother.

I hope you right. But wait! What happened to your stammer?

I shrug and smile.

The house looks as if it shrank, concertinaed by the same giant hands that compressed my skull during my illness. Maybe the fever narrowed my retina. Everything I look at seems squashed into an ill-fitting space. I climb the stairs to the kitchen and there is no breeze to disturb me and each step that I make carries my whole body forward. Today is a good day.

Children seated at the long table greet me like a long-lost and just-returned favourite cousin. They pat me on the back, secure enough room for two people just for me on the bench and make sure I have first choice of the sliced loaf on the table: the crusted and crunchy end slice, please. I look round the table and there is my half-brother from the shack in the field looking back at me flashing a half-smile and raised eyebrow. My hands drop to the table and my last spell of flatness floods back. I sense my aunts paused at their stations around the kitchen and my cousins around the table, staring to see what I will do next. The boy's face is clean and I see a little of my father in him. My dead father who is a photograph and a pose and plenty of balcony talk and the first grave in the family plot behind the house is not dead and lost after all. My hands pick up where they left off buttering the bread with a view to dipping it in the tea to reduce the noise of crunching crust and bringing my head close to the cup to feed my face. I smile showing my pink gums.

Good morning, Brian.

Good morning, Bettany.

The kitchen bustles once more. Some children comment on the miracle of my repaired speech. I lift and drop my shoulders and continue to eat, barely able to fill my mouth fast enough to satisfy my empty belly.

The children tell me the news of the demise of the headmaster and what happened to the school. They interrupt each other and repeat key parts of their report several times. I want the repetition from them because on first hearing what they say I cannot believe my ears. Only after the second or third child says the same piece of news I am able to process it as a fact rather than just a shocking revelation. I really hope someone repeating something will say the opposite of what I hear and therefore take it away from the pressure it exerts on my body. But no, each child piles shock on shock, com-

193

pounded by numerous restatements and even actions of their arms. This is what I piece together from what they tell me.

While I am sick in bed and dreaming of everything except schoolwork my uncles march to the school in the middle of the school day and drag the headmaster from it. In the playground and in front of the school children my uncles ask the headmaster to retract everything he said about the Abrahams. The headmaster refuses. My uncles proceed to strip him naked and to beat him with the belts from their trousers. They chase him down the main road in his naked condition until the plantain man stands between the headmaster and them. An uncle owes the plantain man his life and all of the uncles know the plantain man is the strongest man in Boundary so they leave the headmaster alone. But they return to the school, empty all the children from it – most left to view the spectacle of their headmaster getting whipped anyway – and they set the building ablaze. They swear that just as their hands, meaning the wealth of their father, went into putting it up, so their hands will reduce the whole thing to ashes. Rather a pile of ashes than their building used as a shelter to pour scorn on the Abrahams name. The children hooray to a chorus of hip-hip-hip's at the fact that there will be no school until a new building replaces the destroyed one and with no money coming from the Abrahams household the prospect of a new school building is some way off. Another round of hip-hip-hip hooray follows. To save them all from going to jail the uncles strike a deal to join the army and go to the front line immediately.

I leave the table, decline the many invitations to join this group or that group in such and such a thing and complete my homework assignment set by the headmaster. I ask my eldest aunt's permission to consult the one dictionary in the house. She says I know the routine, first I should scrub my hands and dry them thoroughly. I promise to exercise the utmost care. She nods sharply. I run from her before she changes her mind. I wash my hands with so much lather it squelches when I bring my palms together and little bubbles shoot into the air, each with more colours in them than I see around me. Then I dry one segment at a time of each finger and between my fingers, then my palms, nails, and the backs of my hands. I touch nothing on my way from the water barrels, through the half-doors and into the living room where the dictionary takes up pole position beside the leather-bound Bible. I start with the title since the headmaster says it is very important. I write my two names and the word punishment. One word in the book sends me to another in a chain, in ceaseless waves, endless steps, and proliferating bubbles.

PART 1 *Bethany Bettany Punishments*

Slap, spank, push, punch, pinch, smack, thrash, bash, grasp, whack, kick, trip, nip, spit, whip, wallop, bully, elbow, whale, flail, fling, sting, flog, clout, cuff, swat, chop, pound, poke, choke, provoke, stoke, stalk, strike, box, birch, wrench, scratch, scourge, batter, bite, butt, cut, thump, bump, stomp, larrup, amputate, storm, stone, stare, glare, slam, bang, bark, barge, bombard, starve, stifle, scuffle, knuckle, buckle, hurtle, heckle, compress, reassemble, pummel, hammer, mar, scowl, howl, scold, scald, club, jab, berate, frustrate, rap, tap, thwack, trounce, bounce, hound, strap, boot, bruise, burn, ambush, abuse, refuse, confuse, pierce, soil, bawl, maul, nullify, vilify, cremate, bury, exhume, presume, assume, dehumanise, disenfranchise, despise, cut-eyes, switch, bitch, pitch, filch, kitsch, stitch, unstitch, needle, wheedle, spiegel, sulk, skulk, mulch, pulp, purple, pepper, petrify, fry, roast, toast, boast, ghost, lose, hose, freeze, anti-freeze, squeeze, knee, ignore, deplore, floor, spurn, spin, sin, sink, bring-to-the-brink, crank, blank, outflank, flunk, lump, harrump, jack-knife, hoodwink, invade, pervade, tirade, raid, faze, Gorgon-gaze, organise, gormandise, metastasise, proselytise, terrorise, fossilise, fetishise, chide, ride, deride, abide, abominate, bomb, blast, mask, fast, emaciate, suffocate, berate, irritate, masticate, eviscerate, hate, slate, tie, lie, sty, garrote, hurt, curt, squirt, scare, scar, erase, displease, distress, dissect, wreck, rake, stake, fake, fault, halt, stall, corral, demoralise, amaze, mesmerise, mess-up, upset, set up, trap, ape, fake, make, balk, mark, mollify, crucify.

PART 2 *Bethany Bettany cannot imagine ever being . . .*

(Of all the following words under this heading only the last one remains on my list.)
Hugged, named, winked, whistled, smiled, laughed, joked, played, cooperated, squeezed, tickled, rubbed, approved, danced, skipped, twisted, jived, serenaded, lullabied, praised, patted, ruffled, moon-gazed, feather-touched, flower-smelled, honey-kissed, salt-licked, touch-touched, congratulated, consoled, guided, blushed, knee-bounced, arm-cradled, hair-brushed, dressed-up, made-up, advised, splashed, groomed.

Feather Girl

I am a feather. I land softly when thrown. Take my time to drop to the ground when pushed from a tree or a window ledge. Absorb a blow as only a feather can, a feather from the chest of a pink flamingo.

Kind mouth of the trade winds blow on me. Transport me out of this place. I am no trouble. I promise. Sweep me from here. Set me down anywhere else.

Raindrop Girl

See how raindrops fall in a crowd – that's how I want to be – one raindrop like every other drop of rain, part of the crowd and therefore indistinguishable from any other part of it. A raindrop finds a way off a roof, into a slab of concrete, along a plank of wood, into soil, settles on glass and is the colour of glass, falls on skin and seems to soak right in.

What Bethany Bettany never wants to see again as long as she lives

1. Tears
Eyes that belong to tears look out of me at me in a shameless, brazen, way and produce buckets, well up with water, look right through its own drowning in the sorrow of its making and right through the flesh and blood and nerve-bundle of me.

I do not want them. I want my eyes dry as the Sahara. I would rather blink and with each dry blink feel as if my eyelids slide over a razor than have them wet and ready for a factory of tears.

Dreams paint behind the eyelids. I use my dreams as a substitute for tears and paint behind my eyelids so that when I blink I dream and do not think and my eyes stay dry.

2. Copulation. Cannot write about this (yet). It exceeds decorum.

3. Love. I am not sure about this one.

I store away my completed homework and promise myself that I will deliver it to the headmaster. Then I spot some string and thread it through my fingers into a pattern of four diamonds.

Months pass like this, between the dictionary and that piece of string. A month for every diamond I shape with that string, a dictionary for every month. Other rains plaster the earth after the shellac of drought. No more beatings come my way and no more are held up as promises to come. I count the diamond shapes on the string. No matter how much I thread my fingers through that string I cannot exceed four diamonds. Four diamonds for my grandfather to return a rich man, four for my mother to come back. I unravel my handiwork and string the diamonds again, unravel, string, unravel, over and over. Eventually the string breaks or I give up or more rain interrupts me and compels me to look outside, and the rain that always sounds louder than the last time hurts my head and stomach with its noise.

One such storm and a stomach ache keep me up most of the night. At bedtime the children disappear into the bedrooms of their parents, unroll bed things on the floor in a corner of the room and sleep. Some crawl into the beds of their parents when small or sick. As the only child at the house without a parent present I creep into my large closet full of my father's things on the ground floor of the house. I keep an inventory of his earthly possessions. I love the fact that there is always a wall pressing against my back and I cannot stretch a limb or turn over without hitting his boots and shoes, his English winter separates, galoshes included, for those long muddy walks along the Thames on his beat from Tower Bridge to Gravesend. I pretend I bump not so much into these stored tokens of a life but into my father sleeping. I see myself in a big bedroom and those storeroom things of his include my mother. She cleaned those Wellington boots for him so they retain her grip. She held him when he wore those woollens therefore they keep her embrace. She may have rested her perfumed neck and face on his shoulder and on his chest so I know it is her I smell on them, her musty perfume, powder, sweat and maybe even the odourless salt of shed tears. I keep hearing the talk that I am a fast runner because my mother powered my legs or that I owe my rapid-fire tongue to her. I touch my body and think I am less than a ghost, spirit, jumby, buckoo, wraith, because I am not even myself. Lost among the living, I may as well belong to the other world where bodies collide, mix, and melt not just into each other like my mother's scent and my father's property but through things, through his clothes and into me, through me and back to her living body. And that may be how I find my way back to her side.

Morning brings sunshine, outside bright green, oven-warm, inside smelling of toast and boiled milk. The dull ache that radiates from my belly convinces me I am hungry, though it feels unlike a hunger pain. I put it down to something food can cure. I climb and count the stairs to the kitchen, ignoring my skirt blowing about my waist. I grab two slices of bread and retreat from the kitchen. On my way into the yard I count the steps and ignore the morning breeze, one stair is missing but the distance between each step feels the same.

I crawl under the house. It retains last night's cool and a harvest of shadows. I look all around for a spider's web since I hate the clinging sticky feel of cobweb on any part of my body other than on my hands where it feels tolerably silky. Cockroaches, ants, mice, snails, centipedes, scorpions and perhaps a snake or two all reputedly live under here. I lie on my aching stomach and keep my skirt shrink-wrapped around my knees. I eat the outside crust of the slices of bread and work my way to the soft middle. I chew slowly and gaze unblinkingly, seeing myself on all fours grazing in the cow pasture. I utter a long, low moo and jut my neck out, then return to my bread. It occurs to me I am better suited, under the house like this, to playing the part of a pig, but I like the slowness and apparent calm of cows. I love their big and very wet eyes that include everything around them. Moo, I say, more loudly this time. And I finish my bread. But I still ache and feel starved.

Bettany! Somewhere in the house someone calls me. A woman's voice contains my name. But the windows, doors, and creases in floorboards distort the voice beyond recognition. Or perhaps the wax in my ears hardens against the voice. *Bettany!* I try to conjure a face for that voice but I cannot make the room in my head for my many aunts by blood and marriage. *Bettany!* My head extends into the house above me, balloons outward to take on the dimension of the house, slate roof for bone skull. The voice calling me fires from inside the many rooms of the house. My body occupies all the land under my belly and as far as my arms and legs reach out and touch and then beyond my arms and legs to every patch of ground as far as sight. My name spreads everywhere. *Bettany!* A boy's stick-insect legs and bare feet walk along the side of the house looking for me. Another boy checks the pigsty. Yet another sprints towards the cow shed. And another, the bicycle shed. At least two young women run into the barn where the replacement donkey and cart are parked beside a wall of hay. My eyes follow their dusty feet running in all directions in the yard. My ears pick up the tumble of feet down and up the scraped thin wood stairs and along the polished wood floor of the living room in my head. They laugh and place bets about who will find me first. The caller in the house of my head fills my body with my name when she leans out of the kitchen window and shouts for me. She curses the day I was born and promises everyone within earshot that she will give me a good beating when she lays hands on me. Her threat convinces me I cannot answer. I retreat further under the house and align my body with a large post so that I will not be seen if someone looks into the shadows under the house. I pray for all of them to become distracted and forget about me. A fat red and black ant with a big-mandible head crawls up my arm. I aim my middle finger and flick the ant deeper into the shadows. I shudder involuntarily at the thought of more ants on me. What happens if one of them crawls into my crotch and lays an egg? I will become a giant ant's nest and leave a trail of them behind me as I walk. They will gradually consume me from the inside out until there is nothing left of me except perhaps a giant anthill where the house of my head and the land of my body stood. Something trickles between my legs. I giggle nervously thinking that I am true to my name, Pissy-Missy, and have peed myself. But I do not feel like peeing. I run three fingers over the wet spot and bring my fingers up close to my face, Pissy-Missy, antsy pussy. Rawness greets me more akin to turned soil than the way my body smells. My red fingers startle me. I check again. More red. I think I must have been bitten between the legs by red ants, not the usual ones with mandibles but with teeth to break skin and draw blood. I scramble from my hiding place into the open and sprint up the stairs careful to hold my dress down against the breeze that is always there to lift women's dresses and fill men's trouser legs. I skid to a stop on the front porch inches from the friendly aunt who calls me. But she looks displeased to see me. She draws back from me. I regret not answering her call earlier. A bunch of cousins all of whom claim they saw me first follow me. They spot my bloody condition and stare from my aunt to me and back again. They expect me to be in pain or crying. My aunt looks at my stained skirt and she pushes me inside the house and chases the others away.

KIND AUNT

I urge her not to feel bad for hiding from me. It could have been anyone calling her name. When we shout we all sound the same in this house. She bites into her bottom lip afraid that something is very wrong with her. I tell her bleeding colours a woman's reason. We feel unclean. We feel shame. She has not bled before. She wants to know how long blood will run out of her. I tell her she should get comfortable with bleeding that it is a sign of her growing into a woman. I order her to taste her blood. She looks at me and tries to pull away from my grip. I suppose my determination to stop her from adding another thing to her long list of things about herself to be ashamed of makes me do what I do next. I grab her hand and push it between her legs and before I know what I am doing I bring her fingers up to my mouth and quickly lick them and stare at her. She almost faints. I almost laugh out loud. I hold her and nod to her to do the same. She moves slowly like a cold-blooded reptile at sun up. The face she makes has more to do with sticking her fingers in her crotch and tasting it than with the actual flavour of her blood. I lie to her and tell her I tasted my blood when I had my first period aeons ago. She repeats the word *aeons* when I expect her to stick with *period*.

I make her stand in the upstairs shower reserved for adults. The stone-floor cubicle has disinfectant coming out of the walls. I help her take off the dress and I throw it into a bucket and tell her we will deal with the dress later. I turn on the tap, which splutters and coughs up a spludge of rusty water then a few dribs and drabs then a hoarse gurgle of nothing. So I turn to the reserve bucket of water and I pass her a bar of carbolic soap and a flannel and she follows my instructions very carefully about where to scrub and how much and how necessary copious amounts of water are for this form of ablution. I make her repeat my words that she is a young woman now and no longer a girl and therefore she must conduct herself differently. I help her dry her back and she smears the towel with blood before I can stop her from passing it with such vigour between her legs. I raise my eyes to the ceiling in exasperation but quickly smile and tell her it is nothing that cannot be fixed with soap and water. I hold up a pair of panties for her to try on. She complains that the elastic clutches her waist and the inside of her thighs. I give her a pale blue strip of cloth and spell out how she must fold it into a pad. Then I make her position it correctly in the crotch of her panties. I invite her to wear my nice green dress with little white flowers sewn into the neckline. She repeats after me: I will check the cloth whenever I am alone, and if it is soaked, change it before it stains my dress. No, my dress, I remind her, your favourite shade of lime green, but my dress. We laugh. I point to a covered bucket where such cloths are stored for someone to wash. I show her how to wash the dirty cloths and tell her it will be her turn to wash them soon since all the women in the house take turns. From this moment, I say, you are a young woman, not a sixteen-year-old child, remember everything you wear and take care of the items that are yours. Ever the good student she nods to everything. Every few weeks this bleeding occurs. She repeats my words exactly as I tell them to her, every few weeks. I wonder how much she understands when I tell her about men and women and how babies happen. Does she understand my meaning? Yes, she nods and I believe her since her nose is always buried in a book when she is not looking over the top of the book at one of us.

BETTANY

I think it is my mother bleeding in my body and not me, Bettany, bleeding in that involuntary way. I want to check with my aunt if that might be the case but I am afraid to mention my mother to anyone in the house since everyone always takes every opportunity presented to them by my presence or otherwise to mention my mother's infamy. Is my mother trying to kill me? Does she intend to take over my body? There is no obvious bruise from this bleeding for me to heal. My mother injures me and draws my blood and all I can do is clean up the mess afterwards.

I thank my aunt for all her help. I walk as ordinarily as I can with my head full of my new condition. When I descend the back steps I refuse to count them. I keep one hand in front and one behind my dress and for the first time I hate the breeze on these stairs that always interferes with my clothes.

I never crawl under the house again. A part of my attention always centres on the correct fall of my hem. My nose develops an acute sense for any remnant on my body of the particular rawness of blood. I become convinced that I smell blood all the time that I bleed, the turned-soil and over-ripe fruit of blood. I think it distinct and different from everything to do with my body because it belongs not to me but to my mother. Not my blood shed by me but her blood, shed by me. It seems good if I bleed to death then she can no longer live through me.

The blood continues in a trickle. The life-threatening flood that I wait for never materialises. I change and wash the strips of cloth and hang them out at night to dry and take them down first thing in the morning. The blood stems to a few spots then soon dries up to nothing. My old self returns.

Except there can be no going back after the long talk from my aunt.

I begin to help with the hand-washing of clothes on the scrubbing board, only small things at first, shorts, socks, handkerchiefs and underwear. I try to guess people's names from the smell of their dirty laundry. The worst smells always belong to my uncles; the best to the youngest children. When washing the clothes of my aunts and uncles, I pretend as I throw my weight behind the scrubbing board that I am crushing the part of the body covered by that particular item. I see nothing that might be worn by a grandmother cooped up in a darkened room day and night. Perhaps she walks around in her room with nothing on. But she must wear something to greet the priest on his weekly visit.

Washing my own things makes me recognise my clothes on the line from among the hoard of other children's clothes as if mine are in lights or dyed a colour exclusive to my eyes. If I wear a dress no one else wants to wear it after me. The other girls say they do not want to be mistaken for me as long as they walk the earth. They would rather die than be me. The shame of it would be so great. To be me and alive is surely worse than to be dead. They prefer death to my life. I want to tell them I prefer death too to being my mother in me.

Everyone in the house possesses one kind of blood and I another quite different kind. Whereas their blood runs in the family and they share the same genes relayed through time down the family line, my blood is poisoned by its division between my father and mother. Somehow my mother's blood is all the blood I have in my veins. My father's dries up and is nowhere to be found. How else can all my blood relatives over eleven years of looking at me see only her and not a trace of my father in me? There must be something about him somewhere on my body. Whatever it is seems truly hidden, in my armpits, behind my knees or ears, between my toes, on the back of my neck, in the crook of my arms. And as I grow, it shrinks, eaten up by the rest of me, my mother in me.

If the beatings left me thin as the front wheel of a racing

bicycle then bleeding blows me up into the size of the back wheel of a tractor or the rear wheel of one of those massive dump trucks ferrying supplies and troops to the interior. I balloon from the thin rake of a despised child into the plump pudding of a pampered young woman. My chest changes its two buds into flowers and then two ripe fruits the size of oranges. The cricket stumps of my legs with the knot in the wood for knees develop muscles and flesh and curves. The twin, thin saucers of my rear end burgeon with flesh into two dancing soup bowls full of riches for hungry eyes to feast on. In the ten months following my sixteenth birthday I grow three inches. People in the house look at me with dropped jaws. The women circle me and make me do turns for them. They throw open their closets for my delight. I wear shoes, the best ones in the house, after walking around with bare feet since my arrival there at age five. I step into nylon slips for the first time in my life. Aunts queue to prepare my hair and show me an array of pomades, colourful oils, and perfumed Vaseline, and combs with kind teeth, in order to demonstrate their expertise for the job. One aunt grabs my hands and increases the length of my nails instantly by pushing the cuticles back with her thumbnail. Then she files my nails into neat curves and begs me never to bite them again. I refuse to let her touch my toes after the stone she uses to scrape my heels leaves them raw and sore and barely able to take my weight. My weight becomes a state secret. I am never under any circumstances to disclose it to anyone least of all a boy.

Their husbands gone, my aunts branch outdoors and drive carts by standing with the reins in their hands and clicking their tongues. They round up cows for milking, and lasso and brand a newborn calf. They wrestle a pig to the ground, tie its limbs and, as it squeals, they shriek and, with a hammer, drive a ten-inch spike into the pig's skull and extinguish that squeal, and cut the throat over a bucket. They boil huge outdoor vats containing various parts of the other animals that they kill: the goat and sheep and many throats of chickens plucked clean and cut through in one slice of the stone-sharpened knife. And when an army truck knocks down a cow, they hoist that carcass into the barn and skin it with long knives and carve the flesh into portions for the surrounding houses. They all seem to bleed at the same time of the month and I bleed with them and wash the pieces of cloth and hang the little flags of femininity in the morning sun and take them in by midday to make room for other things.

Each week that the men stay away prompts some new endeavour in the women. The more the women work the less time the children have to play among themselves as they are roped into things. To fetch more water for the flagstone to be washed clean of sticky goat's blood. To deliver this message now, not tomorrow or next week, to this woman and no one else and to return with the answer straight to the one who sent you and none other.

With no school to attend the children turn their minds to building weapons for the defence of the house against an army that will have to pass the house on its way from the border deep in the interior to the capital. We make slingshots after hunting for the exact forks of tree limbs and roll scores of mud balls from clay dipped in water and dried in the sun. We use our nails tempered into knives on the railway line to sharpen long sticks into spears and store them under the house. Then we settle on finding hiding places just in case our defences fail to repel the invaders. The idea is that we fall back to the bushes behind the house as far as the railway line and devise a way to slow down and board the steam train on its way to the capital that will take us to safety there.

The men's absence inspires dances at night where some women dress as men in their missing husbands' clothes to partner other women. My seventeenth birthday comes and goes unceremoniously. War preoccupies everyone. I do not mind, except that all the young men who might have cared about me are drafted into the army anyway so there is no one around to make a fuss over me. We group around the transistor radio and hear what none of us wants to hear since all of us hope that the stand-off between the two armies will lead, after months of waiting, to a gradual retreat behind their own borders. The radio announces that the skirmishes between small scouting parties from each side escalated into a full-scale engagement of the two armies. Previous to this announcement these skirmishes sent back a couple of dead soldiers each week to the capital but never to our village or house. We believed these clashes would eventually make it clear to both sides that they had a stalemate and force them to negotiate. We did not entertain the fact that the clashes presaged a real war. Every woman and child wails at the news. We cut our noise and listen when we hear a low moan coming from the locked bedroom of Granny. She groans with no pauses for a breath. Her guttural, the dry sound of it, a moan without tears, starts us all crying again.

I suggest we go to Granny and knock on her door and invite her out of her room, if not all of us then just one of us, Aunt Ethel, the one person Granny trusts most with her meals and laundry. But all the aunts unanimously disagree. No one is to even think of disturbing the old lady. She has been through enough without having to take on grandchildren. I place my hands over my ears and still hear the low moan. I stand and run to her door. My aunts chase after me. I reach it and hammer twice and beg her to let me in but they grab me and pull me from the door with my heels dragging along the corridor. The moaning ceases and we all stop and I know their thinking since it is mine too: that my pounding on the door and calling out to her works and the door is about to open. But we watch and wait for a long time and the door stays shut. We walk away and disperse to complete single tasks like washing up or chopping wood or gathering berries for a pie. Or form groups of twos and threes for jobs such as loading hay from the barn into the donkey cart to take out to the cows in the parched field or fetching barrels of water from the village standpipe. The women stop at the standpipe to gather news about other men from other houses gone to the border dispute turned full-fledged war.

Ambulances pass the house night and day. The field hospital

where the preliminary repairs to men's bodies are carried out soon fills with more injured men than beds to put them in. The one hospital in Mable where the headmaster lives fills up and wounded soldiers are ferried to other large towns with hospitals nearer to the capital. Schools become temporary hospitals but with no equipment they perform the most rudimentary functions for troops and serve as holding places for men too maimed to walk or return home or in need of an operation as soon as their name climbs to the top of the list. Many die waiting. Many leave those makeshift hospitals for homes they prefer to die in. But by coming home in a condition of total disrepair they bring to the outlying villages and towns pictures of a border war no one wants to see associated with someone from their family.

An ambulance stops at the rum shop and we run to meet it and see for ourselves who has become the first village casualty. The back doors open and a man calling out in pain every time he moves emerges wearing a string vest. Three very old men struggle to lift him. Three women in ankle-length faded cotton dresses scream when they see the man and throw themselves at him. They want to know why his head is shaved, why he wears no uniform on his back and why the dressings on his wounds are so dirty. The way they talk to him it is clear they do not expect an answer. I cannot get close and the man's relatives beg us all to give them some room and when that does not work they chase us off by raising their open hands at us. I hear someone say something about exploding mines and another, 'What a disgrace to send home a man in such a bad condition when he give so much to his country.' I catch a glimpse of him as they climb on to a tractor and trailer for the ride along the dirt track to their house on stilts by the sea. The crowd of women and children around the cart salute the man. I spot his face creased in pain and recognise him not by his clean-shaven head and face but by his muscular bare arms draped around two helpers. The old men begin to sing 'Onward Christian Soldiers', and the relatives join in with the singing. I saw those two arms twice before, both times in quick succession, and they terrified me each time because they seemed to have minds of their own. In the cane and plantain fields those arms ruled. They swung a cutlass and heaved branches of plantains and sugarcane. They passed me in a field and spared me. They glistened and pulsed and appeared invincible. Now they look dry and clinging. And his legs that walked those fields knowing every square yard in the dark stepped into another field much like the ones his legs know, but this time a battlefield far away from home, and triggered a landmine. All that is left of the plantain man's legs are two bandaged stumps.

In their talk the old men curse and gesticulate towards the capital. They shout that it is not the land that takes his legs and almost his life, it is his country.

I walk slowly back to the house while the other children race to see why an army jeep idles at the front of the house, all except Brian who lags behind me in silence. I keep my gaze locked at my feet to shade them from the sun's glare.

Who dead?

Who say anybody dead?

Uncle Ray dead?

Nobody dead, Bettany.

Then how come everybody face so long?

Uncle Ray missing, not dead, missing.

They say he leave his post without permission. They come looking for he.

That not like Ray, something wrong.

The four sisters and two sisters-in-law continue to speak softly among themselves. I apologise for thinking Uncle Ray dead but the way you all sit around crying I find it hard to believe that he still living and will soon turn up at the house in one piece. This grabs their attention so I keep talking.

He would love to see us now mourning the fact that he no longer faces the chance to get shot or blown up. If all our uncles had his good sense they too would walk away from the border rather than risk a return like the plantain man's or no return at all, except in a casket. We should be happy that

Uncle Ray is out of it. We should count him as one of the lucky ones who will soon be home with us.

My aunt who from the beginning has always been kind to me looks at me severely and says the awful politician in me spouting those things and that I do not know what I am talking about. Then she turns from me and the women resume their discussion.

Ray would never do a thing unless his conscience tells him he has to do that thing.

Ray too close to his brother and brothers-in-law to take off without them unless he has a good reason.

But the Ray I know dragged me to the back of the house and beat me with a switch and when his switches all broke he beat me with his hands and feet. He can hardly breathe but he can fight for his country. Serves him right for burning down a government building and ruining my education.

AUNT ETHEL

The coalition government the headmaster loves so much, with its many heads on the one glued-together monster body started a war it cannot finish. No one really cares if the border is fifty miles nearer or fifty miles deeper into the jungle. If someone says they do care they are thinking of a foreign bank account in their name, not of the good of this land.

Remember I joined that expedition to the interior that went in search of our father. We came to a place where there were several waterfalls twisting and turning and descending into valleys. We bathed in one, the men changed behind one clump of bushes, the women another, and we drank the fresh, cool water. Later as we sat and lunched within earshot and view of a waterfall our guide pointed out that we crisscrossed from one country to another just by crossing a few rivers and that though we cannot tell it we were eating lunch on foreign soil. The idea made me stop eating and look around me and really search the place for a sign of a new country but all I could see was water, pointed hills and green valleys. There was not a shred of evidence of one or other country's border. That was what the two countries were now fighting over. And though no politician in power would ever admit it, the plantain man has in fact lost his powerful legs for a line that no one can see and for water that cannot be divided. Ray must have run away when he realised that there was nothing to win in this war but the death of the other side, if the other side does not kill you first. The headmaster for all his learning fails to see this when he lends his support to this government. I do not countenance burning our own goods and services but our children deserve better than the propaganda he offered to them on a daily basis.

BETTANY

Slow applause rings out from one pair of hands not present on the balcony but nearby. Our heads swing towards the bedroom window next to the balcony. It remains shut with Granny behind it listening to the talk.

Aunt Ethel shouts at the window, *Stop it Mummy!*

She storms off the balcony via the front steps followed by the other women and the children. I want to believe that the slow hand clapping has something to do with the age of the hands but I have a distinct memory of them as firm and strong on my forehead. She succeeds in driving everyone off the balcony and maybe that is her intention. There is a sour disapproval in the pace of the clapping but I am not sure of what exactly – the failed search for Granddad that turned up the nugget of wisdom for my aunt instead? It cannot be that Granny approves of the border war and not her daughter's anti-government sentiments, not after prohibiting her two sons and two sons-in-law from joining the army for as long as she could.

I remain on the balcony alone and stare at the window. I will her to open it and say something. Staring at the wooden slats on the blind with hardly a blink makes me imagine that they move. The darkened room means she can see me but I cannot see her. I say aloud, *You hear everything and see everything and do nothing about it.* Then I spin away from the window and hop down the front steps counting them to take my mind off of her and come up with a number one short of the back staircase. My mother and my granny are alike.

Radio announcements ask citizens of the young and great republic to further tighten their belts for the war effort. Bernadette, the aunt who spits, shouts at the radio, *If we tighten we belts any more we guts going come out we mouths!* As the days pass, the country's radio and television stations succumb to emergency government control so that wherever the house radio is tuned it keeps asking for sacrifices. Soon fuel cannot be bought anywhere. The government bus service stops running between Mable and the capital and bus drivers lease their buses from the government and operate an independent though itinerant service completely governed by their ability to gather enough diesel fuel. A water shortage results in dry spells that last a few days each when only a hoarse vacuum issues from the village standpipe. The bakery runs out of flour and stops baking and I miss its perfume in the air. The rum shop operated by an aunt who takes the place of her conscripted husband as head bar person, exhausts its stock of soft drinks and then beer and then rum so that the old men meet there to nurse empty bottles and play draughts and dominoes in lamplight and sip mauby and ginger beer. A few of us whenever we hear the radio repeat its message about sacrifices put out by the hydra-headed, glued-together government we shout Aunt Bernadette's phrase in unison at the radio, *If we tighten we belts any more* . . . And laugh about it.

We herd the animals nearer to the house. All children are forbidden to play in the vicinity of the barn or enter it with many threats of the most unforgettable whippings, and the only reason given for the ban is that the unstable stockpile in there is harmful to the eyes, lungs and minds of children. The water truck arrives and we all line up with buckets and walk back to the house as if carrying an egg on a teaspoon in each hand so we do not spill a drop. We dry coconuts in the sun and press the oil out of them and burn it in lamps, cook with it, rub it on our dry scalps and body and drink a tablespoon of it if one of the children eats too many green guavas and becomes constipated. Coconuts, we call each other. We smell like a coconut harvest. Coconuts or their shells or husks, coconut milk and coconut water. We stop counting the army trucks passing the house and forfeit waving at the young men heading to the interior for a silent protest of simply turning our backs to the convoys. The back door of the house remains open at night for the return of Ray, but Ray fails to show up. A goat wanders into the living room and on hind legs extends up to the mantle and chews the entire Genesis chapter of the Bible before Aunt Ethel sweeps it back into the yard with her broom and announces that the goat is the devil incarnate and earmarks it for the next animal sacrifice and meat feast.

The short letters from my three other uncles on the front line cease. Post stops altogether. We dig out the old letters and listen to them read aloud one after the other at night on the balcony. The short letters inquire after the children and are replete with reminders of the jobs that need to be done around the farm. How we must guard against the terrible kick one can get from the replacement donkey if it is harnessed while standing on the left side of it. Not to mention the terrible bite from its huge, stained, unruly teeth if its harness is not fed into its mouth while it chews on a little treat. And we should not forget to strap the barrels together on the cart with a good rope when fetching water otherwise the barrels will tumble off the cart and cause serious injury to life and limb. And how the war is going this way and that but there is nothing to say about war since war is war is war.

We talk about the uncles every chance we get at gatherings for meals, around chores and on the balcony at night. I even tease about the unique manner each uncle has of beating a child, and everyone agrees I should know since I have for years been the queen bee recipient of beatings. Uncle Joe, the eldest, who lashes and pauses and lashes and pauses as if decorating a cake he checks at each stage of his workmanship. And Uncle Stanley who lashes so fast it is difficult to count his strokes as though the body he steadies with one hand and whips with the other might evaporate into thin air and rob him of his delight. And Uncle Ray, the beater who hurt more than his victim from a beating since he ends up crying. We joke about him vomiting beneath the weight of the overturned cart and breathing with difficulty ever since when other men would have been six feet under after such a grave accident. Last but not least there is Uncle Roger of the withering look who sends me to pick the whip he will use to beat me. We decide no enemy bullet or bayonet can harm them. They can defend a hill single-handed and fight off six men from the other side with the same ease and cunning employed by them in whipping a child. I announce that I am proud to be the one on whom they perfected their battle skills. I am thinking more about Uncle Joe driving me home from the railway line on the cart loaded with sorrel and sugarcane and me with his hat (I am told it belonged to my father) over my face than any beating he or anyone else gave me. If the whip is a rifle, I conclude, then the enemy better not make a wrong move and fall into any of my uncles' hands.

An army jeep pulls off the road outside the house and raises a cloud of dust that sails away from it across the fields. Two men in dark glasses, green fatigues and helmets clamber out, wipe their necks and foreheads with handkerchiefs, confer for a while then march to the house. They demand to speak with the parents or spouses of Joe Abrahams and his brother Stanley Lustol. We all fear the worse. I try not to think it. Aunt Ethel says she is the most senior person present and they can talk to her since both parents and spouses are indisposed. What a word for Aunt Ethel to dash on those army officials – indisposed. The last part of the word makes me think of my father with his best foot forward and his hands on his hips. Aunt Ethel always insists that a little learning can go a long way. Her idea to keep a dictionary next to the family Bible provides two sources of self-improvement for the children, one material as she put it, since a head of many words leads to riches, and the other spiritual because Bible stories save a person's soul. She believes that learning sustains the brain just as exercise maintains the body – two types of fuel.

The taller of the two men clutches an envelope to his chest. He holds it out and announces that like their Ray Abrahams before them, both Joe Abrahams and Stanley Lustol are classified as absent without leave. The man might as well have cut a ribbon for a festival to begin because right away the children begin to dance around and the aunts smile broadly and hug each other. Not dead, merely missing. Aunt Joyce, the kind aunt, offers the men a drink of water. They gruffly decline. The tallest man expresses his outrage at the response to his serious news. Do we realise the gravity of what he said? That desertion in a time of war is a capital offence and these men have dishonoured themselves? And the name Abrahams, so respected among politicians of both parties, has now been sullied twice over, no, three times, by Stanley's marriage into the family. Aunt Ethel replies she heard differently. These three men are not the only men to take this course of action. That the men's action brings the tactical ability of the top brass into question and not the men's bravery. (Lash them with a big word, Aunt Ethel!) That if they do not want a drink of water then their business in the Abrahams yard is over as of now. She adds with her penchant for proverbs, 'You come to buy milk, not to count cow.' The men know they outstayed their welcome. They about-turn and march away. We shake our wrists, slapping the index fingers against the thumbs and middle fingers and widen our eyes at each other. We spin in complete circles on a heel or hop on the spot as if on hot tarmacadam and suck in air as though to cool cayenne pepper on the tongue. Go, Aunt Ethel, go!

The army jeep skids from the roadside and whips up a cloud, about turns and accelerates towards the capital. At first the jeep drives through the little storm it brewed so that it is obscured and seems blended with the dirt and about to become airborne too. It drags that dust cloud for several yards before separating at the turn out of town with the cloud continuing on a wind-driven trajectory over the fields and sowing itself there. Aunt Ethel repeats her warning about the barn being out of bounds or face her wrath. We believe she will unleash hell on a disobedient body and the aunts who hear her promise a whipping of their own on top of the one promised by Aunt Ethel. The prospect of a serial whipping scares us so much we circumnavigate a huge invisible perimeter fence around the barn and speculate about the exact nature of the unstable things hidden inside.

It could not be nuclear – even the government, the continent, the hemisphere is not nuclear. It might be invigorating pesticides for the rice and cane fields that put extra grains on the stalks and more sugar in the same amount of juice fed by ordinary manure. Or the chemical bath cows, sheep, goats and pigs experience to kill off the microbes that accrue on their hides and hoofs and brings them down in droves, or barrels of different coloured paints to transform the white house into a rainbow. Even the notion of purifying agents to convert pond water from murky and full of tadpoles to clear and safe for drinking crosses our minds. In the end we settle on the one thing in there that we would be forbidden to see and talk about during the war emergency as being nothing less than the hidden chemical composition of our uncles. All three are secreted in that barn, in three different corners, under some farming implement. Uncle Ray crouches behind the broken cartwheel that robbed him of his lunch and his ability to inhale deeply enough to blow smoke rings when he puffs on his clay pipe. And Uncle Roger will join them soon in a corner reserved for the fastidious, a neat corner with everything in its place and a place for everything.

We swear to keep our knowledge to ourselves and in the company of our aunts loudly blame the slightest rash or itch, sneezing bout, runny nose or red eyes on the 'unstable stable stuff' as we like to joke about the contents of the barn. We make sure the back door is left open for the return, cloaked in darkness, of Uncle Roger, the last uncle left on the front line. We ask a grown-up about it nightly after the animals are all in their pens, after the clothesline is cleared of dry things, after the battening-down of hatches and before we blow out the lamps. A government broadcast on the radio appeals to the nation for donations to help with the war effort and exhorts everyone to practise Spartan vigilance in our use of resources. But it only encourages us to shout at the radio and mime Aunt Bernadette's, 'If we tighten we belts one more notch we tripe going come out we mouths!' When the plantain man passes us in his customised cart, his temporary measure until the government wheelchair promised him materialises, we stand still and salute and love the wooden handles like paddles attached to the wheels for his powerful arms to row him forward. The old men call him Future, not because it is where the country of young men heads for in the border war, but for the marvellous fact that none of them have seen a man row facing the way he is going and on land.

An air of emergency cheerfulness fills us as we dip our fresh-baked cornsticks in our cups of milk and forage for guavas, bananas, mangoes, sapodillas, berries and firewood. My mother dips into and out of my thoughts as the target for my slingshot instead of a canary or an unreachable guava. If she can see me now reconciled with my half-brother and would-be stepmother or in my young woman's body she will not recognise me. An aunt will have to pick me out of the crowd. I will look at her and think of the word for her apart from 'mother', my head full all the while of the wish that my father can stand in her place. If things become worse, if all the wood we gather and all the fruits on the trees and the gallons of milk in the cows run out then there will be her left for me. Her return and my escape route. But the first thing I will say to her will be take not just me, but everybody, not just the children but all my aunts and hidden uncles, and not just all of them too, but the old woman locked away upstairs, take us all or take none of us. There is no longer me, Bethany Bettany, there is the house and all the animals and birds nesting around it and all the people living in it and near it, take too, my half-brother and his mother or take none of us.

I fuse to my last name. In our play around the house on full-mooned nights, Bethany Bettany solders itself to Abrahams. Our aunts turn a long rope for all the children to skip over at once and we link arms, sing and jump in unison. When I look up that rope in that moonlight appears to swing entirely around the house and over the moon. If my mother can retain the name for her use in her public life, whatever and wherever that may be, then surely I too, thrust in the middle of the house and land bearing the name, qualify as a candidate. This is the name we join hands in our games and swear we will die for more than any cause or call of the country.

I picture myself in a grave beside my father. The tent of the horizon that seems so far away when I reached the sea now contracts to within feet of the outlying fields and pegs its flaps into the ground. The border war pitches at such a distance that no reasonable trek would take us there. It seems to me that the only direct route to the war must be through a portal in one wall of the barn. Perhaps I rested my back against that very door when I stayed hidden behind the broken donkey cartwheel until my cousins found me. But none of us children approaches the barn now. Our uncles' lives depend on us keeping away from it. The barn seems distant from the house and much closer to the country's border.

From my promotion to the floor in Aunt Joyce's room I dream up the notion that if I walk into the barn and find my uncles then a similiar journey can lead me to my grandfather and that letter he has for me that I feel ready to read. And all this will unlock the room my grandmother makes her prison. And beyond my grandmother lies my mother. And behind her my father, not ensconced in his coffin and cemented grave, but standing with his arms on his hips and his best foot forward, and a look on his clean face as if to say, 'What took you so long to get here?'

I climb into men's clothing and roll up the trouser legs and do the same to the sleeves of his large shirt and tie a knot in the belt around my waist and knot the long shirttail around my bare belly. I tuck my hair under the felt hat and pin it and tiptoe out of the room with just a glance at her in the double bed surrounded by her three children in a blend of bodies that makes the one body, a knot of heads, arms and legs in a family potpourri of dreams. At the end of the corridor I open the kitchen door in slow motion and fill my left trouser pocket with cornsticks and the right with a mango and two guavas. At the foot of the back steps I drink from the three-quarters empty rain barrel careful to dip the ladle into the barrel without its ringing against the sides. I run across to the barn stopping at the door to take a deep breath of the night air tinged with the luminosity of a crescent moon. I lift the handle and the door is locked. I brace my body against it and there is not the slightest budge. I begin to circle the barn examining every block of wood for one that might be loose. Cicadas and frogs quarrel in a market place of their own making. I take every glistened blade of grass for one of their wet winking eyes. Fireflies dart from one point to another camouflaged by the dark and blaze suddenly as if torching an invisible enemy. The wooden windows are high and commandeering a ladder in the dark is out of the question. I circle the entire barn trying to prise a plank of wood to one side without luck. At the barn door once again, I twist, lift and push the handle rather impatiently and lean on the door all at the same time and fall into the barn as the door swings wide under my weight.

My immediate impulse is to straighten from my forward falter and pull the door back to the doorframe and leave but the door stays open. When I pushed against it I must have hooked the door against something that stops me now from moving it, turning it into a door that opens and refuses to close again. No doubt the headmaster would call this door the country and the force that can do nothing to influence it the nation. I give up trying to close it and release the door handle and step into the barn. The dark outside is thin compared to what I find myself trying to look through inside the barn. I think of the night outside as water in a pot and the darkness in the barn as the same pot of water but thickened with stock. I take no more than five steps inside when the barn door clicks shut behind me and I spin on my heels and face it expecting to see someone operating that door, first holding it against my pull, now pushing it shut with me inside the barn. I surprise myself by thinking and even more by saying aloud, in a voice with a slight tremor to whomever is in the dark there with me playing the doorman, *You dealing with a Abrahams. I take after my mother and she fears no man.* How many times do I say this before my eyes grow accustomed to the dark and I pick out the exact shape of the door and the fact that there is no one there but me? My guess is half a dozen times, maybe more, but the repetition makes me brave. I remind myself that I am not only an Abrahams but I stand on Abrahams property with a house full of friendly souls only a shout away and the spirit of my mother inside me to embolden me. I cannot explain the door to myself but seeing nothing I turn from it and walk deeper into the barn trying to refer to my mental map of the place. There are shapes that I cannot identify. I stand on the spot and wait for my eyes to catch up with my mind.

What I begin to see makes me think one or the other is faulty and deceiving me. If my eyes are lying to me then my mind can put things right tell it otherwise and literally correct my impaired vision. But if what I see is generated by my mind then I have problems because my mind always overrules my eyes, it tells it something and the poor eyes have no choice but to see that thing no matter how contrary the evidence is before them. Uncle Roger strapped wrists and ankles against the broken wheel in the corner with several leaking holes in his chest and stomach. I stare because I think staring will change things, evaporate what I see and restore a bare broken wheel, stripped for its spares and leaning against the wall at the end of a useful cycle. Instead, more of Uncle Roger becomes clear. Vomit bubbles in his mouth, and with his head inclined to the left, runs down his cheek. His wrists are tied and nailed into the round frame of the wheel, as are his ankles. His blood runs everywhere. The holes in his chest and stomach resemble flaps someone lifts to explore the contents of his body and fails to replace properly. My feet become heavy, too heavy to move them and my head so light it is liable to float off its moorings to my neck. I look away to my left and intend to look back hoping he will not be there, but my eyes land on something that keeps them locked to the back of the barn. Uncle Joe, in his felt hat inherited from my father, that keeps both men's oil and sweat, hangs from the rafters on a meat hook driven through his neck. His stomach has been slashed with a long blade and his entrails hang out of him untidily like dirty laundry. I fall to my knees and place my hands on the ground to steady myself but I grab torn flesh, parts of a body, sharp-edged bones broken off in an explosion. Though there is no face to put to those bits and pieces I guess that they belong to Uncles Ray and Joe. I sprint from the barn and slip on wet flesh and lose my footing and scramble to my feet and stumble. The door opens wide, how I do not know, I fling myself through it and fall into the open and my chest burns as though I surface from water after holding my breath under it for too long. I trip towards the house and the distance from the barn of twenty yards stretches to a quarter of a mile. The house is the same size, a stone's throw away, but the darkness between it and me stretches for miles. I glance back sorry to leave my uncles behind and glad to be out of their presence, and the barn looms over me, growing in height as I run.

Bettany! I run towards my name. My body shakes. *Bettany!* The house jumps closer to me as the barn retreats. I sail up the back stairs, my feet not touching any of the steps. I rock from side to side in my sprint. *Bettany!* I open my eyes and see my Aunt Joyce peering down at me and shaking me.

You all right?

Yes, Aunt.

You thrashing around and shouting. I don't want you to wake the others.

Sorry, Aunt.

Don't worry. Try to settle down.

All right, Aunt.

Goodnight.

Goodnight.

I lie still, catch my breath and listen to my aunt settle in her bed and soon start to snort a little then add her snore to a mini-chorus of snores. I raise myself to my elbows and look at her and sure enough she is fast asleep with her children folded in each other's arms. I creep to my father's cupboard and dress in his trousers and shirt and roll up the trouser legs and shirt sleeves and tie a knot in the belt around my waist and a knot in the long shirttail in which I fold my homework book from school. Then I climb into my father's work boots and head for the kitchen. The door is locked. I stand on tiptoe and edge my fingers along the top of the doorframe in slow motion until I feel the key. I put it in the lock as if threading a needle and turn the key as I might reposition a child I do not wish to wake. With equal care I twist the door handle and push the door only as wide as my body facing sideways on, and I slip into the kitchen. Guava, mango and bread aromas fill the dark room. I stuff my pockets with several finger-shaped and sized cornsticks, two guavas and a mango and tiptoe from the kitchen. I lock the door, replace the key on the slight ledge above the doorframe and creep down the back steps, all of me in step with the rest of me.

I relish the cold breeze and my skin picks up, like static, the soft luminescence from a new moon and more stars than black spaces between them. I drink from the barrel nearest the stairs, even more careful than in my dream not to knock the wood ladle against the resounding sides of the barrel, then I trot across the yard to the barn. Cicadas and frogs quiet in my path and quarrel just out of reach. The night dew, beaded and shining, winks as I pass. I hardly try the barn door knowing it will be locked. I circle the barn feeling all the wood for one loose plank. Back at the door I heave at it and shoulder my weight into it and it remains locked. I try a second and third time and cannot budge it.

A bicycle, my uncle's prized Gazelle from Holland, leans against the shed just left of the door. I know it by its lithe shape and feathery feel. The red frame in the night light resembles congealed blood. Only the white tape trimming on the dropped handlebar shines like bone. I am sure it was not there at nightfall when everything was put away and locked down, roped and tethered, scrubbed and swept clear. Never mind or I do mind but I am too enamoured with the fact that the bicycle is available for me at such an opportune moment than I am concerned to speculate about how it came to be there at that time. I stoop next to the Gazelle, manoeuvre my shoulder under the crossbar and stand with the bike on my shoulder. I walk to the road and hold on to the handlebar and pedal to keep the bike steady and the back wheel still and quiet. On the road I point the front wheel towards the interior, grip the steering with both hands, run and jump on to the saddle and push hard on the pedals building fast to a sprint. I do not look back at Boundary. The dynamo sings against the back wheel and the tyres hum against the road as I would sing and hum if I could muster the breath, together, dynamo and tyres sound louder than the surrounding insects.

I chase a beam cast ten feet ahead and creamy-white at the edges. Crushed glass in the tarmacadam glitters in it. I pause in the saddle to adjust the handle of a long kitchen knife that I grabbed in the kitchen without thinking about it and stuck into my waistband. When I see a headlight approach, sweeping the roadside trees and fields in clean curves as the vehicle hugs the turns, I keep to the edge of the road and lower my head and avert my eyes from direct contact with the mesmerising headlights. The odd car or truck heads in the same direction, towards the interior, I switch for safety to the empty lane on the opposite side of the road. When the vehicle passes I swerve back to the correct lane. In the small hours it is never so busy that a move to the wrong side of the road entails a risk. It is more foolhardy to trust a driver at this hour to judge the gap he should leave between my body and bicycle and his vehicle while overtaking me.

Around the outskirts of Mable, the nearest big town to Boundary, the faintest daylight begins to lift the weight of the night off the sky. The road unrolls its invitation to Mable, the last large town before the bush area takes over. I reach behind me and lift the dynamo off the back tyre. I straighten my shirt and tip my hat a lot to the left and a little over my eyes and sport the air of someone on a leisurely early-morning ride. At the first standpipe beside the main road I stop and drink and wash my face and neck. A little distance from the standpipe, and certain there is no one nearby, I stoop at the roadside and relieve myself. What's a girl to do?

Back on my bicycle I pause for a herd to cross the road and

rather than a complete stop I stickle and succeed in keeping my feet on the pedals with only a fractional movement of the steering wheel from side to side. The cow udders bulge with milk and shine in the paltry light. The boy driving them with a stick taller than his five or so feet and a piercing whistle too shrill to belong to his slight body nods in my direction and touches his cloth cap. I nod back and try not to smile too broadly. He names every cow crossing the road. None are called Daisy. A couple of the animals moo loud and long. I ask him if he knows where the headmaster of the school in Boundary lives. He shakes his head and returns to the list of names of his cows and his shrill whistle after each name with a pound of his stick on the road and rapid clicks of his tongue.

I pass vendors pushing carts laden with produce and dry goods on their way to the market. The houses thicken and draw nearer to the road. Dogs sit up in driveways and regard me as if considering whether they should give chase and snap at my heels. I ask a vendor if he knows of any teachers who live in Mable. He says Mable is a big place and there are many teachers, who do I have in mind. I say the headmaster who ran the school at Boundary before it burned down. He laughs mockingly, *What a scandal that people could do a thing like that in this day and age just because squabbling party politics divided their big name when education the key to every door.*

I agree but ask him what he means by politics. He says everyone knows the headmaster supports the new government and Boundary is a stronghold of the old party. He says the headmaster is famous around town for training pupils to take the foreign scholarships and he adds that since the Boundary débâcle the headmaster has not left his house. The man points to a side road and adds that I cannot miss the house because if I know the headmaster then I will know his house. I thank him and pedal down the narrow road. The first thing that catches my eye is a large letterbox more like a container than a letterbox. Clearly this is someone who expects a lot of post. This will be for the many magazines from overseas that the headmaster subscribes to and sometimes read to us in assembly.

At least he received his post. Then I see the motto next to the number of the house, 58. It reads 'Cogito, ergo sum'. I unhook the gate and step into the yard and a labrador on a leash lunges at me and growls but oddly does not bark. Without thinking I reach into my pocket and throw a cornstick at it, which it gulps down in a single swallow. This little detour might cost me all my rations. I reach into my pocket and throw another to get past the dog to the front door where I stuff my homework behind the metal doorknocker. It costs me two more cornsticks to get back safely to the gate and my bicycle.

I push off on the left pedal and swing my right leg over the crossbar. What makes me glance back at the house? Glance back I do, ever so briefly since I fear hitting a rut in the road and ending up on my rear. I pull on the handlebars and stand on the pedals ready to sprint and glance back at the house, more to take in for the last time what I believe I will never see again than to confirm anything. And there he is in the open door, framed as if in a life-sized photograph on account of his stillness, with my homework book in his hand. He looks hard at me, peering, squinting, to match me up to the thousand children who passed through his tutelage in a long life dedicated to the improvement of the species as he phrased it. I want to turn back and identify myself, tell him I completed his assignment to the best of my ability. But I take fright. I worry that he might link me to the house that shamed him publicly and beat me in return. I speed away as if pursued by his dog all the way to the main road.

As soon as I turn on to it I have to pull off to the side to make room for a convoy of army trucks. Each truck carries equipment of some kind inside rather than troops or else pulls covered trailers. The convoy slows to pass through the town. The last truck passes and I mount my bicycle, build to an immediate sprint and catch up with it. Then I slip in behind it and see little of the centre of Mable but notice the bus garage and market much like the market square at the capital but without its tall wooden steeple crowned with a broken clock.

As the convoy picks up speed I grab on to the back of the truck with my left hand and keep a tight grip on the bicycle's steering wheel with my right and hope there are no big potholes ahead. I find moving so fast with no effort on my part exhilarating. I feel I am skimming the surface of the road, like a stone on a pond, only touching the road a few times to make my way along it. The road rushes beneath me so quickly it loses its solid appearance and resembles a liquid, not water, it seems thicker than that, but with a swollen river's fast current flowing under me. I speed along like this for some time with Mable far behind and vegetation thick and close to the road once again and with fewer cultivated fields. I decide to try and steady the handlebar with my legs and use my freed-up hand to reach into my pocket for a cornstick to munch on. Where does the confidence come from to even think of such an action? The truck shields me from the breeze I should feel for the amount of speed I travel at, a high speed without any effort on my part. I ride a bicycle at upwards of forty-five miles per hour by holding on to the back of a truck but the way I think in the situation I may as well be in a cocoon dreaming myself attached to a speeding truck. I lift my left leg first and brace my boot against the steering at a point as near to the bicycle frame as possible, then my right leg with the added difficulty of having to raise my knee between my right arm and the bicycle. I lean forward and this gives me the room to bend my elbow but it makes lifting my knee quite a feat. I brace my right foot against the handlebar and make doubly sure both feet apply the same amount of pressure on the handlebar to steady it and keep it straight. Then I release my right-handed grip of the handlebar, slowly as if putting an egg back into a bird's nest and I straighten my back to the point allowed by my left hand attached to the truck. I dig into my right pocket and fish out the last two cornsticks. The moment I push the cornsticks into my mouth, cigars of sorts that I nibble at and draw into my mouth by working my lips around them, I grip the handlebar again and replace my feet on the pedals. As soon as the cornsticks disappear, I really want one of the fruits in my left pocket. I know I cannot release my hold on the truck so I use my right hand to get the fruit out of the opposite pocket by raising my left leg up to the handlebar, as before, and then my right leg.

The front tyre hits the smallest pebble and jiggles the handlebar. I lean forward and grab it and drop my legs to the pedals. The road is no longer a river, an increase in the morning light changes it into a revolving stone used to grind other stones to dust with little old me balanced on top. I steady the handlebar, the one thing that keeps me from rubbing against that spinning stone and being ground to less than dust, and try once more. My legs shoot up one after another on to the handlebar and I release my right-handed grip on it. Next I reach around my stomach to my left pocket and dig into it and feel the mango and think that I prefer a guava right now. So I twist my right shoulder a little more and dig deeper for the guava and grip it and pull it out. I bite into it, a large bite, leaving just enough for another mouthful, rather than holding the entire piece of fruit between my teeth and trying to dissect it that way. I want the luxury of eating it from my hand. I chew rapidly sensing a need to return to a safer posture sooner rather than later. I stuff the last half of the guava into my mouth and before I chew it I grip the handlebar and drop my feet back to the pedals.

As I chew, feeling the best kind of triumph there is to feel, I decide to change my grip on the truck from my tired left arm to my right. This manoeuvre entails a simple change of grip of hands from one place to the next, a straightforward swap of positions. I think it the kind of move I can perform in a split second without altering any of the variables of my relationship to the truck and my bicycle. The distance from the handlebar to the back of the truck is about a foot. My right hand needs to dart up to where my left grips and my left hand drop down to the handlebar nearest to it. In fact the left hand has less to do, less ground to cover than the right which needs to travel up and across a little as opposed to the left hand's straightforward drop on to the handlebar. I therefore think it prudent to focus on my right hand. I belch and should have heard it were it not for the breeze in my ears and the engine noise. I glance down at the road that boils like white water and spins like a grinding stone but in the new sunlight glitters too, imbued with precious minerals and metals there for the taking. I count to three and flick my hands. The left hand drops as predicted and grips the handlebar and the handlebar barely shudders but the right hand in its slightly more difficult manoeuvre darts up and across and grabs on to air. I stretch and grab again but the differential between the truck's acceleration and my bicycle slowing a fraction in that moment when I release my grip on the truck results in the truck moving inches out of reach and then speeding away. I return my right grip to the handlebar, raise myself off the saddle and sprint, throwing the bicycle left and right and my weight forward to almost over the handlebar, but the truck opens a bigger gap between it and me. I may as well pedal backwards. I sit back on the saddle and curse as the convoy disappears around a bend. The road feels hard under my tyres as if I pedal bare rims up a steep hill. The wheels may as well be squares. I stop pedalling and the bicycle drifts and comes to a standstill. I stickle, unsure what to do next, curse and dismount and push the bicycle telling myself that once I reach the bend in the road and see what lies ahead I will know what to do next.

I reach the bend in the road and have no idea what I should do: there simply is not a road, as I would ordinarily deploy the term. Instead the bitumen surface ends and a mud and sand track begins that widens to a field then wider still to a plain and savannah and narrows again to a single file track then a wall of tall trees propped against the sky. The convoy disappears into the giant green cavern of the trees. I consider myself lucky to be separated from the truck before the convoy reached this track.

The wall of trees runs as far to the left and right as I can discern. A flock of parakeets cackle mockingly overhead. Bright green and in the distance no bigger than leaves, they resemble a portion of the forest in flight and almost with speech. Turn back now, I tell myself, and I can be home for a late lunch, carry on and there is no telling what might happen. I climb on the bicycle and pedal slowly around the ruts and holes in the dry mud and sand. I fish out the mango and roll it on my thigh as I pedal, careful not to break the skin, until the mango softens to pulp. Then I nibble a hole in the top end of the mango, and, quick to catch the juice trickling out, I clamp my lips over the opening and sip and swallow; squeeze, suck and gobble up. A whoop rises in my throat. I suppress it and convert my joy into a burst of speed.

By now they will miss me at the big house and connect my absence with the missing bicycle. Apart from the speculation about my whereabouts I wonder who really worries over the fact that I am no longer there to occupy someone's space on the floor, wear someone's preferred dress and eat what might well be an extra helping of someone's favourite stew, vegetable, or bread. I robbed the kitchen of cornsticks and fruit, my rations for the day, and drank directly from the barrel against the instructions of grown-ups who always caution the children about contaminating the barrels of drinking water. I ride a bicycle that belongs to someone without their per-mission and I wear a dead man's clothes on my back, and his hat and his boots that are too big for my feet. I am entirely a borrowed and stolen personality and I am happy. I tear the mango skin with my teeth and gnaw at the mango seed until all the strands lodge between my teeth and only the furry seed remains. Then I toss the seed into the savannah and bid it grow and fructify (a word Aunt Ethel made me look up after a whipping to do with my body as the fruit of my mother's tree) a seed, as the headmaster would have it, with twigs for legs and twigs for arms and a fruit on top for a head. I sprint off the saddle towards the inviting green wall. My grandfather is somewhere in there and two of his sons and two sons-in-law. And maybe my mother too. A war rages somewhere in there. I veer off the path and hit dry, crenellated mud. I dismount and push the bicycle. A calypso pops into my head, an old hit about a lover who wishes to rekindle the fire with an old flame that he happens to meet at a party. The problem is she is with another man and she appears to forget her former lover. His song reminds her of old times and suggests new ones just as hot and saucy.

> Mud in you eye
> Make you can't cry
> Make you can't see
> You the one for me
>
> Me the eye doctor
> Show me your retina
> Your water run free
> After a spell with me

Before I could flatten and slide under doors I sang this with the other children and saw a man in a white coat correcting the faulty sight of a grateful woman patient. After I saw a few things in my flattened condition I realised there wasn't a stitch between the two and he did not care a jot about her vision, he had bigger things in store for her and him.

I whistle the jaunty tune and mouth the drum solo and try to walk with the necessary bounce in my feet. As the forest looms, I grow louder. I look up as far back as my neck extends and cannot believe that a tree stands so tall. The light darkens under a green filter and cools the moment I step into the shade. The air thickens with moisture. Ziggurat paths lead in all directions. I follow one path that shadows a track for large vehicles. I decide I am a messenger bearing an important message from one Abrahams to another Abrahams and none other. I practise aloud in my deepest voice. The message is a personal security matter and I have the highest authority behind me to convey it. Where is it? Show the important government seal or some sign of officialdom? Ha, there is the catch. This message is so private I have it in my head and can say it only to the relevant party. I have special training and no means can extract this message from me. I am an Abrahams bearing a message of the gravest importance for another Abrahams. Let me pass.

I see the long vines that Tarzan uses in his films to travel first-class in the jungle. They drip and tangle with each other. In the black-and-white films where he teaches a curly haired boy all the secrets of life in the wild I placed myself in the role of that boy as every girl must do, I suppose. Yellow and red flowers with open mouths bigger than my body aim up at me. Some leaves are so broad one of them wraps twice around the child that I once was, the thin slip of a girl, but not around the young woman I am now. One of the leaves might make me a very tight and very short skirt. But then I would need high heels to go with that skirt and a low-cut midriff showing blouse and rouge lipstick and a pimp for protection!

There are long roots above ground, thick as a man's leg, that fold, twist and turn in their growth and seem about to rise up and encircle me and my bicycle and crush both of us. My bicycle becomes an encumbrance, the very thing my Aunt Ethel often accused me of being to the family. I understand I need to get rid of it. Rather than lose it, I decide to take my chances on the main road. I know that a bicycle is worth more than a child, more than a pig, as much as a cow and nearly as much as a donkey and cart; the next best thing is a motorbike and the most luxurious, a car.

When I was a mere slip of a girl I nailed the two joined sawn-off ends of empty tin cans together to make a wheel. And I drove two of these makeshift wheels into a foot-long piece of wood that served as an axle. I attached the two wheels and axle to a long stick. Then with string for a steering mechanism running down that long stick and to the axle, I managed to approximate the motility of a motor car complete with my flapping tongue and rattling lips for an engine. That was back then.

What can I do now to safeguard this bicycle? I look around and feel at a loss. Nothing suggests itself to me as likely to work as something completely different like the ends of tin cans for wheels and string to steer a wooden axle. All I see as I stare is a tangled mass of green, green leaves, green moss on the massive trunks of trees, knotted vines thick as beards, and light painted green. But as I stare at leaves, branches, vines and green light each appears to untangle from the rest and stand out as singular and adaptable. I begin to see each for what it might become. A way to safeguard my bicycle emerges from the separation of all those things even though it lasts for an instant and scrambles back into the chaos of its outward appearance when I blink.

I grab a vine and rustle up a reef knot learned from watching an uncle askance. I tie the knotted vine to the crossbar of the bicycle. Then I walk with the bicycle until the vine extends fully and pulls the bicycle backwards and stops me from taking another step. I reef knot a second vine to the crossbar to hold the bicycle against the pull of the first vine. And I push the bicycle in a direction at a tangent to both vines, one that extends the second vine and keeps the first vine from slackening. When the second vine exerts as much pull as the first and stops me from walking another step I reach for another vine and knot this third one to the crossbar beside the other two. I drag the bicycle over gnarled roots and around the trunks of trees wide as huts, too wide to see behind them, while keeping the two vines extended and lengthening the third until it stops me from moving another inch. I reach for a fourth vine and tie it to the crossbar and this is where my father's boots come in useful since they help me to pin the bike in place long enough to complete this difficult final knot. Then I release my grip on the bicycle and the vines pull on the bicycle and it sails into the air, rising into the green light that cooks high in the trees, sending butterflies scattering out of its path. And the bicycle only stops rising when the three vines pull on the fourth vine until it is taut.

I look up at the wheels turning slowly about thirty feet above me and the bicycle bouncing slightly as the vines sway against the bicycle-weight and each other's torque. In my struggle with the surrounding vegetation to attach the bicycle to one vine then another vine the dynamo must have flicked from its off position to rest against the back tyre. As the wheel turns the head and taillights glow dully. I wait for the wheel to stop and the lights to die but the wheel keeps spinning and operating the dynamo and the bicycle lights continue to shine. Air bike mounted by a ghost rider pulling trees by their vines, relocating a rain forest, take me with you.

I beg the vines to take good care of the bicycle and promise the bicycle to return for it. I draw my knife from my waistband and mark three moss-green trunks nearest to the bicycle with giant A's working around the fat lianas that ensnare the trunks. As I walk I pause every time I cannot see the last tree I marked and I add another A to the nearest mossy trunk. I continue marking my path of palms, bamboo and hardwoods. I pause to scrape one patch of tree trunk clear of a few handfuls of the million beetles that crawl on it, until I reach the makeshift road wide enough for trucks, armoured cars and tanks. There I etch the biggest A of all on a tree too fat for the road to do anything but go around it. This last A is not quite complete. The final downstroke needs to be widened to match the rest of the letter. I take a couple of steps back from my handiwork to inspect it before resuming my digging, carving and chipping at the trunk. As I add the finishing touches to my A, a voice challenges me to identify myself and step into the road and keep my hands in clear view. I raise my arms and slow the action of raising them when I see that both of them are green, even the palms and deep under the fingernails, and my shirt and trousers too, all deep green. I imagine my hair and face to be bright green too. I wonder about my teeth and tongue and eyes. I lick my index finger and the voice shouts another warning to keep my hands up, but it sounds far off. I touch my face and examine the finger and it is as green as before I licked it. I lift my hands over my head until they are straight and shake them so that the sleeves ride up my arms some more and expose a little of the arm above the elbows and sure enough my upper arms are green too. I feel giddy. To stop myself from toppling to the ground I take a deep breath and shout in my deepest rendition of a man's voice that I am an Abrahams. I am an Abrahams. I am an Abrahams and I turn from the tree branded with my initial to face my inquisitors.

The only house I know, where I learned all there is for a girl child to know about running a home and about men and women and the private ways they share, where is it? The house with a name to be proud of, surrounded by land as far as sight and owned by that name known up and down the land, that house now seems far away. Yet I need it now more than ever, its sense of proportion, of fixed angularity and a roof for all weathers. I strayed beyond my name. If the boundaries of it cannot extend this far and I am truly alone, dependent on my own resources, on something other than my name, what would that be but a quality owed to my mother? I ask the spirits of my mother and my father to set aside their differences and join hands on my behalf and help me with all their adult wisdom and strength. I straighten to my full height and I march towards the army jeep and the two soldiers poised around it with their rifles trained on me. As I draw nearer to them they step back and look at each other, utter expletives and holy denominations and make the sign of the cross and without exchanging a word they jump into the jeep and zip away clutching their rifles and helmets.

I chase the jeep at a fast walk-pace, deeper into the forest and walk into the middle of a downpour. From a dry step to a wet one, from one moment walking in humidified air to penetrating a wall of water, it feels as though I crossed from a dry land to a wet land, across a border from one country of air to another country of water, without warning. My upturned face stings with the lash of a torrent of fat raindrops. I soak and drip in seconds. I sink my knife into my waistband, lift my arms above my head and turn, roped to the rain, made airborne by it to spin on the web of this downpour. My mouth fills. I drink. I open my eyes under rain.

My mother and father are in the rain and they hold me by the arms and turn me. I see no more than a few feet ahead. I close my eyes and keep my face upturned and relish the sting and prod of the downpour. Rivulets form in the road and muddy my boots, which double in weight with mud. The fresh water cools me and slows my brisk walk to a stroll. The dark clouds evaporate and the sun falls with the strength of a shower. I cross back to the land of air or walk through the cannonade of a waterfall to the dry and muffled noise behind it. I want my parents to stay but they retreat to the same distance as the rain clouds drifting to another part of the forest with the rain in strings tied to the tops of trees. I march in big strides with a little bounce to my step and add a verse of my own to a calypso beat. A fledgeling calypso, a wisp of a beat, no more, no less than a hop and a drop in my stride and a double click-pause-double click of my left thumb and middle finger, a clockwork nodding of the head and an involuntary smile.

> I cause men to run
> and I don't have gun
> I green like a tree
> Bethany Bettany
>
> I am my mother
> and my own father
> a daughter of air
> with roots everywhere

Engines approach. I pluck my knife from my waistband and conceal it in my left boot and wait for them to clear the bend and find me. Three jeeps with men standing in them pull up. All wear army fatigues but one of them clutches a Bible and a long silver cross on the outside of his uniform. I stuff my wet hat in my waistband and raise my hands above my head, lace my fingers and rest my palms on the top of my head. I lost the pins on my hair during the downpour, stealthy fingers plucked them from under my hat. The man with the Bible points his right hand at my raised arms and then at the ground.

You see anything unusual, miss?

I drop my arms to my side and reply in my sweetest voice.

No, what you mean?

These men say they see a buckoo near here.

I inspect my brown arms and my clothes restored to the white shirt and khaki trousers and hide my surprise at not seeing green from head to toes, no longer the colour of my immediate environment, a characteristic of the buckoo. The heavy rain and the sun treated me like a piece of laundry.

Why you out here in a restricted area, miss?

My bicycle punctured and I had to leave it by the road and now I can't find it.

He orders me to climb aboard. He wants to know my name and where I live. I say I am looking for the Abrahams of Boundary. He replies that everybody is looking for them, orders from the top brass.

You live at the big house in Boundary?

Yes, sir.

Tell me a little about it.

Well, I live there with my uncles and aunts and cousins and grandmother but my grandfather lost in the bush among one of several Amerindian tribes, and my father dead and my mother gone and she left me there for twelve years now.

He raises his eyebrows and announces everything I tell him into the mouthpiece of a radio. After much crackling I think I hear that I should be brought to the camp right away and treated with the utmost care. The preacher-soldier turns to me squashed between him and another soldier and wonders how much of the radio exchange is understood by me. I feign ignorance, say the static spoiled it for me, shrug my shoulders and add that I do not understand what he is driving at. He smiles and I can tell by the half-formed nature of his smile that he thinks I know exactly what is going on, even though I do not. He says his orders from the top brass are to take good care of me and that he and I will find those missing Abrahams together.

The rest of the drive is bumpy with hairpin bends, near misses of oncoming vehicles, all military, and the odd skid off the rocky sand road on to the rockier verge and back again. The three jeeps race along and the art of the drive seems to be to find a stretch of road without a pothole. This entails driving on the left and right side of the road and passing oncoming traffic in single file in places just to be able to use the same patch of good road. Sometimes the jeep veers so far into the lane of oncoming traffic that I fear a head-on collision but at the last moment the jeep gives up right of way. Or else a massive truck comes at us on our side of the road and wins right of way as our jeep veers into potholes in the other lane in what amounts to a game of chicken. Every time the drivers of the passing vehicles gesture madly at each other and complain bitterly to any passenger who notices. Mostly the other passengers seem resigned to this near-death experience and I am the only one who gasps at each near miss.

I look twice at something on the roadside. The preacher-soldier quickly apologises for what I see even before I know for sure what I am looking at. A man is stretched out on his back, his mouth agape, eyes wide, his body neatly arranged with his arms by his side and his bare feet together. I expect him to be in uniform not a simple cloth wrapped around his body. Red sand from the road coats him. Water sprouts in my eyes involuntarily. The preacher-soldier explains how bodies just appear out of the bushes overnight and a truck spends all its time driving along the road picking them up but the truck is late for this one.

He speaks quickly and emphatically as if in a pulpit, I think to calm me, but with me as his only audience since the others pay no attention. He says this country's defence forces are famous for not having an air force or a navy and infamous for producing some of the world's most effective mercenaries from its standing army who end up in conflicts in Southern Africa, the Middle East and the Balkans. Trained largely in Cuba or by Cubans, the army personnel see war as a matter not of large swathes of territory to be won or lost but the land as a quilt to be expanded patch by patch. In this sense the kind of war now being fought suits it ideally; the only problem is the same is true of the other side. It too lacks an effective air force and navy and its forces also employ guerrilla tactics to compensate for other technical deficiencies.

He says I should know all this, if I do not know it already, because of my name. His voice blends with the engine noise, with the shifts of the gear to circumvent an axle-breaking hole or accelerate along a clear stretch. The holes sometimes ten feet wide and three feet deep mark where trees grew. The roots disappeared in the jaws of a bulldozer a long time ago and dirt ferried in by trucks filled in the hole. But sedimentation never stops in the porous ground and after some months a depression appears at the filled-in root base and in another few months a pothole more like a sinkhole. In one hole I spot the top of a young tree peeping above ground. In another the rusty wreck of a jeep stripped of its wheels and trimmings.

I close my eyes for the last few miles and invent a game. I guess how large the pothole might be by how much the jeep veers to the left or right side of the road. It keeps my head clear of that mannerly roadside corpse accruing sand in its open mouth. Failing that I conjure a picture of the big, white house and the yard around it. I slide into a light sleep and dream of my aunts and uncles on the balcony of the big house flinging their words into the night air, so many words that they wrap themselves around the house and find me crouched in a cupboard with my hands over my ears. They talk about my father, mother and me as if all three of us are dead. I think nothing of the murderous actions they credit to my name. In their talk I am nearly five years old and living with my mother and father in London. I know this by heart because I heard it countless times, but in my dream my father lives throughout my childhood to repair his absence from my living memory.

MOTHER

When I first arrived in England with your father you were more than a twinkle in my eye. On the hop-over flight to Trinidad and then Barbados we could hardly bear to sit next to each other and just kiss and hold hands. On the transatlantic leg while the plane slept or a few insomniacs watched movies your father and I burning for each other after hours of kissing our lips raw and squeezing our hands numb made our way to the back of the plane and into a vacant toilet. And there we stayed keeping our voices low and our elbows tucked in away from the thin walls until we had our fill of each other. Going back to our seats and not bothering even a little about what those insomniacs might have thought we were doing back there so long seemed typical of us then. When he was not trying to entice me back to the bathroom he talked about his beloved river surveyor's job and a unique way of coping with big city life. He said he felt so good with me in that plane the jet had to be a submarine flying through the sea, the element he loved, rather than nearly a mile over it.

I must tell you about his madcap scheme of coping with London. Although Georgetown prepared me a little for London I adapted his scheme and even improved it for him. You would find it hard to think that two grown people – your parents – could subscribe to a notion of looking at English people as lost souls only our evangelical gaze could save, but that is how much we missed Boundary; that is how scared we both felt in London.

BETHANY

I thought if I did not look at English people, they would stop living. And since I loved them to begin with, I gave everyone I could fit into my waking hours the blessing of my attention, including my parents, who took on Englishness in one way or another. One look from me conferred a lifetime on them. For this reason South London's high street crowds terrified me. As everybody streamed past me, I feared that I would not fit them all into my sights, and therefore the missed ones would die through no fault of their own. With a new population to save everyday I had no time to devote to the place, its rules and regulations, habits and customs, dislikes and fears.

I worked out a way of assessing souls in one sweep of my eyes over their bodies, from the tops of their heads to the tips of their toes. I tried to think of one fact about each body and this gave them an especially long and charmed life. What full and gorgeous lips on my mother! What long and tapering fingers on my father's hands!

My eyes mopped up a typical high street in groups ranging from five to ten people, otherwise there was no way to get through everyone. I called these instances my mass savings, like the Pope blessing an entire stadium in a few sweeps of his arm, but on a mini-scale. I did not bother to memorise any single feature. They would just have to live and be happy that they were alive. No special gift would be bestowed on them. That would teach them for catching my attention in a public place. They would live ordinary lives, lives without distinction and pass away and hardly anyone would care. But better to have lived than not to have lived at all. At least that's what my mother said, and often: that life was a gift and I was lucky to have it, that it should not be squandered but lived preciously.

That time was an eternal flame but the little sulphur of a life struck up its flare and perished, as fast as a struck match.

I did everything in my power to be cheerful every day. I knew that if I got out of bed 'on the wrong side', as my mother always said when I was in a bad mood in the morning, it would result in several murders as I deliberately ignored approaching footsteps, shadows and voices. All of them begged for confirmation among the living from me. In my anger I would withhold the blessing of my stare, refuse to look around at them, keep my eyes on a spot on the floor as they shuffled around me, and turn my back on the appeal of a voice. And they would keel over quietly and inexplicably and be no more. I decimated Deptford High Street and Lewisham Shopping Centre in this mood, whipped up every time my mother and father quarrelled, which they seemed to do with shorter intervals of peace, greater and greater seriousness and a matching disregard for the witnessing eyes and ears of their only child. Among a crowd in a public place my eyes were open but I didn't see. I allowed the world to become a blur, a glare. It slid off my retina without trace.

The hardest thing was not to be angry with my mother and my father. You see looking at someone once was all right if I did not have to see them ever again, but if I lived with them then I had to give them their right to live on a day-by-day basis. This renewable licence to practise living became a burden for me. I had to remember to take in my father crossing the room to get to the front door as he disappeared for a day of work. Sometimes with a kind word if he and mum were in agreement, but in a huffed silence if they had rowed. Otherwise he would leave the house unseen by me and perhaps never return. If I missed him in the morning I had to make sure I saw him when he returned and before I fell asleep or else he would surely perish in his sleep. This ruined many of my days. I thought about having to see him before bedtime, minute by minute thinking about him as I worked my way through the nursery school day. I wondered how he was getting along wherever he was and even practised seeing him with a theodolite and knee-deep at work in one of London's network of canals or standing over someone in a supervisory capacity as if I could bless him in his absence. I could not. The golden rule in my gift of life-giving sight stipulated that a person had to be there before my eyes, in the flesh and in the same space and at the same hour as me. There wasn't a way to bless them in some virtual reality or imagined incarnation or by remote control. There was no future for my gifts in cyberspace.

My mother was easy to bless because she rarely failed to make me happy. I was not a happy child. I hardly smiled. It's just that my mother knew me so well she knew what to do to draw me out of my sombre shell. I was not a morning child. I woke up feeling I needed to be stirred from sleep in some other less sudden fashion than my alarm clock rattling my brain or my mother shaking me like one of her carpets that she hung out of the window and shook to get rid of the dust. Yet mornings my mother found some exhilarating thing to say, such as, How is my clever girl today? Or if she was in a hurry and had a toothbrush in her mouth or a piece of toast she mustered a big smile and a rapid hug. So I was always able to send her salaams of longevity right away, even before I had said a word to a living soul. Live, mother, live! And she seemed to thrive until my father left her and me. She beamed with youth and energy. She sang or hummed as she tidied the house. When she walked by closely her movements were so brisk I felt a rush of cool air in her wake. But she stepped lightly and moved with economy so that I couldn't match the breeze with her quietness. She talked to friends on the phone beside the armchair and gestured emphatically throughout as if they were seated right there opposite her on the double sofa. Her hands were busy taking things out of drawers and cabinets and putting things away. Delicate things, bulky things, it was all one with her hands, all seemed to be one thing done effortlessly and without any fuss so that I hardly noticed their flurry of activity and the fact that they never stopped. I realise now that I have no picture of my mother ever sitting with her hands resting on her thighs or on a table in front of her. I saw a hummingbird pruning the air in a nature programme on the BBC and decided that my mother with her always-busy hands and still body must be a species of hummingbird.

MOTHER

On our frequent walks along the banks of the Thames at Greenwich, your father always pointed out the watermark and told us that was how high the last tide had climbed. He made us examine the wood (although I never knew for sure what I was supposed to look for) or guess at the percentage of exposed clay on the riverbed. Like me you grew accustomed to the moment that became a standard fixture of these walks when he made his big speech. He stopped us all in our tracks and pointed at the riverbank nearest us, with both of his arms, his palms pressed together: 'This wood bracing these banks comes all the way from the Amazonian basin. Greenheart wood is the toughest wood in the world. It's been here for two hundred years.'

You asked him why the wood was named 'greenheart'. Was it because the heart was really green? He paused and considered your question, then smiled and said, that was correct and you were a clever little girl.

I wanted a piece of the Amazon's greenheart wood, just a sliver, from the banks of the Thames to keep in a pocket next to my heart in your father's absence.

Bethany

When my father walked out of our lives I found myself for the first time not trying to save him and bless him with all the luck a day could bring. I was in the reverse situation of trying to think his life away, will his death in addition to trusting that he was doomed to expire without me around to consecrate his body. In my recrudescent story of double indemnity, designed to get my father one way or another (he would either die from my active curses or from his absence from the redeeming radiation of my sight), there was no room for laughter. I stopped smiling even when my mother greeted me in the morning. I watched her with a long face knowing that I was extending her life for another day of despair at the thought of my father with another woman. I stopped talking. She reciprocated. We seemed to sense in each other a need for extraordinary peace and quiet or a kept silence, like some kind of cacophony-fast, endured in the hope that it would engineer my father's return and we could once again feast on conversation with each other.

But the days accrued. My mother's hands continued to busy themselves. We heard nothing from my father. Every time the phone rang, I held my breath and listened for my mother to say his name but it turned out to be a friend of hers offering commiseration which invariably left her in tears for up to half an hour after she hung up. Even then her hands would fold and unfold one of her embroidered handkerchiefs, or smooth her dress, or put a stray piece of hair off her forehead and back on top of her skull if not behind an ear. I watched her and I knew to stay out of her way. If I lingered too close to her she brushed me off with a wave of her hand. Failing that she assigned me an especially repetitive chore, like washing the cutlery in the drawer to keep it spick and span as she put it, or picking up every little thing around the house that belonged to my array of dolls. It felt worse to earn that dismissive wave of her hand, in the sense that my heart pained me, than the smouldering anger I experienced at having to polish all the black shoes or all the brown shoes in the house on old newspapers spread on the tiled kitchen floor.

The phone gradually died, asphyxiated by the mounting days of my father's absence. No one rang for me. I knew people but they weren't phone types. We were all too young. I saw them and we talked or I did not, in which case we did not talk. In our separate lives we busied ourselves and did not think to pick up the phone and share a thought, anecdote or make a plan. We simply met and talked and parted having said all we needed to say until the next accidental meeting. My father seemed to be such a man. When out of his sight you somehow failed to exist for him. No amount of linking technology could entice him to check on your wellbeing. The phone messages left at his workplace and with mutual friends brought nothing in return. It hardly seemed worth the effort and the disappointment since it left her and me immobilised for hours at a time waiting for the phone to ring with news of him.

My father walked out of the front door to go to work and I watched him cross the room, watched his knuckles whiten around the handle of his mottled leather briefcase. I memorised how his free right hand swung hardly at all and how his long fingers hanging loose appeared boneless and capable of stretching to several times longer than their relaxed state. Him with his briefcase and his huffed silence, too angry with my mother to spare a measly 'boo' for his child watching his departure. Perhaps he left impelled by those hands of his that did not want to be seen by me again. They preferred one long look to the daily routine of life-affirming glances. Maybe he was lying dead somewhere having failed to make it back the next day and for several days after that for the lightning bolt of my renewing look.

I asked my mother if she was certain he was still alive. She screwed up her round face and tensed those fleshy lips as if I'd thrown cold water on them. I was surprised by her reaction to my question. It occurred to me that I had inadvertently revealed something sinister about the workings of my mind to my mother. I immediately sought to correct it.

I mean have you heard from him.

Not directly.

Apparently, Evangeline received a call from him and reported to my mother that he was doing fine in his new situation. I wanted to know when Evangeline heard from him. But Mother walked off before I could blurt out another question, like what exactly was he doing with his time after work. She turned on her heels with such a flurry I knew better than to follow and pester her. She worked on the presumption that the less she said to me the better since every piece of information about him in his other life would only sully his name and poison the days of his eventual return to her and me. What she didn't realise was that I talked to myself, filling in my own details about the situation for those not supplied by her. I overheard my mother on the phone in her bedroom talking to Evangeline as I loitered outside the door. They must be on different shifts. I liked to linger by my mother's bedroom and play boyfriend and girlfriend with a couple of my dolls as I waited for her to emerge and play with me or invite me in to help her with some job around the house. I heard my mother say how she hated my father for walking away from us as if he were discarding rubbish that blocked one of his precious canals. The reply from Evangeline on the other end of the line must have had something to do with changing the locks since Mum added that she would also give away Dad's twenty prized suits and thirty pairs of shoes and forty work shirts to the Salvation Army. She said that as far as she was concerned he was a lousy father to his daughter. Then she said something was dying inside her. And I took her to mean that her love for him housed in her body and fed and watered by her as long as he was by her side was now in his prolonged absence starved to death's door. I peeled myself away from her bedroom door unable to stomach any more. I thought I was the only one willing my father's disappearance off the map. With my mother and her friends pooling their collective venom against him I feared he really did not stand a chance of making it in this life another day, much less of ever coming back to our house.

MOTHER

I sat on a dining room chair combing your hair in the usual way with you plunked on the floor and lodged between my open legs. Sometimes you draped your bony arms over my fleshy thighs. And I wanted to trade some of my flesh for a little of your skin and bones. This time you just sat keeping your arms to yourself. We faced the 21-inch colour television and I provided my usual running commentary about one of my favourite ongoing dramas, interspersed with offers of nuggets of wisdom to you, my only daughter, that were meant to shape the girl into a respectable woman.

Why doesn't she tell him where to get off, there are other pubs out there to find work in.

You should always bend your knees when you pick up something off the floor.

She should have wised up by now about that boy and his gallivanting ways.

After you leave the house don't touch your face unless you can see yourself in a mirror.

This time I did something new, something I had no intention of doing. I trailed away from my television and life commentary combined and held forth on your father.

If he thinks he can waltz in here after a week like nothing happened he has another think coming.

I have never known a man who uses people like your father. He doesn't even have the decency to pick up the phone and ask after you. It's as if we weren't alive. I am not going to wait on him for much longer. Changes are going to be made around here. He's going to get a big surprise.

BETHANY

Then she bent forward and looked around into my face and saw me, the one who should be protected from all things acrimonious and she went dumb and flicked me one of her beautiful smiles that stretched and whitened her big red lips. Her eyes were red and her face was wet. I must have looked bewildered. She invented an instant task for me to complete – I say invent because when she narrowed her eyes and said something I could tell she was making it up as she went along – something I had to fetch for her from a point furthest away from her that would give her time to blow her nose and dry her eyes. And where was my father? Somewhere, looking into salt water, a salt-water pool filled with the product of her eyes. He would have her and the element he loved. Her water sweetened by her.

MOTHER

Your father returned late at night more like early in the morning. You slept through it all. I opened the door for him after he knocked on the frosted pane for ages and pleaded with me to let him in. I could not bear to hear a man beg like that with the song and dance of the Demerara river in his voice. I relented for your sake and with extra care to minimise the noise braced myself against the door and unlatched it and unhooked the security chain just to stop him waking you with his baby talk begging. He tried to put his hands on me but I would not let him touch me in that way. He would not let me sleep and said all he wanted from me was a cuddle. I shrugged him off. He stopped trying to touch me and talked me back to our earliest days together. You pollster you, he said, knowing full well that I would think of my name for him, rooster, and it would make me smile. He mentioned the airplane and I almost doubted him that he and I would do such a thing. He tried to touch me again as I laughed at the picture of the two of us in that cramped cubicle, a flurry of limbs, and I relented. One thing led to another. Afterwards we wondered whether you were conceived at 35,000 feet or in Boundary or Georgetown. We catalogued the occasions we were together in a catholic sense up until that flight. We arrived at a number less than ten but had to multiply it by three or four because on each occasion we made love not once or twice but quite a few times, except on that jet. We decided that you were so special that each of these times only contributed to one part of you, each time we assembled you piece by piece so that you were made whole over several of these declarations of our love.

He wanted to sleep late so he stuck wax earplugs deep in his ear canal and swallowed two of my sleeping pills that I reserve for my sanity when I work nights and sleep days.

BETHANY

I woke up in my bed though I fell asleep beside her. He was asleep in their bed. She ordered me not to wake him. She promised that I would see enough of him when he woke up in an hour or so. I had to prepare for school. She needed a certain brush to style my hair. Would I be a darling and fetch it for her from the bedroom? But I was to be especially quiet and not wake him.

What about his ear plugs. Isn't he wearing them?

Yes, but your father can hear in his sleep.

Didn't he take sleeping pills?

Yes, little miss inquisition, but do not forget your father can hear without paying the slightest bit of attention.

Yes, that's daddy all right.

She sent me into her bedroom to bring the brush with the small pink blobs on the end of the bristles. This would take a minute or two since my mother had the biggest collection of brushes known to humanity. Every week when she gathered me to go grocery shopping in Lewisham or Deptford or both she would be sure to hunt out a new brush if not at the open-air market then in a nearby shop. If she found a brush I ended up getting a treat but if she was luckless I was too no matter how much I begged and whined. This made me hunt with her for a brush, holding up one after another to be flicked a cursory, No, from her, or, I got that one last time, or, I already have two of those, until I struck gold. She would stop and examine my find, while I watched, motionless, and held my breath. She would turn the brush left and right under the shop's fluorescent lights, or the market stall's natural light strained through cloud, and take forever to nod her approval to my immediate reanimation and broad smile.

The brush she wanted had no back to it. It was round and covered with pink-knobbed bristles embedded in rubber and the rubber encased in plastic. The handle was black and made of plastic. I knew it from the times she slumped in her armchair after a day at the hospital attending to the incurably ill and invited me, if I was in her vicinity, to brush her hair by standing behind the armchair. Of all the brushes I happened upon that was one of the few that allowed a child's hand to grip it properly. I dived into her room promising myself I would not even glance at the bed with my father bundled in it. I kept the whole of my head full of a picture of that porcupine of a brush. But I noticed, not her dressing table piled with four baskets of brushes, nor her heart-shaped and pear-shaped bottles of lilac and pink perfumes, nor all the bright Guyanese gold earrings, bangles and necklaces piled up in untidy bundles. I saw four bottles of my father's rum-coloured after-shave grouped on the dresser. He had returned and he had unpacked his aftershave. His razor had to be nearby. I walked up to the dresser with its main mirror and two movable side-mirrors so that three main reflections greeted me, along with their suggestion of infinity. I opened the bottles and sniffed at the sickly-sweet contents and my father streamed out of those bottles. He crossed the room in his dark suit and briefcase. The fingers of his right hand stretched and dragged on the floor like an empty giant's glove. He smiled at me and gestured with his hand brought to his mouth and ear that he would phone me. And instead of replacing the screw top I tipped all of the contents into the nearest basket of brushes and on to the bed. I picked up a book of matches from one of their restaurant visits that was next to the basket. I selected a match from the middle row, had a little trouble tearing it off, heard a recording of my mum's many warnings about the dangers of playing with matches and her addressing me for real now, *Girl, what's taking you so long?* I struck the match, once, twice, along the abrasive strip. It flared and filled my head. I steadied my hand, and the match-head settled into an orange flame and right away changed its mind and began to climb the stalk of itself towards my middle finger and thumb. I flicked it on to the basket. The brushes whooshed into flowering fire. I struck another match, faster this time, and threw it on to the bed.

Girl, what are you doing? My mother again. This time louder and sterner. Her tone harboured an as yet unformatted threat, something she would have to think up on the spot with the help of her narrowing eyes. The basket of brushes with flames in the middle of arranging themselves sprang into three reflections and their multiplication to the nth degree in the two side mirrors. My father stank in that fire. Then the nausea of burning plastic as my mother's brushes began to crumple and melt and smoke. *Girl, if I have to call you one more time it's you and me today.* When my mother utters this ultimatum I know the end result is a painful twist of an ear, a slap on the arms or a quick rap of her knuckles on my skull. But I could go further. I could earn a beating with her belt – a quaint exercise of skipping around her to evade her swipes as she held on to an arm and swung at the legs with one of my father's belts wrapped twice round her wrist. She used this tone when she argued with my father. All I had to do was remain still and quiet and force her to come to me to see who the little woman was who dared to ignore three of her warnings.

MOTHER

Our quarrels began innocently, so innocently in fact that you would be playing in the same room hardly aware of the conflagration. One time your father reported that he saw some new graffiti in the toilets at his workplace. Not new in content since it demanded an England for whites only, but new because he hadn't seen it there before. He wondered if it was related to the march by right-wing extremists at the weekend, a stirring-up of what he saw as futile hostility. He even cracked his usual joke about how he did not come crawling to England, that he was here by express invitation from Her Majesty's Government to save London's blood vessels. He called the canals veins, and the Thames the city's artery, clogged with mattresses and shopping trolleys and old car tyres and the rusted shells of stripped cars.

There was a severe shortage of river surveyors in London at one time. It prompted the government to invite the likes of your father to cross the Atlantic all the way from South America. I never doubted that it was true, that some invitation originated somewhere from England, but I couldn't believe the solicitation had anything to do with a government that condoned public displays of hate against the very same people. The odd thing about your father was that he felt strongly that these extreme organisations should be allowed the freedom to express their views. He said, and I quote, *The democracy is constructed on the premise of freedom of expression.* He thought since they had nothing substantial to add to any political debate beyond their hate-based sloganeering, they would gradually wither and disappear in the heat of daily political life.

Naturally, I opposed this view of your father's. I said freedom of speech was one thing but incitement through hateful language to actual violence against black people (to me blacks included everyone who was a distinct minority, Asians from South Asia and the Far East, Jews and Arabs) was another matter altogether. It had nothing to do with democracy and everything to do with exploiting the goodwill of a system. I had to get this in very quickly. I talked, fearful that I would not be able to complete a thought without interruption from him. But he always listened until I reached a natural pause before he launched his counter-offensive.

We carried on like this for many minutes until things turned from silly politics to trading personal insults. You tried to interrupt us with culinary requests or the rapid onset of ailments like headaches and stomach cramps. You even picked up a valuable ornament that you knew you should not touch and began to play with it hoping that it would distract me. But I took the ornament from your hand and carried on rowing even if it meant shouting a reply from another room. From one calling the other politically naive, it would become that it was really a lack of intelligence that was the root of the problem. Then we reverted to one-word name-calling. His were basically synonyms of idiotic. Mine all had to do with his inveterate womanising. Then your father walked out of the room, and then the house, in a huffed silence.

BETHANY

The stifling heat made me back away involuntarily. I raised my arms as if to fend off the blows of an assailant. I must have bumped into the bedroom door on my backwards retreat and caused it to swing open baring the whole scene to my mother. I heard her scream. She shouted *God Almighty!* Or words to that effect. And she was beside me that instant, moving in leaps and bounds with her lips parted and her dark eyes ringed by white. She dragged me from the doorway, dived into the burgeoning cloud, gathered her quilt off the bed and swooped it over the flames. Then she grabbed a pillow and piled that on top and beat on the pillow with her arms. Smoke billowed from the quilt, so much smoke that I could see nothing but infinite cloud in the three dresser mirrors.

The way my mother rushed into the room to hug the basket of fire I knew my father with his pyrotechnic fingers would have done it differently. During a prolonged power cut when all the houses of Blackheath burned candles, my father went from room to room with me behind him, snuffing out each candle at his allotted 9 p.m. lights-out time. He rubbed out the flame between his index finger and thumb, whereas my mother would blow at the candles a couple of times and tut-tut if she blew too hard and made wax, pooled around the wick, spray on to the furniture. I saw him striding into the bedroom to lace his elastic fingers around the burning basket and snuff it out as if it was one of a number of lit baskets dotted about the house.

I opened the front door and hesitated for a second unsure what to do next. I thought I should shout, *Fire!* or something, to attract people's attention. The first phone was back in the living room that now had a fresh crop of smoke in it. The second was in my parents' bedroom.

I could hear coughing above my crying. I stopped making any noise so that I could listen. I mouthed, *Mummy, Mummy*. I thought of calling my father's name. He would know what to do right now. When Mum and he were on good terms she referred to his quick wits, his ability to think of something to say that managed to be funny the second someone said something to him that called for a funny response. Rather than laugh with the rest of us he would come up with a funnier remark. The same applied to his reflexes. If he dropped something he caught it before it landed on his clothes or the floor. I saw him lift a piece of toast with a sliver of egg balanced on it. The egg slid off the bread, and whereas it would have deposited itself on the front of my shirt or my mother's starched white nurse's uniform, he flicked his hand down in time to catch that egg before it landed and greased his shirt and tie. The same rapid reflex to match his rapid-fire tongue came into play when my mother threw the car keys to him without warning. They quarrelled and came to the end of a string of personal insults and he was about to leave the house and reached the front door empty-handed when he turned to greet my mother's pitch of those keys at him. His right arm darted up as if about to scratch his brow but in actual fact it was to meet those keys in mid-air and pluck them off the stem of their trajectory.

MOTHER

The last time I felt this way I was with you on a grocery shopping expedition doubled as a brush-hunting one too for my sanity and my delight. The high street was busy as ever but a march we knew nothing about entered at the far end of the street and brought the Saturday morning shopping to a standstill. A megaphone issued a call and the marchers responded with a chant. Long before they came into view I could hear the order from the megaphone, *Niggers! Niggers! Niggers!* And the crowd's response of, *Out! Out! Out!* I hauled you in the opposite direction. But there was nowhere to go. The crowd of onlookers stood thick. We pushed forward but bumped against a wall of bodies and turned around to face the street like everyone else and watch the procession, knowing nothing could be done until it passed by us. You kept your head lowered and your eyes planted on the ground as they trampled past. I instructed you to *Look them straight in the eyes and don't blink, don't be the first one to look away.* But you kept your head down, though you were not afraid. I concluded that you did not wish to grant them the least bit of recognition, a little like your father and me using our eyes when we first landed to take in these people as if they could only survive with the blessing of a look from us. In reality we were so afraid and held the English in such high regard we needed a really good reason to look them in the eye. Did your father ever tell you about that madcap scheme of ours? I do not know about your father but I quickly abandoned it. I expect he passed it on to you the way country people believe every shred of their behaviour is God-given and an emblem of generation. Your father was not, like me, a believer in psychology. Whenever I mentioned Freud he quickly shouted 'boiled'.

BETHANY

People stared out of windows, filed out of doors, and crossed the street towards me. I scanned them all to make sure they would survive, even though I had scanned many of them before I couldn't be sure who was a stranger and who familiar and therefore in need of a daily once-over. I looked at my vacant front door with a thin rope of smoke starting to unravel into the open air. I took a deep breath, shut my eyes and ran up the path to the front door to be beside my mother. I heard some shouts from people for me to come back. I decided I could not stop. Things would only be different if I kept running. So I continued up a small step and through the front door. I tried to ignore the two panes of frosted glass annoyingly translucent to make out a body at the door but not sufficiently clear for me to identify the person unless they spoke, at the same time. My left shoulder hit the doorframe on my right.

That's the thing about our front door. A child could enter square on but adults always seemed to offer one shoulder or the other first in their sideways-on entrance. They created the impression that they were entering one of Alice's phases of gigantism as she struggled to be accommodated in a diminutive world. I did not like to see them enter my house in this way for the simple reason that it implied my house was somehow too small. When an adult came to the front door I looked at them as quickly as I could to confer the usual safe passage on them and then looked away fast to avoid the sight of them edging into the house.

I hit a wall of flesh quadruple my size. I could not get around this obstacle, it was planted implacably there and telling me in no uncertain terms that I had to turn back. Arms on this wall steered me from my forward dash throwing me into reverse. I was literally backed out of the house and held up from tumbling on to my back by these strong arms, too many to count.

I still had the sensation of progressing towards the bedroom. I believed that I would be there in my parents' room in a few steps. I knew it from the many late nights I had stumbled from my bedroom half-asleep to climb into their bed only to wake and find myself back in mine with no notion how I'd got from one to the other and back again. Who carried me back to my bed? My mother or my father? Her soft arms or his tapering fingers laced around my body like the ropes of a hammock? It was all the same to my dreaming body. A mother and father indistinguishable one from the other. Two parents, indivisible. Each weighed the same in my dreaming head. Their shared bed with room for one extra that I gripped the sheets of and climbed into on tiptoe, their skin and hair smell in those sheets. The harvest of their collective warmth in that bed sending me instantly into deep sleep.

I told myself to open my eyes. I coughed blindly. My eyes burnt. I squeezed them shut and tried to erase the sting with the backs of my hands. I moved or felt I was moving but without using my legs, airborne, travelling backwards the way I had come, and, simultaneously, in a forward drive towards my parents' room. They were in bed, asleep, I told myself and I merely padding along the corridor from my fitful sleep to join them. Any second now I would be in their bed and motionless, falling, rising into sleep in our commingled body-camphor. One or other of them must have listened for my breathing to right itself before launching me to my room. But which one? Who slept on the side nearest the door? My mother, who had to rise early a couple of days each week for the early nurse's shift, or my father up at 5 a.m. every morning, 'come rain or shine', as my mother would say? In my sleep they were one body. They shared the precious cargo of their baby girl, in those small hours, and, together, brought me back to my bed. My body-weight divided in half between them.

Her arms and his long fingers like the slats of a wooden bed frame and the springs of a mattress, their flesh and bones for stuffing, their skin for fabric, all for me.

I heard noise and people talking. And coughing. An orchestra whose only instruments were a bunch of constricted throats. Familiar intonations. I came to a standstill. Open your eyes, I instructed myself. I had to see whose hands I held. And whose were those strong arms that allowed me to steady myself on them? Open your eyes. They stopped stinging. I wiped them dry and opened the lids slowly as if peeping into a shoebox in which I had trapped a lizard. The soft English light was a blessing to my eyes. A painter's light. It encouraged me to raise those lids even more, as if that box with that lizard was empty after all. I thought I should look for people. Even though I did this not so long ago, others may have arrived in the short interim. Look into their faces. Clock one defining characteristic about them. Then I changed my mind. I decided not to make the effort on their behalf. Just look for Father, and if I saved a few souls by brushing past them in my search for him, all well and good. I saw my mother and I, both of us coughing up a storm and supported by several neighbours. I held out an arm towards my mother who was too distracted to take it. I couldn't see my father. I went against myself without thinking I should do so. I couldn't help it. I took in each face with a slow 270-degree turn of my head. I could hear sirens approaching. Live, I thought, do what you will with your lives.

MOTHER

I told you I called your father a pigeon when he thought of himself as a kingfisher. Well, for all his princely aspirations the most common bird in London seemed to be the pigeon. They flocked everywhere and nested in every nook and cranny of a building. The most majestic thing about them is their ability to fly, otherwise we would treat them as pests and spray them out of existence. I say all this because the one time I saw your father captivated by something to the point of a catatonic disregard for everyone and everything else around him had to do with pigeons, a flock of them. They were circling a tower block on the Pepys Estate in Deptford and we were on his beloved river sailing in his homemade boat (that's another story, but you should know that after he assembled it in the living room we had to take out the window frame to get the boat out of the house). He forgot about us and his need to tack the strong current, and stared at the birds. True they swooped around the tower in unison and even turned as one body with their wings rippling as if they comprised feathers on a huge bird. And yes, when the wings glided and when they began to beat again it all occurred as one telepathic movement. But the boat drifted into the path of a barge and leaned horribly because the current drove into the side of it and you and I clung to each other and screamed for him to do something, anything. And you know what your father did? No apology, nothing, not even an emergency mode in his actions to correct the boat's lean and get us out of the way of that barge. He tacked to the side of the river and corrected the lean of the boat and apart from the odd glance in our direction to make sure the angle of the boat righted itself, he never took his eyes off that flock. I could have killed him. We might have fallen overboard. That barge could easily have hit us. His precious flock would still be circling over our drowned heads. That was the first and last time you or I set foot on that homemade craft of his. I do not think he bothered to get a licence for it. He said it was too small to be detected by the authorities and because it was not motorised no one would care. I told him he needed to grow wings then he could be the bird he always wanted to be and circle his favourite element all day without endangering anyone else.

Bettany

The jeep slows to a crawl. I open my eyes and wipe them dry and when I look around we are in a tented city. A city, not in the sense that the capital qualifies as a city but because compared to where I come from, Boundary, a village, this place of narrow roads feeding off the main road is several times bigger and twice as busy. It does not take much more activity than this for my mind to jump from soporific village to the honorific of bustling city. Above the jeeps and trucks and horns and men shouting I hear thunder in the distance. I say thunder because I associate all the surrounding greenery with natural occurrences; what I hear is a regular boom-boom interspersed with rapid and irregular boom-boom-booms and the sky darkly clouded in the direction of the booms. I decide thunderous weather brews far off.

At this point I do not link the thunder with the guns long as lampposts with open mouths big as house gutters, mounted on wheels and dragged behind trucks. What I hear high above the trees in the sky does not match the machinery that I see on the ground. There is a problem with scale, with volume, with setting, though I can see clearly from the camp that what I take for low-lying cloud is in fact smoke manufactured by small fires in among the trees.

The jeep stops behind a row of other jeeps and trucks. We remain in the jeep parked in front of a tent that looks like all the others, a faded green, except for its larger size and a flagpole with the country's tricolour at full mast and the fact that men stream into and out of the tent carrying envelopes and small packages. Two soldiers stand to attention at the entrance. I keep seeing women and children in jeeps and trucks, on bicycles or on foot heading down side streets in twos and threes. Everyone looks muddy and dishevelled. The preacher-soldier tells me to sit tight and he marches off and explains the nature of his business to the occupants of each jeep and truck ahead of our jeep in the queue formed to visit someone important in the tent. I cannot hear what he says but I know it involves me because the men in the other vehicles look in my direction and nod in agreement with him. When he returns he announces that we are up next and the other two soldiers congratulate him. I ask him how he managed to jump the waiting list and who occupies the tent. He replies that I am an Abrahams and he cannot believe I do not know how important that is under the circumstances. What circumstances? He shakes his head in dismay. Could my grandfather be in there, I wonder. He looks at me and realises I am genuinely puzzled.

Miss, you really don't know who inside that tent?

No, sir.

I decide not to mention my grandfather. How could a failed gambler run a country and war?

Then you can't be an Abrahams. You must be an impostor. Tell me about your mother and father.

My father died. I sometimes sleep on his smooth concrete grave. My mother left me in Boundary but she keeps the Abrahams name.

Everyone within earshot now stares at me. I wonder what I said that merits their attention.

Bettany!

A boy calls my name. In this unlikely place where I do not know a soul I fail to put a face to the voice.

Bettany!

But I need only look at the young man briefly to come up with a name. Then I doubt myself for thinking it and when he signals writing with his right hand I know for sure that it must be him and I hop out of the jeep and hug him.

Fly! How you get out here?

Everybody from the orphanage come here to lend a hand for the minister who keep the orphanage open.

What minister?

He ignores my question and seems much more impressed with the company I am keeping.

Like a true Abrahams I see you riding in style in big army jeep.

I wave his remark away and do not know where to begin. I want to know how he has been keeping since our last meeting in the capital and about this place. Mud on his clothing and bare feet makes him look like a product of the camp, reared in it from birth and moulded from the soil and surrounding trees. The change of routine from his days in the capital scratching around for provisions, to life as a soldier in an army camp in the middle of a rain forest, clearly agrees with him. He smiles and his eyes shine. Despite his old army fatigues and the mud on his bare feet his skin looks smooth. I want to stay in the camp for as long as Fly keeps his smile.

An army truck pulls up and several men bail out and march directly into the big tent. I look at the preacher-soldier who shrugs his shoulders and after staring at the door for some time he turns his back and joins the other soldiers for a smoke. Fly jerks his head in the direction of a side street and on his signal we slip round the other side of the truck and run down the side street as fast as I can keep up with him. I direct my hair under my hat and hold on to the hat and the belt of my trousers. We turn right and left down muddy lane after muddy lane too narrow for a vehicle and dodge between the gaps of tents closely pegged into the ground. We jump over the ropes holding the tents upright. Fly ducks into a small tent and we flop down on to the ground and fight to catch our breaths and control our laughing. With the two of us inside it and sleeping bags pushed up against the corners, the tent is cramped and everything I touch needs to catch some sun and have the damp drawn out of it.

You know how many of we sleep in here?

I make a wild guess.

Four?

Six!

Six!

Six.

We pack in here like sardines. If one man turn we all turn. You taking up two people space right there.

I make myself smaller by drawing up my legs and folding my arms around my knees and resting my chin on them. Then he notices my clothes, especially my boots, his eyes dart over me and settle at my feet.

Why you dress like a man?

Fly, I dream all this. In my dream I come here and look for my uncles. But I never see you in my dream.

How can you say that, girl?

He jabs me on the shoulder with his writing hand in mock battle and lowers his arm before I can brush it away.

Girl, when I reach here from the capital, you the first person I look for – if the minister here, Bettany and the rest of her people bound to be here as well.

They must be looking for me.

They going find you soon enough. Meanwhile we can have some fun.

I smile not sure what he means by fun. An army camp does not strike me as synonymous with gaiety. But this is Fly, capital Fly, market Fly, Fly from the orphanage, so if anyone knows how to find anything in a place, even happiness in the middle of a war encampment, then Fly can do it.

Another boy ducks into the tent and backs up when he sees me and scowls. Fly tells him I am only visiting and we are on our way out anyway. The boy barely nods. Fly introduces me and upon hearing my name the boy whips his head around and stares at me with his mouth wide open. I reach over to him and push his bottom jaw up to rejoin the top jaw. He lowers his head and retreats into the corner of the tent just left of the entrance. I crawl out followed by Fly and the boy, but Fly tells him, 'Later,' in a way that makes it crystal clear to the boy that he is not to join us. I smile at him and he flashes all his teeth at me in an idiotic fashion and waves as if trying to catch my attention on the other side of a crowded square when in fact we are less than three feet apart. Fly tugs my arm and we dive down a narrow opening between two rows of tents. With bare feet he is lithe and difficult to follow over the ropes of the tents pegged to the ground. I call to him that I will buy him some shoes if only to slow him down a little.

I want a knife before I want any shoes.

I stop. And he runs back to join me. I retrieve my knife and offer it to him. He cannot believe it. He refuses it. I push it into his hands.

No one gives me anything.

That's because you mix with the wrong people.

He touches the curved blade from the handle to the pointed tip and whistles. I inform him that it comes from the most industrious of kitchens. He lets me know he will accept my gift since it is obvious I need to be relieved from kitchen duty. I push him gently and he stumbles in an exaggerated fashion.

Where are we going, Captain?

To eat and then see why we all here in the jungle.

I nod pleased with both parts of that equation. My time with Fly will be short. The boy back at Fly's tent will tell his friends he met me and soon the entire camp of young people will know an Abrahams has arrived. I like the idea of my change of status conferred on me by my name from another teenager to *the one*. The name is all I have and if I dissociate myself from it I am nothing in this place or anywhere else. I keep it on the tip of my tongue, turn over each of the letters and conjure the big house and everyone in it. In my mind I round up people who are not at the house – my grandfather, absent uncles and even my mother, and paste their faces in its many windows. The house grows into a fortification of a name.

Fly pulls me into a long tent with two rows of tables pushed together to form two long lines with benches on both sides and heavy wood planks laid side-by-side which shuffle underfoot. Pots steam, rice boils, beef stews, basil and thyme mollify the air. Women and children fuss over the pots.

Fly nods and smiles at everyone. He marches up to the

woman who shouts instructions at the other women and the children and he announces my name along with the fact that I just arrived at the camp. The others turn away from their pots and pans to stare at me. The woman orders them to get back to work or get out of her kitchen. The woman, clearly the chef, seems far too thin for someone who spends all her time around food. She says some men are looking for me. She will feed me on the one condition that I stay in the tent until she sends word to headquarters that I am in her kitchen. I politely decline her hospitality and I pull Fly's sleeve for us to leave when she quickly adds that it is better to feed an Abrahams than be the one who turns an Abrahams away. I thank her and she pulls a cloth off her shoulder and lashes at the tabletop to clear it of crumbs and flies. She calls over a couple of the children and they fetch cups of water and plates and spoons. She brings a bowl and ladles dumplings and meat and vegetables in an oily stew from it. I tell her she is very kind and she may send someone to tell headquarters that I am in her kitchen but not before I acquaint myself thoroughly with her irresistible stew. Fly and I smile at each other and eat. We joke about the fact that this skinny cook can definitely be trusted and how she must have hollow legs and arms not to balloon like a blimp on such sweet offerings from her pot or maybe she has an extra stomach like a cow. The thin chef watches us from her kitchen and continues to fire orders at her assistants. We stop joking and concentrate on our plates. Fly does not say a word to me, nor I a word to him, until our plates are scraped clean the way aluminium spoons do against the enamel of plates. Then we drain our cups and smack our lips and push up ourselves from the table. The skinny cook asks if I am satisfied. I thank her for the best dumpling and beef stew in the southern hemisphere and add she can send word about me now if she wishes. She signals to a child who scoots from the tent. She wants to know where we are going. I say we will not be far and we intend to return soon but right now we need the time to ourselves.

Outside the food tent Fly claps me on the shoulders and

announces that after the way I conducted myself with the cook he now truly believes I am an Abrahams. Drizzle sprinkles my face and clothing, more a mist than drizzle it drifts down so fine, I hardly feel it, except every now and then the sensation of a feather brushing my eyelash.

I always talk like a Abrahams when I am hungry and the prospect of good food presents itself.

I sticking with you, girl, you can teach me a thing or two.

We keep our eyes peeled for soldiers or children and dive out of sight down another lane or along the sides of tents if we catch sight of them. The spray flies horizontally and swirls with the wind and high up it resembles the merest veil flung over the monocot trees. I ask Fly to tell me where we are going but he begs me to trust him and I calculate that since the food half of the equation exceeded my expectations, the journey part of it cannot be all bad. Where the thought comes from I do not know but I want right then for my mother to be a cook in an army camp with everyone dependent on her for their sustenance and for her talents to be such that people flock to her kitchen. My belly feels warm, the rest of me siphons off my stomach's contentment so that I become energised and elated even though my damp clothes cling to my skin.

We push into the trees away from the hubbub of the camp and inherit the thunder of the bad weather. Fly catches me craning my neck at the forest awning that drizzle and light nevertheless manages to find paths through, albeit in depleted and filtered states.

You think that is thunder.

I nod.

Think again.

What you mean?

That's war, girl, that's the front line; we soon reach.

I expect the trees to change colour so close to a war rather than maintain their uniform camouflage green. I think the whole forest should be red or a deep blue and the plaited vines in their tentacle embrace of the trees and casual way of hanging from branches like giant dreads should alter in a war zone into coiled anacondas ready to strike and lasso some prey. In a war the rain burns, not freshens, and the light peels the skin rather than makes it glow. The *boom, boom, ba-doom* of the war does not silence the shrieks of parakeets and macaws, the cries of peacocks, the clicks of cicadas and crickets, the croaks of bullfrogs, the screeches of monkeys, the grunts of wild boar. If the war is not a kind of weather then it sounds like another creature in the forest announcing its presence and staking out its territory as far as it can pitch its vocals. I suppress an impulse to add my own scream to the hullabaloo. I stop smelling the sweet of wild flowers and the dankness of decomposing foliage and can only smell smoke.

We approach a wall of light and Fly crouches down and tiptoes. I copy him and stick close behind him. The thunder is loudest of all the forest noises. Fly parts the branches and holds them for me to catch before they whip back into my face. He freezes and signals me with a slight curl of his palm to step forward next to him to see what stops him in his tracks. I squint at the piercing light that brightens the valley below like a studio. A river tumbles over ladders of rocks and whitens. Fires burn in patches of the forest with large coils of black smoke winding up to join bundles stacked in the sky. Large guns shudder on escarpments and blast wall after wall of sound that crashes down around my head, bursts from rifles and machine-guns add to the bomb blasts. In the distance to my left and right, lines of men with rifles over their shoulders march down into the valley or else limp back up with the help of comrades. Otherwise they languish on stretchers borne with difficulty over the rutted tracks back into the forest. Rain drills its way through the smoke and light. The sun falls in elephantine pillars. There appears to be no order to the firing and movements of men, just a continuous momentum as if pushed from a standstill they now have no way of stopping themselves.

I turn my back and Fly places a hand on my shoulders. He says we can get closer and see more. I shake my head and ask him to take me back to the camp so that I can meet the minister responsible for this. He seems disappointed but obliges right away by leading me into the plush green light of the forest.

That's the border?

No; the front line. We have to push them back to the border.

Push them back to where?

Across the river and up into the hills to another valley.

We turn and head back to camp. I try to ignore the thunder of the guns that replaces the usual bustle of the forest. Fly glances back at me, so I throw him a smile to reassure him. We plod through mud; a narrow winding trail forces not only single-file traffic but a way of walking almost sideways too. We duck under branches and push twigs and leaves from our faces. Fly never fails to keep hold of a branch long enough for me to grab it before it lashes back into my face. The trail peters out, feeding into a side street of the army town.

As we walk along a few people emerge from tents or else duck out of sight into them. My feet, doubly heavy, slow me to a standstill. Fly glances back at me in one of his periodical looks over his shoulder to check on my progress and jolts around when he sees me several feet behind him standing and watching him. Fly's bright face darkens immediately at the sight of me stuck in the mud like a farm animal in the aftermath of a flood. I ask him if it is awful of me to want to rest in his tent for a while. Before I face the minister and the inevitable third degree that will be the result of my presence at the camp, of the fact that I am away from the big house in the middle of a war and me a young woman to top it all. I mean to say more but I start to shake and even though I fight it, my eyes melt and my mouth breaks from speech into a bawl.

Fly holds me or gathers me up with an arm around my waist and his hand clasping mine, which is more my hand clasping his. He steers me off the side street and between two rows of tents. We zigzag along with Fly pushing and tugging me gently this way and that since I am as good as blindfolded with my eyes streaming and my sense scrambled by the noise of guns and the earlier sighting of men locked in combat. He tells me to wait for a minute and not to move a muscle. The way he squeezes his arms around my waist and my hand as he speaks it is as though he plants the post of my body right there in the mud to ensure I do not drift off that spot. He ducks into a tent a few feet in front of me and I feel a little worse for making him bargain with his friends who share the tent to accommodate a seventh body. I want to step from the spot and push my head inside the tent and tell him not to bother that I have changed my mind about resting and feel ready to face the minister, but I cannot move a muscle. Even my lips and tongue refuse to move and call his name. I watch Fly's tent and exclude all other sights and sounds. I do not blink. Blink, I order my eyelids, blink. But I cannot manage even that small function. The only thing that works is my breathing and that becomes shallow and rapid with every second that Fly spends in that tent. I decide that the longer he takes to return the less likely he is to grant my wish. I look at the sky through a slit in the trees by swivelling my eyes up as far as I can push them. A jet the size of a hummingbird streams by soundlessly. I know or think I know the engine sound in my travels backwards and forwards, to and from England. What I hear when I think of a jet's sound is a combine harvester. I lock my eyes on that jet and my head tilts back with the jet's progress away from me. The vapour trail against the sky twists its long white sheet and drops that twisted sheet along the wall of the sky for the jet to climb back down should it change its mind about moving forward. But the vapour loses its thickness of knotted sheets and becomes strands of a long plait undoing itself, sheets strung together or a long plait? Both sheets and plait. Then I see those sheets again but cut into pieces and scattered about. And then that plait and its separated strands blowing away until nothing of the jet trail remains.

One day my mother will be on a jet and another day my mother and me. We will cross the sky on sheets twisted and knotted together and lowered in the sky or at the end of a long plait releasing more and more of itself for us to make it across an ocean reflected in a sky; but not today. Today I am stuck in the mud like a calf separated from its mother. But I do not want my mother, or my father, or my half-brother. I do not even want a lover. I want a friend, my friend, Fly. I scream his name. *Fly!* Four boys emerge from the tent like a centipede and scramble away. One of them carries Fly's knife. The others keep their eyes on him as if to protect their portion of the bargain. Fly appears in a crouched position, springs upright and virtually leaps at me to be by my side before his screamed name completes another circuit around my head. He hauls me into the tent, explains in a rapid burst of words that his sleeping bag is mine for as long as I need it and dashes for the exit but I grab his shirt and beg him to stay by my side.

My head fills with that war valley with bodies of soldiers blown apart, picked off by snipers, men locked in hand-to-hand combat but unmoving, fixed in meting out death on each other, corpses lined up by roads waiting for collection, if lucky, and the smell of burning vegetation and the river choked with military debris, and wild animals fleeing the bombardment and flames. I do not summon up the tears. Those just well up and flow freely. Fly arranges me in his sleeping bag, zips it up to my chin and lies beside me and hugs the bag and me in it. My head clears at the rate it takes a sky to rid itself of a jet trail. The filtered light in the tent grows less and less but not in a way that can be observed as it happens so much as registered after the fact. It grows dark in a fine sort of way as if the night sifts through muslin cloth and falls like the finest of drizzles, a powdered night that settles on my eyelash. My arms are trapped in the bag and though I like the comfortable feeling of being held with my arms pinned to my body I want more. I want to hold Fly. I ask him to unzip the bag and free my arms. He complies.

Slip in here with me oh giver-away of knife.

Fly pauses and looks at me as I wipe my face and when I hold open the sleeping bag and keep my arm up he complies. We fit with something of a squeeze and we both agree that two of us inside the bag means it is surely meant for army top brass, someone with a lot of weight to throw around. And suddenly I am in a tight hug with Fly and it is the easiest thing in the world for me to do and simultaneously have done to me. I served my apprenticeship by embracing young trees, pillars, posts and pillows. And once or twice I hugged the neck of the old donkey before its legs were broken and my uncles put it down but never the replacement donkey that always tries to bite. I learned how strong my embrace can be but my spell of hugging pillars, posts, trees and pillows taught me nothing about the strength of the other party when a hug is returned. Fly's hug, his hold, resists mine. Resists implies opposition and this is true to a limited extent but I really mean the word to convey a strength that comes at the body even as that body exerts a force of its own. We rock a little, the degree of movement brought on by a tight embrace between two bodies finding equilibrium. Then Fly kisses my face, not once or twice but a succession of kisses. I close my eyes and keep my lips together even when his lips brush mine then lands flush on mine and seem to want to open my mouth but only with the slightest pressure applied in a testing way. I open my eyes and he stares at me with his wide brown eyes or so I think in the dark that thickens now to a delicate fabric lodged between all solid objects. The impression strikes me that if I collide with Fly, the darkness, the sheer thickness of it, will cushion the blow. His kisses on my face feel spongy but with the texture of flesh and the moisture of breath and a small electric charge that flies through me from head to toe every time his lips land on me.

The dark claims us completely. By touch alone we remake each other. A picture of each other reconstitutes by the collective effort of our lips, palms and fingertips. The slight protuberance of bone under Fly's eyes is located at the point where two straight lines of equal length intersect, one drawn vertically from the corners of his eyes and the other horizontally from the point where his nostrils curve. So say my lips and fingertips. His lips map my left breast, ever so slightly bigger than my right one. The slope from my collarbone to my attentive nipple produces marginally less of an incline on my left side than the slope on my right breast, this from his lips in collusion with his hands and the side of his face that comes to rest there for some time. Time measures itself by our synchronised breathing. Sleep creeps up on me and before I think *sleep*, I recognise it, even though sleep is a featureless clock face. I disappear. Lost somewhere between my last exhalation and Fly's intake of air.

Morning drops in on us unannounced and tears us apart. We dress in a speeded-up fashion and straighten each other's clothes in a hurry and dive outside and join a busy street. Fly says it leads straight to the minister's headquarters, if I am sure that is where I want to go. I nod. A couple of boys recognise me and fall in behind us. Four more pull up beside us and cause the jeeps and trucks that crawl along the road to sound their horns and shout at us to make way for them. Three soldiers run up to me and keep a few steps away since it is clear where I am going.

I pass the food tent and the smell of boiling oil and fat turns and knots my empty stomach. The cook stands at the entrance of her kitchen with two other women and she raises her eyebrows at me and frowns and waves. I wave back but I do not smile, I eat saliva that fills my mouth and feel bilious. The crowd swells as more boys and girls and women and soldiers meet up with us and fall in behind or beside us until all oncoming traffic stops and the vehicles behind us slow to a walk pace. I spot the minister's tent up ahead. At last the Abrahams of my heritage. The reason this tent city sprouted among the trees. The Abrahams everyone says brewed the weather above the forest of two conflicting armies in the valley below where men and women lie down beside their weapons never to rise again and more of them pour into the valley for the same cause, dedicated to the same name and minister.

I pull off my hat and shake out my hair. As we walk, Fly reshapes my hat for me with a series of little karate chops of his right hand aimed at the front, top and back, and I straighten my mud-speckled clothes. Fly points out that my outfit, with the green of leaves and vines and the moss off trees and the mud, looks like battle fatigues. I ask him if I look like a buckoo. He shakes his head and raises his eyebrows, which wrinkles the skin on his forehead. Do I have mud on my face and hair? No, he answers as he licks his index finger and aims it at my face. I tell him he is the only person on the planet who is allowed to wet my face with his spit. He laughs and for the repeat performance of cleaning me up he directs my finger that I lick, placing it on to the offending spot of mud just left of the bridge of my nose. He says I am fit to meet Her Majesty the Queen. I bow my head and smile at him. He bows back. What about the minister, am I presentable to the minister? Most definitely, he blurts out in a Scottish accent copied off the BBC World Service and with his chest puffed out and his back straight in mock majesty.

He reminds me of my father not seen alive by me for twelve years but who now walks beside me and is my age. I stop and examine Fly and he comes to an abrupt standstill and right away steps back to be beside me. And so does our entourage. Fly juts his face close to mine and whispers in my ear, *I love you, Bethany Bettany*. I whip my face around to see where the word love comes from in relation to my twin name and my body. The sudden movement causes my lips to brush his ever so slightly we are that close to each other, so that it is more a tickle than any real or prolonged contact. And for that reason it cannot be classed a kiss but a brushing of lips, a powdering of skin on skin, a skittering of the lightest, flattest stone over the stillest of ponds. I pull back and he smiles and I mouth in front of all those people, *I love you too, Fly*. We press on in silence, not that we ever really stop for more than a moment for all this to take place. Rather it happens within our strides, as a part of our progress to the minister's tent, as if on the way to it we stumble upon love, an aside, or a temporary distraction.

Why you call Fly?

Cause I never stay in one place for long. While we on the subject, tell me, why you say your name twice? Back in the tent last night you make me say your name twice every time I call your name.

Which was often.

We laugh and he gives me a little push with his left hand, which I return trying to match exactly his velocity.

School make me write my name one way, home another. My mother prefers the school way, so I am told, while my father, the home side. I like both. I belong to both.

A whistle pierces my skull. My eyes lose their focus and burn and my head spins. I shake my hair out to clear the insect of this sound from it but the quick movement hammers the sound and shatters it into smaller pieces, which grow and become louder. I glance at Fly and I see him in a cracked mirror, disjointed and ill fitting. By his wide-eyed look I know he hears the high-pitched sound too. The shrill whistle increases with our awareness of it. Our exchanged looks convert the screech to a screaming that spreads to all the trees, above them and around them. Just as there is a forest of trees, another forest of this sound exists too. It occupies all the spaces between the leaves, branches, vines, and fallen vegetation fitted on the forest floor. The women, children and soldiers following me stop paying attention to me and they stare at this shadow forest by simply looking into space since it seems to be in this space where the sound hatches and it is this growing sound that gives rise to a forest of itself. A woman shouts the name of Jesus. She stands twenty feet from me but seemingly beside me as this sound joins all our separate bodies. I notice her for the first time. Her face opens into a cavern with stalactites and stalagmites. Her tongue splits and forks. All her features disappear or the cave swallows every part of her face. Fly pushes me to the ground or falls into me, we both tumble over with his body on top of mine.

The whistle cuts off. The green of the forest made denser by the sound now seems suddenly robbed of sound. Now everything around me appears stretched and thinned to a transparency that invites me to look not just into but *through* the forest. I can see through one leaf to a queue of other leaves behind it, past one tree trunk to a row of other trunks in a row without beginning or end. Thunder jars the ground and the blast of it injects more fluid into my skull than my skull can hold. My jaw drops and the bones separate and lock. My ears pop and a vacuum fills them, silence and the pressure that accompanies a vacuum. Fly's body doubles in weight and presses mine into the mud. I shout his name but I cannot hear myself shout nor feel my mouth move. Again the thunder, the ground shivers and rocks Fly's body and mine. I shout, *Fly*. The effort involves all of my body but my voice is small and far away and barely a whisper. I struggle to breathe and push Fly from me. To my surprise he rolls off my back. I wipe mud from my eyes, swallow and my ears pop. Screaming women, children and men fill and block my ears again. I look for Fly. I see him in a broken mirror, a mirror with pieces missing so that Fly is in pieces and parts of him are missing. I call his name. His eyes are open and blank. The tip of his tongue peeps out of the corner of his mouth. Red trickles from his lips and ear. I scream and cry his name. More whistles begin and end in thunder that splinters the earth and sprinkles my body with it. There is less of the mirror than the blank spaces of its missing parts. I shut my eyes, squeeze my eyelids and the uniform darkness is a perfect mirror.

I should see nothing but there is a face in the dark. Before I recognise whose it might be I cry for my mother. I turn in the mud on to my back and reach up with my arms and cry my mother's name. Not a cry exactly more a moan, more a way of breathing with a cry for each breath. *Mummy!*

My outstretched arms grip someone or something. I believe a body fills my arms. I grasp and feel how I lift off the mud and into the air in my grip of this body that does the lifting for me. All I do is hold on tight. I move in the air, upwards I think and estimate that by now I should be above the trees. I should be where thunder is manufactured, where rain brews and overflows. And if I keep moving in this upward direction, I should reach the maker of all this weather. A creature of this world, a single creature cannot undo so much, more a constituent of everything in the world. There is no word for it, this thinking thing. I feel it as if Fly lives again, and stands beside me doing the lifting and being lifted just like me. I do not say Fly, nor Mother, nor Father. I feel them all in the grip of my arms and in the lifting that is done of me. I open my eyes and I squint in a glare that wipes away objects, all the greenery of the forest and the mud-coloured ground, the rain and thunder, all melt into the glare whose lightning intensity belongs to a body deeper and wider than the forest.

I cannot see who or what carries me in a direction and at a speed that spins my head. I hold on for dear life. Some faulty reasoning of mine takes hold of me and I convince myself that my life depends on my attachment to the force that transports me out of the obliterated camp. But my eyes are useless. I open them and keep them peeled and yet the same blinding glare fills my head. I try to speak a mixture of queries and assertions, questions about what is happening to me and who I should thank for the help and the fact that I am an Abrahams. Except that I hear nothing of my speech and my tongue feels wooden in my mouth. My body bumps against a hard surface and I assume I am airborne. I might be blind or some outward light blinds me. I blink several times but each time the soft pressure of the squeezed lids makes no difference to the intensity of the glare. I flex my whole face hoping to change the light and see how it remains the same brightness with no single source but spread everywhere so that objects lose their definition and the world its objects and in their place is this light. The forward or upward propulsion bumps and sways me: forwards *and* upwards. The whistles and thunder retreat from me or I withdraw from them. Cathedral bells ring and from their loudness I stand just below them and look up as they swing and bellow. All the bells melt into the one bright light and their sound is the light pulsing. I hear nothing else. What I take for thunder and whistles in the distance might be a memory of both. I try to be still since listening hard always entails stillness. But I am on the move and the idea of stillness only contributes to my sense of being transported against my will in an unknown direction. I think I hear a flock of parakeets, macaws or cockatoos, their particular music. I conjure things in a world of glare, a world of no sound or one sound invites the same varied inventions.

But I am blind and deaf. I breathe but I cannot smell the forest and this I credit to the fact that I might be high above the trees. My tongue freezes in my mouth. My body bumps and sways. I face upwards. These movements resemble my journey hidden in a truck for my free ride to the capital. The way my body moves replicates that time. The camp must be in ruins behind me, all its muddy streets bomb craters, the tarpaulin blown to shreds with their occupants, the minister's tent hit too. Another minute and not just Fly but me too. I do what crying is supposed to be, a combination of breathing and sighing, a groan and contortion of the face, a production of tears and a generalised hurt of the body, all rolled into one but without my hearing, feeling or seeing any of it. I guess my face is wet because salt burns the rim of my eyes. I label the swaying and rocking of the vehicle as my grief since these two in collusion replace my ability to think straight.

FLY

When I could not write I talked a lot to anyone who would listen. I saw how a thought sprang into the gap left in my head by my failure to write it down.

Bethany Bettany helped me to write my name on the dusty side of a bus and spurred me to set aside my days for the task. I went to school and joined a class of children who could barely wipe their noses and pull up their pants. I said the alphabet with them, filled exercise book after exercise book with the same few lines, and read books with more pictures than words.

One child asked me if I was tall for my age or just stupid. I told him I had some catching up to do, and less of the stupid when he addressed me if he did not want a taste of my dumb fist.

I did this to write to Bethany Bettany. Learning to write tried my patience. In my illiterate life I thought something and no sooner thought than done. With this writing thing I needed a long view, a slow march.

BRIAN

The house miss her that very morning. I miss not seeing her and not getting a little smile from her face that I send back tenfold. We search every corner and under every bed. We turn the place upside down and go over it several times. We can't believe she gone now after the air clear and a new page turn. When we realise she really gone I panic. I nearly cry. I feel lost. I win a sister and lose her almost as quick. I want her to know I pray for a father for years and my prayers answered with her, my sister.

I think I know where she gone. I have a mind to follow her and bring her back home. And if she don't want to come back till she find her mother then I going to join her in her search. Four eyes better than two. She can tell me all about her years in England with our father. I want to know what he looked like asleep. The last time I clap eyes on him he was in a box and he looked asleep but he was pale. She must tell me how he looked with fresh air in him and a dream.

I will tell her about her mother. I will take her to meet her mother.

Bethany Bettany

Sex is first a look, then a sound, then a smell. Sex is fury. Casual repetition. The obliteration of differences. A pursuit of skin. A gathering of nerve endings. Sex unfolds, from something compact. Sex heals me as I watch. I always hurt first before I see it and then I only look because I must heal. I watch in order to repair. I cannot close my eyes and cork my ears and hold my breath. I look for as long as it takes me to fix fully. Whatever I see does not compare to feeling a broken part of me heal bit by bit in an accelerated fashion. My mind pools in that part of my body. That broken part of me returns itself to me to make me whole again, though I can only ever see myself in parts, layers of myself ascending, descending stairs and each layer left behind in a race to catch the layer that leads the ascent and simultaneous descent. I map every second of what I feel. My eyes, wide open, see nothing and everything, a diagram of my body and all the wet parts inside trying to rearrange the broken furniture of themselves, trying to go from sprawl to compact, from spread all over a house to concentrated in a can. Whatever transpires before my eyes seems to be laughing at my need to repair fast.

The eyes of sex gleam, the lips of sex turn up, sex-teeth bare and shine in poorly lit rooms. I am in the same room and apart from it. My eyes are open but they do not shine. I repair. I break to see it all. Sex happens because I break and need to fix again. Sex relies on the fact that my body is smashed before sex can happen. Sex feeds on me with whips and fists, punches and kicks. I heal as fast as I can to rob it of a reluctant witness. My body is not made for sex or so I tell myself until Fly appears and shows me parts of myself strange to feel and see but sweet for as long as he unveils them. But only Fly, and no more Fly.

I try to understand how every pore and corpuscle of my body overrules every carefully weighed edict of my mind, to fathom why, when I remember something, my feelings about the memory outweigh all my judgements about the thing remembered. All I come up with, when I think about it, is the memory of the last occasion when I weighed something and made a decision about it: at that exact moment the feeling came along and swept the table clear of my reasoning. A single wave of the hand of passion sends the china and cutlery of reason so carefully arranged by me, scattering around the room with the music of ruin.

My body, small and too little, holds all the things sent its way. My body grows but so do all the things it must contain. They grow proportionately too. In which case I remain the same body. I carry the same things. Though I know those things at a deeper level. On the one hand, two lovers, twenty lovers in their sex parade. On the other, my single witnessing body, bruised, then healed, then bruised again. Right where the old wound lay a new wound flowers and right there on that spot the body must recall how it heals or rot with the new injury of that new wound in that old place. A child's body then a girl's body long before it becomes a woman's. I want to ask Fly how he finds the parts of me that do not hurt when I cannot find them. When I think I run out of places to hurt Fly finds extensions of my body untouched by whip and fist.

Fly? I know we lay in a tent. Maybe the fabric of that tent became skin – our joined skin without our bodies, the two of us clasped inside this new outer skin that we share.

FLY

Let's just say you have something I want. I think it has to be in your hands so I open your hand and kiss your palm – nothing. Nothing there but skin and the perfume of skin. I track along your arms with my tongue. Let's just say this is an unusual search. Again my tongue and lips are my chief tools of investigation, no hands, not even my eyes. I follow a prominent vein along your arm and it brings my tongue and lips to your shoulders and then down your shoulder to your chest and breast. I find something. I linger there for a while. And you let me know that I getting warm but the fire might be some way off. I like the heat. At least my lips and tongue like it and so I hover there for a while and maybe you change your mind about the location of that fire because you let me know in no uncertain terms that whatever I building sure might result in a fire of some sort. I move down to your belly. You pull it in or it retreats or both but my lips and tongue ready for a chase and they follow and soon your belly settle and if anything rise a little to meet my lips and tongue. When I find your navel I know I still need to look for what I want from you and you let me know that I tickle you too much there so I should move on because you cannot take it, not another second of it. So I press on in my search, my investigation of you, my hunt for something I want from you that I sure you have put in some secret place from me. Let's just say my decision to move on, to work my way down your body, to obey your command to leave your navel alone unless I only wanted to make you laugh, comes to me in a flash. My lips part folds of you. My tongue probes and licks. I think I find what I look for going by your reaction and because of you, the effect on me. I find something. Lift your hips some more for me.

Bethany Bettany

What vehicle, I ask myself. And answer myself, one without an engine. Even if deaf and blind I can sense the combustion of an engine. The movement, despite all my shaking, runs smooth, too much without the vibrations, the shuddering, the hum, and the necessary violations of natural muscular velocity associated with an engine.

Now I move as never before. Before, on the back of a mule, in a cart pulled by a donkey, in the trailer of a tractor, secreted in the huge cavern of a dump truck, under my own steam on the saddle of a bicycle and in my father's Bentley. Now this.

When I flatten myself I sail light as air. This forward motion is none of these. It is more like swinging in a hammock. Or lying in one swung by a breeze or a casual hand. Except that instead of swinging backwards and forwards I register a forward movement and the adjustments over rough terrain best called a swaying of the body.

My body rocks and sways at the mercy of other bodies. These other bodies carry me. I float, bob, and bump on my canvas bed, cushioned by several springy feet on the ground. My head clears and the first shadows sweep across my eyes and the first waves of sound wash my ears. I swallow and my tongue scrapes and presses against the back of my throat. Patches of blue show through the green tent of trees. Blue light speckles a green shell. Wind combs the tangled branches and vines with a fine-toothed comb that sounds more like a brush on hide. Breathing to me is both a taste and a touch as I am borne on a canvas stretcher, bitterness and ground glass shape each breath.

A bearded man, long and curly grey hairs, his head brimmed under a wide hat, stares down at me. His lips hide in his beard.

And though his eyebrows seem thicker than moustaches, two fierce bulbs, that brings my father's eyes to mind, burn under the shade of those eyebrows. His hands with grey hairs on the knuckles and back makes me wonder if not him then who carries me? My eyes circle in my head and at four points I pick up the naked brown bodies, laced at wrist, biceps, neck and waist with precious shells, stones and the teeth of prey, of my four stretcher-bearers. A bone or tusk, threaded through the bridge of their noses, protrudes from nostrils, earlobes dangle with huge, vesicular earrings. The men hum and march with me sandwiched between two bamboo poles lashed to the skin of an animal, instead of canvas, for my bed. The rhythmic guttural of the men mimic drums, a bass sound rather than words and yet closer to speech than any drum. The way I rock and sway seems more obedient to this chant than to their movements. Four words jump into my head: Carib, Macusi, Arawak, Wapashani, one of these, all of these, none of these.

My name. If I say it aloud the whole scene and whatever dream traps me in it will dissolve, from this jungle interior to the big house. Once faced with my name the main road, the rickety bridge leading to the two halves of the front gate, the front yard with the straight path leading to the house, and the house itself, white-washed and two-storeyed with its paling fence down two sides, materialises. I shut my eyes and shout as loud as I can that I am an Abrahams. I am an Abrahams. I open them and expect everything to be different from my present situation. But a man speaks. He says what I least expect to hear from a man and therefore fail to link to the boom of the voice and with the bearded head that hovers over me.

I am an Abrahams too, Reginald Abrahams.

Which uncle?

I picture them all and come up with a composite head or a patchwork of mirrors made up of the images of four broken mirrors.

I am your grandfather.

My grandfather?

Yes.

Lost grandfather?

Yes.

This time my open eyes register the prodigious beard which parts for me and reveals all my uncles and aunts, and my father.

And the minister?

No. I am not the minister. You will meet your mother soon enough.

I hear this in my good ear but in my bad ear it is an echo. I ignore it. My mother, the minister. I pretend not to hear and not to care. I want to tell him I do not understand how my mother and the minister can be one and the same. My mother is my mother.

What happened back there?

You would not understand.

I demand to know.

All right. Long-range missiles, launched from an offshore American battleship. Our coordinates must have been betrayed or a US spy plane or satellite spotted us.

I don't understand.

Lie back and don't talk; you have some injuries we need to examine as soon as we reach the emergency headquarters.

I obey keeping all my questions to myself for now and a little startled by his reference to my injuries none of which I noticed on any part of me in the usual terms of pain, bleeding, numbness or lack of movement. I decide to conduct a mental self-examination. My mind begins with the tips of my toes and works its way up my body. I peer along my body to my feet and count two and notice that my boots and socks are gone and my feet are muddy. I wriggle each toe and count them. The nail that never grew back on the toe I stumped looks equally obscured with mud. I arrive at a weird figure, eleven, and count them again. My shins, knees and thighs all twitch as my eyes travel up my body. Then I forget my journey and squirm at a stabbing pain in my right side and right arm. I cannot move my right arm and when I breathe in or out with more than the slightest effort my right ribs burn.

Everything I hear, from my grandfather and the movements

of the men carrying me, to the breeze in the trees and the usual industry of birds, all pour into my left ear and bang against the stone wall of my right. And I see all around me but only through my left eye. I reach up and grab my grandfather's sleeve and cry out louder that I intend, *Help me, Granddad.*

Yes, child. We almost there.

He smoothes my hair off my face with a wooden hand or so his hand seems. His touch, no more than a shadow passing over my numb face, alarms me.

This war is madness, child. It was thrust upon us. A consortium of American logging companies purchased this region from the other side, only it was never theirs to sell in the first place. We are fighting to save it. If these trees disappear this whole region will become a desert.

My head falls back on to the animal-skin stretcher and bobs slightly to the march of my stretcher-bearers. I keep telling myself my grandfather will make me better. I picture the two of us walking out of the interior and collecting uncles along the way. And all of us step gingerly out of the green light of the trees and into the glare of the savannah and across the bridge of a river and along the tarmac road back to the white-washed house. My grandmother throws open her bedroom window to greet us. I want to include my mother in the rosy picture but it seems unrealistic to do so.

Grandfather, am I dying?

No, precious child, I won't let you die.

I feel numb.

We're nearly there. How do you spell your name?

Is he trying to take my mind off my condition?

No. Please tell me how you spell your name.

I ask him to say more.

I can't tell from the way you say it whether it is B-e-t-h-a-n-y, or B-e-t-t-a-n-y. Your father always said, Bet-ta-ny, the local way. Your mother, Beth-a-ny, the proper way.

He pronounces proper as if in quotation marks.

They left it for you to choose one or the other.

He looks at me for an answer – one or the other. I tell him

how for years I am called Bettany though I look like my mother. Now that everyone acknowledges that there are aspects of my father in me this other spelling of my name, this Bethany, preferred by my mother, somehow means I must choose between the two. I weigh the two the way my father wants me to, but not on his scales of either/or.

I am both Bethany and Bettany. Call me Bethany Bettany and drop my last name.

He nods approvingly. The stretcher bearers cease their chanting.

Did you gamble away everything, Granddad?

Yes. I was sick. Your mother talked sense into me, saved my life. What's left of it.

My mother, the minister?

Yes. She convinced me to switch sides. Your mother is a passionate and persuasive politician. I only wish she could have convinced my sons and sons-in-law not to desert. She knows they are all hiding at the house but she refuses to order a search of the property because she does not wish to add to your grandmother's misery.

I feel angry that he sings my mother's praises before I am able to consider her in these terms.

Why did you abandon Granny and everyone at the house?

Your grandmother blamed me for the death of our son, your dear father. She said I did not lift a finger to save him from your mother's clutches. And everyone at the house stuck with a government that was obviously bankrupting the country while it lined its own pockets.

Could you have saved him?

If your grandmother could not – and he was closest to her, he was her favourite – what chance did I have?

Why did my mother abandon me?

She most certainly did not abandon you. They demanded you from her as the price she had to pay for the death of Lionel. I objected and your grandmother turned against me and accused me of showing favour to your mother and doing nothing to save him. They wanted you because you were all they had left alive of Lionel. I wanted nothing to do with it. I left before you arrived.

We move through silence. Not the silence of our surroundings. For this is filled with explosions and gunfire and flocks of screaming parakeets scattering as if the leaves of trees noisily take flight. We move through the tongue-tied silence between two people when there is more to say than can be said in the time that they share. Because that time seems about to run out and words would only squander it. Sometimes a gesture suffices or at least becomes necessary to help words to flow again.

'The damp gets to everything here,' he offers apologetically. 'I carried your father's letter to you all these years to protect it against prying eyes. I do not know the contents myself but I see that you are ready to learn what he has to say. Maybe I am too.'

I try to sit up on the stretcher but cannot. He holds out his arm signalling me to stay put. Would I like him to read it to me? I nod and incline my one good ear towards him. He walks along beside me and unfolds the waxed cloth slowly as if not to spill the eight little diamonds it might contain. He holds up the blue airmail envelope for me to see that it is addressed to me in care of his name. I do not expect him to shake the envelope the way he does by flapping his hand three times and least of all the quick and almost careless way he tears the top off the envelope. He dips two fingers into the opening and fishes out a bundle of pages folded in half. He turns the pages towards me for a moment. The letter paper looks creased and light blue. The black ink writing slants to the left of the page. He glances ahead then at me then at the page and reads aloud. I recognise every word. My father writes to me, his child in a future without him, his hand sets the record straight. The things he did and the things done to him placed on scales for me to weigh, one side supplied by my mother, the other by him, all in his hand, the tall script inclined to the left of the page. And sometimes on this scale I find myself put into the left side and sometimes into the right. Both of them use me to add weight to their argument. But I too have the chance to weigh them both, one in each hand, one in each half of my heart, the right ventricle for my father, for his left-handedness, the left for my mother who never admitted doing anything wrong in her life. My mother leaves the heart to begin the circuit round my body and just as she leaves my father returns from his round-trip and enters my heart. That is how they keep apart and that is how they stay together in me.

I could almost dictate my grandfather's speech as he says it to me, the same speech dictated to me as my thoughts by my father in me. I do not know my thoughts until I hear them from my grandfather even though I am the one doing the thinking. My grandfather tells me what I already know but do not understand until he says it through me. His lips move as I think myself back to when I lived with my parents in London.

FATHER

Dear Bettany,

(Your mother would hate me spelling your name like this. She says it is not proper and you were christened, Bethany. I remind her that we never actually discussed how to spell your name when we named you nor did we make it to the church with you for the proper ceremony. Instead we allowed the priest to conduct a christening right there in the living room of my parents' house before we left for the capital and returned to England.)

Dear Bettany,

If you are reading this then you are the young woman I never lived to see grow up and do all the things I dreamed you would do in fulfillment of the Abrahams name. (Your mother would not like this reference to your surname. She said there was nothing dynastic about the name. I always disagreed with her. How hard it is to talk to you without talking through her.)

Dear Bettany,

I am your father. I hope you have not forgotten me. For the first five years of your life I fathered you. I did my best according to how I was taught. I had very good teachers in your grandparents. My mother and father worked out this parenting thing between them by dividing it into strict areas of responsibility. Each owned an area that the other one never interfered in. My mother allocated chores and ran the house. My father disciplined and ran the fields. Whichever area a child was in at any time, either indoors or outdoors, would put them in the jurisdiction of either my mother or my father. My mother kept a list of indoor offenders and when my father returned from a day supervising workers in the fields she handed him the list and he called out our names and whipped us. We knew not to get on to my mother's list because once on it there was nothing we could say or do to evade a whipping. All of our pleadings took place with our mother at the time of the offence. If that was no good we resigned ourselves to our fate and obeyed my father's instructions to the letter.

I tell you this because your mother never bought into this regime of child rearing. She thought it too regimental. She said a more fluid model made for a happier child and a happier home. I fought her over it because it seemed that she should accept this system of mine that had been tried and tested in a big house rather than adopt a hunch of hers that had no basis in reality other than in her psychology. But there you have it; the difference between us began with your birth. Not your fault, don't worry. You need to know how things went wrong and why it reached the point where I am staring at my last few hours alive.

I never hit a woman until I met your mother. She had a way of throwing her body into my path, I mean blocking me from stepping in any direction that necessitated me having to push her out of the way just to make enough room for myself to take the next breath. She stood as close to me as possible and looked me right in the eye and told me I was wrong. Then when I tried to turn away from her she manoeuvred around quickly so that she was still there. The first time I pushed her away she fell to the ground and bounced back on her feet and planted herself in front of me as before as if to defy me to push her away again. That first time I hugged her quickly and kissed her and begged her to forgive me for laying a finger on her and she went very quiet and allowed me to hug her but she did not hug me back. And when I released her she went straight to you and picked you up and hugged you and sang a lullaby to you and swayed and ducked her face to her shoulders to dry her eyes. I went to the river for a long walk.

The second physical fight took place a few weeks later by a

flight of stairs. You were asleep. I arrived home late. I could smell burning. I knew right away that she had something on the stove waiting for me to return at the usual time and it burned waiting for me. As soon as I walked in the door she barred my path to the bathroom down a flight of stairs. I mean she stood there and stared at me as if I had to explain everything to her on the spot. I apologised for my lateness but before I could offer an explanation she asked me if this was another of my father's ways that I wish to recommend highly to her. Because if it was I could put it in the trash along with the other little bit of foolishness from my parents that I wished to use to tie her and her daughter – meaning you – into knots.

I saw red. I could not believe she would refer back to an old argument in that way and bad-mouth my parents at the same time. What did they have to do with my lateness? I pushed her out of my way, to the side, but she stumbled backwards and before I could grab her flailing arms she fell down the flight of stairs. The noise woke you. You screamed and she screamed and I stood there not knowing which of the two of you to attend to first. Before I could move from the spot she sprang to her feet and slapped at my head and face. I ducked my head in my arms and turned my body away from her and she kept hitting me and cursing my name. I wanted her to stop and attend to you but she did not seem to hear your loud cries. She kept hitting me.

I grew impatient and then angry. I pushed her hard against the wall and she lunged at me again. I began to hit her on the arms and curse her stubbornness, like nothing I had seen in a woman before. I punched her on the arms a few times and she stopped hitting me and covered her arms, but she kept talking about my parents, saying how their ways warped my mind. I walked away from her and picked you up but I was trembling so much and breathing so hard that you screamed harder. She rushed up from behind me, spun me around and glared at me as if I was doing something harmful to you and she could not believe her eyes and ears and then she dragged you from my arms. She walked away briskly and locked the bedroom door behind her. I heard her saying your name and spelling it, B-e-t-h-a-n-y, emptying a nursery rhyme of its words and using the melody with her own words about you squeezed into it – typical of the inventiveness of your mother.

Her arms turned black and blue. She shrank from my touch. She was in the bath and you were asleep when I opened the bathroom door and went in on the pretext of looking in the cabinet over the bathroom sink for my razor. She covered her breasts. I went to her and she ordered me not to touch her but I rubbed her arms lightly with the back of my hands and said sorry as often as I could say it breathing in and out. She leaned towards my touch and I kissed her arms, then her face, which she turned towards mine. Then I climbed into the bath in my clothes, which made her laugh aloud and cover her mouth because she did not want to wake you. She helped me to peel off my clothes and she even had the wherewithal to wring the water out of them before tossing them to the floor. Me, I was too busy climbing out of the weight of my clothing to think about anything other than to marvel at my good luck with her after a week of being ignored by her.

I only tell you this to let you see that we loved each other, wanted each other, alongside the fights. I even confessed to her that she was right about the ancient wisdom and handed down practices of my parents, that we could live without them. But we were in the bath together and I conceded every-thing to her. That's how much I wanted her. She was the most beautiful woman in the world surrounded by soap suds, with her long hair pasted to her neck and shoulders and her skin shining and her curved eyelashes wet and looking longer too. You did wake up but when you opened the bathroom door I was about to shave at the sink and your mother was wrapping her hair in a towel. You stayed and watched me shave. I put foam on your chin and used the blunt back of the razor to scrape off the foam.

The real change happened in her not me. Our fights became routine, a routine part of our love. What changed in her none of us could have predicted. Initially, I put it down to the fact that my behaviour had spoiled her love at the outset. After all I took her home and introduced her to everyone including your brother. (I am assuming you have found out by now that you have a brother almost your age.)

Your mother saw the boy's existence as an early betrayal by me of our love. And she was right in the strictest sense of the term but wrong too, since it had nothing to do with what I had with her. She stormed into my life and returned to the capital with her sheaf of government census forms and left me quite lonely. The boy's mother thrust herself at me and in my condition I lapped up her pitiful attentions. I swear it was the one indiscretion that led to her pregnancy.

My God, I pulled up roots and left everything I knew to be with your mother because she could not stand to be near anything to do with my past. That's how much I wanted her above anything else in my life. She played the part of the know-it-all city slicker and my parents and brothers and sisters hated her for it. They saw how much I liked her and they feared losing me to the big city, I suppose, so they gave her a hard time.

But even my past was not enough to poison what we had together. No. What we had was special: passion that made my head spin, and lust and love, deep, intoxicating love. She really changed for the worse when she encountered a demonstration of fascists in our high street, Lewisham High Street. You were with her. The demonstrators hurled abuse at her and a few of them detached themselves from the march to spit at her. She covered you from the spit and made you cork your ears. She talked to me about it the way someone explains some remote and puzzling experience to you in the hope that you might provide the key. I had no magic insight. I told her what I would have told you. That the country carried a minority of ignorant people who were afraid of what they knew nothing about and rather than find out about that strange thing they reacted by casting aspersions on it. I hugged her but she was not interested in a hug. She wanted an answer. And what I had to say was nowhere near what she wanted to hear.

301

She began making plans to return home, with or without me as she put it. Of course I was more than happy to return to the country of my birth and the people I knew best but I did not want to turn up with nothing to show for all my time away – nearly five years. I begged her to give me a year or two and she asked me if I was mad. She said she had washed her hands of England and could not stay another month, never mind another year or two in a country that encouraged marches against her as a demonstration of its democracy. She wanted to know why the test of the country's democratic loyalties had to be made at her expense. And as for me, she said, granted I know a lot about water but I know nothing about people. Not true.

She took you to anti-racist rallies and some of your first phrases were odd anti-fascist ones. She was proud of the fact that you shouted Down with racism, down with fascism, and thrust your little fist in the air. She said your elocution was perfect even at high pitch. I failed to see the funny side of any of this. She attended meetings in London held by Guyanese dissidents planning a revolutionary transformation of a Guyana leadership they described as corrupt puppets of global corporations. My family had thrown in its lot with the very government she now lambasted. I told her she was using her new political involvement to punish me for my past and for the fact that my family did not take to her as the new daughter-in-law precisely because of her maverick politics. Politics aside, I said I could not change the fact that I had fathered a child that was not hers (nor would I want to change it), nor could I change the feelings of my family. She seemed astonished by my outburst. She repeated my phrase, nor would I want to change it, nor would I want to change it, as if by my saying it I had somehow surrendered my right to alter my past. She held the phrase up at me and dangled it in my face as all the proof she needed of my idiocy and unsuitability to rear her child.

How so? I asked. She scooped you up in her arms, turned and walked away. All the time she whispered into your ears and you became stock-still not even blinking during these episodes. I guessed she was pouring one of her customised nursery rhymes into your ear. I decided to counter her talk by pointing to all the things that I liked about the country. I shaved and let you spread the shaving cream all over my face and yours. I took you on long walks beside the river. We drove to Deptford, parked in a quiet, cobbled side street, that ended at a high wall, and walked down an overgrown and rubbish-strewn alleyway to a path that skirted the river all the way to Greenwich. I pointed out all the industry along the banks of that portion of the Thames, the paper factory, the fishery and the sugar processing plant. And we met two people I knew from my work, men whose families had worked the river for generations and who liked me because I understood it, men who did not care one iota about my race or where I came from.

All this served merely to harden your mother's heart against me. She said I could never build a future in England because those same men who smiled at me now would rip it down the minute I put anything up. They liked me, she said, precisely because I had nothing. I was less than they were and I made them look good. I asked her if she had been drinking or smoking dope or something. I could not believe those things sounded from her. The only drinking she had done she said was a good dose of reality that had served to open her eyes to her hopeless situation in this country and with me.

So you want a divorce, woman? I had to say it, though I regretted it the second it aired. To tell you the truth I did not expect an answer from her. I figured it was the last card in a quarrel that I could play to bring the mêlée to a close. I was wrong, but I thought if I mentioned divorce she would back away from a row that had escalated from us trading casual insults to shouting and sticking our hands in each other's face. But she barely paused in her reply. Yes, she shouted. Yes. Leave us to get on with our lives. Go back to your countrywoman and her godforsaken child and your stupid superstitious family and that overcrowded house in the middle of nowhere. She would have gone on with her list but I slapped her hard in her face and we traded blows for a while and I walked out the door.

I walked along the river. The high tide slapped the wooden ramparts just like a hand playfully slapping a bare bottom. At least that's how it sounded to my ears. I wanted to be in bed cuddled up to your mother with you next to her or between us before I carried you to your bed. I wanted her to come up quietly behind me as I prepared to join her and you in bed and slap my backside just like that tide shouldering up to that greenheart wood bolstering the river's banks.

Dear Bettany,

I eased the key in the lock, sidled into the house on the balls of my feet and fed the lock into the doorjamb as quietly as I could after that long walk only to turn and face your mother ready for a war. I should have run from the house then and there but I was tired and refused to believe she really wanted another fight with me at such a late hour.

I realised she never trusted me from the day she found out about your brother's existence, when all along I feared politics would come between us. (Reassure your brother for me that I love him even though I do not know him. Tell him I heard about his progress from my sisters' letters to me. Remind him that I held him a couple of times when he was a baby and we had gone back briefly to show you off to my parents and brothers and sisters.)

Your mother actually thought I had just returned from seeing another woman. Couldn't she see how my shoulders were hunched from the cold, how my nose reddened from the biting midnight air? Surely the misery on my face was as clear as daylight? I walked and walked to clear my head and returned to double trouble as if my absence simply added interest to the hostility she had in store for me. Couldn't she see my pain?

Obviously not. We were fighting again. Furniture fell out of our path and flew across the room. Your mother and I were in an arena and we stopped caring about the neighbours or even about waking you. I did not see you in the middle of the fight until it was too late. And then when I noticed you I failed to see what you held in your hand. You cut my trousers with my razor. You did not mean to. You simply swiped at the man who had woken you and made your mother cry and upset the furniture in the living room. Fortunately, so your mother was apt to point out later, you missed my goods. No four-year-old should be put in such a position. Forgive me, my daughter. I made you do it. A few months later, a little before your fifth birthday, your mother and I quarrelled again. Much like the times before. A few breakages. Some traded blows. I left again and returned and again I made you act beside yourself. I caused you to enter the room while I slept from the medication recommended by your mother. I made you pour my aftershave on me. My hand, raised against you and your mother, lifted your hand, steadied it and struck the match and flung it over my sleeping body. Over the bedspread actually, and not me. I escaped with the merest singe of the hairs on my head and my eyebrow. Forgive me, Bethany. (You see your mother wins all our battles.)

I left your mother and you and knew I could never walk back into your lives on your mother's terms and therefore that my life without her and you in it amounted to no life at all. Forgive me, Bethany.

Your loving father,
Lionel

Bethany Bettany

My grandfather's voice ends abruptly. The noise in my head continues. Love, I hear myself say, I know a little about love. First the idea of love without my mother, and, second, without Fly. A night sky with me under it and not a star in sight. My life a sky of nights. And me back in the limits of my own skin and in my body no room for love. Love is out of reach in this body.

Where the sky ends, I imagine stars begin and something like love flowers in starlight. To reach that love I join with those stars and my skin spreads and thins into a sky with the stars and me inside that skin. I line up what stars I find so that they spell love on my skin. The stars shine out into the dark beyond my skin, into the unknown, sending their signal to the love hidden in the galaxies with each star as a launching pad for my call beyond my skin outwards into space to join Fly and find my mother. Tentacles of light radiate off my body, sky for skin, sent out to Fly with the stars on my side, from the biggest and brightest and hottest to the faintest and smallest, the firefly I cupped in my hands to see the faint light emitted by it. My elastic sky: light sent out, love let in.

Do I assume too much? Either I love or I stay lost. A fingertip touches my skin without me flinching. The tip of a tongue, not mine, lands on me, and feels so unlike the needle that I expect to pierce my skin that I lose all sense of the bones in my body. My flesh liquefies under that tongue. I am in the open and naked with the sky for skin, Fly's breath on my neck and in my ear, his arms around my shoulders. He feels as hot as the sun. I do not contract my body. I am so easy in my skin I am airborne, one pink feather for a body, one blue sky for skin, and so many stars that the stars are pores on my body. How can love say no to me?

Back in his cramped tent Fly says to me, 'Kiss me.' And I close my eyes. I offer my sealed lips to him for his rose-mouth to drop its offerings on to mine. And he says, 'No.' His refusal opens my eyes. I look at the man who says no to my yes offered to him. And he says, 'Part your lips.' I widen my eyes at his request. And as if he reads my next thought, he says, 'Shush.' I feel his hands on me urging me to cooperate with him, a firm grip steering me in his direction. So I let my lips part. I lower my jaw. My tongue lifts to meet his and he smiles with his eyes on my eyes, which narrow a little before they smile back at him. And when his tongue touches mine I feel a small shock on my tongue, the tip of my tongue held to a battery. But the shock fills my mouth and blazes without hurting and flies through my body. I swear my toes curl with it. My body fills to the brim and then overflows with warmth and then heat and my tongue laps up his tongue as much as his feeds on mine. Our tongues join. I look at myself through his eyes and see – not my mother's eyes, but mine for the first time. My tongue – not my mother's tongue – suddenly reveals itself. Kissing Fly our tongues talk. Fly's tongue on mine makes our two tongues one. This is love's speech, two tongues in one. My lips tingling then numb with the pressure of our faces pressed together and switching angles without losing touch with one another's lips.

I hear a familiar tune, a calypso. I mouth the three words I know, *Ring, ting, ting*. This is talk without words. Two tongues working as one. My tongue twinned with Fly's. I forget my name, I forget my mother and my father, if only for the duration of this time with Fly. My body in his arms, my arms around his body, my tongue mixed up with his, our eyes open and seeing ourselves and each other, our tongues roped together and free.

MOTHER

Your father and I conferred and covered for you. He said he fell asleep with a cigarette. I said you were asleep in your room. We begged you to keep quiet. It was the only time you were not allowed to have your say.

The fire did not touch your father. He escaped with a strong smell of smoke on him just as your cut on his trouser leg only damaged fabric. I told him since we had to find a place to live it might as well be separate places. I said to him that if he asked to stay with us he could not really love you, his child, driven by him not once but on two occasions to do something that frightened us all, that asking to stay showed he cared only about himself. I could not have him in the house until I convinced you he was dear to me and not a pariah. I needed to work with you to remove all the quarrels between your father and me that you overheard and all my bad-mouthing of him in his absence before entertaining any notion of having him back in the house. I said I loved him and he replied right away that he loved me too. I thought that the promise of this love would sustain us during this trial separation. He knew and I knew it was temporary while I worked with saving you, our daughter, from the damage we did to your mind and heart, the confusion that we sowed in them.

That was the last time we saw him alive. So you see, Bethany Bettany (I see now that my name for you and his name for you both belong to you), his death had nothing to do with you and little to do with me but everything to do with his wilfulness.

Your country did not kill your father, or his him. Both countries are yours. I did not kill your father or you him.

After all our fights and your unwitting involvement in them

he took his fate into his own hands. He drove down the A2 out to Dartford. He stopped illegally on the bridge, left his hazard lights on and climbed out of his Bentley on the passenger side. He failed to close the door though he had the wherewithal to push it to. Your father walked briskly to the barrier and climbed up in a hurry. He did not pause or look behind him at the startled traffic. He launched himself over the side. Eyewitnesses swore his arms were spread like wings.

He swooped down, every bit the kingfisher, Bethany Bettany. He did not fall. He swerved upwards with his outspread arms and rode the surface winds of his beloved Thames past Tilbury, past Gravesend, and out to sea and over the sea to the muddy Atlantic shores of his Guyana home.

BETHANY BETTANY

I enter a tent, eucalyptus in the air. Men and women in white uniform and face masks and gloves surround me. A surgical team replaces my stretcher bearers. Just before a mask is placed over my face a voice asks them to wait one moment. I know that voice. It is my own were I a woman about middle-aged. The middle age I hope to attain, vainly, I believe since I think I am dying. But I say nothing. The figures around me begin to blur and turn into a glare of white, one sheet made of all their starched uniforms and head coverings, and I see myself as I would be then, middle-aged, if I lived to see that time. I see her. My mother. She leans over me. Her eucalyptus more fabric than scent now. I am on my back looking up at a mirror brought close to my face for me to see myself as I would become which matches exactly my mother looking down at the young woman she used to be when she was me.

She kisses me on each portion of my face as if to preserve me with her kisses. She smells as I would wish to smell at her age, of eucalyptus. I see how few lines my face gains over the years despite my predisposition to worry too much and ruminate too long. Her grey hairs can be counted if one were inclined to map how time weaves into and out of the skull even as it etches the face, around the eyes, at the corners of the mouth. She cries and laughs at me, the younger version of herself, restored to her at last.

I love you, Bethany. I never stopped loving you. You knew that all along, didn't you, my darling?

Yes, mother. I love you too.

I will see you after the doctors have patched you up.

I say or imagine saying, 'yes' once more and 'mother' like

before, but she blends into the light that suddenly dies in the middle of me trying to wrap my tongue around the citrus bestowed by the word love.

ACKNOWLEDGEMENTS

Dear Rebecca Carter, my editor, I owe you big time for your nips and tucks, prods and nods. You are a writer's dream of an editor. Alison Samuel, thank you for your encouragement and backing. Caroline Michel, I know you are on my side, I appreciate it. Bruce Hunter and Phyllis Westberg, my agents, read and re-read judiciously and with helpful remarks; thank you. Geoff Hardy, you continue to inspire me. My children keep me focussed: Matthew, Cameron, Elliot, Christopher and Nicholas, love and more love. Debbie keeps me strong. Here's to another ten years. And to Guyana: you keep me dreaming.